Taste of Liberty

Nancy Hunter

An Ellora's Cave Publication

www.ellorascave.com

Taste of Liberty

ISBN 9781419968426
ALL RIGHTS RESERVED.
Taste of Liberty Copyright © 2008 Nancy Hunter
Edited by Helen Woodall.
Cover Design by Syneca and Michelle.
Cover Photography by Suteracher, Conrado,
Judy Kennamer/Shutterstock.com.

Electronic book publication July 2008
Trade paperback publication 2013

Dedication

෨

This book is dedicated to Peter, my very own hero and to Augusta, who was the first person ever to think of me as "an author".

Acknowledgements

෨

Thanks to my mother Audrielle Hannigan and my sisters, Lynne DeCriscio and Karen Yeager, for encouraging me to love books and to my editor Helen Woodall for taking a chance on me and reuniting each and every one of my split infinitives.

Special thanks to my fellow Muse and Shmooze critique group members, without whom this book never would have seen the light of day—Shawn Downs, Laurie Edwards, Julie Good, Lisa Hess, Anne Kline, Steve Klotz, Maggie Martz, Lori Myers, Maria V. Snyder, Melanie Snyder, Kim Stanford, Jackie Werth, Mike Wertz, and Judy Wolfman.

Chapter One
November, 1777, Virginia Frontier

ഔ

Sebastian was looking for signs of life. There were only broken bodies, empty eyes. He walked among smoldering embers that hours earlier had been a peaceful village. More than once he dropped to his knees, sobbed, entreated and cursed the spirits in turn.

When he found Sunflower, he knelt beside her and cradled her in his arms. Her skin was smooth and cold, like marble. He pressed her eyelids closed and kissed her cheek, tasting the salt of her dried sweat and tears. He touched her forehead and covered his fingers in her blood, then smeared it on his cheeks like war paint.

His rational soldier's mind dictated what he should do. Return to the fort, report the incident, request permission to take out a search party to hunt down the murderers. But his broken warrior's heart would not stand reason.

He bent to the ground, struggling to distinguish their tracks in the low light of gathering dusk. Darkness would make it more difficult to follow the trail of the killers but it would also force them to stop soon to make camp.

Sebastian swung up onto his mount and prodded the horse to a full gallop. The cold autumn air cut through his buckskins and dried the blood on his cheeks into stiff clumps. Her blood, her life, her child. Sebastian would give his own life to avenge them.

* * * * *

He came upon the men less than an hour's ride away. When he had lost their tracks, he had followed the acrid smell of their campfire. Now, as he crouched in the brush near their encampment, Sebastian watched them gather around the fire with their red coats unbuttoned, their blood-covered hands rummaging through the pelts, tools and weapons they had stolen from the village. In the center of the butchers stood their leader, a man Sebastian recognized by reputation.

Long and lean, with dark hair and a closely cropped beard, Colonel Reginald Winters resembled the devil himself. The man was the root of all the evil gathered around him. He was the beating heart of the beast that had destroyed those innocent lives. And now he was the sole target of Sebastian's rage. Winters' men would close in around Sebastian as soon as the deed was done but that was of no consequence, as long as Winters no longer lived and breathed.

Sebastian had no concept of time as he lay in wait, watching his enemy's every move. Minutes could have passed, or hours but finally the time came. Winters moved away from the fire, away from the men and the few makeshift tents, into the woods alone.

In a flash, Sebastian covered the ground between them. His knife was already poised. The tip met flesh and bone, skidded off teeth as he stabbed wildly and cut Winters' face, then aimed for his heart.

"God damn you," Sebastian muttered. "God damn you!"

Sebastian felt a sting in his back, turned on his heel to find another man lunging at him. And the second man had his own knife. Undeterred, Sebastian slashed at Winters again but he couldn't hold off both men at once. Winters knocked the knife from his hand.

Sebastian's sense of self-preservation was in tatters but his will to live long enough to kill Winters was intact. He ran through the woods, not sure where he was going but determined to live just one more day. The footsteps behind him drew closer, the shouts of angry men overtook him. Then a loud crack. Intense heat flared where the bullet cut through skin and muscle in his back and traveled into one of his lungs.

He gasped for breath, struggled to see what loomed in front of him but the night was dark and the grass was slippery underfoot.

He had reached a clearing but still could not determine where to go, or how to escape the men behind him, or how to draw enough breath into his lungs. Then the ground beneath him gave way to empty air. He kicked futilely as he flew, fell, plunged over the edge of a precipice he hadn't seen.

He hit jagged rocks hundreds of feet below, heard his own bones shattering, felt unimaginable pain. There was nothing. Vast emptiness.

Eventually, there was a point of light. Light growing, exploding into glorious, vibrant color. Every color of the rainbow. Then their faces. His lover, Sunflower, his best friend, Wes, the village elders. And no more tears, no more sorrow. No more pain.

* * * * *

Reginald Winters folded his blood-soaked kerchief and pressed a dry corner to his chin. With his free hand, he unscrewed the lid of his flask and took a swig of whiskey, then grimaced as a drop seeped into his wound. He took a second swig to dull the pain caused by the first and stared into the distance, waiting.

"Is it done?" he called as Norton, his second-in-command, came into view.

"Yessir. The bullet hit true and woulda been the death of 'im, if it hadn'ta been for 'im going over the cliff and landin' on the rocks about a hundred yards down."

The soldiers who had pursued the now-dead man laughed and congratulated each other as they headed for the campfire and the stew that Cook was dishing up for them. Winters did not join in their merriment or their meal.

"You checked, of course?" he asked Norton.

"O' course. With the lanterns. There he was, lyin' in a pool of 'is own blood, eyes open wide, starin' at nothin'."

Winters dabbed more blood from his wounded chin. "I'm going to talk with our guests. Keep everyone away."

"Yessir."

Winters entered his tent, which held the spoils he had taken from the village — an old woman and a small boy. One was going to be with him for a very long time. The other was enjoying the last few minutes of life on earth.

"I will not answer the questions you have." The old woman's voice sounded like stones grinding against each other. "I know that in the end you will kill both of us."

As Winters' eyes adjusted to the near-darkness of the tent, he saw her holding the boy on her lap, staring past Winters, refusing to meet his gaze. The child lay very still, sound asleep.

Winters crouched down to his haunches. "Is that so? You think you're that smart? Or maybe you're one of those medicine women who has visions? Is that it?"

She did not answer, did not move, barely seemed to breathe.

"Because the truth is," Winters continued, "I have absolutely no intention of killing the two of you." He reached out and grabbed the boy off her lap and held him to the ground as the old woman grabbed uselessly at empty air. The boy had not been asleep after all. He had been as tense as a loaded bow and it took a tremendous amount of strength to subdue him.

"Now, medicine woman, in the interest of saving the boy, you'll answer my questions."

She shook her head. Winters pressed his knee into the boy's abdomen.

"We can do it your way," he told the old woman, "but it makes it difficult for the boy to breathe."

The woman did not speak but a tear rolled down her cheek.

"Let's try this again. Are you ready to answer my questions? For the sake of the boy."

She nodded.

"First, who is still alive from your village?"

She shook her head. "Many of our braves were killed by your kind months ago. And now —" She broke off into a sob.

"Now?" Winters put pressure on the boy until he let out a small squeak.

"Now it is just the two of us."

Winters let the boy breathe again. "Good. That wasn't so difficult, was it? Just one more question." He hesitated, unsure of how to ask it.

"The ones who watch you," the old woman said.

"You know about them?" Winters asked. "Who sent them? What tribe?"

"I do not know their tribe."

"But you've seen them."

"I have not seen them."

Winters grunted and pulled out a knife. He rested the point on the child's neck. "First you say you've seen them, then you say you haven't. Are you playing games with me?"

"No!" Her voice was shrill and frightened. "I cannot see them. I only feel them. I only know that the spirits have sent them."

"You feel them?" Winters laughed. "And you believe they're spirits? Because they look like flesh and blood men to me, when I manage to catch a glimpse of them."

"They are not spirits, they were sent by the spirits. It is complicated."

"My patience is wearing thin. Make it simple."

11

She turned her head and looked at him. Even in the low light he could see the intensity of her gaze. "There are legends about men who cannot be killed by mortal men. Evil men who must be stopped but will not be, even at the hands of armies." She looked away, resumed her faraway stare. "If the Fated Ones watch you, you are such a man."

"My, my, they even have a name. The Fated Ones. And tell me, why do they watch me? Is it their job to kill me?"

She nodded.

"Norton!"

Seconds later Winters' second-in-command pushed open the flap of the tent. "Yessir?"

Winters smiled at the old woman. "I have a little job for you that I think you'll enjoy. The old woman needs some fresh air. Take her for a walk. Let her join our recent unexpected visitor."

Norton grinned and grabbed the woman's arms, hauling her to her feet. "Come on, ducky, we'll have a good ol' time, you an' me."

Winters followed them out of the tent and motioned to one of the soldiers lingering by the fire. As Norton dragged the woman away, she reached out a bony hand and snatched Winters' arm.

"They will kill you. It is their destiny, the only reason they still walk this earth."

Winters laughed loudly and yanked his arm away from her. "Well, old woman, then I fear they're abysmal failures." He dropped his voice. "They've already tried. But as you can see, they didn't fulfill their destiny."

Even in the faint illumination from the fire he could see the drastic change on her face. Her eyes flew open and the color drained from her face. "They tried to kill you and failed?"

"That's right."

She made quick movements with her hands — signs to entreat the protection of the spirits.

"Superstitious heathen," Winters said as Norton hauled her off into the darkness. Winters glanced at the soldier who had come in response to his summons. "Feed the boy, then post a guard on him. Tomorrow we deliver him to his new home."

"New home, sir?"

Winters nodded. "He'll even have his own nanny."

The soldier looked concerned. "But sir, lettin' one o' them heathens live — no good can come of it, can it?"

The soldier could not imagine just how much good it would do Winters to keep alive the last tribe member and sole heir to their lands. He smiled at his confused follower. "Do as you're ordered, son, no questions asked."

The soldier stood up straight. "Yessir! We'll see to it that 'e's in good shape. Guess we killed enough Indians for one day anyway. Watchin' that last one go over the cliff gave the boys a good show."

Winters sent the soldier to fetch the boy's dinner. He did not share what he knew about the enemy who had wanted to kill him that night. The man's fighting style and his accent when he'd cursed Winters... That had been no Indian. It had been a well-bred Englishman and a soldier to boot. And one day, someone was bound to come looking for him.

"Did you send him after me, old Barnabus?" he whispered into the wind. "You've wanted me dead for years. No matter. Your hired killer is the one who's dead and you'll not be much longer for this world."

The crazy old medicine woman had been right about one thing — Reginald Winters was a hard man to kill. More men had tried than he cared to count, for more years than he had once believed he'd stay alive. But he had a way of outliving his enemies and destroying anyone who stood in his way. It had taken more than a few staged battles, slit throats and sacked

Indian villages to bring Winters to the rank of Colonel but now he had everything he wanted. Almost.

He looked to the north. They were there, Barnabus' kin, on the rich farming land of the Shenandoah Valley. Now Reginald finally had the wealth and power he needed for his ultimate victory and Barnabus' kin were fair game, like everyone else who stood in the way of something Reginald Winters wanted.

Chapter Two

March, 1778, the Whitmore Estate, Shenandoah Valley, Virginia

ဢ

Liberty MacRae held tightly to her friend Maggie's hand as they waited to be announced at the Whitmores' ball. A chill washed over her, warning her of a premonition. She clenched her fist and fought against it.

"Libbie, my hand!" Maggie pulled away from her. "Are you all right? You're so pale — oh, no. Not here, not now."

"I can't help it." She took deep breaths, willing her mind to stay in the present. The chill receded. The ballroom came sharply back into focus and she realized that Maggie had taken her hand again.

"I'm sorry," Maggie said. "Do you need to sit down?"

Libbie shook her head. "I'm fine now. We can enjoy the evening."

"You're truly all right?"

Libbie smiled to reassure her friend. "Fit as a fiddle."

"Then we can begin our last adventure together before I become an old married woman. You've probably forgotten how boring life can be out here, while you were off at Mrs. Barton's finishing school."

Nothing could compare to the boredom Libbie had experienced at Mrs. Barton's dull affairs but Libbie didn't mention it to Maggie. She was attending Lady Jane's ball for her friend, soon to be her sister-in-law and premonitions and bad feelings be damned, they were going to have a good time.

"My brother adores you. If you had told him to stop being such a stick-in-the-mud and escort you to one of Lady Jane's parties, he would have done it."

"Not happily, though. You know how he feels about fancy clothes and as for wearing a wig—" With her own bright red locks discreetly tucked away under a powdered wig, Maggie glanced at Libbie's uncovered hair. "The aversion seems to run in the family."

"I explained that I left my wig at Mrs. Barton's. I packed in such a hurry—I was so anxious to come home."

"And you didn't realize it until you dressed this evening, when it was much too late to get another one. I'm afraid finishing school has taken the edge off your razor-sharp lying skills."

Libbie ignored Maggie's grin as she handed the liveried servant their invitations. Libbie prepared herself for next few minutes when all eyes would be upon them as they descended the ornate oak staircase and made their dramatic entrance among Lady Jane's bejeweled, wigged, overly perfumed guests. And then there was Lady Jane herself. She was a kind woman and not much older than Maggie and Libbie. But for Libbie's taste, Lady Jane gave too many parties, wore too much red and flirted with far too many men, often right under her much older and overly indulgent husband's nose.

As the servant announced Libbie and Maggie's names, Libbie caught a glimpse of Lady Jane in the midst of the crowd, surrounded by half a dozen grinning young men. She waved to Libbie with a large, sweeping gesture of her hand. Libbie raised one ungloved hand ever so slightly in response.

I'm doing this for Maggie, Libbie reminded herself. And Mama. Mama, who too often had found Libbie shaking and sobbing after one intense vision or another. Mama, who worried that Libbie lived too much inside her own "dark imagination" and that Libbie would never do the right thing and marry the nice boy on the neighboring farm who knew of her strange episodes but professed to love her anyway. For her best friend and for her mother, Libbie would make this night a success.

The crowd gathering below them clapped approvingly as Maggie and Libbie stepped onto the staircase. Maggie was glowing, Lady Jane was beaming and the premonition that had earlier threatened to overwhelm Libbie was long gone.

As they descended the staircase, something in the far corner of the crowded room caught Libbie's eye. She realized in an instant that it was jet black hair in a sea of white wigs. The dark-haired man turned as though he could feel her gaze on him. He had the most remarkable eyes she had ever seen. Even from across the room she could see that they were a deep blue, the color of a mountain lake at dusk. He wore dark blue breeches and a white shirt fastened at the neck with a jewel, perhaps a sapphire. His waistcoat and coat were the same dark, almost dull blue as his pants but all were finely cut to draw attention to the long, lean shape of him.

Something more than a look danced on the air between them. It felt as though they knew each other, as though they must have met but Libbie could not quite place him. She knew her legs were still moving under her, carrying her down the stairs but she felt out of time with them, with Maggie, with the crowd. The only one in the world who seemed to be moving as slowly and purposefully as she, was the intriguing dark-haired, blue-eyed stranger.

Then as suddenly as their eyes had met, he was gone, obscured by the crowd as she and Maggie stepped off the stairs. Only her racing pulse assured her that something had just happened, something amazing and important and more than a bit frightening.

* * * * *

The dull hum of voices and music rose to a crescendo. Sebastian stood in the corner farthest from the sweeping staircase that was the entryway to the ballroom. He took a sip of his aperitif as he turned to see what had caused the unusual change. The sight made his drink catch in his throat. He coughed and swallowed the liquid, then blinked. When he opened his eyes, it was still there. Amid the sea of grays was a color. One magnificent, radiant color. Green — the bright emerald green of her eyes set against the radiant paleness of her face, the dark green of her dress. Then pink — the bright pink of her lips, the soft pink of her cheeks. And copper strands glinting in her light brown hair.

"Sebastian, there you are." Jane, his childhood friend from Brittany, who was now Lady Jane Whitmore and host of the fêted event, laid her gloved hand on his arm. "What do you think of my dress? Isn't it the most wonderful color?"

He glanced at the low neckline of the frock and at the flounce that showed Jane's ankles and smiled. "Everything looks stunning on you, Jane. And what do you call that lovely shade?"

"Red, dear boy. It's called red. I do worry about you these days." She shook her head. "But come along. There's someone you must meet. She's a beautiful young woman and — well, you no doubt heard the stir that she and her friend caused when they made their entrance."

"I noticed a change in the room."

"And she should be of particular interest to you," Jane whispered as they crossed the room. "She is Liberty MacRae, daughter of one Sean MacRae."

"I am interested, indeed," he said. "Does she know?"

Jane shrugged. "I cannot be certain. I will leave it to you to charm it out of her."

The crowd had closed around Miss MacRae and her friend. All was gray again and the sameness was somehow comforting. As he and Jane moved through the throng, Sebastian told himself that surely he had imagined the sudden intensity of sensation.

But when the crowd parted and he saw her, color flooded over him again. There was also a scent, the sweet fragrance of gardenias. He fought to maintain his composure as the strangest mix of emotions washed over him—joy laced with sadness, hope tinged with regret.

Jane spoke to Miss MacRae, then the young woman turned toward him. She reached out her hand, he touched it. He felt it, warm and pliable in his grasp.

Jane touched Miss MacRae's shoulder. "Sebastian, this is Miss Liberty MacRae. She is just returned from finishing school in Charlottesville. Libbie, this is one of my dearest friends in the world, Mr. Sebastian Cole. The two of you will be seated together at dinner this evening."

Sebastian nodded, unable to refuse, yet unprepared for a whole evening of sensations that he couldn't explain and didn't understand. As a servant rang a bell and announced that dinner was served, Sebastian offered his arm to escort Miss MacRae to the dining room. Her fingers rested in the crook of his elbow. He could feel her heat, could feel her very heartbeat in her fingertips.

In an instant, Liberty MacRae had infused Sebastian's world with vivid awareness after months spent in a subtle, muted purgatory. He could not imagine how he would survive the shock.

As he escorted her to the dining room, Sebastian wondered what he would say to her during dinner. She solved the problem for him by taking an acute interest in the old gentleman to her left and consequently ignoring Sebastian. For his part, Sebastian regaled the ladies to his right with tales of Jane's adventurous childhood. But he could not truly ignore Miss MacRae when her very presence allowed him to taste the creamy, delicately spiced potato and leek soup, the roasted game hen and braised pork, the fresh greens and baked apples, the full-bodied wines from Lord Jamison's renowned cellar. And the scents—pungent perfumes, sweet garden flowers, smoky candles—brought back memories of long ago family dinners and younger, happier years.

When the meal ended and guests rose from their seats, he stood quickly to help Miss MacRae with her chair. She stared into his eyes as if she could see his secrets revealed there. He touched her hand, brushed his fingers across the damp softness of her palm, heard her sharp intake of breath.

"Miss MacRae," he said quietly, although no one was near them, "I'm sorry we didn't get a chance to speak during dinner. I had hoped to inquire about your father."

"You know my father?"

Sebastian shrugged. "I know of Sean MacRae. I've heard talk of his involvement in certain delicate matters." Was it his imagination, or did she turn a shade paler?

She took a step back from him and glanced at the doorway a few feet away. "I have no idea what you're intimating, Mr. Cole. Now if you'll excuse me, my dance card is quite full."

He was left alone in the room, now a gray, scentless, nearly soundless place. A minute later he joined the party in the ballroom and sought out the dance partner at the top of his own dance card. Every so often he would catch a glimpse of Miss MacRae, a blur of fantastic color whirling on the dance floor. He did his best to charm Jane's female guests as he met and danced with each one. He could afford to be charming and patient, because he knew his turn to dance with Liberty MacRae was coming.

Sebastian bowed to one more partner, a middle-aged lady with a quick smile who had made a discreet but unmistakable proposition to him. Murmuring something to the effect of giving her husband his regards, Sebastian stepped away from her and slipped into the crowd, finally in search of his long-awaited dance partner. He caught a glimpse of green dress and copper hair at the far end of the room, then watched her slip out a side door that led to the back garden.

Sebastian told himself that he feared for her safety. After all, didn't he know better than anyone what unseen dangers lurked in the dark, waiting to prey on such innocence and beauty? He stepped onto the veranda and glanced up at the night sky filled with tiny stars and dominated by the full, low-hanging orb of the moon. Miss MacRae would look stunning under its glow. He stepped down the wide flagstone steps and onto the garden path, trusting his inexplicable sensory awareness of her to guide him.

He stopped cold and struggled to catch his breath as a different awareness swept over him like an icy river — not a sight or sound but an instinct. The deepest sensation left to him, the ability to feel the dead. But these were not ghosts, nor were they of this place, not like the others he could feel — the souls of Indians and farmers who had toiled and died on this land. These were corporal beings. He could feel their hearts beating in their chests, their cold blood flowing in their veins. They were like him and like him were tied to their killer, his killer. In an instant he knew them, knew of their horrible deaths, knew that they had come back to life for the same reason he had — to wreak vengeance on Winters. But they were different too, somehow more lost, hopeless, desperate. They whispered to him deep inside his mind, begged him to come to them, to help them, to set them free.

I don't understand. Set you free from what?

Before they could answer, something stirred farther down the garden path. Sebastian ran toward the noise, following the twists and bends in the path, expecting to see the sad, dead beings around every turn but wondering why he no longer felt them. Something flashed green and bright in front of him and he tried to stop but he was moving too fast. His foot caught on Miss MacRae's skirt. Sebastian lost his balance and plunged headfirst into an azalea bush in full bloom.

* * * * *

Libbie would have screamed but her throat was frozen in fear. Death had hurled itself at her, had stumbled, had — Landed in an azalea bush? She was still shaking, still felt the

21

cold fear curled in the pit of her belly but the bright strands of red hanging in the air had dissipated. The death that had lurked just beyond Lady Jane's garden was no longer there. And the creature who had frightened her beyond reason and was now struggling to right himself looked uncannily like one of her dinner companions.

Libbie shook again but this time with laughter. She wiped away the tears that had begun to dry on her cheeks. With the threat gone, she felt light again and joyful and invincible. She reached down into the azalea bush and grasped Mr. Cole's hand to help him stand.

"Miss MacRae, are you hurt? I'm so sorry, I didn't see you there." He stopped to catch his breath.

Libbie covered her smile with one hand and nodded. "I'm fine," she finally managed to say. "I daresay you bore the brunt of our unfortunate encounter."

He was breathing normally now. "I do apologize for that. It's just that I heard a noise and I…" He shook his head.

Libbie took a step back from him, hoping to shrink into the shadows. He had heard her crying like a baby, like a lunatic driven insane by the full moon. Like the aberration of nature that she was. But somehow she didn't want Mr. Cole to know the truth about her, to believe anything bad about her at all. It wasn't just that he was handsome, although he truly was. His black hair shimmered in the moonlight, his dark blue eyes were so wide and intense that she felt she could fall into them. He was much taller than she, broad-shouldered and lean. A sleek black panther, tense and still but ready to spring into action at any second.

"Miss MacRae?"

Libbie realized he was proffering his arm to her.

"I asked if I may escort you back to the party."

She nodded and took his arm. As they walked slowly up the garden path, Libbie struggled to find a reason to explain her previous state.

"Were you lost?" Mr. Cole asked quietly.

"Pardon me?"

"On the garden path. I thought you might have been lost, trying to find your way back to the house."

"Yes, I was… I mean, I got turned around on the path." She smiled up at him. She wanted to throw her arms around his neck, to kiss him and thank him for not making her explain herself as she so often had to do. To kiss him…

"Here we are," he said as they stepped onto the veranda. "I wonder if I might ask one favor of you, Miss MacRae."

"Anything," she said quickly, then blushed.

Mr. Cole smiled. "It seems you stepped outside just before we were to share a dance."

Yes. It all came back to her. She hadn't wanted to dance with him. The things he'd made her feel, even from across the room when she'd first seen him, the touch of his hand as he escorted her to dinner, the sound of his laughter as he sat next to her. Something about Mr. Cole made her want to say and do strange things, like kiss him in the garden and dance with him on the veranda. But then he had mentioned her father…

He stepped back from her and stood in position for their dance. Libbie decided she had been overreacting to an innocent comment and obligingly curtsied to him as he bowed to her. They started a minuet, one Libbie had danced dozens of times but she couldn't quite keep the rhythm. The song was slow but she was breathless. As they stepped back and then forward another time, her knees bent under her against her will. Before she sank to the ground, she felt Sebastian's arms around her waist, pulling her against him.

"Miss MacRae, are you all right?"

"I'm fine. It's just the heat. It's unseasonably warm this evening, don't you agree?"

"And you had a fright earlier."

"No, I'm fine," she insisted, steadying herself and pushing away from him. "You merely stumbled over me and I've recovered."

"I meant before that. You were afraid of something. You went out into the garden alone and got frightened."

"I go many places alone and I assure you I don't frighten easily."

"Perhaps then you should frighten more easily, because the world can be a very dangerous place."

Libbie widened her eyes in shock. "I'm more aware of that than you'll ever know, Mr. Cole. I've seen things that…"

She looked away from him. It was more than seeing things. It was feeling unbearable pain, reliving deaths died a hundred years ago and yesterday, feeling evil coming but not knowing when or where it would arrive. She looked him in the eye. "I don't need a lecture from you about it."

He grabbed her shoulders and stared at her with the same determination she saw in her father's and brother's faces when they wanted to convince her that she needed their protection. But as she stared up into Sebastian's dark, hooded eyes, his look changed. Determination seemed to give way to confusion, then to resignation as he leaned closer to her. His soft breath brushed her cheek, his fingertips caressed her shoulders. Libbie closed her eyes, willing him to come closer, to actually kiss her. His lips pressed against her mouth. She tensed from the shock of it, then felt him loosen his grip on her.

Fearing that he would pull away from her and declare it an indiscretion, or worse, a mistake, Libbie put one hand behind his neck and wrapped the other one in his thick, smooth hair. Mr. Cole laid a hand on each side of her face and deepened the kiss, parting her lips with his and exploring her mouth with his tongue.

His kiss was sweet and gentle but she could feel the strain of his self-control in the tenseness of his neck and shoulders. Some deep, feral part of her wanted him to abandon that self-control, to kiss her with all the passion and desperation that she could feel in him, that she had felt from the first second she had laid eyes on him.

Sebastian withdrew from her slowly, carefully.

"Mr. Cole, I-I mean Sebastian..." She could not finish her thought while he watched her so intently.

With his hands still cupping her cheeks, he stared at her with wonder. "Miss MacRae, Liberty, you have no idea how long I—"

They heard the side door swing open, momentarily revealing louder music and laughter from the ballroom before swinging closed again.

"Liberty! Liberty, dear, are you out here?" Jane called.

Libbie sucked in her breath and jumped back from Sebastian.

Lady Jane stepped onto the flagstone steps, made a quick survey to locate them and was quickly upon them in all her bright red glory. "Sebastian, I'm so glad you found Liberty." She squeezed Libbie's hand. "Maggie told me you weren't feeling well earlier and that you stepped outside for some fresh air."

Libbie nodded, not trusting her own voice.

"Well, you must come back inside so that you, Maggie and I can have a little chat before your brother arrives to collect you." Lady Jane looked at Sebastian and for an instant Libbie thought she saw the woman wink at him. "Liberty's brother just got engaged to her best friend, Maggie."

Sebastian raised his eyebrows. "Indeed? Miss MacRae, you must give your friend my best wishes."

Libbie cleared her throat and ventured some words. "Won't you join us, Mr. Cole, to convey your best wishes in person?"

He opened his mouth to speak but Jane interrupted.

"I'd like to give Maggie a little marriage advice." She smiled. "Ladies only. No gentlemen allowed."

Libbie looked to Sebastian for help but he could only shrug. Then he bowed to her as he had when they had danced. She curtseyed back to him and they both smiled.

"It has been my pleasure, Miss MacRae," he said.

She nodded. "Likewise."

She wanted to say more but Lady Jane had fastened her grip on Libbie's arm and deftly maneuvered her to back to the house.

As they stepped into the stifling ballroom, an idea occurred to Libbie. If she could find excuses to visit Lady Jane frequently during Sebastian's visit, she could see him as well. They could spend more time together. Perhaps he would like to ride with her around the perimeter of the Whitmore estate. Libbie knew the lands better than Lady Jane, having grown up on the farm next to them. The thought of spending more time with him lifted her spirits.

"Lady Jane, how long will your friend be staying with you?" she asked as they moved through the crowd.

"Hmm? Oh, he—" Jane spotted Maggie. "There she is. Maggie, dear, come chat with us!"

A strand of hair fell into Libbie's face as she hurried to keep up with Jane. She tried to discreetly pin it into place but one of her hairpins was missing. Heat flushed her face as she realized the pin had probably fallen out when Sebastian had kissed her.

With Jane distracted by the task of threading her way toward Maggie, Libbie slipped away from her hostess and moved to the veranda doors. She hoped to find her hairpin but it was a secondary consideration. Sebastian was still out there, she was sure of it. He would flash his brilliant smile at her, she'd run into his arms, they would share another breathtaking kiss. Her heart raced as she stepped outside.

He wasn't there, at least not where they had left him. But the low hum of voices came from somewhere in the garden. A cold fear gripped Libbie as she remembered the horrible presence of death that she had felt earlier. She felt dizzy as she frantically looked around for Sebastian. She forced herself to regain her composure and tried to feel whatever was out there. Death had not returned. There was nothing more sinister lurking in the darkness than some party guests who, like her, had needed a breath of fresh air.

With a sigh of relief, she stepped onto the garden path, determined to find Sebastian. She hadn't gone far when she recognized one of the voices as his. A pang of jealousy shot through her. Then she heard another voice—a male voice. A very familiar male voice. Sebastian was speaking with her brother.

Now her mind raced with new fears. Had Johnny arrived early to collect her and Maggie, come around the back of the house, seen Sebastian kissing her? She crept closer, step by step, until she could peer through some hedges and see and hear them clearly.

Sebastian handed something to her brother. It looked like a paper or an envelope. Before she could identify it, it disappeared inside Johnny's waistcoat.

"Thank you, Lieutenant. My father will be happy to see this. It will save a lot of lives."

"Yes, well, I'm glad Jane was able to arrange our meeting. I had hoped to meet your father as well. I've heard talk that he's one of the best leaders the Virginia militia has."

Her brother was having a secret meeting with Sebastian. Johnny called him Lieutenant. They spoke of her father and the militia. The man who had kissed her was involved in one of her father's secret missions. Libbie touched her lips, wondering if she had unwittingly been part of it, a patsy used to create a cover for the Lieutenant.

Johnny was smiling. "My father is the best leader. And Lady Jane has said nothing but good things about you. I never would have taken information from a Redcoat if she hadn't vouched for you."

A Redcoat. Libbie shook her head, backed away down the path. For decades, the MacRaes had been sworn enemies of soldiers of the British Crown. Now Johnny was conspiring with one and Libbie had kissed him.

She heard Sebastian's voice. Something about Jane, then a laugh. It made Libbie think of the brooch he wore to fasten his shirt, a brooch she was sure she'd seen Jane wear. There was something she should put together about that, about him, about Jane but her head was swimming. A vision was coming. She fought it, tried to close her mind to it, like she had earlier. But it was too big, too strong. She sank to her knees.

Death hung like thick red fog clinging to the earth and obliterating the sun. Bodies — some whole, some broken, some barely recognizable as human — littered the once peaceful meadow. Someone called out her name, reached out a hand. She instinctively grabbed it but it was wet with blood and slipped from her fingers. He called out her name again, she reached for him but he went still. She saw Johnny's face, Johnny's blood. Nearby lay her father and a few feet from him, Tom Donnelly. The neighbor who had grown up with her, the boy who wanted to marry her.

It was the first of May. May Day. They were to be home by now, joining in a celebration but their orders had changed. They had ended up on this field and now could never come home again...

"Come back," she whispered to her brother. "Come back and I'll do anything you and Papa ask. Papa please, come home. I'll marry Tom, just like you wanted. Anything you want. Just don't leave me."

The ground was suddenly firm beneath Libbie. She lay curled into a ball in Lady Jane's garden. Johnny and Sebastian's voices were gone and she was alone and shivering.

It had never happened like this before—twice in one night. If the vision were true... But it couldn't be. Her premonitions had been wrong before. Still, something evil was approaching and Libbie knew with every fiber of her being that she would be powerless to stop it.

Chapter Three
November, 1778, Virginia Frontier

ഽ

Death hung in the air. Not the bright red haze of certain death but a thin scarlet wisp of the possibility. Every instinct told Libbie to rebuff it but Mother Cloud Dancer, the Occaneechi medicine woman, had taught her that her instincts would not allow her to harness her ability. Control would. Libbie let the death sign vibrate through her, held it in place with her mind and wrapped her will around it to keep it from overwhelming her.

The rumble of horses running at full tilt came from Libbie's right, the direction of the American encampment. Hiding in a copse of trees, her belly pressed against the cool earth of a small knoll, she breathed a sigh of relief. So Clay Pipe, her Saponi guide, had relayed the message to the regiment that Redcoats were planning an attack on the Saponi, friends of her adopted tribe, the Occaneechi. She turned her gaze to the left.

When a dozen Redcoats rode over the forested southern ridge and revealed themselves, Libbie strained to see a dark-bearded, scarred face. But like the other times over these past weeks since she had begun watching his fort, Winters did not join his soldiers in their raid.

The two groups of men charged toward each other over the flat clearing a quarter of a mile away from Libbie. Mist rolled from the horses' nostrils and sod flew from their hooves. A shot rang out and smoke rose from a Redcoat's gun. Winters' men were more prepared this time than last and for a few minutes they made a good show of fighting the Bluecoats who blocked their path to the Indian village. But outnumbered and out-positioned, the Redcoats soon turned tail and galloped back over the southern ridge. By the time the smell of burnt gunpowder reached Libbie, the British soldiers had disappeared.

When the smoke cleared and she could again breathe in the soft smells of dirt and leaves, the scarlet wisp was gone. She spotted Clay Pipe with the Bluecoats. They would camp near the village and keep watch in case the raiders made another attempt. Libbie would not join them. She spent most of her time alone now, communicating only with Clay Pipe and seeking him out only when it was necessary. Clay Pipe respected her privacy, kept his distance and proved invaluable each time Libbie spotted Winters' men on the move.

Libbie was waiting for the day that Winters joined them, when he left his den and ventured out into the world where he would be vulnerable to her attack, her revenge. But today, like every day for weeks, Winters' men had attempted their raid without him.

Libbie jumped up and paced around the small clearing. She was running out of time. Soon it would be too cold for her to continue living off the land, sheltered in her hidden cave. She would have to abandon her quest until the spring thaw, leaving precious little time before the next May Day, when Winters would again strike her family.

Just thinking about it could bring on the vision these days — Winters and his men storming their farm, she and her mother and sister no longer protected by the men Winters had already cut down. *You left us too soon,* she heard Mother Cloud Dancer whisper in her mind. *Come back, daughter. I have so much more to teach you.*

"No," Libbie said out loud, shaking her head. "I'm running out of time. My family is running out of time."

She took deep breaths, forced away the darkness crowding in at the edges of her vision, focused on the sun high in the sky, on Winters, on coming up with a new and better plan.

Twigs snapped close by. Too close.

Too deliberate to be an animal. Had Mother Cloud Dancer given up on persuasion and sent braves to retrieve Liberty by force? She dismissed the thought—the noises were too loud to have come from well-trained braves.

Libbie desperately scrambled toward the nearby overgrowth of shrubs but her hesitation had cost her precious seconds. Strong hands clamped around her neck, yanked her backward and flung her to the ground.

She stared up into the faces of two men she'd seen several times over the past few weeks. Two of Winters' soldiers. The smell of blood and heated combat wafted from them, reminded her of another battle that she had only seen in visions and made her gag.

"Well, well, look what we got 'ere," the younger, grimier man leered at her. "Must be a half-breed squaw, with that pale skin. She's just waitin' 'ere for us, like she's expectin' us, Norton!" He fumbled with the buttons of his trousers, his eyes glowing with a wildness that terrified Libbie.

"There's no time for that!" Norton answered. He surveyed the clearing and woods around them. "The Colonel's been lookin' for this bird. Tie 'er up. Make it fast."

The other soldier grunted and stared sullenly at Norton. "No need to rush. She's alone 'ere." He licked his lips as he ran his eyes over Libbie's supine form.

Her flesh crawled. She inched one hand closer to her waist, near the knife tied there, cursing her decision to leave her pistol in her saddlebag. Without warning, Norton's booted foot landed on top of her hand, sending heat and pain radiating through it. She screamed. Cold sweat and hot tears streamed down her face.

"I said tie 'er up," Norton repeated, his voice low and even. "Then take that knife she's got on 'er waist and wrap 'er in a horse blanket. We don't need Cole seein' 'er."

The pain in her hand made her head swim. The smothering heat of the rough blanket drove her to the edge of consciousness. But there was something that would not let her slip into the blackness. Something Norton had said. She struggled to remember it, tried to focus on it.

One word. A name. It came to her in jolting clarity—Cole.

* * * * *

Four months spent working for a cold-blooded killer and Sebastian had nothing to show for it. So many times he had come close to just trying to kill the bastard but if it wasn't the right moment, if he failed in his task, no one would be left to finish it. At least for now his very presence was keeping Winters and his men in check. Sebastian had ties to General Gordon. The General had made it his personal mission to destroy Winters' military career after the General's nephew had died mysteriously while under Winters' command.

Still, there had been small skirmishes and unexplained absences of some of the men. A small group had left the fort earlier that day and Sebastian had not been able to learn where they'd gone.

Thundering hoofbeats drew Sebastian to the window. The missing soldiers rode into the fort, their guns smoking, a few of them balancing wounded men on their mounts. Sebastian grabbed his coat and ran out the door. He reached the main building in the center of the fort just in time to see the soldiers carrying in the last wounded man.

"What's going on here, Norton?" he demanded. "I'm to be kept informed of the men's movements. Why wasn't I told that soldiers were outside the fort?"

Winters' second-in-command stopped and stared at Sebastian with narrowed eyes. "It was a huntin' expedition. Didn't seem necessary to consult the 'ole o' the British Army on the matter."

"Hunting? Those men took gunshots while hunting?"

Norton shrugged. "We ran into some unexpected trouble."

The man's face was impassive, unreadable. Winters had taught him too well. "From now on, I'm to be told," Sebastian said but he knew it would do no good.

Norton ambled away without another word. Sebastian stepped to the doorway of the building and peered into the large room lined with cots where six wounded soldiers now lay. He watched as Winters made his rounds among the men.

Before leaving the room, Winters stopped to consult with the army surgeon. "Norton will help you keep watch on the men overnight."

"There's not much to worry about, sir. Mostly superficial wounds."

"Just the same, he'll be here." Winters turned to his corporal who was always nearby, taking notes. "Send commendation letters to the wounded men's mothers. Make it clear that their boys are fine but they've earned a little bonus pay for their bravery."

"But sir," the corporal protested, "the army won't allow it."

"The army will never know." Winters spotted Sebastian as he exited the building. "Lurking in doorways again, Cole?"

"Just waiting to speak with you, sir."

"Come to my office, then."

Minutes later, Sebastian followed the commander into his office. It was stark and functional but the glasses Winters pulled from a shelf were of finest crystal. He poured two bourbons and pushed one toward Sebastian.

With a swift motion, Winters tossed back his drink, then leaned forward and stared at his empty glass. "Why are you here, Cole?"

"It's my job to review the duty roster. I should know when men are leaving the fort."

"I'm the commanding officer. I'll make sure you know all you need to know. And nothing more." He leaned back in his chair and narrowed his eyes. "You served under General Gordon. Why did you leave his command to come here?"

Apprehension crept up Sebastian's spine but he made his face expressionless. "My assignment there was finished. I could have stayed on longer but I missed the frontier."

"Ah, yes. You were assigned to a post near here. I never had dealings with you. Still, there's something about you, something familiar."

Winters' hand flickered over the scar on his chin as he spoke. For the briefest moment, he looked distracted. Sebastian took a flavorless sip of his bourbon and willed himself to remain calm. Winters came back to himself and continued as though he had never paused.

"Your record indicates that you are an excellent soldier. I have a lot of those under my command. Unfortunately, what I don't have are educated men. You, Lieutenant, are that as well. You could be a tremendous asset to me and believe me, I could compensate you well."

Sebastian sat forward and studied Winters' face. The man could be bluffing. After all, he was a cold-blooded killer, why not a liar as well? But it was his first opportunity to gain Winters' confidence and Sebastian was sure he wouldn't get a second.

"I'm listening, sir."

"There are conditions," Winters continued. "You must prove your absolute loyalty to me and you must never question my orders. I'll have no dissension in my ranks. And you are to stay away from the Indians. I'll have no squaw-men in my fort."

His last words made Sebastian clench his fist, recalling the sight of a village razed to the ground and the unprotected women and children lying in pools of blood and dirt.

"Colonel!" Winters' corporal called as he knocked on the door. "Pardon me, sir but it's urgent."

Winters shoved his chair back from his desk and stood. "Lieutenant, we'll continue this later. You are dismissed."

Sebastian left without another word. When he got outside, he quickly crossed the expanse of the fort to the stables. There he found Matthew, a young soldier Sebastian had first met through Jane and had come to know while serving under General Gordon. The young man had been eager to accept the frontier post as Sebastian's assistant and now served as Sebastian's eyes and ears among Winters' younger, less experienced soldiers.

"What have you heard, Matthew?"

Matthew led a lathered horse into its stall. "Heard and seen, sir. Norton and the others didn't come back alone. They brought a prisoner."

Sebastian raised his eyebrows. "A Bluecoat?"

Matthew shook his head. "An Indian."

"Bloody hell. A brave won't last long at Winters' hands."

"It's worse than that, sir. It's no brave. It's a squaw."

* * * * *

Libbie stood in a dark corner of a squalid cell — a dank, moldy room in a dugout cellar. From her brief inspection, her prison seemed to offer no means of escape. But would it be the place her life ended? She closed her eyes, searching for a truer sign but the spirits denied her a clear answer.

Winters was coming closer, she could feel him. She reached for the small, sharp knife hidden in her moccasin. Voices rose outside the cell, then the thick wooden door scraped over the dirt floor.

"Turn around and let me see your face, white squaw."

Libbie could barely hear his words because her heart was pounding so loudly. She turned slowly, willing her eyes to focus on him as red spots floated in front of her. The premonition she'd sought but predicting whose death?

In the low lamplight, Winters' dark features looked cruel and the pink scar on his chin gleamed menacingly through his short beard. Smells of sweat and horseflesh mingled with sweet liquor emanated from him as he circled her. He left a wide berth between them, making it impossible for her to strike at him.

"Just as I thought. Miss Liberty MacRae."

Her breath caught in her throat. How did he know her, know her name?

"I am Walks-in-Two-Worlds of the Occaneechi." She kept her voice steady and calm.

"Do not play games with me." Winters' mouth twisted into a snarl. "I am easily bored. I know you ran away from your family farm after your father's and brother's deaths and took up with an Indian tribe but it doesn't change who you are, Miss MacRae. And lucky for you, because I've come here with a proposition for you."

She shook with rage at his audacity to mention Papa and Johnny's deaths, their murders at Winters' own hands. "You might as well kill me where I stand, because I want no part of any proposition from you."

"My, my, you are a beauty when you're indignant."

"Indignant? How dare you even speak to me."

Winters struck her across the face with the back of his hand, moving so fast that she didn't have time to brace herself. She staggered backward, silenced by the surprise and pain of it.

"You and I have much in common, Miss MacRae," he said as he backed away from her. "Perhaps even more than you will ever know. It is such a pity that it has come to this."

"I have no idea what you're talking about. We could not be more different, Colonel."

Winters sucked in his breath. "A spitfire. I do so like my women with bravado. Perhaps I won't kill you instantly, after all. Don't look so surprised, white squaw. You have been spying on my men for weeks now, interfering with their duties, sending information to the Americans. Certainly you didn't think that could go unpunished."

"I've only prevented your men from killing women and children."

Winters smiled and his smile was more frightening than his snarl. "Don't be so sentimental, Miss MacRae. We have business to tend to. As I said, I have a proposition to offer you."

He waved a paper in front of her. "If you sign this, I promise you your death will be quick and painless, when the time comes. If you do not... Well," he looked her up and down, "no doubt that in your time with the savages, they taught you something about slow, agonizing death."

She considered her options. If she lunged at him, he would have time to sidestep her and pull his own weapon. But if she could get him to step a little closer, she could plunge the knife into his belly and eviscerate him before he had the chance to lay a hand on her.

"What is it you expect me to sign? A confession that I'm a British spy, just as you claimed my father and brother were? One more lie to add to my family's shame? You might as well begin your torture now, because I'll never do it."

He moved a little closer but still remained out of her reach. "No, Miss MacRae, I think two spies in the family are enough, don't you? Nearly everyone in the community has turned against your family. Oh, the Continental Army may sort it all out one day but the damage is done. The MacRae name is as good as mud in the Shenandoah Valley. No, my sweet, what I want from you is much, much more important."

* * * * *

Sebastian flattened himself against the side of the building that housed the fort's food stores. He waited impatiently to see signs of the fire Matthew was setting outside the munitions building. It was a dangerous assignment that he'd given to the young man but not half as dangerous as one he'd left for himself. Moments later he saw the thick gray smoke billowing upward on the wind and he slipped into the building.

Sebastian crept down the narrow stairway into the dugout basement, careful not to make a sound. A lantern hanging on the wall illuminated one soldier guarding the heavy wooden door of the root cellar. The man spotted Sebastian as he emerged from the shadows. He opened his mouth to shout a warning. Sebastian smothered the man's attempted yell with his hand. With his other fist he landed a blow in the man's midsection that dropped him to his knees. The *coup de grâce* was a blow to the man's head that rendered him unconscious.

Sebastian pressed his ear to the door. He was relieved to hear Winters talking and a woman's voice responding. It proved the squaw was still alive. Sebastian couldn't make out their conversation and couldn't imagine what Winters would have to discuss with a captured squaw but that was the least of his concerns. The spirits had given him no signs to indicate that he should confront Winters now but if the commotion over the fire didn't draw out Winters before he attacked the woman, Sebastian would have no choice. He pressed himself into the shadows beside the door and waited.

* * * * *

Just come a little closer, you miserable bastard, Libbie thought but she remained silent.

"Now, how could I kill you," Winters said. "Let's see, I could cut off your eyelids and tie you to a post, then watch while the sun burns out your eyes and you slowly die of thirst. Very long business, that — takes about a week. Or I could skin you alive, inch by beautiful inch." His eyes raked over her. "But I would rather see every inch of you under more pleasant circumstances."

He took another step toward her and Libbie breathed faster.

"I understand your name is beside your mother's on the deed to your family farm. You simply need to sign over that deed to me. Then you and I will get to know each other better, much better." He grinned wickedly. "It will almost be a shame to kill you but when it's time, I'll make it as painless as possible." He waved the paper in the air again.

She shook her head, trying to make sense of it. "The deed? What good would my signature do? My mother will still own the farm."

He shrugged. "Perhaps she could be persuaded to forfeit her share, as well. Especially if she believes it will save your pretty neck."

Libbie fought to keep her wits about her as he stepped closer, almost within striking range. He wouldn't go to the farm, not yet. Her dreams, then later visions, had always been clear about the timing of Winters' attack—it was in springtime, after the first planting. On the first anniversary of her father's and brother's deaths.

Libbie's fingers coiled expectantly around the knife hilt and her heart pounded hard but slowly, like a ceremonial drum. All else was quiet, the deepest quiet she had ever heard.

An explosion shattered the silence. Shrieks, howls and running feet shook the ground above them and then a soldier was calling for Winters. Something about a fire in the munitions building. And then he was farther away from her, throwing a promise to return over his shoulder and disappearing through the cell door.

Libbie turned to the wall and let out a shrill scream. She pounded her fists against her earthen prison walls, re-igniting the pain in her injured hand. She cradled it against her and dropped to her knees. So close. She had been so close, had nearly felt his blood flowing over her fingers, had almost avenged the deaths of her loved ones and saved those few still living. But the chance had passed and she had failed.

With a loud clang, her prison door swung open again. Libbie straightened her back, slipped the knife into her sleeve and waited. She slowed her breathing, tensed her muscles, prepared for a fight. Perhaps she would have another chance after all.

"Miss MacRae? What are you doing here? Did he hurt you?"

That voice. No, it couldn't be. Her mind was playing tricks on her. She'd thought she must have imagined hearing Winters' men say his name but now the months fell away as she turned to see that he truly stood in front of her, taller and broader than she remembered, hair as black as night, blue eyes preternaturally bright. Her vision narrowed until all she could see were Sebastian Cole's hypnotic eyes.

She could almost smell the flowers in Lady Jane's garden as he moved closer. She opened her mouth to say his name. The word did not come from her. Just a gasp as he pulled her close. He crushed his lips against hers. His mouth was cold and hard but warmed and softened as he deepened the kiss.

Terror and pain and fury and exhaustion swept over her at once. Given no time to think, only time to respond, she kissed him back. Passion rose to the surface of her skin under the touch of his fingers, just as it had that night.

But that night had been a lifetime ago, when she was barely a woman, just returned home from finishing school. Now her tranquil life had been shattered, her family destroyed, her mother's and sister's lives made pawns in some perverse game of a madman. And that naïve young woman was no more.

Libbie pushed him away from her and for the first time noticed his long, red coat. A sobering reminder of who and what he was. "How dare you?"

"You're right. This is no time for a reunion. We have to get out of here." He grabbed her hand.

A cold chill started at the point where he touched her and crept up her arm. She pulled away from him, then flung her open hand across his cheek. "I'm not going anywhere with you!"

He touched his reddening face and stared at her with those unflinching blue eyes. "Miss MacRae, Winters will soon return. Do you trust him or me?"

How could she respond when she didn't know the answer herself? That Sebastian was a British soldier and a spy was clear. But one of Winters' butchers? Was he more treacherous than she'd realized? And why did she still react to his touch? She backed away from him, ready to pull her knife.

He clasped her hand again and this time pulled her with him through the cell door. She nearly tripped over the guard lying prostrate on the floor as Sebastian dragged her to the cellar stairs. She did not fight him anymore. The moment for claiming her vengeance had passed. Now she must think of self-preservation. At least Sebastian had released her from her cell and she still had her knife if she needed to use it on him.

"I suppose they confiscated your horse?" he whispered as they climbed the stairs.

"She's too well hidden for them to have found her. If you can get me out of the fort, I can get to her."

"I will. And then get as far away from Winters as you can."

She didn't answer him.

The two crept out of the building. No one was near them. The soldiers still shouted and battled the distant blaze. Sebastian led her to a small tunnel that led under the fort wall and explained that it was there to allow messengers to sneak out of the fort during a siege. It looked frighteningly close and dark but still, it was an escape route.

"Are you sure you can find your horse from here?" he asked her.

Glancing at the position of the sun to find due west, she nodded and moved toward the tunnel. Then she turned to face him.

"Thank you for saving my life. I don't know why you did it but thank you."

He reached for her face but he didn't touch it. A shot exploded and he fell to the ground. A spot of bright red emerged and spread on the left leg of his breeches.

"Stop! Both of you!" The guard from Libbie's cell ran toward them with his rifle trained on them.

"Go, Liberty. Damn it, go!"

She dropped to the ground and crawled into the hole. The blackness swallowed her, then receded, replaced by a red haze. It was all around her, choking the breath out of her. Libbie heard another gunshot. A shriek. Was that Sebastian?

"Matthew, get that soldier back to the root cellar." Sebastian's voice. So he lived. Libbie could not explain why relief filled her as she inched forward, pulling herself on her elbows.

"Winters will be after her, sir! Go with her."

Another shot rang out. Then no voices, no sound. Libbie was too deep in the tunnel to hear any more. And still the red haze penetrated the darkness to taunt her.

Something clawed at her foot. She screamed, tried to kick it away from her. It tightened around her ankle and she realized it was a hand. Someone had followed her. Someone who might kill her here, strangle her and leave her deep in this cold, close grave. She panted. Kicked. Cried out to no one. Death tightened its icy grip on her leg.

Then it pushed her from behind, propelled her forward. Sharp shafts of moonlight penetrated her tomb. She struggled forward and emerged into the brush that lined the outside wall of the fort. She was free.

Her attacker-turned-savior crawled out beside her. She gripped her knife and held it over his back until she saw that it was Cole. He was breathing hard, too hard, even for the effort of pushing them both out into the fresh night air. She should run as fast and far from him as she could. But she couldn't. The red haze settled around him like mist hovering over a cool lake on a summer morning. If she left him, he would die. She did not take the time to ponder why she cared.

She helped him to his feet and pulled his arm over her shoulder. They had only taken a few steps when he doubled over as though overwhelmed by pain. At the same time, Libbie saw a flash of red and felt her legs go weak.

"Not now," she muttered. She focused on the feeling, tried to tame it but it was different from what they normally were. Still, there was something familiar about it. She had felt this before, that first night she and Sebastian had met.

"They're here," he whispered. "What do they want from me? I can't help them."

He was muttering nonsense. Libbie feared he was delirious from the pain. She stopped fighting the feeling of dead souls who were reaching out to her and focused her energy on dragging Sebastian into the woods, onto forest paths that white men's eyes never detected. The farther they got from the fort, the easier it became for her to breathe.

At the same instant Libbie felt the dead ones release their tenuous hold on her, Sebastian muttered, "They're gone."

She stopped walking and stared at him. Had he felt them? It wasn't possible. Unless he was closer to death than she thought, so close that he could feel the dead reaching out from the other side.

She dragged him through the forest as quickly as she could. By the time she propped him on a large rock and traveled the last few hundred yards to her well-hidden horse, Libbie's buckskins were soaked with sweat. She led Black Thunder, who had been her brother's prized mount, back to Sebastian. The moon hung low on the horizon and its light showed her what she had feared — he was losing far too much blood.

She reached into her saddlebag and pulled out the medical supplies that Mother Cloud Dancer had insisted Libbie take with her. She wrapped strip after strip of cloth around Sebastian's wound but the blood soaked through each one before she even had it securely tied. After several tense and fearful minutes, the blood covered the cloths more slowly and Libbie felt sure her handiwork would sufficiently stanch the flow until she got him somewhere safer, somewhere far from Winters.

"Come on, up into the saddle," she prodded him.

He swung his wounded leg over the horse and Libbie pushed him into an upright position. She climbed up behind him and reached around him to gather the reins. Then she slipped the knife from her sleeve and held it at the side of his throat to ensure that he did not try to hurt her. She didn't have to hold it there for long. Sebastian slumped forward over Black Thunder's neck in a dead faint.

Chapter Four

ﾏ

All was dark. The ground shifted under him. The blackness paled. He opened his eyes to see a thin line of trees in soft gray light. A horse jostled under him. And warmth pressed against him. Liberty was truly with him again.

A quick turn in the trail made his leg bump the horse's side. Pain flared. He groaned, closed his eyes. Pain. Always pain. The rest of the world was fading away from him but pain was his constant companion.

Sebastian stirred as Libbie turned Black Thunder onto a steep, stony trail. He had faded in and out of consciousness throughout the long night's ride. She hoped he had not lost too much blood. She would know soon.

In the dim light of early dawn, the mouth of a well-hidden cave rose above them. For Libbie, it was a homecoming. Things from her former life — a few dresses from home, her favorite books, her silver hairbrush and a looking glass — were here, as well as fur blankets and stores of food and medicine from the Occaneechi village where she'd learned to heal, to fight and to control her visions.

She and Sebastian would be safe, at least for a while. They had passed into Saponi territory an hour earlier. Clay Pipe's people, friends of her adopted tribe, the Occaneechi, would know she was here. If British soldiers ventured into the area, the Saponi would alert her.

"All right, Cole, time to get down," she said as she climbed off the horse.

Her tired muscles ached as she reached up to help him dismount. She led him to a pile of blankets and left him for a moment while she tended to Black Thunder and lit a fire in the stone circle outside the cave. As she gathered salves and clean cloths, the first rays of sunlight were stealing into the cave, adding to the glow from the fire.

In the light, she examined his wound more closely. She cut away the stained bandages and gently probed the bullet holes. There was one on each side of his calf. She breathed a sigh of relief, grateful that he had been hit with a well-formed British bullet, not grapeshot. The bullet had exited cleanly and had not shattered any bone. Still, the sinew and muscle were severely torn and as she swabbed the wound, the bleeding began anew.

Sebastian groaned and opened his eyes. He looked confused, disoriented. He tried to pull his leg away from her but he was weak and she could easily restrain him.

"I have to dress your wound. Try to lie still."

He was staring at her, disconcerting her. "Liberty, I never thought I'd see you again. Why were you there? In the fort?"

She shook her head at him. "Don't try to talk. Save your strength. I'll make you some tea that will help you recover from the blood loss."

She felt him watching her as she hung a pan of water over the fire, stirred herbs into it and ladled the liquid into a cup. He dutifully sipped it when she held it to his lips. She felt the pressure of his shoulder as he leaned into her for support. Now that the danger was past, she was acutely aware of his every touch. She wanted to move far from him but she had to be sure that he drank all the tea. Finally, mercifully, he drained the last drop from the cup. Then he smiled at her and moved his mouth as if to speak but his eyes rolled back and his body fell sideways.

She laid him on the blankets and pulled her own sleeping mat close to the fire. Exhaustion settled over her flesh but doubts and fears made her restless. What had Sebastian been doing at Winters' fort? She knew the kind of men that served under Winters. Was the man she had rescued, had dragged with her, had brought to her camp, a murderer?

She would get a few hours of rest, then would plan her next move. At least Sebastian would not be able to hurt her while she slept. Perhaps it was unfair of her to drug him but until she knew whether she could trust him, she had no choice.

* * * * *

Sebastian struggled to lift his heavy eyelids. When his vision cleared, he saw Libbie bathed in color, leaning over the fire, her long coppery hair hanging damp and loose down her back, tan buckskins clinging to the curves of her legs. So it had not been a hallucination.

But he had dreamed, had remembered every moment of the night they'd met.

His heart skipped a beat when Liberty turned to face him and he stared into the green eyes he had thought he would never see again. There was no denying it. This was no trick of memory or wishful thinking. The nearness of her drew him out of his strange half-existence and brought him back to the world.

"You woke up just in time for dinner." She moved slowly toward him. "But first, I'll check your bandage."

He could smell the soft scent of flowers in her clean hair. He tingled when her fingertips brushed his leg, then winced when she unwrapped the wound. It hurt more without the bandage and he imagined pressing his mouth against hers to help him forget his agony. He bit his lip to control the impulse.

She quickly redressed his wound and helped him to his feet. With her arm around him, she guided him toward the fire. She helped him sit near the flames with his leg stretched out in front of him, then handed him a small cup of water and a larger one of stew.

"Aren't you having anything?" he asked.

"I've already eaten."

The losses she had suffered had taken their toll. There was a hardness in her eyes now. It had not softened once since they had met at the fort.

"So, you are one of Winters' men," Libbie interrupted his thoughts.

The words cut into him. But how could he tell her his story? He could never expect her to believe it. Instead, he nodded.

"Then you can tell me something I need to know."

"All you need to know about him is that you have to stay away from him."

She wrapped her fingers around the hilt of the knife she wore at her waist. "No! What I need to know is how he killed my brother and my father and our friend. Did he torture them? Shoot them? Run them through with a bayonet?"

Sebastian grimaced as understanding dawned on him. "It was Winters? I should have known. If I had been there—"

"You were in his fort, with his regiment. You must be one of his butchers. Tell me, did you watch my father die? And my brother, just a month after you'd met him? Did you set them up? Those papers you gave Johnny, were they full of Winters' lies?"

The knife blade flashed as she lunged at him and pushed the point against his chest. The hardness in her eyes had changed to something worse—molten fury, sheer hatred.

"I didn't betray them, Liberty, and I wasn't there, I swear it."

"Why should I believe you? You're a liar!"

"Look into my eyes. Whatever you think of me, do you truly believe I could watch your brother die? Johnny and your father didn't think I was a threat to them. Do you really believe they were wrong?"

She dropped to her knees. He could see her resolve fading.

"I joined Winters' company four months ago. He killed a general's nephew. I went there to find the proof. The general, General Gordon, was my commanding officer."

There was more, so much more and he longed to share it with her. But the more she knew, the more danger she would face. She had already suffered enough.

"General Gordon? You were spying on Winters for Gordon?"

"I swear it to you. You know Gordon?"

She shrugged. "I know of him. Some information I saw in my father's papers after..." She coughed as the words stuck in her throat. "He was a hero, my father. Everyone knew it. But after their deaths there were accusations, lies."

"Jane wrote to me about their deaths. But lies... She didn't write about that. Tell me."

He wanted to reach for her, to embrace and comfort her but she didn't even look at him. She stared at the distant mountains, her eyes again hard. It made him shiver as he thought that her fury might in fact be less lethal than this strange detachment.

He opened his mouth to speak, to bring her back to him but he could not form words. His eyelids drifted shut against his will and his muscles felt too heavy to move. He had the vague impression of her hands on him, then of movement and finally of lying back on soft furs.

"I will trust my instincts on this," she whispered to him. "As long as you don't get in my way, we won't be enemies."

"Good," he said, struggling to form words. "I hope this means you'll stop drugging me."

* * * * *

Libbie woke with a start when a deep groan tore through the quiet veil of night. She crawled to Sebastian's side. He lay perfectly still but his breathing was fast and shallow. One touch of her fingertips against his hot brow told her the reason.

She rummaged through her medicine bags to find a pouch of ground willow bark. She mixed some into a cup of cold water, then shouted and shook Sebastian until he responded. With little help from him, she cradled his head on her lap and managed to force some of the liquid down his throat.

She lay him gently back onto the blankets, then stoked the fire. In its bright glow she cut away his bandage and surveyed his leg. There was no question about the cause of his fever. The bullet wound was red and pus-filled and nasty red streaks snaked in all directions from the torn flesh.

Libbie took a deep breath and recounted all the things Mother Cloud Dancer had taught her about infection, wishing for a moment that she had cared as much about those lessons as she had about learning to fight from the braves. She rummaged through her stockpile of sacks, this time the food stores. She mixed a concoction of corn meal and lard in a pan and stirred it over the fire until it was pasty and hot. Then she spread it on the infected area and wrapped his calf tightly in a bandage.

"No!" Sebastian moaned as the heat penetrated the inflamed wound.

"Shh." Libbie doused cloths in cold water and wiped his face and neck with them. When the dressing on his leg cooled, she redressed the wound with hot ointment. When the cloths on his head warmed, she replaced them with cold ones. She repeated the process time and time again, into the wee hours of the morning.

Finally, Libbie could stay awake no longer. Sebastian's skin was cooler, although not nearly as cool as she would have liked. And the streaks on his leg were smaller, with most of the infection collecting on the wound in a pus sack. She would try to draw it out in the morning, in the brighter light of day. She did not even have the strength to crawl to her bedroll. She collapsed beside him.

* * * * *

Libbie knelt on the trampled grass and took Johnny's hand. It was still warm but his eyes were wide open and unblinking. She ran her hand over his eyelids and closed them for all eternity. She heard a noise behind her and jumped to her feet, warily surveying the battlefield littered with broken bodies. There he was, just five feet away from her—her father. She didn't know how she had walked right past him without seeing him.

"Come closer, lass," he told her.

She sat in the grass beside him and took his hand. They were silent for a moment, her father breathing heavily with the effort of staying alive.

When he finally spoke, his voice was hoarse. "Johnny and Tom were good men. The world has to know it. I canna do anythin' about it now. It's up to you, lass."

"Me, Papa? What do you mean? What do you want me to do?"

"Avenge them. Avenge me."

Libbie shook her head. "But, I wouldn't know how."

"Ya must! You're the only one who can now. Ya must swear ya will. Swear it to me, Liberty!"

She obediently nodded her head and struggled to project her voice. "I swear it."

He closed his eyes and squeezed her hand. "I love ya, lass. And I love Annalee. Tell her. Make sure she knows how much her Papa wished he could ha' lived to see her grown."

Her voice cracked uncontrollably. "I'll tell her. I love you, Papa." She kissed his sweat-soaked brow.

The heat flared, coursed through her veins.

There was no escaping it. And there was something she needed to do, something she could not remember. Something about Sebastian. She ran from the battlefield, through foothills and deep into mountains. She stood by a river, which was swiftly turning red. Mother Cloud Dancer was there, speaking to her, telling her she must touch the red water. A river of blood, of death. Libbie dipped her arm into the current.

The water burned her skin and jarred her awake. The heat radiated from Sebastian's fevered body.

Libbie stoked the fire, mixed more willow bark into a cup of water and this time forced twice as much medicine down his throat. Knowing that it would not be enough to bring the fever under control, she removed his shirt. She sucked in her breath at the sight. Dark hair curled over his chest. The thatch narrowed as it went lower, forming a thin line just below his navel. It grew out of golden skin that was taut across the defined muscles in his chest and belly.

There was a scar—a pink, puckered remnant of some long-ago wound—at the bottom of his left breast. She touched it carefully with her finger and felt a surge of pain and death so powerful that she doubled over and nearly blacked out.

He ran until his lungs burned, the cold air drying the blood caked on his cheeks. There was a crack, the explosion of a bullet from a gun. Searing pain cut into his chest, then spread through his entire body. He could not draw another breath, could barely keep his feet under him. The ground shifted, gave way and he tumbled over a precipice, landing on sharp rocks. Pain, so much pain. And then darkness.

A full minute passed before Libbie could straighten herself after the vision and then she was shaking so hard that she could barely get to her feet. It made no sense. The gunshot and the fall over the cliff were real. They had to be. The bullet scar proved it. How, then, was he still alive?

There was no more time to ponder it as another groan snapped her mind back into focus. Libbie dragged a bucket of fresh water to Sebastian's side, then gently poured water on him from head to foot, soaking the blankets under him as well.

Next, she exposed his calf to find the wound as inflamed as it had been before her hours of treatment. When she probed it to determine whether she could lance it and drain the infection, Sebastian thrashed wildly. He groaned and muttered barely coherent words and kicked at her each time she touched him. His ravaged body possessed a tremendous amount of strength and she was not sure she could restrain him well enough to make an incision and squeeze out the pus.

"Mother Cloud Dancer, I wish you were here with me," Libbie said into the dark cave. "I know there's something I'm forgetting."

As she concentrated on the Occaneechi medicine woman, tried to hear her voice, a thought came to her. She rustled through first one bag, then another, looking for the large tobacco leaves that Mother Cloud Dancer had insisted she take with her. In the third sack she found them.

She tried to apply more corn meal mixture to Sebastian's calf but he kicked too violently. Finally, she had no choice but to straddle both his knees and use her weight to hold down his legs. She managed to coat the wound well and already some of the pus burst forth. Not enough drained and she packed on another layer of ointment and wrapped it all in tobacco leaves. She secured the leaves with a strip of cloth that she knotted over the wound.

"Walks-in-Two-Worlds." Sebastian's voice was strong and clear behind her.

Libbie blushed at the awkwardness of her position and jumped to her feet. She backed away from him, wondering how he could know her Indian name. He spoke coherently but his eyes were unfocused.

"You're forgetting something, Walks-in-Two-Worlds. You haven't said a prayer over me."

The words came from his lips but their rhythm, their tone, were Mother Cloud Dancer's. Her fear was replaced by relief.

"Of course. Thank you, Mother, thank you." She poured water over Sebastian's left hand. "Father River, bring your cooling kiss to your burning son." She pressed dirt into his palm. "Mother Earth, bring your healing strength to your injured son." Libbie reached into her shirt and pulled out the small, flattened bag tied with around her neck with a cord — her own medicine bag, blessed by the tribal elders. She removed it, pressed it into Sebastian's right palm and placed it over his heart. "This is strong medicine. Feel its power flowing through you."

She turned to leave him to his rest but he grasped her wrist with his muddy hand.

"A mistake!" His voice had regained its normal timber.

"Sebastian, rest."

His eyes were closed but his voice was loud. "Sir, those boys were set up for that attack."

Libbie dropped to her knees. "Johnny? Are you talking about Johnny?"

He tightened his grip on her. "Shot him... So sorry... Tell his wife...his son."

Sebastian's hand dropped to the ground and he fell silent. Libbie pressed her palm to her cheek and stared at him. His fevered hallucination could not be about Johnny but it bore an eerie resemblance to her brother's tragedy. Had Winters killed someone Sebastian loved? Could that explain the haunted look in his eyes?

* * * * *

Sebastian moaned from the depths of the cave. Libbie mixed more medicine for him and went to his side. In the morning light she could see that his eyes were clear, his pupils normal. With one shaking hand, she touched his brow and found it cool and dry. She quickly pulled away, afraid to touch him for too long. There was so much she didn't know about him, there were so many secrets he wouldn't share. She had realized it the first time they had met, although at the time she had convinced herself that it didn't matter.

"The fever is gone," she said, unable to think of any other words.

"Fever? Is that what it was? All I remember is heat. And pain. It hurt more than when the bullet went in."

"It was an infection." She reached for his leg. "I should check it, make sure it has drained."

She peeled back the tobacco leaves. The wound was a paler red and the edges were clean and smooth.

"I had such strange dreams," he told her as she bandaged his calf with cloths. "There were Indians. And a medicine woman. You were there and a friend I once knew…"

Her hands stopped moving when he stopped speaking. She feared he would hear her heart beating against the walls of her chest.

"Well anyway, they were strange dreams." He cleared his throat. "By the way, I seem to be missing my shirt."

She didn't answer him. She silently finished tending his wound, then stepped away from him. He had already closed his eyes and was breathing deeply. This time he looked peacefully asleep.

She wondered if he ever truly felt at peace. How much blood and horror had he seen? She wanted to ask him if it ever left him, or if it crushed the breath out of him as it did her. And the rage—did it consume him? Did the pain overwhelm him, so that the only reprieve was to feel absolutely nothing at all?

Libbie stepped out of the cave and sank to the ground. She covered her face with her hands and wept.

Chapter Five

ഔ

The soft light of dawn roused Sebastian from his shallow sleep. He sat up straight, stretched and rose cautiously to his feet. He shifted his weight to his wounded leg, testing it as he did every day. It ached with each step he took but it was healing well. A few weeks after being shot, he was able to walk by himself, thanks to Libbie. The Occaneechi medicine woman had taught her well.

He crossed the narrow width of the cave and stood over her, watching her. He longed to stroke her cheek and feel her soft breath against his palm. But he couldn't do it. From the moment he had met her, he had known he couldn't have her.

When his leg was strong enough, he would take her somewhere safe, then be on his way. The sooner he could leave her, the better for her. To that end, it was time for a tougher test of his recovery.

He set off on a footpath that followed the course of a mountain stream running through their camp. He moved slowly but steadily and reached his destination by the time the sun was fully visible over the mountain peak above him.

Liberty had described the beauty of the lake to him, with its rich jewel colors and fragrant earthen banks. That beauty and scent were lost on him but not the tranquility of the small oasis. He dipped a foot into the water and sent gentle ripples, growing ever larger, lapping against the far shore. This was a sacred place, a healing place.

Sebastian pulled off his coat, then slipped off the buckskins given to him by Clay Pipe. He rinsed the tunic and breeches and laid them out on a large rock to dry, relishing the return of self-reliance.

He stood at the edge of the lake took a deep breath and plunged into its calm depths. He sliced through the water, stretching his atrophied muscles. The heavy water parted easily at his body's command. He played as if he were a child with no cares, no ghosts. It seemed so long since he had been without them. She had done that for him. Libbie had brought light into his world to chase away the shadows. He only wished he didn't have to leave her so soon.

He stepped out of the lake and picked up the dry cloth he had brought from the cave. He rubbed it vigorously over his hair, then moved it over his face and shoulders, wiping the water droplets from his skin. As he bent toward one foot, he heard a small noise from the other side of the lake. It came to him sharply, clearly. That meant it could only be Libbie.

He moved slowly, waiting for her to announce herself, or to discreetly leave. She did neither. He knew she was watching him, studying him. His blood surged through his veins from the thrill of knowing her gaze was on his bare skin. His body throbbed with intense desire. He panted to catch his breath, overwhelmed by feelings he hadn't enjoyed for more than a year.

If it was a show she wanted, it was a show she would get. He rubbed the towel over his arms, his legs, his buttocks. Then, with the towel hanging around his neck, he turned slowly, deliberately, letting his hidden watcher admire him from every angle.

He stood tall and proud, facing the trees that covered Liberty, pretending to take in the view. After a long, still minute, she moved. He could not see her but the trees shuddered as she passed them, going away from him. Judging from the ripple she made in the forest, she was running and at quite an impressive speed.

When he knew she was beyond earshot, Sebastian broke into laughter. It was pure joy to imagine her face, wide-eyed and slack-jawed, tinged with a deep blush, as she watched him turn in her direction. She might still have concerns about the condition of his leg but at least she now knew she didn't have to worry about the health of any of his other body parts.

After dressing, Sebastian spent nearly an hour sitting on a long, flat rock at the edge of the lake. He watched the wind ripple the water's surface and shake the tree tops.

Libbie would soon wonder what had happened to him. He hated to worry her. She would never admit it but her eyes brightened and her lips lifted slightly with the relief of seeing him every time he returned from one of his short outings. Not into a true smile — he hadn't seen that since the night he'd met her. God, how he missed that beautiful smile. He longed to hold her against him, soothe her pain, assure her that it would get better, easier. But he couldn't bring himself to lie to her.

And now he waited, even knowing that she would soon be concerned. He had no choice. Someone was coming. He couldn't say who or why or even precisely when but they were coming.

"You took a bullet for her."

Of all the possibilities, he had not considered that it would be Johnny MacRae. Sebastian turned to see the apparition.

"She saved my life afterwards. Or at least she believes she did. She certainly relieved the pain." Sebastian furrowed his brow. "I have to ask, why you? Why now? They haven't sent anyone for so long."

Johnny shrugged. "You haven't needed guidance."

"And now?"

Johnny wore the same intense look that lately defined his sister's face. "What are your intentions where she's concerned?"

Sebastian laughed. He couldn't help himself. "That's why they sent you? Well, since you've asked, I plan to take her somewhere far away from Winters, somewhere she'll be safe while I go after him."

"I thought maybe you'd know her better than that by now."

"Meaning?"

"Meaning that it will never work. My sister won't give up. The man killed us, planted lies that ruined the MacRae name, destroyed our family."

Sebastian frowned. Libbie had finally told him about the lies. Winters had declared the MacRaes spies, his spies. He had told the surviving members of Sean MacRae's regiment that he had paid Sean and Johnny to tell Winters and his men where to find the regiment and attack them. It was hard to understand how Sean's men could believe such lies. But then again, most of those men were really boys and seeing the horrors of battle could do strange things to anyone's mind.

"There's more," Johnny continued. "She fears for those still alive. My mother and other sister."

Sebastian clenched his fists. "Are their lives in danger? Is Winters after them? Is he after Libbie?"

Johnny looked as though he was about to speak, then shook his head. A moment later, he spoke. "Libbie believes he will try to kill them. It informs every move she makes."

"Then I'll protect them. And her. I'll handle Winters. She's no longer in it."

Now Johnny laughed. "Are you planning to order her away from him? I'll have to come back just to watch you try that."

Sebastian's patience was wearing thin. "Fine, then. Guide me, if that's why you're here. What I am to do with your headstrong sister?"

"Stay with her. Don't let her go after him alone."

Sebastian shook his head. "I can't do that. You know how dangerous it is."

"She'll either be in danger with you, or she'll be in greater danger without you." Johnny stepped closer, crossed his arms over his chest. "They'd say I can't force you to do it, you still have free will. I'm saying that she's my sister and I can make this existence even more miserable for you if I have to."

Sebastian turned to stare out across the lake as he considered the words, wondering what, if anything, Johnny could truly do to him. But it wasn't the threat, idle or not, that swayed Sebastian. It was the truth of Johnny's assessment of his sister, a truth Sebastian could not deny. She wouldn't give up her quest, futile as Sebastian knew it to be. The best he could hope for was to protect her, to take more bullets for her, to keep Winters from destroying her.

He turned to tell her equally stubborn brother of his decision. Apparently Johnny knew Sebastian's answer, because he had already left.

* * * * *

Winters sat up in his bed, pulled out of a sound sleep by voices. He did not bother to light a candle and check the room. When he was still a boy he had given up trying to see the ghosts who spoke to him. He didn't fear them, couldn't remember ever having feared them.

Then had come the fateful night when they had whispered, "Pledge your loyalty to us and we will give you your heart's greatest desire. You need only wish for it."

"Revenge," he had whispered back and the next day his life had begun to change.

This time, the voices were excited, frenetic. "Come, come quickly," they whispered. As if in a hypnotic trance, Winters threw back his blankets and hopped from his bed. Within minutes, he was fully dressed and leaving his quarters, barely noticing the cloud-muted half moon as he relied on his familiarity with every inch of his fort to navigate his way to the small side entrance on the western wall. Whatever was calling to him waited in the forest on the southwest edge of the fort. He could not explain how he knew, he just knew that they were there and that if he could get to them, if he could finally discern what they wanted from him, they would stop haunting him.

He slipped out of the fort and quietly identified himself to the sentries keeping watch. The men saluted him, then looked concerned as Winters moved into the darkness. "Sir?"

"As you were, soldiers."

Winters walked beside the high stone wall, then crossed into the thick copse of trees that marked the edge of the untamed forest. His black wool cape billowed in the frigid breeze. He took a deep breath, savored the sweet smell of evergreens and impending snow. Once he had thought he would never get the stench of urine and vomit and drunk, unwashed bodies out of his nostrils. But the dirty, diseased London streets of his boyhood were far behind him now. He was wealthy, powerful, a master of men.

Winters had lost count of the number of times men had tried to kill him. He had been a better fighter than most, not as good as some but every one of those enemies was now dead while Winters still walked and breathed. He had been born for greater things and the spirits who had called to him would protect him so that he could achieve them. Perhaps he had been born to lead the entire British army. He grinned as he thought of sniveling dogs like General Gordon bowing down in front of him. Not that Gordon or any of the other men who had dared to cross Winters would live long enough to do so, once he held their destinies in his hands.

He was deep into the forest, consumed by his own thoughts when he felt their presence like a cold draft on bare skin.

"Who goes there?" he called. No one answered.

"I know you're here," he muttered. "Show yourselves, you bloody cowards."

He had barely finished the whispered command when they materialized out of the dark and knelt before him. They were brown-skinned and lean, with stringy black hair and gaunt faces. They smelled of sweat and dirt. Ragged, filthy buckskins hung from their thin bodies. They bore no resemblance to the specters of insubstantial mist who had visited him so often. He reached out and touched one on the shoulder, met the firm resistance of flesh and drew his hand back with a gasp.

"You look and feel human, yet you appear out of the darkness like ghosts." The kneeling beings remained silent. "What are you?"

"We are human."

Winters' heart pounded so fast it was hard to catch his breath. "You are the ones. The ones who have been following me, who tried to kill me. Why… How did you call me here?"

"You called us."

"That's not possible." Winters clenched one fist and laid the other hand over the hilt of the knife he wore at his waist. "If that's the case, how did I call you? And why did you respond?"

"We are at your service," the same man who had spoken before answered. "We are bound to you now."

At the words, Winters felt the power surge through him and he knew it was true. "On your feet." They instantly obeyed. "At my service, eh? Then explain all of this to me."

The man who had spoken stared at Winters with eyes as black as onyx. But those eyes held no depth, no spark. They were flat, unblinking. Dead. "Our futures, our destinies, what is left of our lives are tied to you. While you live and breathe, we live and breathe. If you call us, we come, if we are able. If you command us…" He hesitated, then continued, "We obey, to the best of our ability."

"You're not my soldiers. You've pledged no loyalty to me. You're Indians, for Christ's sake. Why do you obey me?" He held up his hand to the man who had spoken. "Let the other one answer this time."

He looked at the man who was not quite as tall or thin as his companion but who had the same dead black eyes. The man didn't speak. He gasped, grunted and moaned until tears rolled down his cheeks but he didn't get out a word.

"What's wrong with him?" Winters asked.

The struggling man lifted his chin, exposing a thick seam of scar tissue.

"He cannot speak," his companion answered. "He lost the ability when you slit his throat, when he tried to kill you but failed."

Winters' legs no longer felt stable beneath him. The mute man grabbed his shoulder to steady him. The sight of the man's face brought back a night months earlier, when one overzealous brave had lunged between Winters and a squaw whom he had hit to the ground with the butt of his rifle. The brave had been furious, distracted. And Winters' knife had been poised in his other hand.

Winters struggled for words. "I killed him, I know I did."

"The first time, your men killed him and he went to the spirits. They sent him back, as they did me, to fulfill a destiny to defeat you. But, in different times and places, we each failed the charge the spirits gave to us. Now we have no way back to the peace and contentment of the spirit world. Now we dwell here as long as you do."

"And someday, if I die?" Winters asked.

The man shrugged. "Our time in this realm will end but who knows what price we will have to pay. This life cannot truly be called that, as all color and scent and now even feeling have been drained from it, yet it may be better than our eternal fate."

As the words sank into Winters' mind, he pushed away the mute man, perfectly able to stand on his own. "And you will obey my every command."

The mute man nodded slowly.

"To the best of our ability," the other man said. "But we lack the strength we had when we pursued you. And we grow even weaker in the daytime. Like the ghosts we cannot become, our strength gathers at dusk," he glanced at the night sky, "and is magnified by the moonlight. It is greatly augmented by your close proximity and is slightly affected by the nearness of another with the ability to feel the dead."

Winters felt the blood drain from his face but did not confirm nor dispute the man's claim.

"We realized it when the other one was near. She felt us but she did not call out to us."

She. The man could only mean one person. "So, dear cousin, we are more alike than either of us realized," he whispered into the wind. To the men he said, "You have served me well tonight but it was only the beginning. Be prepared to respond to my call at any moment."

Of course he would test their abilities soon, perhaps as soon as Gordon sent another spy into Winters' fort. A spy like Cole had turned out to be, even after Winters had offered to make him one of his own. As soon as he got his hands on that traitor who had helped Liberty MacRae escape, the insolent son of a bitch would pay.

"M'lord?"

Winters liked the sound of that. "Yes?"

"There is something you should know, one of our limitations. We cannot help you kill the other Fated One."

"Fated One?"

"That is what the spirits have named us."

"And you say there's another one? Sent to kill me?"

The mute man nodded vigorously.

"And he is strong, sir," the speaking man continued. "Perhaps stronger than the two of us together. Or perhaps it is just that he travels with the other one who feels the dead."

Winters narrowed his eyes. "Liberty? He's traveling with Liberty?"

Both Indians nodded.

Winters shook his head in disbelief, then nodded, finally understanding. Sebastian Cole was more than a mere spy whom Winters needed to kill. He was a Fated One, a man who had already died.

* * * * *

Libbie lay alone under her blankets, shivering. It had turned bitterly cold but since sundown, they had been unable to light a warming fire. A Cherokee hunting party was nearby, on the southern edge of Saponi territory. Clay Pipe had come to warn her. She had found him waiting at the cave when she had run back from the lake. He had been worried, sure that Libbie had stumbled upon the Cherokee herself. She had assured him she had not, although she never did tell him what had sent her scurrying through the woods.

Clay Pipe had also told her something that she already knew. A fierce winter storm was on its way. The cave would not protect them from it. So tonight, she and Sebastian would huddle in the dark, hiding from the Cherokee. And in the morning, they would begin their journey out of the mountains. She would find someplace safe for him, where he could convalesce and she would get back to tracking Winters and seeking out his weaknesses, preparing for their ultimate confrontation.

Alone. Just as she preferred it. Yet there was an emptiness, a deep loneliness about the prospect of it. She determined to dismiss the foolish thoughts as she tossed and turned, telling herself that the cold and the proximity of the Cherokee were the roots of her discontent.

"You can't sleep?" His deep voice echoed in the quiet cave.

"I'm sorry. Am I keeping you awake?"

She heard no response from him, just a rustling in the dark. And then she felt him against her. He climbed under her blankets with her and covered them both with his furs. She was breathless, unable to protest as his body, at first chilled, warmed beside her.

"I'm afraid this is the only way to survive this frigid night," he whispered.

She lay rigid and silent beside him. In her mind she knew he was right, that this was strictly a matter of survival. But her body—that was a different story. Sebastian's form was long and sturdy, hard muscle and roughened skin, such a contrast to her own. How could a woman sleep with such a beast pressed against her? And why did she suddenly feel flushed and disoriented, as though she had drunk an entire flask of her mother's homemade claret?

"You're frightened of the Cherokee?"

She took a deep breath, then cleared her throat but her voice quivered when she spoke. "I've seen them in battle. They're fierce. Relentless."

"You've seen battle? I didn't realize."

"It isn't something I like to discuss."

"Especially with someone you don't trust?"

Libbie frowned. He sounded hurt. Somehow, for all the distance she kept between them, she couldn't stand to hurt him. There was more to him than met the eye, something that went beyond secrets and espionage. A sadness, a longing. A world-weariness that tore at his soul.

"If I didn't trust you, you wouldn't be here," she said.

"I wasn't sure you believed me."

"I do." It was not a lie. She believed the things he had told her. What concerned her were the things he hadn't explained, like how he could swim in an ice-cold mountain lake in late November, why he carried the scar of a bullet that should have killed him, what loved ones he had lost at Winters' hands.

"The Occaneechi had joined with the Saponi in battle," she told him. "A matter of honor. Although how anything honorable can come out of such horror, I still don't understand."

"Why did they take you with them?"

"It was my final test before being adopted by the tribe." She smiled. The night the Occaneechi had finally accepted her as one of them was the happiest memory she'd had since Papa and Johnny had left for the war.

"You were there to treat the wounded?"

"Yes and..." She let her voice trail off. How could she tell him the rest of it? Her death vision had saved the young chief's life. He was her friend's husband, father of a baby daughter and he was destined to die that day but she had interceded. It had earned her more than the tribe's acceptance. It had earned her their respect.

Libbie felt Sebastian move and prop himself up on his elbow. "Thank you for telling me, for trusting me. Much has changed in the past few weeks."

Liberty wanted to ask what he meant by that. But then, of course, a few weeks ago he had been a healthy soldier in the British Army, living in a bona fide shelter. And with no woman to share his bed, except on the occasions that he visited his "friend" Lady Jane. The memory of seeing the two of them together after Libbie had thought he had feelings for her made her skin crawl.

She rolled over away from him to give herself a few inches of distance and to clear dangerous thoughts that could be misconstrued as longing or jealousy from her mind.

"When you have completely healed, what will you do?" she finally asked. "You can't go back to Winters' camp. He'd kill you on sight."

"He could try. It's not that easy."

She turned toward him again. "What do you mean?"

"Nothing. I meant nothing. As for my plans... Hmm. No doubt I should take you somewhere safe, then find a way to watch Winters while staying out of his reach."

Libbie sat up. "Take me somewhere safe? Excuse me but who saved whom back at that fort? You're still recovering from nearly dying. If anyone is being taken somewhere safe, it's you."

"Is that what you are planning?" His voice sounded more amused than upset. "As I recall, I did rescue you from Winters' dungeon."

"Yes but then I dragged you for miles and miles through the woods and rode all night to get you here and tended your wound and treated your fever."

She heard him chuckle. "All right, I concede. But truly, you cannot go near Winters. He'd kill you on sight, as well. How on earth could your family survive that?"

He had asked the one question that haunted her. But she would trade her own life a thousand times over rather than lose another loved one to Winters. Her course was set, her destiny was sealed. Winters would die at her hands. To hell with the risk to her own safety or even life.

She pushed thoughts of the consequences from her mind and tried to make her voice sound light. "You know, there's a terrible flaw in your plan to watch Winters. If you're nice to me, I might reveal it to you."

"Oh really?" Sebastian's fingertips brushed her forearm, sending first ice, then flames through her body. "And what, pray tell, must I do to be considered nice?"

A list of wholly inappropriate and unladylike suggestions occurred to her, accompanied by the vivid memory of Sebastian standing by the lake, healed, strong, naked. A rush of feelings and sensations washed over her, feelings she hadn't felt since...since Sebastian had kissed her, first at Lady Jane's ball, then at Winters' fort. She'd seen him half-naked when she'd tended his wound and his fever but she'd been too consumed with healing him to notice the incredible breadth of his shoulders and flatness of his belly. Or at least to dwell on them overmuch.

But today had been different. So different. He had been so healthy, so exposed. And so utterly virile.

She focused on keeping her breathing normal and her voice steady as she spoke so she wouldn't give herself away. "You must treat me like the woman I am." She paused for a moment as she considered the irony. In order to treat her like the woman she truly was, the kind of woman who could have the thoughts about him that she had just had, Sebastian would have to be something that his respectful and chivalrous behavior had proven he was not—a lecherous cad.

"You were saying?"

She was grateful for the darkness when she felt her neck and face flush with heat. She cleared her throat and concentrated hard to remember the point she had been about to make. "You must, um, you must treat me like a woman. A capable woman. Not a child. Not a helpless young girl."

She felt his body tense beside her. "I am well aware that you are a woman. Too well aware," he added softly.

Libbie's heart pounded. What did he mean by it? She wanted to ask him, wanted to know if had ever thought of her the way she had been thinking of him that night. The way she'd been thinking of him all day, if the truth be told. She wanted to ask the question. The words were on her lips. Common sense caught up to her just in time. What would she say if his answer were no? And what on earth would she do if it were yes?

His voice had regained its normal timbre when he spoke again. "You said my plan is flawed."

The words brought her back to reality, the cold, stark reality of her life. She sighed and lay back. "We keep watching him and waiting for him to make a mistake. He won't. I wasted a month of time, you wasted four. And he's still alive and well. There's nothing more that watching and waiting will reveal to us."

"You make a good point," Sebastian said. "Although I thought I was making headway for a time. He made me an offer to join his inner circle."

"It was a test. To gain his trust would take years. And the things you would have to endure in that time…" She couldn't explain how but she knew it was true.

"Yes, I had the same feeling after I thought about it. When I regained consciousness after one of his men shot me and I found myself under your expert care."

"Winters knows you're nothing like him. You're much too good, too kind."

"You don't know what it means to me to hear you say that." His voice had taken on the soft, sentimental tone again.

Libbie refused to dwell on it, as it would only make her lose her senses again. "He made me an offer as well," she said.

Sebastian sat bolt upright beside her. "What kind of offer?"

"He wanted my mother's farm. In exchange, he would give me a quick, painless death."

"That miserable bastard," Sebastian muttered. "He has to be stopped."

"We need another plan."

"Perhaps we do have another option…"

The way he said "we" made relief flood over Libbie. Suddenly the prospect of facing a cold-blooded killer alone seemed too overwhelming and the prospect of having someone to watch her back seemed immensely appealing.

"What is it?" she asked Sebastian. "We have to do it. Anything at all."

"I can go back to Gordon, give him what I know. You're a colonist, still under the Crown's protection, despite the uprising. And Winters kidnapped you."

"I'll have to give Gordon my side of the story." Libbie turned toward him, her heart pounding with sudden hope. "Your word won't be enough against a colonel. My testimony will be necessary as well. And then the British Army will have to go after that monster they've created."

To save the rest of her family, Libbie would make a deal with the devil himself. So making a deal with the next closest thing — the British Army — seemed wholly reasonable to her now.

Sebastian was silent for so long time that she worried he had fallen asleep. When he finally spoke, his voice was low and controlled. "It's a possibility," he said.

"It's a good idea!"

"Maybe General Gordon can provide some measure of protection for you. And his men could certainly contain Winters' soldiers."

"It's a plan," she said. A plan that has to work, she didn't add. "But first we must survive this night."

"Ah, yes. The Cherokee. The enemy at hand. Lying in wait under cover of darkness."

"When I was a little girl, I was afraid of the dark. My father sat with me and told me stories until I fell asleep."

"Really? What kinds of stories?"

"Oh, ones about the Highlands, mostly. Whimsical stories about the fairies who lived there."

"Tell me about them," Sebastian whispered.

"I don't remember many of the details. But there is one story I'll always remember. He told it whenever he wanted to remind us of the importance of family. And he wanted to remind us often. Even Annalee…"

She choked back tears as she thought about her eight-year-old little sister whom she hadn't seen for months. There should have been more children, many more children. But frontier life was difficult, and after Johnny and Libbie, none of

72

her parents' other babies had made it to term. Until their beautiful, happy little Annalee came along to complete their family. Now there were only three of them — their mother and two daughters — to keep the family, its name, its traditions and stories, alive. "Even Annalee could tell that one by heart."

"Then tell it to me. Just the way your father would have told it."

Libbie smiled and invoked the sound of her father's brogue. "There's no land on earth so fair as the Highlands o' Scotland. No Scot who e'er laid eyes on them could leave them again without feelin' his heart break. An' near the edge o' that fair land, beyond the sharpest crags and the deepest lochs o' Scotland, lie the fairest fields of all, the heartland o' the Clan MacRae.

"And there lived in those lands the wisest man of all, a man revered by kings and guarded by the sprites and fairies who resided in the rocks and trees o' those lands, a man named Ian MacRae. And he would ha' lived forever, if he'd not been lured off his land by rabid British dogs, who hunted down innocent clan folk and killed them in cold blood.

"The dogs were on the heels o' Bonnie Prince Charlie himself when Ian MacRae joined the bloody battle to drive them out o' the Highlands. But without the magic of his fairies to guard him, he was as mortal as any man. And the dogs turned on him, slaughtered him as they had so many before him, cut him down in front of women and children, then turned on the women and children as well.

"When Ian's widow learned of his death, she nearly died herself from grief. But she couldna do that — she had a wee bairn to care for. An' she knew the British dogs would kill him too, if they found him. So she sent him away, had a farmhand smuggle him to Ireland, then settled in to protect the lands of Ian MacRae. She called on the fairies to protect her and their homeland but the fairies were so aggrieved by the death o' their fair master that they failed her and she was slaughtered like her husband before her.

73

"And so, all that was left o' the line of Ian MacRae was one wee bairn. With no money and no kin, he shoulda perished but he was as strong as his ancestors. He worked his way to the New World and after years o' back-breakin' labor, he went to the fairest valley in the land and bought the best farm in that valley. He married a lass who was brave, strong and beautiful, as his mother had been and together they founded a new homeland for the Clan MacRae."

Sebastian was silent for a long time. Then he sought out her hand in the darkness. "I'm sorry about your family, your grandparents. What you must think of me, a Redcoat."

"I know you're not like them, not like Winters." She felt her fingers tremble and he withdrew his hand.

"Nothing like Winters." His voice was harsh. The tone was softer when he spoke again. "My father comes from a long, proud line as well. Farmers, most of them. My two older brothers still work the land with him. My younger brother studies at Oxford. And I…well, I suppose I've taken up the family's past profession."

"Past profession? Didn't you just say they were farmers?"

He laughed softly. The sound of it comforted her. She relaxed and closed her eyes, letting his voice wash over her.

"When I couldn't sleep, my mother used to tell me stories, as well. Her favorite was one she learned from my father's grandmother. It's a family legend about the Black Knight."

"Black Knight?"

"Yes, well, family legend has it that the dark hair — mine, my father's, some of his forefathers — comes from the Black Knight. He was the son of a Cole who fought in the Crusades. The soldier fought well and bravely for the Pope, until he fell in love with a Moorish princess."

"A princess!"

"A Moorish princess — not the kind of woman a Crusader should really be courting. Well, they ran away together, got married and lived in exile. Years later, their son — Byron was his name — returned to the British Isles to reclaim the family lands from thieves who had usurped them.

"First, he appealed to the king for help. The Coles had served the king faithfully in years gone by and he promised not to interfere with this quest but he was not about to offer support to the half-breed son of an exiled man.

"So Byron was left to his own devices. Nearly a year passed and still he had persuaded none of his family's old allies to join him. It didn't help his cause with the gentlemen that his mixed heritage proved an endless fascination to the English ladies. But it was actually that which gained him his first supporter. He was discovered in, um — shall we say a compromising situation? — with a very beautiful and very betrothed young lady.

"When her fiancé learned of the offense, he promptly challenged Byron to a duel. Unfortunately for the fiancé, Byron was a master swordsman and although Byron did allow him to live, the man was humiliated. Fortunately for Byron, the fiancé was a highly unpopular man. The brother of the woman who was at the center of the duel was the first to offer Byron a congratulatory drink and over that drink he heard Byron's tale.

"By the time that night was through, the Black Knight, as they began to call him, had many well-heeled and stout-hearted supporters. Weeks later, he led a small band of men north to his homelands and after several days of vicious, bloody fighting, they rousted out the men who had taken over the Cole lands and the Black Knight reclaimed his birthright. When the king validated his claim a few months later, the Black Knight took a bride, the same young woman he had dueled over months earlier and vowed never to take up his sword again. And the Coles were farmers ever after."

"Until you."

"Yes, I suppose so. But this is all legend, of course. My father never put much stock in it. In fact, he even told my mother she shouldn't put such ideas in my head. But sometimes, when my mother was describing the Black Knight's triumphs, I would see my father hovering in the doorway, hanging on her words, smiling. The way that a man can only smile when he's deeply in love."

His story ended there and they fell silent. Libbie thought of the way her father had smiled at her mother, remembered the tenderness between them. And for the thousandth time since her father's death, she marveled at her mother's strength, her ability to carry on after the loss of the love of her life and of her only son.

I will protect you, Mama, Libbie thought and hoped that her mother could somehow feel her words. *I'll save you and Annalee. I swear I won't let Winters take any more from you.*

Sebastian's soft breathing beside Libbie soothed her. Tomorrow they would resume their crusade against Winters. They would carry out their vendettas together, or they would die trying. But tonight, just this one night, Libbie would escape into a pleasant dream of a valiant black-haired knight and his green-eyed Scottish lover.

Chapter Six

ဆ

Sebastian watched Libbie, curled into her bedroll on the opposite side of the campfire and waited until he heard her deep, even breaths that assured him that she was asleep. He'd been watching her sleep for weeks now, knew that her deepest sleep was early in the night, knew that her nightmares came closer to dawn.

But this past week, as they'd climbed down out of the mountains and crossed the foothills, he'd been unable to let her suffer them alone. He had taken to holding her hand, stroking her arm, murmuring soothing words. His ministrations didn't wake her but they did seem to chase away the demons that haunted her sleep.

He had to return before the hour of her nightmares, which left him precious little time. He slipped away from her and moved to the edge of the small clearing where'd they'd made their camp. He peered into the surrounding woods and gave a low whistle. A few seconds later, he got a familiar response and his old friend, Fox, slipped from between two trees and reached out to shake Sebastian's hand.

Fox looked surprised. "You just came away from the fire but your hand's like ice, boy."

Sebastian pulled his hand away and shrugged, then launched into conversation before Fox could pursue it.

"How did you find us?" he asked.

"The Saponi Indian who was lookin' out for Miss Libbie. I do a lot of tradin' with the tribe, so they trust me. Don't trust you, though, by the sound of it. Clay Pipe said the medicine woman took an instant dislike to you."

Sebastian furrowed his brow. "Medicine woman? I never even met their medicine woman. Only Clay Pipe and I only met him once."

Fox shrugged. "Who knows what got into her. Visions or somethin'. I didn't used ta put much stock in it but after what happened at the village..." His voice cracked and he had to take a deep breath before he could continue. "Well, Little Doe had been tellin' me for weeks that somethin' wicked was in the air. I didn't listen."

Sebastian gripped his friend's shoulder. "We made a pact, you and I. We said we'd stop blaming ourselves."

Fox nodded. "Yeah. And that's workin' for you about as well as it is for me. I can see it in your eyes. And I know where you've been these past months. I know you got yourself assigned to that son of a bitch's regiment."

"I'm going to take him down, Fox. I'll avenge them, I swear it."

Fox nodded. "And so you're off to meet with that drunk bastard Jackson at his usual haunt, hopin' to find out what Winters is up to these days?"

Sebastian nodded. "It was a godsend, hearing your signal this afternoon, knowing you'd tracked us. I can't leave Libbie out here alone and unprotected but I sure as hell don't want her anywhere near the likes of Jackson."

Fox inclined his head toward the fire. "And Miss Libbie? Did she hear my signal? Did you tell 'er you'd be leavin' 'er under my care while you're off playin' the spy?"

"She doesn't know anything about that life." He bit his lip, remembering what she'd learned about him from his association with her father and Johnny. "Not much, anyway. There's no need to drag her any further into my world. She's been through enough."

When Fox scowled and rubbed the back of his neck, Sebastian knew he'd hit the man's soft spot. "I knew her pa a little. The MacRaes are good people. What Winters did to them... Fine, I'll stay 'ere and baby-sit—or lady-sit, as it were—while you try to find out somethin' about that son of a bitch."

"Just watch her from here. Keep your gun drawn, just in case. She doesn't sleep well."

"That's fine," Fox muttered. "She'll wake up, find out you left without tellin' her and she'll bite my head off."

Sebastian shook his head. "As I was about to say, she doesn't sleep well toward dawn. I should be back before then." Sebastian hesitated. He trusted Fox more than anyone else left on earth. One day he would explain to the man how he and Libbie had come to be traveling companions. Hell, he might even tell him the whole sordid story about his "death". But not tonight. There was no time. "She'll never know I was gone."

Fox narrowed his eyes. "If she wakes up, I'll tell 'er where you've gone. I'm not keen on secrets between friends."

Sebastian got the distinct impression that Fox was referring to their friendship as much as he was to the situation with Libbie.

"I understand, Fox." He glanced at the moon rising higher in the sky. "But it's getting late. I have to get to Jackson."

"Fine." Fox patted his musket. "I'll be here watchin' over 'er when you get back."

"Thank you. I wouldn't trust anyone else in the world to do it."

Fox nodded. "One more thing," he called as Sebastian mounted his horse.

"What is it, Fox?"

"You watch yer back. I don't want to be the one who has to explain to Miss Libbie why you went off and got yerself killed."

Sebastian nodded to his friend but sighed as he spurred his mount into action. "Not to worry," he mumbled to himself. "There's not a man alive who can truly kill me."

* * * * *

Sebastian flattened himself against the side of the tavern when the front door swung open. Two laughing patrons stumbled into the road, then disappeared. Sebastian stepped away from the wall and surveyed the dark landscape. Confident that no one else was near, he slipped to the side door. With two well-spaced raps followed by two quick ones, he announced himself. The door creaked open just a crack and a round, sweaty face peered out at him. The obese man pulled the door wide open.

"He's not expecting you," the man said as Sebastian brushed past him. "You didn't send word—"

"It was unavoidable. He is here, isn't he?"

"Always is." The tavern owner jerked his head toward a closed door.

Sebastian entered the room without knocking. He found Colonel Jackson sitting at a small table in a private room. The man's coat sleeves were pushed up to his elbows and his shirt was unbecomingly loosened about the neck.

"Cole, is that you?" Jackson squinted at him. "Have a seat, old man. And a drink."

Sebastian stood his ground. "No thank you, Colonel. I just need to know if any of your men have brought you information about one of the British commanders along the frontier."

Jackson reached into his jacket pocket, pulled out a stack of tattered papers and tossed them on the table. "Help yourself. See if there's anything in there."

As Sebastian scanned the papers, Jackson stared at him. "It's always business with you, isn't it, Cole? That's your problem. You never take the time to enjoy the finer things in life—a good whiskey, a good pipe, a good woman." Jackson leaned back and took a deep drag from his pipe.

Sebastian watched Jackson blow puffs of smoke into the air. He could not discern the slightest whiff of tobacco. His senses were duller than the last time he'd met Jackson in this place. Or perhaps it was just the contrast of his normal state to the overwhelming sensations he'd been experiencing in Libbie's company.

He turned his attention back to the reports from the frontier scouts. Nothing on Winters. Still, there was useful information. Some American regiments were on course to intersect British troops near the northwestern border of the Virginia colony. Sebastian had seen the spilled blood of too many young men. He'd have no more of it on his own hands. He would do everything he could to make sure General Gordon got the British troops out of the Continental Army's path. The number of lives that would be saved on both sides would make the risks and this unpleasant interaction with Jackson worthwhile.

"You're sure this is good information?" Sebastian asked.

Jackson moved as if to stand but he swayed and fell back into his seat. "Have I ever given you bad information? Are you accusing me of lying?"

Sebastian reached forward and patted Jackson's shoulder in a friendly gesture. As much as he hated to touch the drunken sod, he had to calm the man before he did something foolish. Or loud. "You've always given me good information, Jackson. One just can't be too cautious these days."

Jackson stared at him for a moment, then nodded, lifted his glass toward Sebastian and downed the last drops of his spirits.

"There's nothing in these reports but maybe you've heard something about Winters? He's the commander of the fort where I was serving."

Jackson nodded. "Yeah, Winters. Holed up in his fort, last I heard."

The information was no help but Sebastian thanked him anyway.

"One more thing before you go, Cole."

Sebastian stopped with his hand on the doorknob, wishing he could ignore the man and keep walking.

"I think you can help someone I know."

Jackson picked up his walking stick and pounded it on the table. The sweaty tavern owner burst into the room and Jackson motioned him closer and whispered to him. The tavern owner disappeared through a second door and, before Sebastian could take his leave, reappeared with a short, full-bearded and obviously inebriated stranger. The drunken man had dandified clothes and a pompous demeanor and Sebastian didn't need to hear his heavy accent to know what kind of man he was. The tavern owner helped the stranger into a chair, then left the room.

"Monsieur Cole, I am Marquis Phillipe de la Beaulieu. I am here to offer you a proposition."

Sebastian stepped behind Jackson and spoke in a low tone. "A Frenchman? What does he want from me?"

"Relax, old man," Jackson said, slurring more with every word. "Hear him out."

Sebastian considered the wisdom of the suggestion. Better to hear what the dandy had to say, to make sure the fool wasn't going to get in his way.

"He is to be trusted, yes?" the Frenchman asked Jackson.

Sebastian bristled but Jackson nodded.

The Frenchman spoke to Sebastian as he held out his empty glass for Jackson to fill. "Please, Monsieur, you must help me. I have acquired hundreds of guns through many backers in France who…well, let us say they have a great interest in seeing the Continental Army succeed. Our plan is to distribute the guns to the Indians along the Ohio frontier so that they will rise up against the Redcoats."

Sebastian widened his eyes. "Indeed? Last I'd heard, those tribes were in league with the King's army."

Beaulieu smiled. "For now they are with the British but when we give them guns, they will come to our side. We just need someone to make the arrangements, a man who can slip past the British and get to the tribes."

Sebastian forced a smile. "That is a daring plan. But something else comes to mind, something much bigger and better."

Beaulieu propped his forearms on the table and stared, wide-eyed, at Sebastian. "What is this plan?"

Sebastian glanced over his shoulder. "Not here, not now. I'll get word to you when the time is right. But for now, you must listen very closely."

Sebastian paused.

Both men nodded and waited for him to continue.

"For now," he whispered, "put those guns in a very safe place. A place where no one will find them or even think to look for them."

Beaulieu nodded again. "*Bien sur.*"

Sebastian glanced from Beaulieu to Jackson and back again. "And not a word of this to anyone, not until I contact you. I'm counting on you both."

Beaulieu placed his right hand over his heart. "Monsieur, you have my solemn vow."

Jackson mumbled something incoherent but looked as grave as the Frenchman.

"Goodnight, gentleman," Sebastian said as he moved to the side door. "And remember, not a word to anyone!"

Sebastian stepped out into the night. He silently cursed the men's stupidity — planning to give guns to tribes who wanted to kill settlers and soldiers alike to drive them away from their lands. He could only hope that when the men sobered up in the morning they would actually hide the guns where they would never be found. Otherwise there'd be more dead soldiers like Johnny and Sean. And Wes. And civilians like Sunflower and her tribe. Some would be killed by design, others by accident but all would be dead just the same.

Sebastian pushed down the rage and sadness as he untied Black Thunder and climbed into the saddle. He tried to ignore the searing pain burning in the scars in his chest and back as he rode into the dark night, away from the memories of death, toward the only woman who reminded him of what it meant to be alive.

* * * * *

"Lady Jane is here?"

Libbie stared across the tavern table at Fox, a well-known trapper who knew almost everyone in the Shenandoah Valley. Fox was a big bear of a man, with grizzled red hair and a full beard that glinted like copper in the low lamplight of the heavily shadowed room.

"She's here for th' big to-do." He nudged Sebastian in the ribs. "Knew you'd want to be apprised of the situation."

Fox's intimation only fueled Libbie's anger, which she had been wearing close to the surface for days. First, there'd been the close proximity she and Sebastian had been forced to keep every day as they rode Black Thunder down out of the mountains, sharing one mount because the Occaneechi and Saponi had none to spare. Sleeping on the other side of the fire from the man was no easier, as her mind was far too busy concocting elaborate seduction fantasies to allow her to fall asleep easily. Then there were the dreams, just glimpses of terror followed by the strangest sensation of calm and the feeling that someone was with her, taking care of her, protecting her from the evil portents.

So that morning, when they had finally arrived in town, Libbie was looking forward to a brief meeting with Sebastian's General Gordon, followed, she hoped, by a hot bath and a soft bed. Instead, they found Gordon's headquarters bustling with activity and bursting at the seams with all sorts of British officers and dignitaries. Of course, it was only then that Sebastian had informed her that they could not just walk up to Gordon's office and knock at the door. No, Sebastian was on a clandestine mission and was sworn to the strictest secrecy.

"I suppose you'll be pleased to see your," Libbie stopped herself just short of using the sort of term that would have made her mother cringe, "childhood friend."

Sebastian looked at her, wide-eyed, as if surprised by her tone.

Fox pulled an envelope out of his pocket and held it in his huge, paw-like hands. "When I told her you'd be comin' into town to see Gordon, she said you might need special arrangements. She told me to give this to you."

He glanced from Libbie to Sebastian, as if unsure who should receive the note. After a moment, he handed it to Sebastian. Just as well. Libbie had no desire to read the man's love letters.

But like it or not, Sebastian soon held out the message to Libbie. She snatched it from his fingers, admitting to herself that perhaps she wanted to know what Lady Jane was up to, after all.

"A soirée? That's what you meant by 'the to-do'?" Libbie raised an eyebrow at Fox.

Fox shrugged. "Some fancy party at the Gordons'. His missus just arrived in Virginia and wants to announce herself. I expect that's causin' most of the ruckus over there."

Sebastian smiled. "Well, that explains why Jane is here. She does so hate to miss an important social engagement."

Libbie frowned. "It doesn't explain why she sent you an invitation to the Gordon's party."

"Actually, it does," Sebastian assured her. "You just have to know how Jane's mind works."

"No, thank you."

Sebastian seemed not to hear her and pointed to the invitation. "You see, this is addressed to Count and Countess Ashland von Herscher, of New York."

"Ah." Fox nodded.

Libbie was too surly and exhausted to follow their thinking. "Please elaborate."

"Mrs. Gordon is unlikely to know many of the guests she'll have invited to her party," Sebastian said. "And while many of the Virginia upper crust will be familiar with each other, they are not so likely to know those from someplace farther away."

"From say, New York," Fox added.

Libbie caught and held Sebastian's gaze. "We are going to be the Count and Countess von Herscher?"

"Exactly." Sebastian touched her hand, sending the now familiar cold-hot flash through her. "You said you would do anything to finish this with Winters. Certainly being a countess at the event of the year is not too high a price to pay."

"No, of course it's not. But Lady Jane will have to make arrangements for our attire. It will cost a pretty penny but one cannot be a countess," she looked pointedly at Sebastian, "or a count without dressing the part."

"Thatta girl," said Fox.

Now Sebastian looked surly but he nodded his agreement. "Dressing like a bloody dandy is a small price to pay for something this important. By the way, you will need to become accustomed to your name, Countess."

"Countess. There. I'm already used to it."

Sebastian shrugged. "Husband and wife would use given names. You may call me Ashland."

He looked too happy for Libbie's taste. "And you'll call me?"

The serving girl approached, interrupting the conversation.

Sebastian smiled at the girl. "Another round of ale, please." He turned his smile on Libbie. "You would like another glass of ale, wouldn't you, Brunhilde?"

Chapter Seven

ဆ

The countess shifted on the seat of the rented carriage. The short ride had been bumpy and she patted her skirt to ensure that the layers of petticoats and underskirts were still in place. Then she touched her head, scratching carefully along the edges of her heavy, powdered wig.

"Brunhilde, you'll move it out of place," the count said.

"Stop calling me that, Ashy."

"Libbie, don't be upset. This will all be worth it."

"I'm not upset. I was never upset. But I don't understand why Lady Jane insisted on sending such a frilly, ridiculous dress for me."

Sebastian nodded. "As long as you're not upset."

"I just wasn't prepared for the sacrifices that espionage requires. Really, three layers of petticoats? Even at Mrs. Barton's school, one layer sufficed. And underskirts were wholly unnecessary. And don't even speak to me about this wig— Is yours itchy? Because mine is incredibly itchy. I don't think you're having nearly as many problems with yours."

"Brunhilde, you're rambling."

She scowled at him. "Easy for you to say. Your suit is beautiful." She touched the black silk lapel and ran one finger along the gold thread applique. "The tailor Lady Jane hired to make this outdid himself."

"Is that jealousy I see in your green eyes?" He was smiling at her as he said it.

Her stomach twisted. She hadn't seen Lady Jane since Papa and Johnny's funeral. Then Libbie had been so immersed in grief that she could barely remember why she had come to hate Lady Jane. But tonight's encounter might prove thorny. Seeing Sebastian reunited with his lover while playing the role of Libbie's husband was too ironic and cruel to bear. Yet bear it she must.

They arrived at the Gordon house in the center of town and the coachman helped them alight. Holding the von Herscher invitation firmly with one hand and taking Sebastian's arm with the other, Libbie walked with him to the front door, where they were announced by an armed soldier. They stepped into a room so large that it still seemed imposing despite the heavy antiques, silk tapestries and sea green velvet curtains that adorned it. The furniture had been moved to the edges of the room to allow for the large crowd of dignitaries, many of them in military uniform, to mingle and dance, although the music had yet to begin.

"You didn't tell me that Mrs. Gordon has such extravagant tastes," Libbie whispered.

"I didn't know, having never met her. The general didn't see fit to share details of his wife's decorating or entertaining habits."

"Do you see him yet?"

"Not yet but we're barely in the door. Jane should already be here and knowing her, she'll be able to tell us who is who and who is where in astonishing detail."

With the words barely out of his mouth, Lady Jane was upon them. As she always did at parties, she wore a shockingly red gown with a low décolletage. She hugged Libbie and Sebastian and kissed them on their cheeks.

"I've been so worried about both of you," she whispered. "Don't you look the part of a count and countess. It's just amazing!" Out loud she said, "Count, Countess, how lovely to see you."

Thankfully, Lady Jane had no opportunity to say more or to exchange lovelorn looks with Sebastian. A plump, dark-haired woman in an elegant blue dress was making a beeline for them.

"Your hostess," Lady Jane whispered.

The woman stopped in front of them and took Libbie's hand. "Countess, it is a pleasure to meet you. I'm Mrs. Gordon." She turned to Sebastian. "Count, I am so pleased to meet you."

Sebastian kissed the woman's hand.

Libbie hesitated before speaking. She had to remember to use the clipped vowels and hard consonants of a Northern accent. "It is a pleasure to meet you as well, madam." Libbie tilted back her head and looked down her nose at Mrs. Gordon. The countess was a notorious snob and was reputed to have become more of one since her arranged marriage to a Hessian count.

Their hostess spoke with them briefly. As much as Libbie hated to admit it, Jane was a great help, keeping up much of the conversation so that Libbie did not have to struggle overly much with the accent. For his part, Sebastian smiled and nodded frequently. It was well known that the count spoke very little English.

"Oh, here comes my husband," their hostess told them. "Count and Countess von Herscher, may I present my husband, General Gordon."

A tall, barrel-chested, grandfatherly man in the full dress uniform of a British officer reached for Libbie's hand and kissed it. "Delighted to meet you, Countess." Upon seeing Sebastian, he raised his eyebrows, then nodded. "And you, Count von Herscher."

The general turned in his wife's direction. "Madam, perhaps you would introduce the Countess and Lady Jane to some of our other guests."

His wife, obviously accustomed to such requests, reached out to take Jane's and Libbie's arms to lead them away from the men. Libbie threw a desperate look in Sebastian's direction.

They had agreed not to separate at the party unless it was absolutely necessary. Now he gave her the slightest nod. She scowled but went with Mrs. Gordon just the same.

A few minutes later, Libbie looked away from a new acquaintance to see Sebastian watching her. He moved his gaze from Libbie to Jane and back again, then indicated a nearby archway. She gave him a nearly imperceptible nod and he moved through the doorway.

Libbie gave the same eye signals to Lady Jane, then excused herself from Mrs. Gordon's company. She made her way through the crowd and passed through the archway Sebastian had indicated, which led to a less formal sitting room with several doorways leading to other parts of the house. Not spotting him, Libbie stayed her course through the room and stepped into a narrow corridor at the back of the house.

Sebastian was waiting there for her. "Bad news," he whispered.

From the grim expression on his face, it was worse than bad. "You mean terrible."

He frowned. "Gordon can't help us."

Libbie gasped. "But why —"

"Winters has pull with some people in very high places. He's managed to turn the tables. Gordon's inquiries and complaints regarding the man have gone unheeded. It's been made clear to him that he is not to get involved in Winters' business for fear of swift and serious reprisal."

"That miserable bastard. How did he know to go after Gordon?"

Sebastian shrugged. "Gordon has been watching him for a few years now. That's why he sent his nephew to Winters' fort in the first place. The boy's death was proof that Winters was onto Gordon. That's why my mission was so secretive."

In that moment, Libbie realized the danger Sebastian had been living with every day under Winters' command. It made her want to reach for him, hold him, keep him safe. The impulse shocked her.

"And there's more," Sebastian continued, pulling her attention back to the moment. "Winters reported me as a deserter. There's now no one in the whole of the British Army who can help us without facing the risk of being charged as my coconspirator."

"Then there's no way to —"

Men's voices echoed in the corridor. They seemed to come from the room at the far end of the hall, which appeared to Libbie to be the kitchen. Sebastian lifted his finger to his lips, warning her not to speak, then bent to whisper in her ear.

"Gordon's men. If they recognize me, they'll arrest me and Gordon won't be able to stop it."

Over Sebastian's shoulder, Libbie could see a shadow moving across the room's entryway. She raised her eyebrows at him to warn him. He stole a glance over his shoulder just as the soldier stepped into the far end of the hall.

Sebastian wrapped his arms around Libbie and pulled her against him. He pressed his mouth against hers in a hard and sudden kiss. It had been weeks since he had kissed her in Winters' fort. Now that she felt his mouth opening into hers and his tongue slipping between her lips, stroking the crevices of her mouth, she knew that she had wanted him to kiss her again for a very long time.

She was so consumed by the feel of his hard muscles against the length of her body that she lost track of time and place. When he finally pulled away from her, it took her several seconds to remember what had happened before that kiss.

"The men?" she whispered.

"Could have seen us," he said in a low tone. "They've gone now — surely they didn't want to interrupt an intimate moment and risk upsetting any of Mrs. Gordon's important guests."

"Yes, of course."

He put one hand under her chin and lifted her face so that she would look at him. "I'm sorry to surprise you like that. Please don't be angry."

"I'm not."

Strangely, it was the truth. There were myriad emotions tumbling around inside her but anger was not one of them. Confusion, hope, sadness, desire—especially desire—but not anger.

"We're fortunate that Lady Jane seems to have been delayed."

Sebastian grinned. "You needn't worry. Jane is not very easily shocked."

"I meant that you—"

"Sebastian, Libbie, thank God you're hidden back here!" Lady Jane bustled into the corridor. She was out of breath and speaking quickly. "I was afraid he would see you."

Libbie pushed away the emotions stirred by Sebastian's kiss. "Afraid who would see us?"

"Not Winters," Sebastian said. "He can't be here."

Lady Jane nodded. "From the looks of it, he wasn't invited but Gordon seems unable to get rid of him."

"Damn it. He's bound to have spies here as well, now that he's out for Gordon's blood."

Libbie's heart pounded. Her mind raced. "We have to get out of here. The back door."

"Too risky," Sebastian said. "There will be soldiers there."

"You know the house from your time spent here," Libbie said. "Is there another way out?"

He glanced up and down the hall. "Perhaps. Jane..."

She held up her hands. "I have it under control. A little feminine distraction for Colonel Winters coming up." She gave them each a quick kiss.

"There's also the matter of Libbie's horse. She's boarded at the inn."

Jane nodded. "When you know where you're going, have Fox get word to me and I'll have the horse delivered to you."

"Wait, Sebastian, what are you planning? Where are we going? How are—"

"We'll work out the details on the way."

He took Libbie's hand and led her to the kitchen. A few servants were arranging platters of hors d'oeuvres at one end of the room but they did not look up to see Libbie and Sebastian moving quietly along the wall at the opposite end. They came out into another corridor, this one running along the side of the house.

They stopped outside a closed door. With one last look over his shoulder, Sebastian opened the door and they tiptoed into the room.

It took a moment to adjust to the darkness but soon Libbie's eyes could distinguish a large desk, several upholstered chairs and three bookcases straining under the weight of hundreds of thick tomes. A thin shaft of moonlight sifted through the window.

"You're sure you didn't see them?" Winters' voice came from the hallway. He couldn't be more than a few yards away.

Sebastian stood completely still. Libbie held her breath and waited.

"No, sir," another man answered.

"Keep looking," Winters said.

"Colonel, there you are! I've been looking for you!"

"Lady Whitmore," Winters answered. "I was taking a moment away from the crowd. May I escort you back to the party?"

Libbie and Sebastian waited another minute, then exchanged a glance. He moved to the window behind the desk.

"What are you doing?" she asked.

He opened the latch and tugged. "Readying our escape route. Or at least attempting it. It's stuck."

There was a noise just outside the door.

"What do you mean stuck?" Libbie whispered as panic seized her. "Someone's coming!"

Sebastian budged the window mere inches. "It'll take another minute."

They didn't have another minute, or another second. She would have to take matters into her own hands. The doorknob turned. Libbie flattened herself against the wall just inside the door.

The soldier stepped into the room and spotted Sebastian. He opened his mouth as though to shout.

Libbie pushed the door closed and jumped to the soldier's side.

The man looked from Sebastian to Libbie. "What th —"

Libbie slammed her elbow into the soldier's gut. He doubled over and grunted but reached out to grab her. She kicked hard at his ankle. His leg collapsed under him. From a deep pocket in her dress Libbie drew out her silver pistol.

"Libbie, no! Don't shoot him!" Sebastian commanded in an agitated whisper.

She raised the gun above the man and cold-cocked him with the butt. "Don't be ridiculous," she said as she joined Sebastian by the now open window. "A shot would be much too noisy."

Sebastian stared at her, his mouth hanging open.

"Sebastian, snap out of it! We have to get out of here before that soldier wakes up."

"Of course. I just…" He shook his head. "You'll never believe this but the night I met you, I worried that you were an unprotected young girl who would be unable to defend herself."

"Men," she muttered.

Libbie peered out the window. The drop was more than one story. She glanced down at her overly frilly pink party gown and back up at Sebastian.

"Hmm. That might be a problem," he whispered.

"Well, turn around."

"What?"

"Be a gentleman and turn around. I can't go out the window in this get-up, so it will have to come off."

He obeyed her without saying another word.

She pulled at her dress, glad that she had insisted on a front-buttoning gown and dropped it to the floor. The petticoats came off next, layer by layer, until she stood in her buckskin pants and the low-cut blouse that she'd had the seamstress fashion to be concealed under the gown. With a soft but triumphant grunt, she pulled the wig off her head and let her long braid fall down her back.

She gathered her discarded clothes into a ball in her arms and surveyed the ground below them. "You can turn around," she said to Sebastian.

When he turned to face her, she handed him some of her petticoats. "They'll make for a softer landing. I'm aiming for that bush a few feet over."

She hoisted one leg over the ledge, straddling the window, then positioned herself with her excess clothes under her. She launched herself a bit sideways and landed in the bush with her clothes cushioning her fall.

Sebastian was seconds behind her, choosing to land on the harder ground but also using the cushion she had provided. When he was on his feet, she grabbed the petticoats from him.

"Hurry, Liberty. Jane can't hold off Winters all night."

Libbie headed for a thick hedge. With a shove, the pile of clothes and the wig fell deep into the tangled branches where they were swallowed by the green foliage.

Sebastian looked appalled. "Those were expensive!"

"And itchy and entirely inappropriate for a narrow escape."

He groaned as he grabbed her hand and dragged her through the dark garden. "Tell me something," he said. "If you were wearing buckskins under all those clothes, why did you make me turn around?"

"Modesty. I'm not a sniveling young girl but I'm still a lady."

"Women," he muttered.

"Tell me something," she countered. "Where are going?"

"To the stables."

"Why?"

"To steal two of the general's horses."

"Horse rustling?"

"Just this once," he said. "There's no other way to get out of here ahead of Winters."

"Hmph. Men. And I suppose you have considered our next move."

"We get out of Winters' sight, then try to stay one step ahead of him."

"That's rather vague."

"Do you have any suggestions?"

The briefest glimpse of a dream from her deep sleep flashed through her mind. It was shortly after Christmas and her mother and Annalee were packing to leave Charlottesville, heading back to the family farm months ahead of schedule. And they were going alone and unprotected. With Winters on the prowl, they were in terrible danger. If the premonition held true, it would just be a matter of weeks until it came to pass.

"It would serve to kill two birds with one stone," Libbie muttered to herself.

"What are you talking about?" Sebastian asked.

"In answer to your question, yes, I have a suggestion."

Sebastian glanced at her as they stopped outside the barn to check for soldiers. "Well, don't keep me in suspense, Brunhilde."

"Just get horses for us, Ashy, then follow me."

Chapter Eight

ജ

"Your aunt is a gunsmith?"

Sebastian pulled his horse to a halt beside a tall wooden sign with block letters burned into it, "Caroline Holling, Gunsmith".

Libbie started in her saddle at the sound of his voice, then stopped beside him but she did not answer. She had fallen into a sullen mood on the long ride to Charlottesville. No doubt she was exhausted and saddle sore from the unbroken hours of riding. But he was more concerned about her emotional state after their horrible luck with Winters. Sebastian wanted to rub her sore muscles and kiss away her fears. He wanted to hold her in his arms and make love to her. The thought echoed in his mind as loudly and undeniably as a cannon shot. He wanted her, yearned for her, not with simple need but with desperation. He gripped his reins more tightly to stop himself from touching her.

"Libbie," he said again, fighting to keep his voice calm. "Did you hear me? You seem a world away."

"My aunt... Yes. The women in my mother's family are not known for sewing quilts and throwing tea parties."

"Really? I wouldn't have guessed, after watching you stalk a frontier regiment, heal bullet wounds and pistol-whip a soldier."

"About that... My family is not completely aware of what I've been doing these past several months. My mother only knows that I went to stay in the Indian village with my friend. Aunt Caroline probably suspects more, seeing as she gave me the pistol."

"Like any good aunt, I suppose."

"I keep it in my saddlebag most of the time. I need more practice with it. I'm much more proficient with a blade."

"I didn't realize what a chance I was taking when I kissed you in Winters' dungeon. I'm glad I escaped with only a sore cheek."

He smiled at her but she looked even more dejected. Perhaps it was the wrong topic to discuss but he wished she could feel happy about the thought of his kisses. Right or wrong, he very much wanted to kiss her again and soon.

She pulled her horse to a halt. "Are you sure Winters will believe the story that Lady Jane fabricated about our whereabouts? I realize that Lady Jane means well but bribing one of Winters' spies…" Libbie shook her head. "If he suspects something and decides to look for us with my family —"

"Jane has taken care of it, Libbie. And between the Continental soldiers guarding the town and Fox and his son keeping watch, we'll know if Winters gets within a day's ride of Charlottesville."

He snapped the reins and guided his horse into Aunt Caroline's lane with Libbie following just behind him. Snow crunched under the horses' hooves and wet, heavy flakes drifted down around them. Libbie shifted impatiently as they trotted down the lane. When she caught a glimpse of Aunt Caroline's house, she sat up straighter, then ducked to elude a small white object flying in their direction. The snowball narrowly missed her and landed squarely on the top of Sebastian's head.

The child running after them with another snowball clutched in her hand had to be another MacRae. Her face was a younger version of Libbie's, at least as far as Sebastian could tell, although he wondered if her eyes were the same gorgeous shade of green. As he wiped the snow from his hat and hair, Libbie — wearing her first real smile since he'd met up with her again — jumped from her horse and enveloped her sister in her arms. Within minutes, their laughter and shouts rose over an impromptu snowball battle and attracted the attention of two women who ran out of the house. Libbie embraced them, wiping the tears from her face and theirs.

"Oh, Libbie, I do so hate to see you in pants," her mother told her. "Just look at her, Caroline. She looks more like an Indian boy than a young lady."

"Nonsense, Anna, she looks wonderful," her aunt insisted.

Sebastian dismounted but hung back from the women, not wanting to interrupt the private reunion. Any lingering doubts he'd had about coming to Libbie's family instead of disappearing into the wilderness evaporated as he watched their joy. They'd been apart too long.

After a few minutes, Libbie extricated one arm and motioned toward him. "Mama, Aunt Caroline, you must meet…" She stopped.

"Mr. Cole, madam," he said as took Anna MacRae's hand and bowed.

Libbie raised her eyebrows in silent question. They had agreed to keep the true purpose of their visit hidden and Libbie had probably expected him to use a false name. He just couldn't bring himself to deceive her family any more than was absolutely necessary for their own protection.

He bowed toward Aunt Caroline. "It's a pleasure to meet you. I believe Miss MacRae wrote to tell you I would escort her to your home on my way east to visit relatives."

"No, I don't believe she did," Libbie's mother answered.

"Ah!" Aunt Caroline threw her arms into the air. "I did it. I surprised you! I kept the letter from you because I wanted to see the joy on your face when Libbie came to us out of the blue."

Libbie seamlessly followed her aunt's lead, which had just saved them from spinning awkward excuses about the slow speed of the post. "So you didn't tell Mama that Mr. Cole would be staying for a short time before continuing on his journey? You see, Mama, Mr. Cole is a frontier farmer, who was on his way east—"

"To visit relatives," her mother finished for her. "Yes, I heard."

Libbie's mouth went dry. She feared her mother could see through the charade. Her head throbbed when she thought about pretending that Sebastian was merely an acquaintance.

"Well, let's move inside before we all freeze to death," Aunt Caroline urged. "Mr. Cole, would you take the horses to the stable behind the house?"

As Sebastian silently obeyed, Aunt Caroline took one of Libbie's arms and Annalee took the other. They led her inside the two story, whitewashed house decorated with Christmas greens and red ribbons. Anna walked silently behind them.

"I got your gift!" Annalee told Libbie as they pulled off their coats. She reached into her bodice and pulled out a thick string threaded with large, colorful beads that Libbie recognized as her own crude handiwork.

"Someone named Mother Cloud Dancer asked that trapper, Mr. Fox, to bring it down to the valley with him," Anna told Libbie. "He brought it straight to Annalee."

Libbie smiled. No doubt Fox had also delivered news of her wellbeing to her family, probably at Mother Cloud Dancer's insistence. She was about to ask but did not have the chance.

"Libbie, is it really you?"

Out of the corner of her eye Libbie caught the flash of bright red hair. Tears pricked her eyes when she recognized the once round, pink-cheeked face that was now pale and gaunt.

"Maggie! I had no idea you'd be here!" She embraced her friend. "How are you?"

"Some days I'm fine. Other days..." Maggie shrugged.

Anna put her arms around both of them and pulled them close to her. "Libbie, you've become so thin! I think you need some of your mother's cooking. Girls, let's take her to the kitchen for some fresh biscuits and jam."

As they walked, Maggie grabbed Libbie's arm and held her back from the others. "Libbie, why on earth did you bring that man here? When I saw him through the kitchen window, I couldn't believe my eyes!"

Libbie pulled away from her friend's now tight grip. "He is an enemy of Winters, the man who killed Johnny and my father. He's promised to help me make that bastard pay for what he's done to us."

Maggie scowled. "Just because he is Winters' enemy does not mean he's our friend. He's British. He's a spy. And he has lied to you in the past. You can't trust a word he says."

"Johnny trusted him and so will I."

"Johnny needed information that Cole had. But he never claimed to trust him. And he would never approve of this...alliance you've forged with him."

"You don't know that."

Maggie tossed her head angrily. "I do know it, because I knew Johnny. I loved him and I respect his memory."

"You had better not be implying that I don't," Libbie said through clenched teeth. "Not after I have risked life and limb to salvage his and my father's names."

Maggie bit her lip, then sighed. "I'm sorry, Libbie. I missed you so much, I really did. But there's something odd about Cole."

The young women rounded the corner into the kitchen. Libbie's mother and aunt were busy laying out biscuits and tea.

"Well, it's about time you caught up to us," Anna said.

Annalee appeared from somewhere behind them. "Maggie doesn't like Mr. Cole. But I do. He's handsome. And he called Mama 'madam', the way Papa always said a gentleman does."

"I agree with Annalee," Aunt Caroline told them. "I like him. He's charming. And he certainly has eyes for Libbie."

Libbie blushed. The rush of blood made her head ache. She dropped heavily into a chair.

"That makes it even worse!" Maggie insisted. She trained her gaze on Libbie. "After all, what do any of us really know about him?"

Libbie's mother held a hand in the air. "Enough about Mr. Cole. Libbie, you don't look well."

"It's just a headache, Mama, from the long ride." And the unanswered questions, she thought to herself.

"Maggie, Caroline, will you prepare her bed?" She took Libbie's hand. "You had better get some rest before it turns into something worse."

Libbie nodded, unable to refuse. She wondered how her mother did it, where she found the strength to get out of bed every day and be the matriarch of the half of her family that was left.

"Stand up, dear." Her mother grasped Libbie's arms. "Here, I'll help you."

Libbie was glad for the support as her mother guided her out of the kitchen. At the bottom of the staircase, Libbie leaned into her mother and hugged her.

"Mama, wait. You must tell me, how are you?"

Anna sighed. "I'm as well as is to be expected. Some days are terrible, other days are better." She squeezed Libbie tightly. "Today is a good day. I hated to see you leave us but I knew you needed time away from the farm. But having you back is the best gift I have ever received."

Annalee hopped out of the kitchen and joined them. She took Libbie's hand and helped her mother guide her big sister up the stairs. "Mr. Cole has an accent doesn't he, Libbie?"

Libbie could barely nod.

"It's like the man who wanted to buy the farm," the girl said.

Libbie grabbed her mother's arm tightly. "Buy the farm?"

Anna shrugged. "That was weeks ago. Don't worry. We refused in no uncertain terms."

"And Aunt Caroline told him never to come back," Annalee added. "I was glad she did. He scared me."

Libbie stopped in the middle of the staircase. "Did he have a scar? On his chin, running through his beard?" she croaked.

"A scar?" Her mother shook her head. "No. And he was clean-shaven. What on earth made you ask such a question? Libbie, do you know who he was?"

It was not Winters but still, it was too coincidental. He had probably sent one of his underlings to the farm after Libbie had slipped through his fingers. It was a warning. He could get to her family.

"No, Mama, I have no idea," she lied.

* * * * *

"Are you awake, dear?"

"Yes, Mama. Come in."

Libbie sat up in her bed as Anna entered the room and headed straight to the window. She grasped the thick crimson drapes and pulled them open wide, letting sunlight spill into the room.

Libbie groaned with pain and slung her arm over her eyes.

"Libbie, darling? Oh dear." Libbie heard the curtains slide back into place and mercifully the light dimmed.

She carefully opened her eyes. "It's so bright outside. What time is it?"

"It's half past nine." Anna crossed the room and laid a cool hand on Libbie's face, then touched her shoulder and her pillow. "You've had a fever and it has broken. Your nightdress and sheets are soaked through."

Libbie tried to shift her legs over the edge of the bed but even the slightest movement caused a stabbing pain in her temples. "I'm all— Oh, perhaps I'd better lie down."

"After I change your sheets." Her mother took her arm and helped her out of the bed and into a chair. She left the room and came back a minute later with an armful of fresh linens.

"Mama, let me help you with that," Libbie said but her body was refusing to obey her command to stand.

"Nonsense. You're ill. You haven't been taking care of yourself. But now you're back where you belong with your family and I'm going to take care of you."

After her mother had helped her change her nightgown and crawl back into bed, Libbie said, "I'm sure I'll be fine by tomorrow."

"Yes, well, we'll see about that."

There was a knock at the door.

"Come in," her mother called.

On cue, Annalee entered, balancing a tray with a bowl on it.

Anna took the tray and set it on the bedside table. "Thank you, dear." She kissed Annalee's forehead.

Annalee smiled and jumped onto Libbie's bed. "I've learned two new songs on the spinet since we've come to Aunt Caroline's!"

Libbie took her sister's hand. "That's wonderful! Perhaps you can play them for me this afternoon." She shot a pleading look at her mother. "Assuming I'll be allowed out of bed to sit in the parlor."

Anna frowned. "We'll see. Now, Annalee, you run along. Your sister's going to have her broth, then we're going to let her rest because she's not feeling well."

Annalee's face fell. "Oh. You won't be sick for Christmas, will you Libbie?"

"Of course not," Libbie promised. "I'll be fine in no time."

Annalee leaned toward Libbie to hug her but Anna intervened and set the child on the floor. "Not today. Libbie's fever could be catching and if you come down with it, there'll be no one to help me make the mincemeat pies. You know your Aunt Caroline is helpless in the kitchen."

"I'm going to tell her you said so!" Annalee giggled as she scampered from the room.

Anna sighed. "It's done her a world of good to see you."

"How is she these days, Mama?"

"She's doing better than I am," Anna answered and for a moment she looked so lost and alone that Libbie wanted to cry. But her mother quickly covered her pain with a smile. "And you are doing better, I can tell, even though you've come home thin and ill."

"Really, Mama, I don't think I've lost a pound. The Occaneechi fed me almost as well as you do."

Anna nodded as she stared at some point on the other side of the room. "It was the right thing, letting you go with them. You were so strong, hiring the farm hands and overseeing the planting. Then we got the news and you were still so strong for the funeral. But by June, I could see it taking its toll on you..." She broke off in a sob.

Libbie sat up and hugged her mother. The first week of June, one month after Johnny and Papa's deaths, Libbie's friend Bird-in-Flight had arrived at the farm with her husband, who was a young Occaneechi chieftain, their baby daughter and two braves. Libbie hadn't laid eyes on Bird-in-Flight since the Occaneechi had fled their village near the farm three years earlier and had moved up into the mountains, out of the reach of the encroaching white settlers. But the girls had sent letters back and forth and when Libbie had received the horrible news about her loved ones, she'd felt compelled to write to Bird-in-Flight about it.

Libbie had hoped for a response, no more. But instead, her old friend was there on the doorstep and within days, Bird-in-Flight and her husband were explaining to her mother why Libbie should go with them. A week later, Libbie was settling into the lodge of Mother Cloud Dancer, the tribe's wizened old medicine woman. Shortly after arriving in the village, Libbie had learned that it was Mother Cloud Dancer's directive, not Libbie's letter, that had prompted Bird-in-Flight's visit and convenient invitation.

"It was the right thing to do," Libbie told her mother, remembering all the lessons she had learned from the tribe.

Mother Cloud Dancer had insisted that learning to use her "gift", the second sight that Libbie had tried to deny and then to suppress for so many years, must be Libbie's top priority. Libbie had submitted to the old woman's lessons and had achieved some sense of peace about her visions. At least she no longer felt crazy and with the Occaneechi she didn't have to hide her abilities. But she had relished her time with the braves, who taught her to track and hunt and fight, because she knew those skills would be her key to destroying Winters.

Anna pulled away from Libbie's embrace and held both of her daughter's hands. "Now that you're home, we can be a family again. We'll give Annalee a wonderful holiday. Then when the weather clears, we'll go home. The MacRaes will be back on our own land, where we belong."

Where Winters would find them, would hunt them down, would kill them. Libbie wrapped her arms tightly around herself to keep from shaking. She was not going to allow it. She was going to stop Winters with Sebastian's help.

"It's just the womenfolk today," her mother said, as if reading Libbie's thoughts as she wondered about Sebastian's whereabouts. "Your Mr. Cole has taken his leave for the day — something about meeting with friends in the area."

"He's not my Mr. Cole," Libbie said quickly, without thinking. She felt heat flush her cheeks and hoped her mother wouldn't notice.

As usual, though, her mother caught every detail. "It's a turn of phrase, darling."

"Yes of course. I'm just not thinking clearly. It's probably the fever."

"There's no use pretending, Libbie."

Libbie felt her heart drop into the pit of her stomach as she waited for her mother's next words.

"Even Annalee can see that the two of you have feelings for each other. Now, if you've fallen in love with that man — "

Libbie sucked in her breath and pressed her hands to her cheeks. "Love? Why would you say such a thing? I assure you, whatever is between Sebastian and me has nothing to do with love! It's a business relationship, of sorts. A travel relationship."

"Sebastian, is it now? No longer Mr. Cole. I worry that you don't know your own heart, Libbie."

"Mama, I promise I'm not lying to you. Mr. Cole is not the sort of man whom a girl should fall in love with." Lust is another matter, she couldn't help thinking. "But he is honorable, at least as far as our business dealings are concerned and you can rest assured that he has absolutely no interest in me beyond that."

Sadly, she wasn't lying. He had kissed her on several occasions but each time there had been a motive behind it. Except, perhaps, when he'd found her in the fort. But then again, he had needed to persuade her to trust him. And when left alone with her any other time, he remained the perfect gentleman, uninterested in kissing her again, unaware of the thoughts she'd had about him, unlikely ever to think of her as a desirable woman.

But they had developed a rapport, even a friendship, or so she liked to think. And she had come to trust him, perhaps even to rely on him.

"Your father could never keep secrets from me. I heard the name Sebastian Cole from Sean himself. And then I learn that he, of all people, has escorted my daughter to Charlottesville."

Libbie's throat was parched as she choked out a lie. "He had business near the Occaneechi village and then was heading east. It was just a convenient arrangement."

"Yes, very convenient." Anna frowned. "I have the most awful feeling that this has something to do with unfinished business of Johnny and your father."

Libbie could not look her mother in the eye.

"I see," her mother said. "Libbie, I fear that you're putting yourself in harm's way." She dropped her voice to a whisper. "I can't bear to lose anyone else. If you tell me that your Mr. Cole will protect you, then I'll trust him."

Libbie wrapped her arms around her mother's neck. Her mother was warm and soft and her dress held the scent of the pumpkin pies she'd already baked that morning. Libbie could instantly see her family gathered around the Christmas dinner table, could hear her father's deep, booming voice singing carols he'd learned in his childhood, could see the Johnny plucking bits of crisp skin from the goose when he thought no one was looking.

Libbie swallowed hard, choking down sobs. She had known the first Christmas without them would come but her heart had refused to accept it. Now the emotions had caught her off guard and were threatening to consume her. But Libbie couldn't further burden her mother by breaking down in front of her. Anna MacRae was holding together what was left of their small clan and was doing everything in her power to make this Christmas a happy one for Annalee.

Libbie squeezed her mother tightly. "Sebastian would protect me with his life if it came to that."

She felt her mother shiver and regretted her choice of words. But Anna pulled away and gave Libbie an encouraging smile. "I'm glad we've had this talk. Now, you have your broth and get some more rest. And if you're up to it this afternoon, you can sit in the parlor and Annalee will play the spinet for you."

Libbie smiled back at her mother so intently that she could almost convince herself that all was well, that they would enjoy this holiday without the men of their family, that Sebastian would be able to keep her one step ahead of Winters and out of harm's way. But the minute her mother left the room, her self-control lost its battle with her emotions and she fell back against her pillows.

"Papa, why aren't you and Johnny here with us?" she said, her strength dissolving with her tears. "What are we going to do without you?"

A morning of rest did little to relieve Libbie's headache and by late afternoon her fever had returned. It broke again that evening but still Anna insisted on sleeping in the same room to keep watch over Libbie, just in case.

Libbie didn't have the energy to protest and she didn't know if she would have, anyway. It was comforting to have her mother and all the overprotective love that came with her so close. All day, Libbie's sleep had been fitful, full of half-dreams and terrifying images whose details she couldn't recall upon waking.

She was running, panting. There was heat—a fire, smoke, so much heat.

Libbie sat bolt upright in her bed and sucked in a deep breath. The night was dark and still. Her mother breathed slowly and evenly beside her. Libbie's head still pounded. She closed her eyes and rubbed her temples. The vision hit her harder and faster than any ever had.

Libbie was on her family farm. It was May. The first of May. Anna and Annalee were somewhere nearby, not in danger. Heat flared. Fire raged. Smoke burned in her nose and throat.

Winters was there. "It's mine!" he shouted. "Your lands, your name, everything that was ever yours is mine!"

"Libbie, I have to do this." Sebastian's voice.

She looked for him, couldn't see anything through the black smoke. "I have to go," he whispered. "Libbie, let me go."

Libbie opened her eyes. She was lying on the floor, shivering. The headache was gone. She touched her face. The fever too, had disappeared. But the memory of the heat, of the fire…it felt like the flames had singed her skin.

She knew Winters wanted their farm but even more than that he wanted to destroy them. The vision proved she could change everything and make her mother and sister safe, just as Mother Cloud Dancer had told her she could. But that wasn't enough. She still had to find a way to stop Winters and she had to do it by herself. Otherwise, the rest of her vision would come to pass, as well.

And Sebastian would die instead of her family.

Chapter Nine

ജ

"Are you sure this is appropriate?" Libbie asked her mother two days after her "miraculous" recovery.

"Yes, it's appropriate." Anna glanced down at Libbie's gray frock. "And absolutely necessary."

Anna knocked on the door of the seamstress's combined house and shop. The woman lived on the edge of town and despite knowing that American soldiers patrolled the town's borders, Libbie couldn't help glancing over her shoulder, fearing she'd see Winters around every corner, just as she saw him in her dreams and visions. "I really don't need another dress, Mama. Aunt Caroline won't mind what I wear to Friday night's dinner."

"We'll all want to look our best, dear." Her mother smiled at Libbie. "Mrs. Barton will be there."

At the mention of her finishing school headmistress, Libbie straightened her posture. "Well, maybe something a bit more suitable would be nice."

The shop door swung open to reveal Mrs. Mitchell, the small, bird-like seamstress who was Anna's friend from her own stay at Mrs. Barton's school.

Mrs. Mitchell greeted Anna and Annalee, then turned to Libbie.

"Adele, you remember my older daughter," Anna said.

"Oh, Libbie! Let me look at you." Mrs. Mitchell shook her head as she took both of Libbie's hands. "It has only been a year, hasn't it? But you've gone from a lovely girl to a beautiful woman!"

Mrs. Mitchell invited them into the house. Libbie let out her breath in a sigh of relief as the door closed behind them and she and her family were safely hidden from prying eyes.

Mrs. Mitchell patted Libbie's sister on the head. "Annalee, your mother can take you into the next room to try on your dresses while your sister and I consider fabrics for her new gown."

When Anna was out of earshot, Mrs. Mitchell stood close to Libbie and spoke softly. "I'm glad you've come to Charlottesville. Your mother looks so much better than she did when I saw her last week. I'm sure it's because you're here."

"She wasn't well?" Libbie asked.

"Oh, I didn't mean she was ill. She just looked," Mrs. Mitchell shrugged, "she just looks happier today than I've seen her look since your father died. I know this time of year will be difficult for you. I remember the first Christmas after my Harold died."

Libbie remembered the day her mother had told her about Mrs. Mitchell's husband Harold. Libbie had been about Annalee's age and had asked how Mrs. Mitchell had a son without having a husband. Harold Junior had been a rude boy with a penchant for pulling Libbie's hair and she had been fully prepared to hear that he was a changeling that Mrs. Mitchell had selflessly rescued. Instead, Libbie heard the sad tale of Mrs. Mitchell losing her husband when her child was just a few months old. She'd had to sell the family's large home that had been just blocks from Aunt Caroline's house and had moved across town into a small cottage and had become a seamstress to support her son.

Anna had described her friend's courage and fortitude with pride but the story had depressed Libbie. It had also made her think of Widow Mitchell as old and pitiable. But in truth, the woman was the same age as Libbie's mother. And now Anna was a widow as well.

A stabbing pain cut through Libbie as the horrible sadness of their losses washed over her again. But she swallowed hard and willed the pain to stop. She even managed a smile for Mrs. Mitchell.

"How is your son?" she asked the seamstress. "I haven't seen Harold Junior for years."

Mrs. Mitchell stared out the window but her eyes were unfocused and shiny with tears. "Harold Junior died last year. Shortly after the last time I saw you."

Libbie touched her hand. "I'm so sorry. My mother didn't mention it."

"He died in the fighting up north. I don't like to talk about it." Mrs. Mitchell shook her head and looked at Libbie. Her tears were gone. "Now, about this dress, I'd like to do something with lace edging on the sleeves and neckline. That's such a becoming look on you."

Tears stung Libbie's eyes. Anger fueled by pain swelled in her breast—anger at the men who left them, who went off to war without looking back and expected the women to pick up the pieces after them. Mrs. Mitchell tightly clenched her jaw, biting back her own anger but neither of them would speak any more about it. Instead, the women did what was expected of them—they went about their business, which today was to get new dresses.

Anna and Annalee returned from the adjoining room. Annalee, wide-eyed and smiling, skipped to Libbie's side.

"I can't wait for you to see my new green dress!" Annalee told her sister as she wrapped her arms around Libbie's waist. "It makes me look almost as beautiful as you."

Libbie kissed her sister's head and hugged her. "You are beautiful. And I've missed you."

Libbie only wished that she could share more of her sister's joy but she had no idea how much longer she could stay with her family. As soon as the opportunity presented itself, she would have to leave them and leave Sebastian, as well. It was the only way she could save them.

"Adele, my daughter looks too somber," Anna said. "I think a dress in some cheerful color," Anna ran her fingers over a bolt of gold silk, "something like this, might be just the thing for her."

Mrs. Mitchell clapped her hands together. "Yes that's perfect. Your mother has always had such exquisite taste."

"I don't know, Mama. It's only been seven months."

"Nonsense. It's time you stopped dressing in mourning colors. Your father never stood on such formalities, and he'd have a conniption if he knew I'd let you celebrate Christmas in a sad dark frock."

Mrs. Mitchell put her hand on Libbie's arm. "Your mother is right, Libbie. Such a lovely young woman should wear beautiful colors. At least for Christmas."

Annalee tugged at her mother's sleeve. "Please, Mama, can I have a gold gown too?"

"'May I', dear and no, you may not," Anna told her. "Two new dresses are enough for now. You can wear the green one for the party."

Mrs. Mitchell clapped her hands together. "So you will be attending the party? How very grown-up."

Anna patted her younger daughter's head. "She's talked of nothing else since Caroline and I started planning it. I could hardly refuse her request to be there."

"I'll be the one in green, not gold." Annalee pouted but her disappointment evaporated when she saw Mrs. Mitchell's small white cat enter the room.

Libbie smiled. "Annalee, why don't you play with the kitty while Mrs. Mitchell is busy with me."

The suggestion distracted both her mother and her sister as Anna picked up the cat and carried her to a chair where Annalee could hold her. Minutes later, Libbie stood in her shift with her arms raised to the ceiling while Mrs. Mitchell took measurements and pinned fabric. The noise of something hitting the ceiling above them startled the seamstress and she sank a pin into Libbie's backside.

Libbie shrieked. Annalee jumped up from her seat. The white cat fell to the floor, hissed loudly and streaked across the room.

Anna put her hand to her heart. "What on earth?"

"I'm so sorry." Mrs. Mitchell took Libbie's hand in apology. "That must have been one of my other cats."

Libbie grimaced. "Would you kindly remove that pin?"

"Oh, yes, of course —"

Mrs. Mitchell was interrupted by a louder noise that did not sound as though it could have come from a cat. It was followed by a decidedly human cry that sent a chill down Libbie's spine. She whirled around to face Mrs. Mitchell.

"Surely that is not one of your cats!"

"Oh, of course not." The woman wrung her hands, then took a deep breath. "You see, I have a nephew visiting, a young boy. For obvious reasons, he can't be downstairs while I'm working."

"Perhaps he needs a playmate," Anna suggested. "I'm sure Annalee would like that, as well."

"Oh no!" Mrs. Mitchell looked frightened but again recovered. "The poor thing came down with the pox shortly after he arrived. His parents will be coming to take him home soon but in the meantime, we can't expose him to anyone. He's quite contagious, you know. I'll just send my girl to check on him."

"Adele, since when do you have a girl working for you?" Anna asked.

"I've just hired her," Mrs. Mitchell answered quickly. "I'm so busy right now and then my nephew came to visit… If you ladies will excuse me for just a moment, I'll take care of this."

When she was gone, Anna stepped close to Libbie and took her elbow. "Adele is not at all herself. She's obviously lying to us. When she returns, I'm going to demand she tell us what's going on here."

Libbie knew what it was like to keep secrets. Was the noise made by a hidden spy? A wounded American soldier with an innocent face and dedicated heart like Johnny? Or an escaped British soldier?

"No." She took her mother's hand. "These days there are secrets that even our friends can't share with us. We're better off not knowing."

Anna nodded, her face softening. "And who are we to judge others when we can't imagine what their secrets really are? You're right, Libbie. We'll speak no more of it."

Libbie knew her mother would be true to her word. And she also knew Anna was not just referring to Mrs. Mitchell.

* * * * *

Sebastian stood in front of the looking glass in Caroline's foyer. He struggled with the top button of his ruffled shirt, once again trying to play the part of the gentleman. Entertaining Anna and Caroline's guests at a dinner party could not have been less appealing to him but he and Libbie had been unable to think of a way out of it. At least their worried conversations about it had given him a chance to see her and talk to her, a rare treat these days as she had been avoiding him since they had arrived in Charlottesville.

Not that he sought her out. She needed time with her family and they needed her as well, for as long as they could have her. Despite making quite a show of it, the family was dreading the holidays without Sean and Johnny.

"Blast it!" Sebastian muttered as his fingers slipped across the shirt material.

"May I help you with that, Mr. Cole?"

Sebastian turned around to see Anna and Caroline. Anna reached up to adjust his collar for him, then imparted a motherly smile of approval.

He took her hand and bowed. "Thank you, madam. And may I say, you look lovely."

She gave him a small bow in return. "Thank you. I do hope you enjoy the evening."

As she walked away, he stood in stunned silence.

"I told you my sister would warm to you," Caroline said. "She only wants what's best for Libbie."

"And you believe that's me?"

"Of course! Don't you?"

The question hung in the air, unanswered. "Of course not" was the only reasonable response. He couldn't have her, no matter how much he wanted her. And he did want her, with every fiber of his being that was so fully alive when she was near him.

A swish of skirts pulled him from his reverie. He lifted his gaze to the staircase. A glorious golden vision floated above him, moved, descended took the shape of the most beautiful woman he had ever seen. Strands of copper sparkled in the dark mass of curls that framed her face. Her flushed cheeks approached the color of her rosy lips. As she reached the last step, the soft scent of gardenias enveloped him.

He reached out to take her hand, almost expecting it to slip through his fingers like one of the ghosts that haunted him.

"Don't you have anything to say?" she whispered.

Maggie flounced down the last step and stood with her arms folded in front of her. "Hmph. Some gentleman. He doesn't even greet ladies properly." She stormed past them into the drawing room.

Caroline patted Sebastian's arm. "Please make allowances for Maggie. She hasn't been herself since… Well, if you will excuse me, I'll get back to our guests." She kissed Libbie's cheek.

When they were alone, Sebastian lifted Libbie's hand to his lips. Her soft skin tasted sweet, enticing. For a moment he forgot himself and bent toward her mouth, meaning to kiss her. She did not move, as though she would allow it.

Giggling broke out behind him and the moment passed. Libbie stepped off the staircase and glanced at three young ladies standing in the doorway to the drawing room.

"I'm afraid Mrs. Barton's charges have seen more than they should have," Sebastian whispered to Libbie. "I may have permanently sullied your reputation in their eyes."

Libbie licked her slightly parted lips. Her blush deepened. "Nonsense. Nothing happened. But perhaps we should join the other guests before Mrs. Barton comes to the door to see what's so interesting."

She turned to leave but he grasped her elbow.

"First, you must promise me something."

He could hear her breathing quicken when he spoke to her in a quiet, urgent tone. It made his heart pound and he longed to pull her closer.

"Caroline has asked Fox to play some music this evening. Actually, I asked her to invite him. I feel safer having him here."

Libbie shivered. "Yes, I do too. I haven't felt safe since…"

Sebastian wanted to take her in his arms and make her feel safe. Instead, he did the best he could. He bent over her hand and kissed it again. "Promise me that we'll dance again, like we did the first night we met."

Her eyes widened and he was sure his words had had the intended effect—to conjure up images of that night that had nothing to do with the minuet. Then she dropped her gaze and shook her head.

"It's only been seven months —"

"Caroline told me that your mother asked you to wear something colorful for the occasion, in honor of your father's memory. Perhaps a dance would be acceptable under the circumstances as well?"

"I'll consider it." She quickly turned away from him. He followed her into the drawing room, where the giggling girls fell silent and parted to let them pass.

Fox, wearing the cleanest, and probably most uncomfortable clothes Sebastian had ever seen on him, was just warming up his fiddle and broke into a lively jig. Mrs. Barton's charges joined hands and swirled in the center of the room. Sebastian followed Libbie to the side of the room where Anna and Caroline sat in upholstered chairs that flanked a divan. On the divan sat the three ladies who were their guests. One of them was tall and hawk-like, the others smaller and well-coifed.

Caroline introduced Sebastian and he went down the line, shaking the ladies' hands. Mrs. Barton and Mrs. Mitchell showed little interest in him. The tall woman, Mrs. Jackson, held his gaze for a moment, then turned her thin, angular face to Libbie and then back to him. Caroline had told him that the ladies who would be joining them were also graduates of Mrs. Barton's finishing school but she hadn't mentioned their husbands. He wondered if the hawkish woman was Colonel Jackson's wife. He certainly didn't want to run into that drunken sod in front of an audience.

"This must be the gown you've been telling me about, Adele!" Mrs. Barton said, drawing Mrs. Jackson's attention away from him. "I couldn't believe it when she told me she was making it for Liberty MacRae. I didn't even know you were in town until yesterday, dear."

Pink color tinged Libbie's cheek. "I haven't been here long, ma'am. Barely long enough for Mrs. Mitchell to finish my gown. My mother chose the color. My father so loved it when I dressed in bright colors."

As Libbie spoke to her former headmistress, she visibly straightened her back and stood with her hands demurely clasped in front of her.

"Your mother has already explained, dear." Mrs. Barton patted Libbie's hand, the spoke to the seamstress. "You really have outdone yourself, Adele." The woman blushed and smiled.

"Thank you, Mrs. Barton. I told you she would look like a princess in it."

"Ah, our last guests have arrived!" Caroline announced.

Sebastian glanced over his shoulder and saw two people entering the room. He had thought he was prepared for anything this night but their entrance made his jaw drop.

Pierre de la Beaulieu bowed dramatically in front of Mrs. Barton's charges. Beside him, Lady Jane Whitmore surveyed the room. Sebastian excused himself and made his way to her.

"Monsieur," Beaulieu said to Sebastian before he could speak to Jane.

Sebastian scowled at him, hoping the man would take the hint.

"I am sorry," the Frenchman said in a whisper. "Of course, we should be as strangers. It is not yet time for your plan." Pierre bowed and turned his attention back to the young ladies.

Sebastian forced a smile for the sake of the curious eyes that might be upon them and took Jane's hand. "What are you doing here?" he asked through clenched teeth. "And what the devil are you doing with that pompous ass?"

Libbie smiled politely at the ladies who were making such a fuss over her. As soon as there was an opportunity, she quietly asked Aunt Caroline for a private word. They walked arm in arm to the far side of the room.

"Thank you for throwing this lovely party for me," Libbie said.

"I just provided the house, dear. Oh and the music, the charming Mr. Fox. You know your mother arranged everything else."

Libbie raised her eyebrows. "Charming, is he?"

Aunt Caroline cleared her throat. "I know you didn't want to speak to me about that. You want me to assure you that I posted your letter to Mr. Donnelly. And I did."

"Thank you so much, Aunt Caroline."

"But I still don't understand why you are asking him to perpetrate a lie. You know your mother will never sell the farm, whether Mr. Donnelly finds an interested buyer or not."

"I know that but... If I tell you a secret, do you swear to keep it from Mama?"

Aunt Caroline frowned but she nodded.

"I've asked Mr. Donnelly to help me give the impression that the MacRaes are ready to sell the land. There's a man, a terrible man..." She closed her eyes and took a deep breath, then opened them and plowed on. "He killed Johnny and Papa."

"Winters. But what does he have to do with the farm?"

"He wants it. Very badly. Badly enough to kill for it. And I think he'll go after the rest of us if he thinks that's the only way to get it."

Aunt Caroline went pale. Libbie couldn't ever remember seeing her look so close to fainting. The woman didn't have a fearful bone in her body but Libbie's words had obviously cut her to the quick.

"Anything you need from me Libbie, I'll give you. Anything to protect the three of you."

Libbie nodded. "I need you to keep them here as long as possible after I'm gone. Mama and Annalee." She swallowed hard. "And Sebastian. He cannot follow me when I leave."

"When you— Libbie, you're in danger too! You can't go off unprotected."

"My life is not in danger, not right now. I have my pistol and Black Thunder's speed on my side. And I won't be alone long. I'll go back to the Occaneechi. If anyone can help me figure out how to fix this, it's Mother Cloud Dancer."

"The medicine woman? Help you fix what? Dear, you're speaking in riddles. Has your fever returned?" Aunt Caroline reached up to feel Libbie's cheek.

Libbie grabbed both her aunt's hands. "Aunt Caroline, promise me you'll keep them here."

"I can exhibit great influence over your mother but the only one who can influence your Sebastian is you."

The words stunned Libbie. "I don't have any…and he's not my…"

"I've never thought you foolish, Libbie but you certainly do delude yourself about your feelings for him. And perhaps even more about his feelings for you. Is that why you're going to leave? Are you running away from the feelings the two of you have for each other?"

Libbie didn't know what to say. She desperately wanted to tell her aunt that she had learned that her "episodes" were real, that she could see things, had seen terrible things. But as much as her family loved her, they had never understood that part of her.

"That's it, Aunt Caroline. I just need time. I need to sort out my feelings. So please help me. Help me keep him from following me."

"He's a good man. He could make you happy."

Yes, he could. Libbie could feel the truth of the words down to her bones. But she could destroy him.

"I just need some time. And to know that Mama and Annalee are safe."

"All right, dear. I'll do what I can. Just don't stay away so long this time." She kissed her niece's cheek. "But you think long and hard about Sebastian while you're gone. And dance with the man tonight, for pity's sake."

Aunt Caroline returned to her guests. Libbie took a steadying breath and set off toward Sebastian. He seemed to be involved in a conversation with Lady Jane but Aunt Caroline had prescribed a dance and Libbie had promised him that, as well. Now was as good a time as any.

Maggie stepped in front of Libbie, her pale cheeks stained with color, her blue eyes twinkling. "Libbie, you simply must meet this Frenchman — he's a true gentleman!"

"I was just on my way to dance with Sebastian."

"Sebastian?" Maggie glanced over Libbie's shoulder. "It appears he's busy. The three dowagers on the divan have certainly noticed."

Libbie followed Maggie's gaze. Her breath caught in her throat. Sebastian and Lady Jane were bowing and curtseying, obviously preparing to dance together. "You were about to introduce me to a Frenchman?" she said to Maggie.

Maggie smiled and led Libbie to him. "Monsieur Beaulieu, may I introduce Mademoiselle Liberty MacRae?"

The man took her fingers, bent deeply at the waist and pressed soft lips against her hand. He straightened himself, still holding her hand. "*Mon Dieu*, such a beautiful woman! And in the loveliest dress I have ever seen!"

"Thank you, Monsieur."

"You would do me a great honor by calling me Pierre."

Libbie wanted to pull her hand out of his grasp until she realized Sebastian was staring at her from across the room. His jaw was set and his blue eyes were hard as stone. The dowagers too, now focused their attention on her.

"Well then, Pierre, are you going to ask me to dance?"

She saw the shock cross his face but he quickly recovered. "But of course."

Before Libbie and Pierre could begin, Sebastian and Jane twirled into the midst of Annalee and Mrs. Barton's charges, forcing the girls to part in their wake. The gazes of the three ladies on the divan were riveted to the pair.

Libbie turned to Pierre, who was watching her stare at Sebastian and Jane.

Pierre took her arm. "We should move to the center of the floor, *n'est-ce pas?*"

As they took their place for the dance, Pierre's deep bow was matched by Libbie's dramatic curtsey. With every move they made, they threw their arms wider than they needed, stepped higher than necessary and drew as much attention to themselves as possible. Libbie vaguely noticed that the dowagers had turned their heads to keep their eyes on Pierre and her.

Just when she was sure Sebastian would be overwhelmed by the scene and come to cut into the dance, she caught a glimpse of a red dress spinning endlessly. She and her partner slowed their steps and watched as Sebastian and Jane circled them. The ladies on the divan no longer seemed to notice Libbie and Pierre.

Libbie grabbed Pierre's hand and spun in a wide circle. She threw her head back and laughed and her dancing partner followed suit. When she caught a glimpse of Sebastian, he was standing stock still, scowling at Pierre.

Before Sebastian and Jane could retaliate, the music ended. Libbie laughed again, feeling triumphant. She curtsied and Pierre bowed as light applause broke out in the room.

Maggie rushed to join them and compliment them on their dance. Pierre basked in the attention of two women and was as charming as any man could be. As long minutes passed and Sebastian didn't join them, Libbie smiled with gritted teeth and wished she could find a ladylike way to escape

Pierre's well-rehearsed banter. When she felt a tug on her skirt and looked down to see Annalee looking up at her, she breathed a sigh of relief that salvation had come.

"Can I dance with the Frenchman too?" she begged.

"Annalee, what would Mama and Mrs. Barton say about your manners, interrupting this way?" Libbie said but she winked at her sister.

"But Mama sent me. She needs to see you in the kitchen."

Libbie's spine stiffened. Mama would be furious about her audacious behavior and in front of Mrs. Barton, no less. One dignified dance might have been acceptable. But Libbie's exhibition with the Frenchman had gone too far. She suddenly felt very foolish. She glanced around the room to see if Sebastian was watching her but she could not find him. Fox was gone too, which meant that he and Sebastian were probably comparing notes about something. Libbie sighed, deflated.

"Please excuse me, Pierre."

She slipped out of the room and hurried down the corridor to the kitchen, preparing herself for the tongue-lashing that no doubt awaited her. By the time she realized someone had stepped out behind her, it was too late to scream.

One strong hand covered her mouth and another wrapped around her shoulders and pulled her into the dark shadows of the kitchen doorway. Libbie sighed with relief when she looked up into Sebastian's flashing blue eyes. Seeing her relax, he loosened his grip on her.

"Liberty, what do you think you're doing with Beaulieu?" he demanded. "That man is a menace, perhaps even worse."

She smiled. Jealousy was quite becoming on him. "We were dancing, of course."

"Stay away from him! He's dangerous."

She raised an eyebrow. "If he's so dangerous, perhaps he knows something of Winters. I should try to charm some information out of him. After all, you seem to have your hands

127

full with Lady Jane. Not that anyone could mistake her for a lady after the way the two of you behaved tonight."

"The way we behaved? I'm not going to argue with you about it. But you'll do no more charming where Beaulieu is concerned." He grabbed her hand and pulled her with him through the kitchen and out the back door.

The cold night air cut through her dress and petticoats. "What on earth do you think you're doing? Unhand me or I'll scream!"

"I'm saving you again," he muttered.

"How, by dragging me out into the winter night to freeze to death?"

They rounded the corner of the barn and Libbie was shocked to see Black Thunder and one of the general's stolen horses saddled.

"Sebastian, what on earth—"

Fox stepped out of the shadows. "You're all set, Cole, Miss Libbie." He doffed his hat to her.

"I don't understand…" Libbie started.

Sebastian took her arm and led her to Black Thunder. "There's no time to explain. Just mount your horse. We have to go."

She crossed her arms in front of her. "Not until I get an explanation."

Sebastian glanced at Fox, who shrugged his shoulders, then nodded. The two men stepped forward, picked her up into the air and placed her firmly on the saddle. Fox threw her cloak around her without bothering to explain how he had sneaked it out of the house. Then Sebastian swung onto his horse.

She glowered at Sebastian. "Just because I'm on the horse doesn't mean I'm going anywhere with you until you tell me what's going on."

He smiled and leaned toward her. "If you must know, we're eloping. At least, that's what Annalee will tell everyone in an hour or so. I'm sure Mrs. Barton's charges will support the story, given what they witnessed earlier this evening."

And Aunt Caroline would probably confirm it, as well, judging from the conversation she'd had with Libbie earlier. "You cad! Have you been planning this all evening? Making them believe we'd had some lovers' quarrel which will end in a passionate elopement?"

Fox stepped forward. "Stop teasin' the young lady, Cole. Truth is, Miss, this came up all of a sudden. My boys have contacts in these parts who saw British soldiers a few miles out of town. At least one of 'em is Winters' man."

"Winters? How did he find us so fast?" She turned to Sebastian, who was now astride his mount.

He shrugged. "He has spies everywhere and one of them is obviously too close."

"But my family! He can't get near them…" She shook her head. Her visions had never shown them in danger anywhere but on their farm.

"With the militia controllin' the town, this is the safest place for 'em," Fox said. "And me an' my boys'll keep an eye on 'em too."

She looked at Fox. "Tell them the truth. I mean, not all of it. Just that we had to leave. Nothing about an elopement."

"That's our cover story and Fox here is going to back it up," Sebastian said. "It's the only way to avoid questions about what's really happening. Now, enough of this nonsense. Let's go!"

Libbie gasped. "No! I'll have none of this!"

Sebastian leaned closer to her, so close that she was sure he would try to kiss her. She prepared to turn her face away from him but the romantic attempt never came. Instead, a riding crop swished behind her and landed squarely on Black

Thunder's flank. The horse reared. Libbie grabbed the reins, holding on for dear life, cursing Sebastian as the horse bolted.

Behind her, his voice rose above the horses' pounding hooves. "Is that any way to talk to your future husband? If you keep that up, you might spend your wedding night sleeping alone on the floor!"

Chapter Ten

ও

Libbie twirled in front of the long mirror in the small room she and Sebastian had taken at the inn and observed herself in the flickering candlelight. The borrowed gown, pale blue with white lace accents on the bodice, sleeves and hem, was a bit wide for her through the waist and hips but it was lovely. It was also freshly pressed by its owner, the innkeeper's wife. Libbie touched her lightly powdered face with a gloved hand and smoothed a wandering strand of hair into place.

Mrs. Jarvis caught her eye in the mirror and smiled wistfully. "It's lovely on you, dear. Your husband will be pleased."

Libbie frowned, then quickly covered it with a smile. She doubted that he was the least bit pleased. In fact, she was sure that he had conceded to spend Christmas Eve in a real inn instead of a makeshift camp not only because the weather had turned dangerously cold but because he also hoped to appease her after her third attempt to slip away from him. No doubt having Fox enlist Aunt Caroline to send along some of her things was for the same purpose. He thought she meant to get back to Charlottesville. He had no idea that she was actually trying to get away from him and it was for his own good.

But tonight she would stay put, safe and warm. It was not a time to be sleeping on the frozen ground and there was always tomorrow to make her get-away.

"Thank you for lending this to me, Mrs. Jarvis," Libbie said as she caught the woman's eye in the mirror. "We didn't think to pack anything quite so fancy."

"How long ago did you say you married?" Mrs. Jarvis asked, for at least the third time.

The woman was sweet, if a bit addled and Libbie hated to lie to her but Sebastian had insisted they keep up their cover as a newlywed couple traveling to visit relatives.

"We married in November."

"But you've known each other a long time?"

"Just since March," Libbie said, glad to have at least one truth to tell.

"I see." Mrs. Jarvis sighed. "You know, dear, marriage is a difficult thing."

"I suppose it is."

"And there may be times when it seems too difficult. You might even want to run away from your husband and your problems. But you must work on it, dear. You've taken vows in front of God. You have to honor them. Do you understand what I'm telling you?"

Libbie raised an eyebrow quizzically at Mrs. Jarvis. In fact, she had no idea what she was telling her but she attributed it and the woman's repeated questioning to her advanced age. Then again, perhaps the woman was merely insightful. The tension between Libbie and Sebastian had been thick enough to cut with a knife. Perhaps those around them could sense it.

"Yes, ma'am, I understand," Libbie said.

There was a knock at the door. "Helen, it's me," Sebastian called from the hallway.

"You may come in, Seth," she answered. "Mrs. Jarvis, thank you for helping me with my dress."

"Of course, dear." The woman smiled at Sebastian as she took her leave, closing the door behind her.

Libbie breathed a sigh of relief. "She's a sweet old lady but a bit strange," she told Sebastian. "She asked about our courtship and marriage over and over again."

"Really?" He rubbed his chin. "Mr. Jarvis acted the same way. Very odd. This may have been a bad idea, after all."

"What was our alternative—freezing to death?" And because her harsh words made him flinch, she added, "And besides, I'm looking forward to this evening." The words came out quickly, before she could carefully consider them.

He placed a hand over hers and pressed his fingertips into her palm. "This is so unfair to you. This year of all years, to be away from your family on the holiday."

"It's what we have to do, I understand that. And now we can celebrate. I even have a lovely gown to wear."

Blood coursed through her as Sebastian surveyed her from head to toe.

"You are truly stunning, Liberty MacRae."

He placed a gentle kiss on the back of her hand, then stepped away from her, as he always did when she most wanted him to hold her in his arms.

The thought startled her. She so often wanted him to kiss her but when had she begun to long for his embrace as well?

"I've seen Fox again," he told her as he pulled off his overcoat. "Nothing new about Winters. But I do have some news that should make you happy."

She swallowed, intent on sounding unflustered despite the wild racing of her pulse. "Really?"

He smiled. "Fox and his boys will be staying at his house over the holiday. It's about half a day's ride from here. I've never been there, so we'll have to follow him. We leave first thing in the morning."

"And my family…"

"Under the watchful eye of some of the militiamen that Fox trusts."

Libbie glanced at the knife in the scabbard at Sebastian's waist. It was a harsh reminder of the danger that permeated every moment of their lives. "We really should leave tonight, shouldn't we?"

"No. Fox says it's not an easy ride. It's best not to attempt it in the dark." As he spoke, Sebastian donned the black jacket embroidered with delicate gold thread that Lady Jane's tailor had made for him to attend the Gordons' ball. He took care to conceal his weapon well.

He peered into the mirror and smoothed back his hair, then struggled to gather it in a black ribbon. Libbie stepped forward to tie it for him. When she brushed her fingers across his neck, their eyes locked in the mirror.

"Enough about Winters, Libbie. This night is for us, for celebrating. And what would a Christmas Eve celebration be without a gift?"

He turned toward her and pulled out a small package from his pocket.

She smiled and reached for his hand.

"Oh, no you don't! Sit down first."

Her heart pounded with excitement as she perched on the edge of a chair. She held out her hand, barely able to contain herself. Sebastian laughed as he dropped the small gift into her palm. It was a hard, oddly shaped cylinder, wrapped in a delicate kerchief and secured with silver thread.

"The kerchief is from your aunt," he told her. "She made Fox promise you would receive it on Christmas Eve."

Libbie traced the pattern of the cloth's lace embroidery. "It's beautiful. Just beautiful."

"Yes, it is. But what about the rest of the gift?"

She pulled the kerchief aside and held up a lead crystal perfume bottle engraved with winding, flowering vines. "Oh, Sebastian," she breathed.

He bent on one knee in front of her and held the bottle steady while he unscrewed the top. The scent of the clear liquid inside it wafted into the air. He touched the lid to her wrist, leaving the enticing scent on her skin.

"Gardenias," she said.

"Your scent. Such a beautiful, delicate perfume."

"Thank you so much for this."

"There's one more thing," he told her. He went to his overcoat and pulled out a small wooden box.

"Another gift? Oh, Sebastian, I didn't even get you one."

"This isn't really a gift. It already belongs to you. I had this box hidden in my room at the fort. Matthew found it after I left. He passed it along through Fox."

Libbie laughed. "Fox does get around, doesn't he? When does he have time to check his traps?"

"His sons help him." As he spoke, Sebastian lifted the box lid and withdrew something that he covered with his fingers. "The box held some letters from my family. And this."

He held his hand out to her and slowly opened it. In the middle of his palm, a small hairpin decorated with delicate green and pink flowers glinted.

"I have a pin just like this! I had two but I lost one the night that...oh."

He gently lifted a wayward curl from her face and secured it above her ear with the pin. "I saw it on the verandah after you left. I should have given it back to you then but... It's difficult to explain. It was just something of you that I could take with me. I didn't think you'd miss it."

She threw her arms around his neck. He had answered the questions she had been afraid to ask. "It wasn't all a lie."

He wrapped his arms around her, surrounding her with hard muscle. "A lie? Is that what you thought? No, Libbie, I never lied about my feelings for you. In fact, that night, I felt —"

A series of loud raps on the door interrupted him. "Mr. and Mrs. Parker, will you be joining us now?" It was Mrs. Jarvis. "We're all waiting for you!"

"We'll be right there," Sebastian answered. To Libbie he whispered, "We'll discuss this later."

She nodded, unable to conceal her smile of joy as he led her down the stairs to the inn's tavern room. Soon, much too soon, she would have to leave him. But not tonight.

"Ah and here we have the newlywed couple!" Mr. Jarvis said, raising a glass to them as they entered the stone-walled room that glowed in the light of a blazing fire in the hearth. "Come, come." He motioned for Libbie and Sebastian to sit near him at the head of the table.

Mrs. Jarvis and two serving girls scurried around the table, heaping mounds of succulent roasted goose, apple-nut dressing, white and sweet potatoes and creamed corn onto every plate. While they worked, Mr. Jarvis introduced the other guests to Libbie and Sebastian — a young farmer dressed in work clothes, an elderly lady traveling with her niece and nephew, a sour-faced middle-aged couple who nodded stiffly toward them and a young couple with their three small and energetic children.

Libbie could barely hear Mr. Jarvis over the music of two minstrels who stood in one corner of the room but she smiled amiably at the other guests. Dinner was a loud and boisterous affair, especially for those seated closest to the children, and conversation was difficult. As Libbie took another drink from her wineglass, which never seemed to empty, she laughed loudly and reveled in the chaos of it all. It was truly a celebration.

After sampling Mrs. Jarvis' pumpkin pie washed down with hot spiced apple cider, Libbie grabbed Sebastian's hand and pulled him to the center of the room to dance. The young couple and their children were already dancing a jig. Soon the farmer and the elderly lady's niece joined them.

When the jig ended, the troubadours changed tempo. They sang a sweet, simple song about two lovers destined to be together forever. This brought the rest of the guests and the innkeepers as well, to the dance floor but Libbie barely noticed them. She only had eyes for Sebastian as they stepped to and fro, constantly joined by their clasped hands. When the song ended, he held her hand tightly and bowed to kiss it. He held his lips against her skin long enough to make her stomach flutter.

"You're pale," he whispered to her when they stepped off the dance floor.

"I'm fine. In fact I feel wonderful! But I am parched." She reached for another glass of cider.

He grabbed her hand holding the cider glass and pulled it close to his nose. He smiled. "Be careful. There's enough mash in that cider to make a Scotsman stagger."

She laughed. "Perhaps that's why I feel so warm. I'd like to step outside for a breath of fresh air."

"Of course." He took her by the arm and led her toward the door.

Before they could reach it, Mrs. Jarvis stepped into their path and addressed Sebastian. "My husband is about to make a Christmas toast with the gentlemen. Won't you join them? It's a tradition at our inn."

"Actually, Mrs. Jarvis, I was just going to take my wife outside for a breath of fresh air."

"I could use that, myself," Mrs. Jarvis said, smiling at Libbie. "Why don't I go with you, dear? We'll just check on things in the kitchen first."

As she spoke, Mrs. Jarvis shooed Sebastian toward the men and pulled Libbie with her. Libbie wanted to protest. After all, she expected that Sebastian would kiss her under the moonlight. But when she tried to move her mouth, the muscles would not respond. Her legs felt heavier by the second, like she was wading through very deep water. The music faded, replaced by the noise of clanging pots and dishes as they entered the kitchen.

"Have a seat here for a moment," Mrs. Jarvis' voice said from somewhere far away.

Libbie felt a hard chair under her but did not remember bending her legs to sit. Her eyelids dropped shut against her will.

Sebastian was in front of her. He looked serene, angelic. Then a haze enveloped him. He was immersed in a thick pool of red, of death. She struggled desperately to open her eyes, to move, to scream but no sound or movement came. She lurched forward and her limbs went limp as she fell into a deep, black hole.

Sebastian glanced anxiously at the kitchen door. It had been several long minutes since Mrs. Jarvis had taken Libbie through that door. Long minutes of waiting for Mr. Jarvis to find enough snifters and the right bottle of brandy and to unsteadily pour out the liquid as he patted each man on the shoulder and chatted with him. When this prolonged ritual was over, Sebastian planned to storm the kitchen and retrieve Libbie.

"Drink up, my boy," the innkeeper told him with a slap on the shoulder.

Sebastian sighed in relief and prepared to toss back the drink in one gulp but the man continued speaking. "You barely touched your wine at dinner. So please, sir, drink up!"

It might have been a friendly invitation but it made Sebastian's muscles tense. His heart pounded as he remembered Libbie drinking her wine at dinner, growing more giddy with each small sip.

He pretended to take a sip of the brandy, then slammed his glass onto the table. "If you will excuse me, gentlemen, I must tend to something."

He rushed to the kitchen despite his host's protestations. On the other side of the door, he frantically scanned the room. His gaze rested on Mrs. Jarvis, standing with one of the cooks at the stove. Libbie was nowhere in sight.

"Where is she?" he demanded as he reached Mrs. Jarvis.

"Now, sir, calm down," she told him. "Have a seat and I'll explain everything to you."

"I don't want to sit! I just want to know where she is and I want to know right now!"

The woman wrung her hands in her apron. "Now sir, please try to understand. A woman's place is with her husband. I know you may think you love her, may think you can give her a better home but she took vows."

"What? What on earth are you babbling about? Where is she?"

"She's gone. With her husband. He came to take her home."

The world dropped out from under him. He grabbed the woman's arms, to keep himself anchored as much as to hold her attention. "Her husband? Who? When?"

She trembled and pulled away from him. "He was her husband," she said in a small voice. "He came here looking for her just last week and described her to us, described you too and asked us to watch for her."

"What did he look like? For God's sake woman, answer me!"

She pressed her hands to her cheeks. "He was young, perhaps your age and he wore his hair long and untied. And he had the most piercing eyes."

Sebastian clenched his fists. "My God. Norton. Do you have any idea what you've done? That madman will kill her!"

Chapter Eleven

℅

In less than a minute, Sebastian ran from the inn to the barn, pulled Black Thunder from her stall and mounted her bareback. He rode off screaming Libbie's name, disrupting the quiet night. In the distance, to the east, there was a shrill scream, like an Indian battle cry. Sebastian nudged Black Thunder with his knee and dug into her sides with his heels, clinging to her with all his strength as the mighty beast charged toward the sound.

Sebastian heard faint hoofbeats somewhere nearby but he did not pay them any heed. He could think of only one thing — saving Libbie. There was no other choice. He knew now that she was part of him, part of his destiny.

"Cole! Where in the hell are you going?" It was Fox's voice.

"Winters' second-in-command has Libbie!" Sebastian shouted over his shoulder without slowing his pace.

"My boys and I are coming right behind you!" Fox shouted.

Sebastian hoped they were but he could not wait for them. Black Thunder's speed was Libbie's only hope. Minutes later, with Fox far behind him, Sebastian spotted a horse in the distance. As he closed the gap between them, the moonlight illuminated a cloaked rider with a prostrate form balanced in front of him.

Sebastian dug harder into Black Thunder's sides, hanging on to her mane with one hand, reaching for his knife with the other. And then he was upon them, his fury overwhelming him, nearly blinding him. Sebastian slashed at Norton but barely grazed him.

Norton pulled on his mount's reins and the horse skidded to a halt. "Stay back!" he shouted as he reached into his pocket. "'E wants me ta take 'er alive but I'll gladly slit 'er throat!"

Sebastian did not hesitate. He pushed himself off Black Thunder and lunged at Norton, knocking him off balance. The two of them crashed to the frozen ground. Norton's hand slammed against the hard surface and a pistol flew from it. Sebastian's knife skidded away from him.

Out of the corner of his eye, Sebastian saw Libbie slide from the saddle, stand unsteadily on her feet, then drop to her knees. Norton lunged at him and wrapped his hands around Sebastian's neck.

"I'm not that easy to kill," Sebastian gasped.

"But you'd die for her, wouldn't you, squaw-man? Like I thought you did for that damn Indian squaw of yours."

Shouts and gunshots echoed in the distance. "Hang on, Cole! We're coming!" Fox called.

Sebastian twisted free and smashed his fist into Norton's face. Norton hit the ground but rolled out of Sebastian's reach.

"Another time!" Norton called over his shoulder as he bolted for the woods. "Then we'll discuss 'er boy that we kept alive."

The words made no sense, yet they slammed into Sebastian's belly like a fist. "What boy?" he whispered, stunned motionless.

But Norton was gone and men and horses were closer and Libbie was lying a few feet away from him. Fox arrived, firing shots into the trees after Norton.

Sebastian took one staggering step, tears clouding his vision. "Fox, he's alive. Daniel is alive!"

Another shot rang out above Sebastian, sailed into the trees. It was too loud, too close. Black Thunder reared up on her hind legs, then came crashing down. Sebastian felt a powerful hoof slam into his shoulder. Pain radiated through him, knocked him flat. He heard the thud of his own head against the ground, then the world disappeared.

* * * * *

Voices. Deep, unfamiliar voices. Libbie floated in inky blackness, listening to them. Where were they? Where was she?

She had been dancing with Sebastian, she could still feel the pressure of his fingers around hers. She had needed a breath of fresh air, had followed Mrs. Jarvis into the kitchen. And she had seen Sebastian—his face, the blood, the death vision. There had been a flash, a brief moment when something had pulled her out of darkness and she had peered up into a wicked face.

Libbie woke to her own screams. Strong arms encircled her, pulled her against an unyielding chest. Still screaming, she kicked and punched with all her might. Her fist connected with a shoulder and her assailant crumpled away from her.

"Libbie, it's me. It's Sebastian."

The words were meaningless to her but the smooth, familiar voice penetrated her fear. She reached for him, clung to him, felt him shake in her arms or her shake in his. They were both alive and his arms were around her again, calming and protecting her.

"Is everything all right in there?" a man called from the other side of the partially opened bedroom door.

"We just need a moment," Sebastian answered.

Libbie's blood pounded in her ears. "Who is that? What's going on? Does Winters have us?"

"Shh. We're in the mountains with Fox and his sons. We're safe for now."

"How? I can't remember… I thought I saw the man who kidnapped me." She hugged her arms around herself, then glanced down, realizing she was wearing only her shift.

"You have no broken bones," he told her, as though answering her question about her state of undress.

She nodded but couldn't keep her limbs from trembling. Sebastian held her shoulders and stared into her eyes. When she touched his cheek, she felt the stickiness of dried blood.

"You're hurt," she whispered.

"Not too badly." He smiled as he touched her face. "Norton didn't want to give you up without a fight."

"So it wasn't a wine-induced nightmare."

The room door creaked open. "More like a drug-induced one." Fox's son Scott, a tall, broad man with a long beard, strode toward them. Fox's second son, Grayhorse, a thin, copper-skinned man with a hairless face, followed his half-brother into the room.

"Is your father back yet?" Sebastian asked.

Scott nodded as he set a lamp on the bedside table and turned the knob until it lit the room brightly. "He's gone to bed. Gettin' too old for this kinda excitement, I reckon."

Sebastian laughed. "You're looking awfully tired yourself, old man."

"But I still look a damn sight better than you, Cole." Scott's small smile belied his gruff tone. "And as soon as Grayhorse gives Miss Libbie a once-over, we'll both get outta here and let you rest."

Libbie blushed as Grayhorse stepped toward her, wondering what the "once-over" would involve.

"Not to worry, ma'am," Grayhorse said gently, in a tone Libbie had heard Mother Cloud Dancer use many times. "We just want to make sure the opium has worn off."

"Opium? He gave me opium? How do you know that?"

"Norton didn't give you the drug," Sebastian answered. "The innkeepers did. Norton lied to them, told them you were his runaway wife."

"They sent their apologies and your belongings here with Fox, after he showed them the error of their ways," Grayhorse said as he examined her eyes.

"Fox got to the inn just in time," Scott added with a grin.

"Some farm boy was about to pay 'em a pretty penny for Cole's ridin' boots and they were goin' to auction off the trunk full o' ladies' things next."

Their voices faded as Libbie struggled to keep her eyes open. The pillow came up under her head suddenly, unexpectedly, and she sank into sleep once more. The only sensation that followed her into unconsciousness was the warm, safe grasp of Sebastian's hand in hers.

* * * * *

Libbie's hand was empty and cold. When she opened her eyes, Sebastian was gone from his bedside chair. Frantic, she scanned the room. Through the open door, she saw him in the next room, crouching by the hearth to stoke the flagging fire. She crawled slowly from the bed, not quite trusting her wobbly legs.

Sebastian did not notice her as he coaxed the flames into a blaze. He had traded his fine embroidered suit for the simple breeches and tunic that he wore while they traveled. His face was slightly stubbled but clean, devoid of any trace of the blood that must have come from the small cut under his eye, where a purplish bruise had formed. His movements were slow and graceful but Libbie could see stiffness when he used his left arm.

"Does it hurt?" she asked him.

He turned quickly, swept his gaze over her scantily-clad form, then averted his eyes. He touched the cut. "It looks worse than it is."

"I meant your arm. You're favoring it."

"It's actually my shoulder. It got caught between Black Thunder's hoof and the frozen ground."

144

"You'll have to tell me the details." She shivered as the danger of their situation came back to her.

He was immediately on his feet, striding toward her. "You're cold. Come closer to the fire. I'll get some blankets."

He disappeared into the bedroom before she could protest and returned with quilts, which he arranged on the floor near the hearth. She sat down and pulled one quilt around her shoulders.

Sebastian stood near her, rubbing his hands as if to warm them and stared at the flames. He was quiet for such a long time that she wondered if he remembered she was in the room.

"Where are Fox and his sons?" she asked when she could no longer stand the silence.

He pointed to a window, indicating the darkness beyond it. "In the main house. There's more room there. This cabin is left over from Fox's bachelor days."

"Of course he would have been married, to have two sons. I just never pictured it."

"He was married twice. Widowed both times."

"Well, he's full of surprises." She touched her hair. The pin Sebastian had returned to her was still there. "And so are you."

He was silent again.

Libbie could not tolerate the distance between them. She needed him to hold her and look into her eyes the way he had at the inn, to make her feel as safe now as she had then.

"At the inn, you were going to tell me something about the night we met."

He leaned toward the mantel for support but winced when his shoulder brushed against it.

"You can tell me while I check that."

"No, it's fine."

"I'm in a better position to judge that than you are. My skills saved your life in that cave. You trusted me then," she told him as she stood and stepped in front of him. "Trust me now."

Her hands trembled as she reached for his tunic and lifted it over his head.

She noticed bruises on his neck and gently touched one.

"A souvenir from Norton," he answered her unasked question. "No damage done."

He did not pull his gaze from her as she reached toward his shoulder but he lifted his hand in the air to protest. She slowly pressed her fingertips against his. Sparks danced between them as she pressed the length of her fingers to his, then flattened her hand until they stood palm to palm.

Sebastian pressed his free hand against the small of her back and pulled her body against his. He moved his face slowly, carefully, toward hers. She stopped breathing as their lips touched, then pressed more firmly together. His mouth was strong and demanding. She responded in kind, blocking out everything in the world except the warm feel of him.

He moved his mouth over her cheek and chin, planted gentle kisses along her jaw, ran his tongue down the length of her throat. With one last lingering kiss he lifted his head and looked into her eyes.

"You made me feel alive that night. I can't explain to you what that meant, what it means to me to be near you, to touch you, taste you."

She reached up to wipe a tear from his cheek. He caught her hand and kissed it, then closed his eyes, pressing out more tears.

"But knowing me put you in danger. I had to get away from there, from you, to protect you, to keep you safe. God, I wanted to give you that but I couldn't."

"No one could." She leaned against him. "I know how fragile life can be. I know that no one can keep me safe every minute of every day. But there are things you can give me. Important things."

His lips nuzzled her ear. "Tell me," he whispered.

She swallowed hard. "This heat. This passion."

He ran his fingers down the length of her spine. "Is that what you want from me?"

She nodded. "Since the moment I met you."

"Libbie, I know I don't deserve you. I don't deserve these feelings you bring to me. But I was so afraid I'd lost you tonight. I prayed I could hold you just one more time, even though I know it's wrong of me..."

"No, Sebastian, this is right. So right."

Their lips met again in a deep kiss that left her quivering. She pulled away from him just long enough to let him lift her shift over her head and drop it to the floor. His gaze roamed over her, leaving a heated blush in its wake. He pressed his bare chest against hers as he gently kissed her eyes, then nipped at her earlobe. He ran his tongue over the pulse in her throat.

Libbie gasped at the small, scintillating touches.

Sebastian stroked her back, her buttocks, her thighs, pausing only to pull off his own breeches. Then he bent lower until he was kneeling in front of her. With his upturned mouth, he kissed one breast, then the other, flicking his tongue teasingly over her throbbing nipples.

Libbie moaned as he pulled her down to kneel with him, his hands caressing every inch of her. Her unpracticed touches were less gentle as she rubbed his dark chest hair and small, smooth nipples, which rose to hard points under her fingertips. She lingered over his rippled stomach and slowly traced the soft line of hair that began under his belly button.

With one hand supporting her back and the other wrapped in her hair, he crushed his mouth against hers. His erection pressed insistently against her belly. She leaned back, pulling him toward her. Her desire for him had turned into a feral, instinctive need to feel him deep inside her.

He stopped, suspending her just above the blankets. "Are you sure? There will be no turning back."

"I don't want to turn back. The past is full of pain. I just want this time, this place. This moment with you."

"I'll be gentle, love."

She dug her nails into his back. "No! Not gentle. I want your passion. Make me feel it. Make me burn!"

He groaned as his mouth covered hers again. His kisses were hard and frenzied. Libbie returned every bit of his desperation. He laid her on the makeshift bed. The heat from the hearth licked at her naked skin but the real fire burned inside her, under her flesh, in the tips of her breasts and the crevice between her legs. Sebastian ran his fingers up her thigh, then slipped them into her slick, tight channel. Pain and pleasure rushed through her, dragging ragged cries from her throat.

As he positioned himself above her, Sebastian balanced on his injured side. He cringed and sank back on his knees. She cried out from the pain. She could feel it in her own shoulder. And other sensations — all that he felt, she could feel. The passion raged inside him, obliterating the momentary distraction of his injury. He kissed her and pulled her with him until he lay on his back with her above him.

Libbie moved her hips over his and stopped on the precipice of joining. Her nerve endings sizzled with his desperate need as well as her own. She quivered as he helped position her, guiding the tip of his penis to her moist folds. Their combined sensations made her suck in her breath and groan with the pain of their overwhelming need. A throbbing pressure built inside her, urging her to sink against him, to sheath him with her flesh.

She looked down into his face. His mouth was parted in anticipation and his eyes were hooded with desire but he lay still, waiting for her. The sweet, smoky smell of the fire, the soft crackle of splintering wood, the audible hush of the snow-muted outside world — she wanted to memorize everything about that moment, to suspend it in time. Then all external feelings ceased. The world faded to gray silence. Only their passion existed, blazed, vibrated around her.

She moved herself over the tip of his cock and felt an uncomfortable resistance to his penetration. She wiggled, pushed, felt a sharp pain as he broke through the barrier. With a cry, she stopped. His fingers brushed her face, his eyes asked her a question that he started to form with his lips. Before he could speak, she kissed him. She focused on the feel of his tongue in her mouth, of his hands on the small of her back. And sank completely against him.

Sebastian made a small gurgling sound as she encompassed him. But he remained unmoving, except for his mouth, which he used to sprinkle kisses onto her face and throat. With her body fully acclimated to his, she moved against him, slowly at first, then harder, faster. They were heat and light and color. The world was nothing, they were everything. Their yearning, their desire, the sensations swelling inside of them — only these existed.

She moved faster. He grasped her hips, drove himself deeper into her. Every fiber of her being tensed, then let go, releasing her from the exquisite torture.

She closed her eyes as powerful waves of desire crested and broke into cascades of pleasure, drowned her in ecstasy that she had never imagined. Moans rose from deep inside her, matching the rhythm of his thrusts. She leaned against his chest and kissed him hard and long as the ripples subsided. He grasped her hips, lifted her from him and pulled her back over and over again, refusing to let her slow her pace. The waves rose again, spread from her toes to her thighs, lapped across her belly, swelled in her breasts, then crashed over her entire body at once.

Sebastian tightened his grip on her. He pulsed deep inside her, filling her, pushing her further and further into their combined pleasure.

Gasping for breath, she collapsed against him. His heart still pounded wildly in his chest as he gently stroked her hair and face with a featherlight touch. Several minutes passed in blissful, satisfied silence.

"How do you feel, love?" he finally whispered.

She propped herself up on one elbow, grimacing slightly as she felt the strain in muscles she had not used before. "Like I've died and gone to heaven."

His face darkened. "Please, don't say that."

She kissed him. "I mean heaven on earth. That's how it feels to make love to you." She closed her eyes, still barely able to believe it. "I've never said those words to a man before— 'make love'. And I never imagined it would be like that, so…delicious."

"Hmm. Delicious. Yes, that's what it was." He kissed the top of her head as she nuzzled against his throat.

"And more. It was as if… I can't explain it. As if I could feel your pleasure as well as my own."

"We were connected, as one," he said. "You made me feel things…" His voice trailed off, then came back stronger. "I've had so much pain, so little else for so long. Then I met you and I saw beauty and I felt joy. I could feel again. And now we've had this perfect moment and it's as if nothing else exists in this world."

She kissed him gently, sweetly, with her eyes closed, savoring every second spent in his arms. But her body, still suffering the effects of the opium and adapting to the rigors of lovemaking, was on the brink of exhaustion. She tried to roll off Sebastian so she could curl up beside him but he wrapped his uninjured arm tightly around her.

"Stay here, just like this. I want to wake up this way, still inside you, feeling your heartbeat against my chest."

She didn't protest. Although she was too overcome with fatigue to tell him, it was what she wanted, as well. And what she wanted just as much was to wake up with him and pursue another perfect moment.

* * * * *

Libbie woke up on the bed, the blankets heaped on top of her. Her stomach tightened as the familiar smells of eggs, sausage and strong coffee coaxed her to rise. Her feet touched the cold floorboards before she realized she was still naked. With a small smile, she lifted her shift from the chair where it lay tangled with Sebastian's tunic.

The sound of voices beyond the closed bedroom door raised a concern about dressing, since her clothes were still packed with the other belongings from the inn, all of which were piled near the fireplace. But Sebastian had thought of everything. Her simple gray frock and her brush both lay at the foot of the bed and a full water pitcher and basin were on a stand by the door. She managed to wash herself, dress and brush her unruly hair in a matter of minutes.

She smiled broadly as she reached for the door and gently tugged it. It was heavy and did not move far. Before she could open it wider, she heard Sebastian speaking.

"I cannot tell her that!"

She froze, her hand still on the doorknob.

"You owe her that much." It was Fox's voice. "Miss Libbie deserves to know what she's in for."

"All she needs to know is that Winters is still a danger to us and we have to stay at least one step ahead of him. Everything else is off limits."

Through the cracked doorway she could see Sebastian frowning deeply. "You are to swear you won't tell her."

"Sebastian—"

"Swear it!"

"All right, I swear it. But I don't like lyin' to the likes of Miss Libbie."

"I don't do it because I like it," Sebastian said. "Hell, Fox, I'd trust her with my life, fleeting as it is. But right now, I can't tell her about this."

Libbie could not stand to hear anymore. He was still hiding things from her. More secrets and deceptions. How could she have let herself forget who and what Sebastian was? A spy. A liar by definition.

Why hadn't she left him by now? Why hadn't she devised a plan to sneak away from him and pursue Winters on her own, to save the life of that liar on the other side of the door?

Because she hadn't wanted to leave him. In the light of day, that truth was startling and harsh. Despite her doubts and her cautionary visions, she had wanted him more than she had wanted her own safety and she had failed to protect her heart.

She had tied herself, heart and body, to man who might never love her enough to tell her the truth.

Chapter Twelve

ॐ

"We can't stay here long," Sebastian called to Libbie. "We should travel a bit farther before dusk."

The late afternoon sun was sinking. If they wanted to find a secluded spot to make camp, this would have to be their last stop for water and it would have to be a short one. He knelt beside the small stream to splash water on his face and to lift it to his lips. It would be cold, so he did not linger over it, since she was watching him closely. She'd been doing that for days as they'd traveled west from Fox's home, moving closer to Occaneechi territory.

"We should be able to get better sleep tonight, now that we've come this far." He stood and walked toward her as she knelt on the bank of the stream. "I know it's been difficult, barely taking time to rest these past few nights."

Or perhaps it had made things easier. Since the moment she had emerged from the bedroom in Fox's cabin, he had known that she regretted their night of passion. Her red mouth, so recently swollen from his kisses, had been twisted into a frown. She had barely turned the gaze of her alluring green eyes on him. And while she was polite enough, she had said little more than ten words to him or Fox that entire morning.

Sebastian had hoped that the privacy of their ride would bring her out of her melancholy but it only seemed to make it worse. For his part, he could think of little to say to her. Small talk was sheer hell when all he wanted to discuss was that night and the passion and the connection that they had both felt. And he wanted to hold her, kiss her, make her look at him with hope and desire as she had that night.

She rose to her feet and brushed a small clump of mud off her gray frock. Not the best riding attire for such a grueling trip but that and her fancy party dresses were all she'd had at the cabin. "I'm ready," she said softly, without looking at him.

She took one step, then stopped. She furrowed her brow, then knelt again by the stream.

"Libbie," Sebastian said, then called more loudly, "Libbie!"

She did not respond as she scooped up water in her palms, then let it flow through her fingers. Slowly, wordlessly, she turned her hands over and over, inspecting them, seeing something that Sebastian could not.

His voice sounded distant. "Libbie, what is it? Speak to me, please!"

She couldn't answer as she scooped up more water and saw it again—the red liquid like blood in her palms. She bent closer to the stream and saw scarlet rivulets growing thicker by the second, cutting through the clear water. She jumped back from the blood-soaked bank but Black Thunder did not seem to notice it and drank greedily from the tainted water. Of course the horse could not see or smell the blood. No one else could.

Libbie climbed on to Black Thunder. She prodded the horse to a gallop along the stream's edge.

"Libbie! Hell's bells, what are you doing?" Sebastian shouted behind her.

His voice faded as she felt it all around her—the death that she knew was near. The air was dank and close. She tugged at the strings of her cloak, desperately trying to pull them off her throat so she could catch her breath. She had no concept of time or distance, could not have said where she was going or from where she had come but she kept riding. There was something pulling her to it.

The first things she saw in the field were the patches of pink snow. They were covered by a gray mist and made beautiful patterns on the barren earth. But the field was not really empty. Torn clothing and discarded weapons littered the ground. The gray mist enveloped her, choking off her breath with its pungent smell of burnt gunpowder and spilled blood. Libbie dismounted, leaving Black Thunder to wander back to the shelter of the trees.

She stepped close to the nearest pile of rags. It was soaked in blood that still seeped and bubbled through the ripped fabric. And she realized the truth.

The soldier dressed in those shredded rags was dead at her feet, his eyes flung open with terror. She looked out across the field and saw that all the piles — at least fifteen with blue coats, nearly as many with red coats — had bodies and faces but none had life left in them.

A low, throaty moan reached her, struck her to her soul. It was a death song without words or tune. And it was coming from her.

There were two Continental soldiers, boys really, lying just in front of her. It made her think of the way Johnny and Tom had died beside each other on a battlefield far too similar to this one. But these deaths were recent, and soldiers would soon return to claim the dead. She had to leave this place, had to get away before someone found her here.

There was so much smoke, such a thick red haze, too much death. Libbie couldn't will her legs to carry her back to her horse. She dropped to her knees in front of the dead soldiers.

Sebastian had called her name but Libbie had not responded, had instead knelt in front of the dead boys. Sebastian climbed off his horse and ran toward her but they surrounded him. Dozens of souls, all of them confused, walking in circles, calling out the names of missing friends.

In the midst of the newly released spirits appeared two more young men. One of them moved among the confused specters, speaking to each one in turn and pointing toward the horizon. The other ghost, one Sebastian recognized, knelt by a dying boy.

"Let him go!" Sebastian touched the blood on the boy's cheek, saw his eyelids flutter. "Let the boy live, Johnny!"

Libbie's brother looked up from the nearly dead boy. "It's too late, Cole. This is his destiny. There are rules. You know that better than anyone."

As Johnny spoke, the boy's spirit left his body and moved toward the other spirit guide.

"Tom Donnelly," Johnny answered Sebastian's unasked question. "It's a comfort to them to take direction from other soldiers. Somehow they understand it better this way. When death is so fast, so unexpected."

Sebastian nodded. Of course he knew. "But that's not the only reason that you're here."

Johnny was watching Libbie, who still knelt on the ground across the field. "I wish she hadn't seen this."

Sebastian clenched his fists at his sides. "It's because of me. She's been subjected to all this death because of me."

"No, Cole. This moment is part of her destiny as well as yours. But it has to end soon. More Redcoats are on their way."

Sebastian's stomach twisted. "Winters?"

"Not this time. But still dangerous."

Sebastian nodded. "I'll get her out of here."

"There's more."

Sebastian scowled. "Isn't there always?"

"You didn't tell her what Fox told you. The Occaneechi are in danger."

"I'll tell their chief when we get there and then Libbie and I will disappear into the wilderness," Sebastian said. "With us gone, Winters won't waste his time going after the tribe."

Johnny shook his head. "Winters will still attack them. You can't run from him anymore. When you get to the Occaneechi village, stop, hold your ground, gather all of your resources. Then it will be time to turn the tables and pursue him."

"But, I don't know—"

Johnny held up one hand. "You'll know all you need to know when the time is right." He glanced at his sister as she crawled away from the dead boys. "Now it's time for her to know your secret. And what started all of it—Wes and Sunflower."

Sebastian sucked in his breath. "I can't. The rules—"

"Aren't ours to make. They say she has to know." Johnny met Sebastian's gaze and held it. "Winters already knows what you are. He has found others, the ones who came before you."

"There were others?"

Johnny nodded. "They failed and now their souls are his. You cannot fail, Cole. And you cannot hide the truth from my sister any longer."

"But why did they fail? How do I avoid—" He felt a hand on his shoulder and realized he was speaking to empty air. Johnny, Tom and their new charges were gone.

Libbie felt lightheaded as she knelt on the frozen ground. She just managed to turn away from the brutalized bodies in front of her when the contents of her stomach spilled out of her. The convulsions continued, although her insides were empty and her head was throbbing from the exertion. When they subsided, she found herself prostrate on the hard ground.

She picked up her head, her stomach still churning, her mouth full of lingering foulness. Sight and sound returned to her and she realized Sebastian was also in the field, kneeling beside a very young-looking dead boy. She tried to push herself off the ground, failed, tried again. On the third attempt she rose unsteadily to her knees, then more solidly to her feet.

As she stumbled toward Sebastian, she saw that he was talking. Not to himself but to the empty air in front of him. When she knelt beside him and touched his shoulder, he jumped as though he'd seen a ghost. The thought made her shiver. But the ghosts were gone. Death still surrounded them, but the spirits of the dead soldiers had moved on.

"Sebastian." Libbie touched his shoulder.

He turned his gaze slowly in her direction and focused on her face. "I'm so sorry you saw this."

She shivered. "I've seen the horrors of death before. But this is too much like the battle that killed Papa and Johnny and Tom."

"I know. I know so many things, and I have to tell them to you. I have to tell you the truth about myself."

Despite the horror around them, Libbie's heart felt lighter at the sound of those words. "Yes, the truth. But not here."

He jumped to his feet and pulled her up beside him. "You're right, not here. They're coming—more soldiers."

"But how—"

"Just trust me, Libbie. I swear you'll understand all of it very soon."

She clung to his hand as they crossed the field and mounted their horses. Before she could nudge Black Thunder to a gallop, Sebastian grabbed the bridle and leaned close to her. He lifted one hand, sticky with blood from the dying boy he'd touched, to her cheek.

He had that faraway look again. "I pray she can accept it."

Libbie shivered and looked over her shoulder, almost expecting to see someone there, someone to whom Sebastian was obviously speaking. She turned back to find his gaze fixed on her.

"I pray you can understand, that you won't hate me."

She pressed her hand over his fingers, which still lingered on her cheek. "I could never hate you, Sebastian." She swallowed hard, forcing herself to say the words, to admit what she'd fought so hard to conceal from him. "I love you."

He pulled his hand away. Tears filled his eyes. "I don't deserve it, Libbie. And you can't promise that you won't hate a man who killed his own best friend."

Chapter Thirteen

ဆာ

Sebastian leaned close to the campfire and stoked the kindling, then added thicker branches and watched the flames catch and grow. With the fire burning steadily, he sat down on a rock and stared into the flames. He was not alone. He sat with the shadows of the ghosts he had made and waited for Libbie.

She was feeding the horses and checking the perimeters of their makeshift campsite. Not that there was much chance that any of the soldiers would come after them. They had covered the tracks they had made on and near the battle site. The task had given them a reason not to speak, not to face the demons for a little while longer. Then they had ridden in silence, each immersed in their own thoughts. And now they were deep in the forests of the foothills, sheltered from sight by a thick ring of evergreens, safe from everything but his past.

She touched his cheek with cold fingers. He turned to see her as she sat down beside him. Her face was an emotionless mask as she stared at him, waiting. There was no turning back.

"I don't understand why you're still here," he whispered. "Why didn't you turn and run when I told you I'd killed my best friend?"

She widened her eyes. "Is that what you thought? That I would run away? Is that why you didn't tell me before?"

"How could I tell you? You barely trusted me as it was, even after… I couldn't possibly ask you to understand this." He dropped his head into his hands.

She touched his shoulder. "I knew you were hiding something from me. Still, I believe you're a good man. Tell me about your friend."

Sebastian took a deep breath. "His name was Wes Bradley and he was more than my friend. He was like a brother to me. We met when he was seventeen and I was eighteen. He had just joined the militia. American and British battalions worked together then."

Libbie nodded. "Keeping the French from crossing borders or inciting Indian attacks were the main concerns of Papa and his friends in those days."

"Much has changed in seven years. But Wes and I worked together. Our regiments patrolled along the Ohio frontier. What a time we had! Not long after that, he fell in love with an Indian girl. I stood up with him at his wedding and sat up with him all night when his wife was having their son."

Sebastian took one of Libbie's hands in his, needing its soft strength. He prayed she would not pull it away from him when he told her the truth. If only he could hold her, just hold her, could forget about his past, even forget about his future for just a short while. He wanted to stay in the shelter of the evergreens and her arms and never think of anything else.

"Please go on."

The words jarred him. He cleared his throat and stared at their joined hands. "Everything changed a little over a year ago. It was early November, on a devil of a night. The weather was unbearable. There was an ice-cold rain that hadn't let up for days. My regiment had spent the week driving a small band of French soldiers away from a frontier settlement and we were on our way back to our post.

"We were exhausted, sick, hungry. That's when we got the orders to help out a nearby patrol. Local Indians had joined the French in terrorizing some settlers.

"We rode on through most of the night but when we got to our position, the other British patrol was nowhere to be found. Then we heard the horses. We gave the signal for the British troops to answer but got none. At that point, we could only assume it was the French and Indian contingent. By the time they crested the hill close to us, we were ready.

"The battle was short. We'd surprised them and far outnumbered them." He swallowed hard to fend off tears. "One of them rode straight for me. He was waving his arms and yelling. But there was so much noise — the horses and the men and the guns exploding all around us. The smoke stung my eyes and stuck in my throat. All I could think was that this screaming man with a long braid and buckskins was going to kill me. So I aimed. And I shot. He fell backward out of his saddle. By that time he was close enough for me to hear him. He was screaming my name."

He covered his face with his hands. Tears spilled into his palms and ran down his wrists.

"It wasn't your fault. You didn't know."

"I knelt on the ground beside him and held his wound shut with my hands," he shuddered, remembering the horrible feel of it, "but I couldn't stop the bleeding. Wes' life slipped right through my fingers." Sebastian stood up and paced in front of the fire, hoping the movement would help dull the pain of the vivid memory.

"It was my fault. And what happened afterward only made it worse, if that's possible. Our commander wouldn't let us bury the dead. We were ordered straight to our camp and didn't even leave for our normal duties. All of us were asking questions. Where was the other British patrol? And what about the French troops? We never saw any sign of them, or of any destroyed towns.

"Weeks went by before we finally got our orders. We were to tell absolutely no one about what had happened. The army promised they were investigating the matter."

"An investigation? I don't understand."

"Everyone realized by that time that the information about the French troops had been false but no one knew why. I could have done something, should have done something but I wanted to forget about that night, that battle, about killing Wes. Because I did nothing, the man who had set up Wes and the others was able to come back to finish the job."

"Winters." Her voice was soft. The word was a statement, not a question.

Sebastian nodded, then continued. "Most of the braves from the tribe were killed by my regiment. It left their village vulnerable. Our fort was close by and we tried to keep an eye on them but in the end, we couldn't protect them. Winters murdered them. Women, children, old men. All of them." Except perhaps one child, he wanted to add but he could not bring himself to discuss Daniel.

He sucked in air through his teeth, then exhaled slowly. He watched her face, trying to assess how much more she could bear to hear. In the firelight, her face was beautiful, still, unreadable.

"I found them." He could not make his voice louder than a whisper. "The embers were still burning."

"He..." She sucked in an unsteady breath. "Winters killed them, the whole village? But why?"

He shook his head. "I can't pretend to know how his evil mind works but the tribe must have had something he wanted—probably their land. Nothing is sorted out yet but when it is, no doubt Winters will swoop in to stake a claim on the deserted village."

"And you found them, your friends. You saw what he'd done to them." A tear rolled down her cheek. He wiped it away with his thumb.

"It didn't take long to find Winters and his men. They hadn't gone very far. I watched them, waited for Winters. I wasn't afraid to die but I wanted to kill him first, so I had to get him alone."

Libbie shivered and leaned closer to the fire. "What happened? You're still here and so is that murdering bastard, so—"

"It's not that simple. I didn't kill him, as you've seen but I sure as hell tried. I put that scar on his face. But his second-in-command found us fighting. I couldn't beat two of them."

"You were lucky to get away with your life."

He sat on the rock beside her but left space between them. When she heard his next words, even that distance may not be enough for her.

"I didn't."

She stared blankly for a moment, then blinked. "Didn't what?"

He breathed deeply, trying to calm his pounding heart. "I didn't get away with my life. I took a bullet first."

"The scar!" She touched his chest.

Heat spilled from her fingers. He was shocked to realize how cold he was, now that he felt the contrast of her warmth.

"But you survived it. You're here with me now."

He shook his head. "I didn't survive it, or the fall I took when Winters' men chased me off a cliff. Libbie, the truth is that I died that night."

Libbie shrank from him and shivered again.

"I don't understand."

Sebastian let out a hollow laugh. "Of course you don't. I don't either."

He got to his feet again and rubbed a hand over his unshaven chin. "The night was dark, cold. I felt the bullet, then felt the ground disappear from under me. I flew. Fell. Felt my body crumple into a heap. But there was no pain. Just color and light. And then their faces.

"I saw Sunflower first." He brushed away tears. "She was Wes' wife. And she was—" He shook his head, not ready to explain that part of it yet. "And the elders and Wes. I felt such peace, such joy to see them."

Libbie stood beside him and laid her hand on his shoulder. "A dream, then."

"No Libbie, not a dream." He grabbed both her hands in his, letting her warmth thaw the iciness of his fingers. "My death. I was dead. But it wasn't meant to be. My rage and pain had blinded me, had made me risk my own life and I'd left this earth without fulfilling my destiny."

He moved closer to her.

"I know this is difficult to understand, believe me. But they — the spirits — told me I couldn't stay there, couldn't have eternal peace unless I made it right. I couldn't bear to leave that place to come back to the pain and loneliness of this life but I had no choice. This is my only chance to find peace for my soul."

"Winters. He's your destiny. Killing him, avenging them."

Sebastian sighed. "They gave me no clear directive but it is the only thing that makes sense. Sometimes I get signs that let me know I'm on the right path to my ultimate destiny."

She shivered and he drew her close to him.

"What kinds of signs?" she asked.

He held her tighter. "To understand the signs, you have to understand my existence. I am flesh and blood, Libbie. You've seen that for yourself. I can feel pain, tremendous pain. I can bleed, heal, scar. But this is a life of half-measures. I cannot taste or smell, cannot see color, can focus on only a small amount of sound at one time. And I can barely feel touch, even that of extreme cold or heat. I must remind myself to eat because food and drink hold no appeal for me. I must look at what others are wearing to know whether I should don my overcoat or sit close to the fire."

A wave of nausea swept over her. She had given herself to him, had shared the most intimate of sensations with him.

She pulled away from him. "You can only feel pain? But I... We... How could you..."

165

"Oh, no, love, it's not what you think! That night, in Fox's cabin," he took her hands in his and she felt how truly cold they were, realized that they only warmed from contact with her, "when I made love to you, I felt every incredible sensation. I told you then that you made me feel things—and make me feel things—that I haven't felt in a very long time. I can't explain it, except to say that perhaps you're tied to my destiny."

Relief washed over Libbie. Still, there was so much to absorb. She had thought that all she could ever want from him was the truth but she was beginning to believe that she was not equipped to handle it. She could barely follow the logic of it all, if there were any logic.

"It happens," he continued, "when an opportunity presents itself that will take me down the right path, like when General Gordon offered me the post at Winters' fort. Suddenly I could feel the glass I was holding and could taste the brandy he'd given me."

"So when you saw me, you knew we were destined to cross paths."

He smiled but even his smile seemed tinged with sadness. "With you, Libbie, it was so different. There were no subtle impressions like the other times. There was so much sensation—every one of my senses came back to life near you. So I suppose I knew even then that we were destined to meet but frankly, I was so overwhelmed that I didn't dwell on that aspect of it."

She stared into the flames. "It seems so," she shrugged, "planned. Not by you but by them, whoever or whatever they are."

"Look at me, Libbie."

She did look at him, truly looked at him. She stared into the depths of his intense blue eyes took in the downturn of his sensitive mouth, noticed the fine lines of worry and pain etched into his face. And her own pain lessened, replaced by sorrow for Sebastian, for all he had sacrificed and lost.

He laid a cold hand on each side of her face. "What you said to me earlier—I said I didn't deserve it but I want it more than I have ever wanted anything in this world. You have to believe me that whether it was pre-planned or pre-arranged by anyone or anything else, all that matters is how we feel." The heat of his hands blossomed against her cheeks. "I love you, Liberty MacRae."

He intended to tell her the rest of the story, about the other woman he had loved and how he had destroyed her. But when Libbie leaned closer to him, her tongue darting out to wet her lips, he could not bear to tell her any more, not that night.

Instead, he dug his fingers into her jaw and lifted her lips to his. She pressed hard against him, her tongue running across his lips and slipping into his mouth. Nothing else mattered to him in that moment except her—the sweet taste of her, the soft feel of her skin as he pulled at the bodice of her dress, the pressure of her fingers in his back, his aching need to sink into her and possess her. In one swift motion, he laid her on the ground and settled over her.

Her passion rose to meet his as she clawed at his shirt, scraping her fingernails across his bare chest. The sensation brought him unexpected ecstasy and he moaned with pleasure. It took all his concentration to pull off her riding boots. He ran his hands up past her stockings and grasped her bare thighs, which parted easily under his touch.

She pulled off her shift and tossed it aside, then pushed his breeches down over his hips and lifted her hips toward him, entreating him to come to her. She met his thrust as he plunged deeply into her. Their strangled cries mingled as her wet heat enveloped him. He rocked against her savagely, desperately, seeking solace and release in the intensity of their joining.

167

He kissed her breasts, her neck, her lips, all the while aching with the sheer bliss of being one with her. Her breath came in ragged gasps and her muscles spasmed around his cock as he pushed her over the precipice of passion. Her body writhed under him, demanding he come with her over the edge. His body could not deny hers. He left the world of substance and reason behind him. He turned to heat and liquid and tumbled with her into an abyss of pleasure deeper than any he had ever known. His soul was laid bare, his inhibitions were turned to dust.

"I love you," he whispered. "I love you. I love you."

Lying under him, more a part of him than not, she whispered back. "I love you too."

* * * * *

Libbie stirred from her sleep. Sebastian's arm was still slung across her shoulders, his body still pressed along the length of hers. His admissions, their words, their pledges of love still lingered in her ears and on her lips. She smiled, remembering the half-dressed, unbridled passion they had shared, followed by a silent undressing and snuggling into soft blankets where they gently came together again. Sweet, satisfied sleep enticed her to return to it. A soft noise broke the spell, registered more in her spine than in her ears and brought her senses to a state of acute awareness.

She reached under the rolled blanket that pillowed her head and wrapped her fingers around the hilt of her knife. Beside her, she felt Sebastian tense. Fear of revealing their exact location kept her from making any movement or sound. She took a slow, steadying breath and waited.

"Walks-in-Two-Worlds."

The words floated to her on the wind. She wondered if she were actually still asleep, hearing the name in a dream. All wonder ceased when the words came again, this time stronger and closer, followed by a greeting in Occaneechi. She relaxed her grip on the knife.

"Swift Bow? Is that really you?" she whispered.

She heard the muffled wolf howl that was the brave's signal to others who were with him, then the rustle of the leaves as he moved closer to the low flames of the campfire. Sebastian jerked upright just as Swift Bow stepped into the light.

"Sebastian, this is Swift Bow, from the Occaneechi tribe."

Both men remained perfectly still, eyeing each other in the fire's dim glow. An embarrassed silence hung over the three of them until Libbie feared it would smother them. She coughed nervously. The distraction seemed to rouse the men. Sebastian reached for his breeches as Swift Bow discreetly turned his back.

"Mother Cloud Dancer sent us," he said, a bit more loudly than necessary. "She said you were coming with important news. And she said you might like to travel in this." He reached into a sack that he wore strapped over his shoulder, drew out a buckskin outfit and dropped it on the ground behind him. "She didn't send anything for your...your traveling companion."

Blood rushed to Libbie's cheeks as she snatched up the clothing and hurried into it. She was glad for the warmth the buckskins provided now that Sebastian had moved away from her to pull on the rest of his clothes. By the time they were fully dressed and wrapped in their cloaks, three more braves had joined them.

While Swift Bow had been mature and self-assured in all the time she had known him, still she was surprised by the ease with which the young man took charge. He was almost exactly the age Johnny would have been and he'd been like a brother to her as well as a mentor when she'd lived with the tribe. Now he commanded the braves in packing up the camp and preparing the horses as if he'd been doing it for years. His position of authority suited him, although Libbie wished he would speak to her with his usual chiding banter instead of the reserved speech he now used.

"We will leave immediately," he spoke more to Sebastian than to her. "There will be a snowstorm coming in two days. We will want to be in the Occaneechi camp before then." He moved away to help the other braves.

The sun was just beginning to cast a surreal glow on the horizon when Sebastian covered the embers of the fire with snow. Libbie took advantage of the last vestiges of darkness to reach out to him and steal a hug. He enveloped her in his arms and placed a long, lingering kiss on her lips.

"Libbie, there's something else I need to tell you, something I meant to tell you last night but…"

Her legs felt weak under her. "Something more?"

"Yes. I'm sorry I didn't tell you then but under the circumstances—"

She pressed a kiss to his cheek. "Last night was fraught with emotion. Had you told me one more thing, I'm not sure I would have survived it. I'm much more prepared to hear it now," she finished, although she was not entirely sure it was true.

"What the brave said about the message we have for the Occaneechi—I have the message. Matthew managed to get word to Fox. Winters has scouts looking for the Occaneechi camp. They aren't safe, at least not much longer."

Now Libbie's legs did buckle slightly and she leaned into Sebastian's chest to keep her balance. "Winters knows about them because of me. I told him about them. He'll go after them because of me."

"We're ahead of him this time. Finally, we know his next move before he's made it. We'll help the Occaneechi any way we can, then we'll figure out how to go after Winters on our terms. Are you prepared for it, love?"

A tingle ran up Libbie's spine when she heard the gentle endearment. She hugged him more tightly. "As long as we're together, I'm ready for anything."

* * * * *

Reginald Winters held his mistress's hairpin between his thumb and forefinger. He twisted it, pulled it free and sent silky hair streaked with silver spilling over her bare shoulders. He wrapped one hand in it and tilted her head back, planting a soft kiss on her lips.

"So," he whispered, "they have slipped through my fingers again." He tightened his grip and twisted the hair until she gasped. "I would have had them in Charlottesville had your message been timely."

"I did the best I could. I sent word as soon as I learned they were in town."

Her eyes were wide with fear and her lips parted enchantingly. Desire raced through his veins. He kissed her again, this time with a hard and unyielding mouth.

"My messengers tell a different story. They say they only learned that my prey had been in Charlottesville after Liberty and that traitor had escaped."

His mistress gulped. Reginald traced the outline of her Adam's apple, mesmerized. "Messengers? You mean those Indians? I didn't speak to them, thank God. There is something so strange and horrible about them." She shivered and closed her eyes. "I sent the message with Norton."

"Indeed?" Reginald twirled her hair in his fingers, considering it. Norton had failed him too often lately. He'd already given his underling more chances than most who dared cross him. "Are you sure you don't have some misguided affection for that little MacRae tart?"

She was breathing faster. She shook her head. "No. I promise you."

Winters watched her pulse throb furiously in her throat. He ran his tongue over it until she relaxed. Then he sank his teeth into the creamy flesh and she stiffened in his arms.

"That's good, because we can't afford to have her and that deserter she's taken for a lover running loose much longer. I don't like loose ends."

"I will help you find them again, I swear it."

He kissed her cheek, then her eyelids. "You had better, my dear, or I may begin to think you a traitor."

Her breaths were ragged and shallow. Winters could smell her fear as she trembled under him. God, how he wanted her. He pulled at the thin shift that separated her skin from his.

"Reginald, I swear that my loyalty lies with you."

"Good. Then you won't object to my plan to draw our wayward lovers out of hiding. Norton will handle the dirty work, of course and this time he'd damn well better not fail me. We'll need your cooperation."

She swallowed hard and nodded. "Anything you say."

"That's my girl." He grasped her trembling shoulders and pushed her thighs apart with his knee. "Just remember that— anything I say. I am an enemy you cannot afford to make."

He plunged into her and she made a slight cry at the intrusion. The sound sent a wave of pleasure through him. He laid his hands gently on her throat as he rocked harder against her. "Oh, yes, my sweet, yes. Always remember that I can kill you at any moment."

Chapter Fourteen

ॐ

The mountain mist thinned as the small party cleared the pass and caught sight of the Occaneechi village. Libbie wished Sebastian could see it as she did, with the big circular lodges covered in white skins fanning out from the large council hut in the center of the village, looking like distant pearls lined up against the blues and purples of the mountains and the oranges and reds of the sunrise.

As they neared the village, one solitary figure stood waiting for them, silver hair flowing in the breeze, arms outstretched to receive a prodigal daughter.

"Mother Cloud Dancer." Libbie could not contain her smile as she leaned forward in the saddle and urged Black Thunder to gallop across the clearing between her and Mother.

She pulled her horse to a halt and jumped to the ground to embrace the old woman. Just three months had passed since Libbie had left the Occaneechi village, yet so much had changed. But Mother Cloud Dancer remained as she always had been, as she always would be. Strange, though, Libbie thought, that she didn't recall the medicine woman being so thin and frail.

"It is good that you have come home, daughter," Mother Cloud Dancer said as they ended the hug. "You have ridden far these past few days. You are tired."

"Yes, I am. We all are."

"Then you shall rest before the council meeting." She turned her attention to the approaching men. "Swift Bow, inform the elders that the meeting shall commence at sundown."

Swift Bow left to inform the council and the other braves took the reins of all the horses to lead them to the corral. Sebastian dismounted. Libbie introduced him to Mother Cloud Dancer as he stepped forward to take the woman's hand.

"Yes, it is as I thought," Mother Cloud Dancer said, then turned toward Libbie. "Both of you need sleep but first we must talk."

Libbie took her arm as they walked toward the old woman's lodge. "Yes, Mother, Sebastian has important news to share."

"It will keep until the council meeting." Mother Cloud Dancer glanced at Sebastian. "It is about him."

They stepped into Mother's lodge, which was as neat and spare as ever. Libbie pulled off her cloak and gloves and warmed her hands by the hearth in the center of the hut.

"So, Sebastian Cole, you are not cold?"

He cleared his throat. "Well, I—"

"There is no need to make up stories. I know what you are." She turned to Libbie. "Perhaps it is right that you left, after all. It is obvious that the spirits intended you to find this one."

Libbie blushed. "Yes, I'm sure that I was meant to find him. In fact, we met last spring, before I came here. Even before Johnny and Papa..." She felt a lump in her throat as tears welled in her eyes.

"But you did not know what he was until you met him again."

Libbie shook her head. "I didn't know until a few days ago, when he told me."

Mother Cloud Dancer shook her head. "Shameful. It should not have happened that way. I should not have let you go out into the world so unprepared."

Libbie sat on the furs by the fire, too tired to stand or to follow Mother's logic.

Sebastian sat down beside Libbie. "Mother Cloud Dancer, what are you saying? Why should Libbie have thought me anything but a normal man?"

Mother Cloud Dancer glared at Libbie. "He does not know?" She looked at Sebastian. "You do not know why she is called Walks-in-Two-Worlds?"

He shrugged. "Well, she's a white woman in an Indian village."

Mother shook her head. "It is much more than that. She sees what others can see and what they cannot." She fixed her gaze on Libbie again. "And if she had learned all her lessons, she would know when she is seeing one from the other world walking in this one."

Now Sebastian stared at Libbie as well. "A seer?"

"It's not an easy thing to explain."

Mother Cloud Dancer clicked her tongue. "Shameful," she muttered. "Shameful. Bound together, fighting the same battle but neither seeing the truth. An inexcusable lapse for a seer and a Fated One."

"Fated One." Sebastian rolled the words over his tongue. He would have guessed it to be something different, perhaps "Cursed One", if he'd had any notion that there was a name for his existence.

Mother Cloud Dancer stirred stew in a pot that hung over the fire. She ladled some into a bowl and handed it to Sebastian. "You need strength. Your kind never eat enough. You might know that if you had learned more about your existence."

Libbie put her arm around him as if to protect him. "His kind? You make it sound as if there's a whole race of them out there in the world."

Mother shook her head. "Oh, no. There are very few. Mostly they live in legends. I myself have only met one before today."

175

"Yet you say I should have known more about my own condition, as it were," Sebastian said.

Mother nodded. "One might be curious about such a thing."

He frowned at her. "Whom would I have asked? Who would know about such a thing?"

Mother shrugged. "I knew."

Libbie put a hand over her mouth but Sebastian could still see her smile. He sighed loudly and set to eating the stew, hoping it would satisfy the exasperating woman who was Libbie's mentor. But exasperating as she was, she must be a wise and skillful woman, to teach Libbie as well as she had in the short span of time that Libbie had lived with the tribe.

Libbie had told him, while they were still hiding in the cave waiting for his leg to heal, that after Sean's and Johnny's deaths, her Occaneechi friend Bird-in-Flight had come to visit her and Libbie had returned to the Occaneechi village with her. The tribe's braves had taught her to fight and the medicine woman had taught her to heal. Of course, Libbie had not told him she was a seer but he of all people could not fault her for keeping secrets.

"What do you know?" the medicine woman asked Sebastian, interrupting his thoughts. "The loss of senses, the need for little food and sleep of course, and the ability to see ghosts."

He nodded, then glanced at Libbie. "And the fact that I can't die. At least, not until I confront my ultimate destiny."

Libbie's jaw dropped. "Can't die? But the bullet and the infection..." She looked at Mother Cloud Dancer. "The death warnings around him."

Mother patted her shoulder. "You relieved his pain and quickened his recovery."

"You were brilliant, Libbie," Sebastian added.

"As for the death signs—" Mother started.

"Indications that he is a Fated One," Libbie finished. "They happened when my defenses were low, when I couldn't protect myself from the truth."

"Good. You are beginning to understand." Mother rose to her feet. "When you have finished eating, you will sleep. You must be well rested for the meeting at sunset."

"But Mother," Libbie said, "I need to see to Bird-in-Flight."

Mother shook her head. "Later, Walks-in-Two-Worlds. First eat, then sleep." She looked pointedly at Sebastian. "Nothing else."

When Mother had left the lodge, Libbie broke into laughter.

"Sebastian, I do believe she thinks you have other things on your mind."

He set down his bowl of stew and scooted closer to her. "She is a very, very wise woman."

Libbie lifted her eyebrows. "Oh, is she now?"

He kissed her neck and ran his tongue over her breastbone, relishing her small, seductive moan. His erection was instant.

"I have some very specific other things on my mind," he whispered as he nipped at her earlobe.

She wrapped one hand in his hair and kissed him hard on the mouth. Her other hand slid under his tunic, grazed one nipple, then the other, sent sparks dancing over his skin. When she slid her fingers into his breeches, his entire body pulsed with pure desire.

"Tell me what you have in mind," she said in a low, throaty tone.

"Oh, no." He pulled her buckskin shirt over her head, then took her round, full breasts into his hands. He nuzzled her neck, tasting the sweetness of her soft skin. He moved lower, circled the nipple of one breast with his tongue, gently grazed it with his teeth, felt her arch toward him.

"I'll tell you nothing," he murmured. "But I will show you everything."

* * * * *

"There is little more we can accomplish tonight," Chief Soaring Eagle announced.

Sebastian had spent more than an hour explaining what he knew to the council. Winters was looking for maps, directions, descriptions of any kind that would lead him to the Occaneechi camp. Sebastian knew too well what that meant and he shared that knowledge openly. Their only hope was to be prepared for Winters and his onslaught. Even then, Sebastian feared for them, although he held his tongue on that matter.

The elders watched Mother Cloud Dancer. She stared at the flames, her sharp cheekbones standing out starkly on her thin face. The warriors, young and old alike, waited, backs straight, faces unreadable.

When she finally spoke, she looked at Sebastian. "Stay a bit longer and speak with the chiefs. The other men should rest now."

The elders rose first and silently filed out of the council hut. The braves, many of whom were not seasoned and respected enough to have a voice in the proceedings, had sat cross-legged on the floor during the gathering. Now they rose and filed out of the lodge as well. They did not presume to speak until they were outside. Their voices, animated after such long disuse, clamored in the night air, faded, then disappeared. Only the old chief, Soaring Eagle; the younger war chief, Bird-in-Flight's husband Red Wolf, the medicine woman and Libbie remained with Sebastian.

"You have more to tell us, Mother Cloud Dancer?" Red Wolf asked as he stood to stretch his legs.

Sebastian followed the young chief's lead. His legs were stiff and sore and his back cracked as he rose.

Mother Cloud Dancer spoke again. "We must hear the truth from you, Cole. You have told us that Winters is dangerous, that he has attacked unsuspecting villages in the past. The braves should believe that our pre-knowledge changes that. They should go into battle believing that they and our spirits working together can win. But the five of us in this room must discuss whether our warriors stand a chance against a regiment of the British Army."

Sebastian shifted his weight from one foot to the other, wishing she had not asked him the question so bluntly. "I'd like to believe that the braves can beat him. They know he's coming and each of your warriors individually has more heart than Winters' entire regiment put together."

Soaring Eagle had been sitting still with his eyes closed, looking so peaceful that he could have been asleep. But now he spoke loudly. "You have not answered Mother Cloud Dancer's question. We can all sense that you are troubled but you must prepare us. Tell us what we need to know."

Sebastian sighed and rubbed his jaw. "I have two concerns. The first is that your braves have never observed white men's wars. Winters has the advantage of having seen many Indian tribes fighting. His men know what to expect, your men do not.

"The second concern is the lack of weapons. Winters' supply of weapons and ammunition is among the best of all the regiments in the British Army. We, on the other hand, don't even have a musket for every man."

Red Wolf smiled. "I am glad you include yourself with us, Cole. Mother Cloud Dancer has said you will be a great help to us."

Mother Cloud Dancer stood slowly, waving away Red Wolf's hands when he tried to help her. "Indeed. There may be no help for our lack of weapons but you will help eliminate Winters' other advantage."

Soaring Eagle nodded. "We can train now, while the hunting is not good."

Sebastian widened his eyes. "You want me to train the braves to fight Winters? By myself?"

Red Wolf shrugged. "We have no other option. First you will train Swift Bow and me to be your assistants. There is a flat, open area less than a day's ride from here. When the weather clears, we can train there."

"But I can't—"

Mother Cloud Dancer held up a thin hand. "If you deny us, Cole, what hope do we have?"

Sebastian stood up straight. "Of course. Red Wolf, you, Swift Bow and I will begin tomorrow. And I would like to start working with the men in a few days. There is much we can do here without an open field. When I feel they are ready for mock battle, we'll make the journey."

Mother Cloud Dancer nodded, then left the lodge.

Libbie stood and took Sebastian's arm, leading him out into the snowy night. "Thank you," she whispered.

They walked without speaking for a few minutes, unconcerned with the snowflakes that drifted onto their cloaks and into their hair. Libbie seemed as pensive as he felt.

Finally, she broke the silence. "Despite the plans to protect the tribe, you're not feeling optimistic."

"No, I'm not. We've both seen what Winters is capable of. The man will do anything." He thought about the child, Wes and Sunflower's son. "I don't know how to help him."

"Him?"

"Them," he recovered quickly. "The tribe."

She stopped walking and turned toward him, throwing her arms around his neck. Standing on her tiptoes, she kissed him, her mouth hard and demanding against his. Heat and desire flamed through him, temporarily obliterating all else.

"No more about Winters tonight," she said when the kiss ended. "Tell me something about you. One thing that I don't already know."

He smiled as he took her arm and started walking again. "Well, let's see, you already know about my family — the farmers and our sordid past — the Black Knight. Something about me... Well, I met Washington a few times."

"As in General Washington?"

"He wasn't a general then, of course. He was with a surveying party. He was a normal man, intelligent and ambitious but just a man. Now, your turn. One thing that I don't know about you."

She laughed. "There are many things you'd probably never care to learn. Hmm. One thing... There was the incident that got me sent off to Mrs. Barton's finishing school."

"Sent off? I was under the impression that it's a family tradition, of sorts."

"Yes, well, I suppose it is. But not the way you think. My mother got sent there at age sixteen for going on an unchaperoned carriage ride with a man. Mrs. Barton's mother ran the school back in those days."

"Your mother was that rebellious?"

Libbie nodded as they stopped outside Mother Cloud Dancer's lodge. "Mama did marry the man — my father — two years later, after her refinement was complete. Aunt Caroline had gone to the school years earlier for... Well, you've met Aunt Caroline."

He laughed. "Indeed. And what was your crime, pray tell?" When she glanced down at the ground, his heart sank. "It wasn't the sight, was it? They didn't send you away for that."

"Not directly. I'd known Bird-in-Flight since I was about ten. The tribe lived just a few miles from my father's fields back in those days. I was so jealous of her freedom, of the way she could stay out late into the night, that I began sneaking out of my window and down the trellis to join her.

"Then about three years ago, I had this awful vision of death, of her tribe being attacked and killed. I sneaked out to tell her and found the whole village preparing to leave. Settlers wanted their land. They had to go or face dire consequences."

"Hence the death vision."

Libbie nodded. "I was so depressed about losing my friend that I was careless. My father caught me sneaking back into the house. And the rest is family history. Holling family history." She smiled. "I did have a wonderful time at Mrs. Barton's, though I daresay she didn't enjoy my stay nearly as much."

Sebastian wrapped his arms around her and kissed her. "Well, she seemed to remember you fondly. You're an easy woman to love."

"It is late!"

Mother Cloud Dancer startled them and they stepped apart.

The old woman continued. "Sebastian Cole, you will stay with Swift Bow until your own lodge is prepared. Walks-in-Two-Worlds, you will stay here. Our day begins before the sun breaks the horizon and we need rest."

Sebastian bent over Libbie's hand and kissed it. "Until tomorrow, Ms. Holling MacRae."

* * * * *

Libbie felt the full womb of the expectant mother who had come to Mother's lodge. "The baby moves often?" she asked.

"Not as much when I am walking but when I sit or lie down, he does not stop," the woman answered.

"That's perfectly normal," Bird-in-Flight said as she stepped into the lodge and shook snow off her boots. From the sack strapped to her back, Little Lark cooed.

Libbie smiled. "It certainly is normal. Everything seems to be perfect. Remember to steep and drink a cup of those herbs twice a day, morning and night."

She walked the woman to the door and peered outside. Evening was approaching but still the sky was darker than normal. More snow would be upon the village by morning. Libbie sighed. Harsh weather made training the braves slower and more difficult. And while life had been blissfully peaceful during the weeks Libbie and Sebastian had been with the tribe, they all knew that it was merely the calm before the storm.

Libbie closed the flap and rubbed her hands over arms to warm them. She helped Bird-in-Flight remove Little Lark from her carrier, then they unbundled the child and placed her on a fur blanket. Libbie sat with the baby for a short time, tickling her and making her laugh.

"You're good with her," Bird-in-Flight said.

Libbie kissed Little Lark's cheek. "She's amazing. A little miracle. I remember feeling the same way about Annalee when she was a baby."

Bird-in-Flight laid a hand on Libbie's shoulder. "You miss your family—your other family."

"Very much." She took a deep breath and glanced about the room. "Keeping busy helps, though. And to that end, I'll begin an inventory of the medicines tonight. We won't be able to replenish the stores until the spring thaw but at least we'll know what's left to dispense until then."

Bird-in-Flight grinned. "Does that mean you will still be with us for the spring thaw?"

"I wish I knew. Nothing is clear yet. Sebastian doesn't know how long he'll need to train with the braves. In the meantime, Mother is working with us..." She stopped herself just in time. She could not explain Sebastian's secret, not even to her dear friend. "She's teaching me more about my gift."

"Is Mother at the council meeting this evening?"

"Yes, and Sebastian too. So if you and Little Lark don't have other plans while Red Wolf is there, you're welcome to join me."

Little Lark crawled toward Libbie and reached out a hand to her.

Bird-in-Flight smiled. "It seems my daughter has made up her mind and you have just gained two helpers."

* * * * *

The women had been working for a few hours when Libbie heard a small rustling noise outside the lodge. Bird-in-Flight did not seem to notice it but Libbie motioned for her to be silent. Libbie tiptoed out of the hut, her hand poised around the knife at her waist.

"Very good, Walks-in-Two-Worlds. Your senses are keen."

Libbie relaxed and smiled at Swift Bow as he stepped out of the shadows. "I thought my days as your student were behind me."

He smiled back at her. "Never."

"So, is the council meeting over?"

Swift Bow nodded. "For most of us. Cole and Red Wolf are discussing more training strategy. Mother Cloud Dancer should be along shortly."

"Swift Bow, I thought I heard your voice." Morning Dove, one of the women vying for his attention, came down the path.

Swift Bow's eyes danced and his smile broadened. The two began a conversation that did not involve Libbie. Feeling like an intruder on a private moment, Libbie turned to go back inside the lodge just as Bird-in-Flight, carrying Little Lark, stepped outside to join them. The assembly seemed too much for Morning Dove, who quickly bade them all goodnight.

Swift Bow turned to Libbie with a serious face. "Do not make more of this than it is."

Bird-in-Flight began to laugh but covered it with a cough. "I don't think she could."

"And do not ask me any questions about it."

"Of course not!" Libbie agreed.

Swift Bow rubbed his neck. "I really should be going. I will speak with you tomorrow."

When he was out of earshot the two women smiled, then giggled, then laughed.

"I have never seen Swift Bow nervous about anything before," Bird-in-Flight said.

"Perhaps he's in love."

"Do you think so? I was beginning to worry that there would only be one woman in his life. A woman who is obviously in love with another man."

Libbie scowled at her friend. "I have told you time and time again, nothing happened between Swift Bow and me."

"Yes, and everyone wondered why. But the minute you arrived here with Sebastian, we all stopped wondering."

"It was that obvious?"

Bird-in-Flight nodded. "And no one could be happier for you than I am. When you came to us last summer, you were more alone in the world than I have ever seen anyone. But now your heart is full." She hugged Libbie. "I will sleep well tonight, as I have every night since you returned."

Libbie went back inside the lodge and neatly restacked the medicines. Then she picked up her hairbrush and ran it through her tangled curls. She toyed with some tendrils, deciding whether she should pin it into a bun. She smiled. What would be the point? Sebastian would just pull it loose later.

"So, you will not sleep here again tonight?" Mother Cloud Dancer stepped into the lodge.

"Mother! How are you feeling? How was the meeting?"

"I am fine. It was not. The weather has made things more difficult."

Libbie's heart felt heavy in her chest.

Mother Cloud Dancer patted her shoulder as she passed. "Do not blame yourself. This is a trial. The spirits are testing us."

Libbie did not argue as she poured a cup of hot water from the kettle over the fire and handed it to the old woman. Mother Cloud Dancer reached into a bag behind her bedroll and pulled out a pinch of ground herbs, which she stirred into the water. Libbie was too far from her to determine what the herbs were.

"You will leave soon?" Mother asked.

"After you've fallen asleep. Unless you wish me to stay."

"Nonsense. What purpose is there in watching an old woman snore?"

"I just thought...if you needed me..."

"I am fine. We will talk no more about it."

Libbie twisted her lips into a frown. Mother looked frailer by the day.

Mother's voice interrupted her thoughts. "There is work to do before you go, though."

Libbie nodded and sat cross-legged beside her teacher. They both stared into the fire and Mother began to speak in a soft chant that was almost a song. Libbie's limbs grew heavy. Her eyelids drooped.

"Focus, Walks-in-Two-Worlds. Focus on someone close to you. Ask them a question, silently. Open your mind, listen with your heart."

Libbie obeyed, choosing her mother. *Mama, do you know that I'm safe and well? That I'm happy?*

Libbie waited, listened, heard nothing but the wind rising outside the lodge.

"Again," Mother Cloud Dancer said.

Libbie tried again. For a brief, fleeting moment, she thought she smelled her mother's fresh-baked bread and heard Annalee's voice. Then nothing.

She breathed deeply, exhaled loudly.

"No," Mother said. "Do not be angry with yourself. Anger, pain, hatred — these are the things that block your path to connecting with another. To truly connect, you must find another path. What is your path, daughter?"

Love, Libbie thought. *Mama, I love you. I miss you. Please speak to me, tell me that you know I am all right.*

Again she relaxed, focused on Mother Cloud Dancer's chant, let heaviness ground her body while her spirit floated above it.

Mama, do you know that I am safe and well? That I'm happy?

Her mother's scent and voice came to her clearly. Anna was speaking with Caroline, laughing, sharing a bottle of claret while sitting by the fire. Annalee was curled into the blue settee. They were in Aunt Caroline's parlor. The sisters raised their glasses in a toast. It was a toast to Libbie, to her new life, to her happiness. Anna's heart swelled with joy, the joy of knowing that a child is safe and well. There were tears too — a dull ache for the distance between mother and daughter.

The vision faded to darkness. Libbie's body and spirit were fully one again and she opened her eyes to see the small fire sputtering in Mother Cloud Dancer's hearth.

"Mama," she whispered. "And Annalee and Aunt Caroline. They're all together, this very minute. And they're thinking of me."

Mother Cloud Dancer placed an arm around Libbie's shoulders and hugged her. "You have taken the next step, daughter, as I knew you would."

"I wasn't as confident. I thought that the first time," she blushed at the memory of the intimacy that she had been unable to hide from Mother, which had accompanied her first full connection, "might have been an aberration. There was no rhyme or reason to it."

"But there was, daughter. You gave yourself over completely to your emotions. That, along with the tie between you and Cole, opened the channel. Now you are learning to choose this connection."

"Thank you for helping me see my other family."

As Mother nodded, Libbie noticed the deep circles around her eyes.

"You're exhausted," Libbie said.

"Yes. I must rest now."

Libbie helped her to her sleeping mat, then sat beside her as Mother closed her eyes.

"A question, Mother, before you sleep?"

Mother nodded.

"It's about the Fated Ones."

Mother opened her eyes and pushed herself up to a sitting position. She held Libbie's hands. "I know your heart, daughter. I know that you want to believe that you are his destiny."

"I know I'm his destiny."

"Yes, I too, believe that you are." She sighed. "But that may not mean what you wish it to mean."

"You've spoken of Sebastian's ultimate destiny. You believe that his life with me isn't part of that."

"A Fated One's ultimate destiny arises from the reason for his death. You did not cause his death."

Libbie nodded. "I understand. But when he has met his ultimate destiny —"

"I cannot predict it, Walks-in-Two-Worlds. I only know what I know from the legends and the things I have seen in the past."

"And?"

"And in my experience, once a Fated One has fulfilled his ultimate destiny, his reason for being in this world no longer exists."

Mother squeezed Libbie's hand and pressed her dry lips to Libbie's cheek. Then she lay back down, breathing heavily at first, then more easily.

Libbie held Mother's hand and stared into the flames. She hadn't told Mother about the vision of Sebastian's death on her family farm, or that it had come to her again while they'd been in the Occaneechi village. Speaking of it would do no good. Only changing it would. And Libbie would change it. She would break all their rules, if need be, to fulfill what she knew was her destiny — to spend her life with the man she loved.

After several minutes of silence broken only by the old woman's deep, even breaths, Libbie reached behind Mother and pulled out the pouch of herbs. When she sniffed them, her worst fears were confirmed. Foxglove. So it was her heart.

"Don't leave us now, Mother Cloud Dancer," she whispered. "We need you. I need you. I have to keep Sebastian in my life and only you can help me do it."

Chapter Fifteen

☙

For three days, snow had fallen on the village. When the skies had finally cleared, the braves had begun their preparations for traveling to the training ground. Sebastian had been packing his supplies and ruminating over how he would bid Libbie goodbye when he'd received a summons from Mother Cloud Dancer. Now he sat cross-legged in front of the fire in her hearth.

"You're sure I can do this?" he asked.

Mother Cloud Dancer's nod was barely perceptible. "You have done it before."

Sebastian shook his head. "No. When the ghosts have come to me in the past—"

"It was when you summoned them." She looked at him with her small, intense eyes. "When you needed them, when you needed an answer or their guidance, part of your soul instinctively called to them."

He considered it for a moment, then nodded. "I can see that it's possible. Still, I don't know how to go about intentionally bringing them to me."

Mother laid a hand on his shoulder. "That is why I am here. Shall we begin?"

He nodded.

"First, prepare yourself for the feeling that will come. It will be like that moment between this world and the next, when you have not quite died but do not yet live."

He frowned. "That sounds like the definition of a Fated One."

"But it is not. Do you recall that moment? You fell over the cliff, your body collapsed but you felt nothing, sensed no one. Close your eyes, Cole and go back to that moment."

He breathed deeply, focusing on that void.

"Good. Now keep breathing, just like that. Next, you must picture the one you summon, the one you have chosen."

He remembered her as she had been, not on the night he'd found her but on the first day he'd met her. So young, so beautiful, so full of life and hope.

"Now chant her name softly. Feel your heart calling to hers."

He chanted Sunflower's name, reached out for her essence.

"I wondered when you would call to me."

"Sunflower. It's truly you!" He meant to jump to his feet but he felt Mother's hand on his shoulder.

"Touching me would do no good," Sunflower explained. "To you, I would feel like morning mist. It is more important that you ask the questions that you want me to answer."

"There are two things. Surely you know what they are. First, your son. Is he in my world or yours?"

"He is well. I cannot tell you more than that."

Sebastian felt a wave of panic wash over him. "But you must! Why else would you come to me? What did they think I would ask you?"

"You have another question. That I can answer."

He took a steadying breath and blinked back tears.

"I do not blame you. Neither does Wes. It was an accident, a horrible mistake. He is where he should be. He is with me and we are at peace."

"But I didn't tell you, Sunflower. I never told you how your husband died."

She knelt before him. "You must listen to me, Sebastian. You and I loved each other as young lovers often do. But when Wes came into my life, you stepped aside. You knew he and I were meant to be."

"And I wished you well. I swear it." Tears slipped down his cheek. "I loved you both and I truly felt joy for you."

"Then let it go. I can see your heart. There was not a moment that you wished you could stand in Wes' stead. You never wished to kill your best friend. Please, Sebastian, forgive yourself."

He nodded. "If you can forgive me."

She smiled. "There is nothing to forgive. There never was."

As quickly as she had come, she was gone. Sebastian closed his eyes, then opened them again. Mother Cloud Dancer sat beside him, the fire danced in front of him. The world was as it had been before he'd gone into the trance.

But his heart was different. Sunflower had released him from the soul-wrenching guilt that had consumed him since Wes' death. He was forgiven. He was free.

* * * * *

Libbie had been waiting for Sebastian for an hour, anxiously glancing at Mother's hut every few minutes. When she finally spotted him leaving the Mother's lodge, she dropped the flap of the small hut that had become his temporary home, pulled her buckskin dress off her shoulders and let it fall to the floor, then lay down naked on the thick furs lining the floor. She fanned out her hair behind her, pulled the blanket up to her chin and waited for him.

Seconds later, he opened the flap and stood in the entryway, framed by bright moonlight. His black hair hung plaited down his back and shone in the soft glow. He closed the flap behind him, covering them in darkness. She could not see his beautiful blue eyes but she could imagine them, flashing with desire, as he searched the small space for her, hoping she was there as she had promised she would be.

The golden glow of a lantern sprang from his hands. Now she could see his taut muscles rippling under his formfitting buckskins. When he turned, his gaze immediately rested on her. She threw back the blanket and felt cold air rush over her. Sebastian sucked in his breath as he surveyed her naked body.

"Come to me," she whispered.

"In a moment. Let me enjoy you like this first."

Blood rushed to her skin under his admiring observation. Her lips parted as he peeled his shirt from his torso and revealed dark hairs curled against his skin. He knelt down beside her and ran one hand over her shoulder and down to her breast. He placed both hands around her waist and pulled her up to sit beside him. She rubbed the hard muscles of his arms as he kissed her.

He pulled away from her kiss but still held her body tightly. "Wait, love."

"I've been waiting. I've been waiting all day. I can't do without you for one more minute." She pressed her mouth hard against his and slipped her hand between his legs.

He moaned and sat back."I was working with Mother Cloud Dancer," he told her.

She moved toward him but he caught her arms and held her just inches from him.

"Yes, I know. I've been waiting for you for the past hour." Her gaze searched his face. "You seem…different, somehow."

"How?"

She shook her head. "I'm not sure. The lines on your face don't seem so pronounced. There's a light in your eyes. Is there news? About Winters?"

"No, love. Nothing like that. Mother helped me find out that Wes and Sunflower don't blame me for his death. They know that I loved them both."

"Of course they don't blame you. And now you can forgive yourself." She kissed his cheek. "And what about the rest of your day, your work with the braves?"

He kissed her lips. "We'll discuss it another time. That and my leaving."

He moved toward her to kiss her but she blocked him with her hands at his chest. "Leaving? So soon??"

"Or we could discuss it now." He pressed his hands against hers and sighed. "The braves are ready to learn more, and the paths to the training field should be passable soon. We leave in a few days."

Libbie slumped against him. "It seems like you just started teaching the braves." She closed her eyes. "Like we just came here."

He kissed her forehead. "It's been a month and a half."

"I know. So, will they be ready for Winters and his men?"

"A few more weeks and they will have learned all that I can teach them."

"And then it will be time for you and me to leave the tribe," she said. "And still we have no plan."

She sighed as his long fingers traced her cheek and traveled over her eyelids, her brow, her hair, caressing away her fears.

"Mother Cloud Dancer believes we'll be ready," he whispered. "Let's not discuss Winters tonight."

She opened her eyes, nodded and ran her hands up his bare back.

He pulled her face to his and kissed her deeply. He laid her on the blankets as she had been earlier and slowly, lingeringly ran his hands over her, from the nape of her neck to the tips of her toes. She wriggled restlessly under his touch, longing to stroke him, hold him, pull him inside her. But he kept his body just out of reach, taunting her.

When his hands had traced every inch of her, his tongue followed suit. He nibbled gently on her neck and shoulders, then pressed soft kisses up and down her arms. She closed her eyes as he covered the tip of one breast with his mouth. He circled the nipple with his tongue until it throbbed, then gently held it between his teeth.

A throaty moan rose from her as he lingered over the other breast and traced his tongue over her midriff, her navel, her hip. He shifted her weight so he could sink a soft bite in the roundness of her buttocks, then kissed his way down to her thigh.

She drew ragged breaths as his tongue, lips and teeth grazed her inner thighs. Pleasure coursed through her. He moved his mouth higher. She wrapped her hands in his hair and arched her spine as his tongue caressed her throbbing loins. Heat, pressure, need and bliss tumbled around inside her, fanned out over her body, then exploded into waves of ecstasy.

She lay still, feeling his kisses on her moist skin. Her muscles gently contracted in the aftermath of the intense pleasure. He hovered above her, his hooded eyes swirling with desire for her. He pressed one knee between her thighs and eased his body over hers. She spread out one hand in the center of his chest.

"Wait," she whispered. "Lie back."

He silently obeyed. She knelt over him, poised in position to allow him to sink deep inside her. He arched upward but she withdrew and pressed him back into the blankets. She ran her hands over his chest, his thighs, his full erection.

She pressed her lips against the salty skin of his neck, lapped her tongue over his heaving chest. He smelled vaguely of earth and snow and campfires. On his thighs, she mimicked the licks, kisses and small bites he had placed on hers. He wrapped his fingers in her long, loose hair and lifted his hips. She reached out to stroke him, led his firm flesh to her mouth.

She flicked her tongue across the tip of his cock, then swirled it over the shaft. Underneath her, Sebastian writhed in ecstasy.

She willed herself to share his senses, to feel her touch on his skin. It flooded over her — pure desire so intense that it took her breath away. Her own skin tingled in the places she touched him — his belly, his thighs. And between her legs, that sweet need, that building pressure swept over her again. It was true. If she willed it, she could become a part of him. But in that moment it was too much to feel her passion combined with his. She retreated into her own body and relished the sensation of his hands in her hair and his taste on her tongue.

He pulled away from her and grabbed her by the waist. Rising to a sitting position, he brought her hips to his, pushing himself deep inside her in one swift motion. She gasped with surprise and delight. She lost all sense of time and place. She threw her head back and cried out as exhilarating sensations pulsed through her with every deep, hard thrust.

When he had nearly brought her to her peak, he stilled her motion and laid her on her back. Above her she could see his sparkling eyes, his parted lips, one small bead of perspiration running down his cheek. He thrust into her again and she wrapped her legs around his back, forcing him as deeply into her as he could go. His face contorted in rapture, a strangled cry rose from his throat, his rod convulsed inside her. The rhythm of it carried her along on its waves and she tightened herself around his cock and thrust against him. The explosion came again, this time rocking her to the core.

Minutes later, Libbie opened her eyes to find that he was lying beside her. He brushed a strand of hair from her cheek.

"I thought you might never open your eyes." He pushed himself up on one elbow and smiled down at her.

"I might not have, if it weren't for the chance to see your face again."

"Have I told you how much I'll miss you when I'm gone? The weeks we've spent here haven't been nearly enough for me to have my fill of you."

"And how long would it take to for you to have your fill of me?"

He laughed. "It could never happen. Especially when the alternative is spending my nights sleeping on the hard ground, surrounded by dozens of snoring soldiers."

"So, I'm more appealing than snoring soldiers. Sir, you flatter me."

He laid back and closed his eyes. "Hmm. Yes. And you don't snore nearly as loudly."

Libbie gave him a swift nudge in the ribs with her elbow as he chuckled. She closed her eyes and settled against him, smiling.

"Are you asleep?" he whispered a few minutes later.

"No, I'm just thinking how strange it is being here like this. Months ago, I came here alone, with a broken heart and an impossible mission. Now I'm back here with the same mission. But this time it feels possible because of you. You've renewed my faith."

"You've renewed my life, Libbie."

She kissed his fingertips, then pressed his hand to her breast. "You've healed my heart. It's yours to keep."

* * * * *

Much later, they lay in each other's arms on the verge of sleep. Libbie drifted into a shadowy dream full of spirits. They danced and howled and reached for her, then brushed past her. Mother Cloud Dancer stood behind her. The spirits embraced the old woman and carried her away with them. Libbie woke with a start.

"What is it, love? What's wrong?" Sebastian tightened his arms around her.

197

"It was just a bad dream about Mother Cloud Dancer. She's ill."

"How ill?" He ran his fingers through her hair and down her back as he waited for her answer.

She snuggled against him. "I don't know. But if she were dying, she would tell me, wouldn't she?"

He kissed her. "I don't know. I wish I had the answer for you. I wish I had so many answers for you tonight."

She closed her eyes for a moment and reveled in the warmth and safety of his arms.

"There's more, isn't there?" he finally asked. "Other nightmares. You toss and turn with them every night."

She didn't want to say it, didn't want to put it into words but she couldn't hide from the truth. "It's me. I can feel it. Winters wants me. At first it was about my whole family and the farm..." She sat up and ran her hand through her hair, still unable to make sense of it all. "But since that day we met in his fort, what he has truly wanted is me."

"Winters has many enemies. He pursues them all with equal vitriol."

She shook her head. "There's something more with me. Something else between us. And now I've dragged so many others into it. He'll go after everyone I've turned to for help."

Sebastian sat up beside her and wrapped his arms around her. "That's why you wanted to run away by yourself. You thought you'd be protecting me."

"How did you know? I didn't tell anyone my plans. Not even Aunt Caroline."

He shrugged. "I could feel it. But I knew running away wouldn't stop Winters from coming after me or your family, or even the Occaneechi." He grabbed her shoulders and looked into her eyes. "You could have run off alone into the mountains for the rest of your days but it wouldn't have protected anyone. Winters would come after your families—

the MacRaes and the Occaneechi—without mercy, hoping to draw you out."

A chill ran down Libbie's spine as she recognized the truth of his assessment of Winters.

"We're making them all as safe as we can," he said softly. "And when we feel they are prepared, you and I will leave and go after Winters together."

"Yes. Of course. But I've dragged you into it. I lost Papa and Johnny to that monster. I can't lose you to him as well!"

"But you couldn't keep me out of it. Libbie, he killed me, ended my life. I'm only here now because my destiny lies in destroying him." He laid his hand on the side of her face and kissed her lips. "And in keeping him from destroying you. I'm sure of that now."

She threw her arms around his neck. "We'll protect each other. He won't take anyone else away from us. We won't let him."

"I just want to spend every moment that I have on this earth loving you."

Sebastian held her tightly. His doubt that he would survive their encounter with Winters hung heavily in the air. But she wouldn't waste time and energy trying to convince him that he would. Instead she would have enough faith for both of them.

With a resigned sigh, she pulled away from him. "There is no more night. It's nearly dawn. I should check on Mother Cloud Dancer."

They washed and dressed in silence. By the time they stepped outside, the stars were fading and light was breaking on the edges of the horizon. He draped his arm around her shoulders, shrouding her with warmth as they walked toward Mother Cloud Dancer's lodge. They hadn't gone far when the sound of ice crunching under feet caught her attention. She stopped short and whirled around. Two wide-eyed faces stared back at her from several yards away.

"Walks-in-Two-Worlds!" Swift Bow stood shirtless in the cold air, apparently trying to entice his visitor back into his lodge.

Beside him, her arms wrapped in his, Morning Dove giggled.

"Oh," Sebastian stammered. "Well, we were just…"

"We were just leaving," Libbie pulled Sebastian along with her.

Once safely out of earshot, Sebastian laughed out loud. "Well, it's about time!"

"What are you talking about?"

"Swift Bow. It's about time he turned his attention to one of those lovely girls chasing him."

"Why should that concern you?"

He grabbed her shoulders and planted a firm kiss on her cheek. "Because, my dear, it means he will finally stop fawning over the woman I love!"

"The woman you love? Hmm. Oh, that would be the one who snores quietly!"

He kissed her hand. "The one who means more to me than life itself."

Libbie clung to his fingers and his words and silently pledged that he would have both — her and his life.

* * * * *

Norton leaned against the stone wall of a barbershop, one foot crossed over the other, a half-smoked cigarette dangling from his lips.

"Damn scratchy shirt," he muttered, running his finger under the collar. But as much as he hated them, the patched pants and shirt, worn boots and fraying cloak made him look like just another down-on-his-luck farmer visiting the big town of Charlottesville.

Winters had assured him that he would eliminate the biggest obstacle in Norton's way and true to his word he'd somehow made the MacRaes self-appointed protectors disappear.

Norton pulled his hat down over his eyes when he saw two women approach. The ones he'd been waiting to see. They weren't half bad, especially the thinner, younger one, from what he could make out through her thick coat. Too bad Winters didn't have any special plans for him to carry out on her. No doubt she'd be a better roll than those damn screaming squaws. And in the middle of it, he could describe the look on her husband's face when Norton had slit his throat and drained the life out of him.

Norton shook his head, regained his focus. The women were past him now. No child with them. All was going according to plan. He waited a few minutes longer to ensure that they would not return to fetch a better pair of gloves or some other such nonsense, as rich women were wont to do. Then he dropped his cigarette onto the street, turned up his collar against the cold wind and set off to finish his task before it was time to take his dinner.

A red-headed wench answered the door of the large house. He recognized her as the one called Maggie. Not one of the MacRaes, so Winters hadn't wanted her. Seemed a shame, Norton thought as he sized up the tasty morsel.

"Can I help you, sir?" she asked.

Norton smiled. "Well, miss, I'm 'ere to see the owner of the gun shop. Seems I've got a sticky trigger on me shotgun. I was 'opin someone could help me wit' it."

The wench wasn't smiling back at him the way women normally did. "But I don't see your shotgun, sir."

"Per'aps I could just step in and leave a note for Miss 'olling."

She shook her head, about to refuse him. He didn't give her the chance. He pushed the door inward, knocking her off her feet. Now inside the house, he slammed the front door shut and slid the bar across it.

Norton stood in a large foyer lined with furniture that would fetch enough at auction to keep his mother in her cups for the next year. The sound of a coach outside told him that the well-bribed driver was right on time. Norton took a quick survey of the position of the downstairs rooms, then drew a rope out of his pocket and stepped toward the wench.

Her eyes grew wide. "Sir, please, there's a child in the house."

"Oh, I know all about 'er." He tied the rope tightly around the woman's wrists and ankles and pulled a knife from his pocket. "Now if ye want to keep 'er pretty little throat from bein' slit, ye'll keep yer bloomin' 'ole shut."

She nodded, shaking furiously. It made it difficult to tie the rag around her mouth but soon enough it was secure. He picked her up like a rolled up rug and carried her to the hall closet, then changed his mind. There they'd find her as soon as they got home. Better to put her in some remote part of the house.

She wriggled as he carried her up the stairs but the tip of the knife that he pressed against her backside calmed her. He checked several bedrooms before he found one that looked unused. The closet was empty, as he'd suspected. He dumped the wench unceremoniously on the floor, dropped the pre-written note on top of her, then shut and locked the door.

"Now, for the brat." There was a horrible looking red bedspread on the bed that would make a perfect sack for the girl. He grabbed it and headed for the stairs.

"Maggie? Maggie, where are you?" the child called.

Norton stole down the steps, not wanting to scare the brat too soon. But he reached the last step just as she came around the corner into the foyer and the two nearly collided. The child shrieked.

202

"Gawd, this is what I was afraid of." He grabbed her and shoved one hand over her mouth, while he fumbled for a kerchief with the other. Before he could gag her with it, she sank her front teeth into his hand.

"Yoww! What is it wit' the birds in this family? 'Ave ye no manners?"

He tied the gag on her while she punched and kicked at him. Most of the blows missed him but a few found their mark with surprising force.

"'E'd better give me a 'ell of a bonus for this one," he muttered as he rolled the child into the bedspread. "Now, ye listen to me, ye little brat, if ye keep real still and quiet, I'm gonna take ye somewhere safe. But if ye don't, I'm gonna dump ye in the nearest river. Then I'm gonna come back for yer Mom, slit her throat and dump 'er in straight after ye. Ye got it?"

The child stopped struggling and lay limp against him as he carried her to the waiting coach. He shoved her inside and gave the coachman his orders.

When they reached their destination, Norton pulled the still bundle from the conveyance.

He handed several coins to the driver. "Here's an extra shillin' for ye to forget ye ever saw the likes o' me."

With that, he slung the bedspread and its contents over his shoulder and strode away. He walked several blocks in the quiet neighborhood, which was deserted at tea-time as Mary had said it would be. Minutes later, he knocked on the door of the seamstress' shop.

"Norton, ye made it safe and sound!" The girl opened the door wide. "The old lady went off this mornin', just like we planned. Bring that upstairs." Mary closed the front door behind him.

She led him through a long hallway to the kitchen, where she unlocked a door and pulled it open to expose a staircase. Norton followed her to the top of the stairs, where she pulled out another key and unlocked and opened the attic door a crack. She peeked into the room before entering it.

"Ah, now, there 'e sits, actin' like the gentleman. Knew ye were comin'. 'E's a son o' the devil most other times."

Norton unrolled the bundle and pulled out the little girl. He untied her ropes and gag. "This is yer 'ome fer awhile, little miss. Don't ye go makin' any noise, or ye remember what'll 'appen to yer mom. Now, yer roommate 'ere is Daniel. Daniel, this 'ere is Miss Annalee. Don't ye be teachin' 'er none o' yer bad behavior."

He crossed his arms and glared at the room's other occupant. At age six, the boy was only two heads shorter than Norton. Had damn scary eyes too. Norton had warned Winters to kill that one but the old bastard never listened to anyone. Before Norton could chastise the boy, he spoke.

"I have no mother to threaten. I have nothing to lose."

The boy was right. There was nothing to hold over his head. A chill ran down Norton's spine as the child's flint hard eyes bored into him.

Norton cleared his throat. "Some other day, Master Daniel. C'mon, Mary. Let's leave the guests alone to get acquainted."

They locked the children in the room and made their way downstairs to Mary's bedroom. Now Norton could turn his attention to other matters. He would have to leave town in the next hour, before the women returned to find the redhead unconscious and the youngest MacRae snatched right out from under their noses. He would return to the fort, then ride out again on his next special assignment.

He grinned as he thought about what was in store for the two men who would go with him on that next adventure. Both had raised Winters' suspicions. One of them would take an unfortunate walk off a cliff. But not Matthew Nichols. That one would have an accident and end up with a broken neck. That was Norton's favorite way to do it. The thought, coupled with

Mary's ample ass being bared directly in front of him, gave him an erection so hard that it hurt.

Mary pulled down his breeches and reached between his thighs to grab his aching rod. "It's been awhile, ain't it, ducky?"

Norton pushed her against the wall and rammed himself inside her, finishing the job with his first stroke.

"Don't worry," he told her. "There's more where that came from."

He closed his eyes and pictured Matthew standing in front of him, eyes bugged out, face purple, begging for the life that Norton would squeeze out of his throat. He felt the blood rush back into his groin, heard Mary gasp as he pushed her onto the bed and rode her hard. He could hear it — the raspy breaths, the strangled pleas for mercy.

Mary dug her nails into his back and screamed, begging Norton to come with her. Eyes still closed, he pictured his hands twisting around Matthew's neck. His muscles tensed, his blood pumped harder. He felt the pressure build to an unbearable level, thought of the neck resisting his force. He imagined the neck snapping like a twig, felt his cock pulse. The boy's nose and ears leaked blood onto the hard ground. Norton's rod convulsed, spewing his semen deep into Mary's ripe, welcoming body.

He struggled to catch his breath and finally managed a whisper. "Gawd, Mary, it's never been that good before."

Chapter Sixteen

§Ŋ

Sebastian leaned close to Mother Cloud Dancer's fire, watching the wise woman. She stared into the spitting flames, nodding her head as though listening to something they said to her.

At length, she leaned back from the fire and turned to him. "Something has happened. A friend needs to reach you but the snow east of the mountains makes the trails to our camp difficult."

Sebastian's heart pounded. "Is it about Winters? What has that bastard done now?"

Mother Cloud Dancer shook her head. "I do not know. The flames hold many secrets tonight and they reveal few of them to me."

"There has to be more. What shall I tell Libbie?"

"For now, nothing. Not a word until we know more. I am sorry, that is all I can see. The spirits do not speak to me as they once did. It is no coincidence that Walks-in-Two-Worlds has come to the Occaneechi now. She is learning to see the spirits in ways my tired old eyes no longer can."

"So she's here to do more than fend off Winters."

Mother Cloud Dancer nodded. "The Great Spirit always brings us what we need. It is our duty to take what is given, to learn all we can about our own special gifts."

"You're speaking of me now."

"There is more that you can do. Now is the time to show you." Mother leaned toward the flames again, humming a strange tune, seeming to forget Sebastian's presence. Finally, she leaned back. "My husband died ten years ago."

The revelation surprised him. Sebastian could not picture the old woman as she must have been years ago as a young bride. "I'm sorry."

She shook her head. "That is not why I tell you. I would like to speak to him tonight, as I often do. But this time, I would like to hear what he says, as well. That is your gift, not mine."

Sebastian felt great sadness for the old woman. Beloved as she was by the tribe, hers must still be a lonely existence.

"I do not seek your pity," she said loudly, making him jump. "I seek your assistance. You will summon my husband."

"I know now that I can do that but how will you —"

"It is time for you to learn. You will summon Great Bear now."

Sebastian closed his eyes and listened as Mother Cloud Dancer described her husband. He'd been tall and lean, had liked to fish more than hunt, had been a council elder. Sebastian chanted his name, beseeching him to come. He felt a cold breeze, opened his eyes. There was an apparition in the guise of a man Sebastian had never met.

"Now, Cole, he is here?" Mother asked.

Sebastian nodded.

"Tell him you have brought him here to speak to me. Then close your eyes, breathe deeply."

Sebastian did as he was told.

"Very good," Mother spoke again. "Now, relax, silently invite him into you. No, do not tense. There is nothing to fear. He will not possess you, he will simply pass through you."

Sebastian focused his energy on breathing, on dropping his shoulders, on relaxing his tense muscles.

A cold breeze rose around him, whistled in his ears, cut through his skin. He involuntarily gulped in frigid air. It lightened him, made him feel as though he floated off the ground. And then he felt still and peaceful. He could hear their voices, Mother Cloud Dancer and Great Bear, although he could not distinguish their words.

Sebastian dropped to the hard floor. He opened his eyes.

Mother Cloud Dancer stared at him. "You did well, Cole."

"You spoke to him? How long? I had no concept of time or place."

She smiled. "Long enough to make an old woman feel young again. Now you must rest. Tomorrow you will leave with the braves before the sunrise. Do as you have planned — go to the distant fields to train them to fight these white men who seek to destroy us. Your friend will come to you there. Be prepared to leave with him. That is all I can tell you."

He shook his head. "There is something more I need to know. Not about your visions. About Libbie, about our future together."

Mother sighed. "You want the same thing she wants but you know better than she that it is not meant to be."

"Why can't it be? We've found each other. We work so well together." He gulped down the thick lump in his throat. "We love each other."

Mother nodded. "Her love ties you to this world. My greatest fear for you is that you will not be able to release it when the time comes. But you must." She grabbed his hand, stared intently into his eyes. Her voice grew strong and loud. "If Winters holds you here beyond your time, he will have won. You cannot let that happen. The stakes are too high. You are fighting for your very soul."

She released his hand and backed away from him. Sebastian stared into the flames as he fought back tears. They had taken everything from him — color, scent, taste, hopes, dreams, a future. But Libbie — they couldn't take her from him, or him from her. He would never allow it.

"Now you must rest," the medicine woman whispered. Her words flowed over him and wrapped around him like a blanket.

He could do nothing more than nod and rise to leave her. By the time he reached his lodge, his limbs were heavy and his eyelids drooped. It was a feeling that was completely foreign to him now, one that he hadn't felt since the night he'd gone after Winters to avenge Sunflower's tribe. Sebastian crawled gratefully into the fur blankets. His movements made Libbie sigh in her sleep and cuddle against him. He placed a firm kiss on her lips, then for the first time in more than a year, fell into a deep sleep.

* * * * *

Libbie awoke in Sebastian's lodge and blinked the sleep out of her eyes. There was nothing around her but blankets and gray morning shadows. Two full days and nights had passed since he had left and still she was surprised to wake up alone each day. Her original plan had been to stay with Mother Cloud Dancer while he was gone but she had missed him too much there. Here she could take comfort in the subtly lingering scent of him.

Mother Cloud Dancer did not seem to mind, in fact showed relief to be left alone at night. As Libbie pulled her dress over her head and fastened her leather boots on her feet, she thought about the wise woman. She worried about her long silences and extended walks. Libbie relished taking over the healing tasks for the tribe but the one patient she would have most liked to heal preferred a solitary communion with nature over the skills she had taught Libbie.

Fresh, cold air stung Libbie's face when she pushed open the door. Through the silver clouds, bright rays of sun slanted toward the earth, dissipating the ground's thin layer of frost. Spring was still many weeks away but today the spirits were giving them a taste of that promise to come. And long before that, Sebastian would return.

She smiled as she walked, stopping to greet the children who gathered at the outer edge of the meadow to play. One of the older boys held a long, thin stick over his head and launched it, throwing all his weight into the act. A few more boys took their turns while the smaller children judged their form and measured the distance of each throw. It was at moments such as these that Libbie missed her little sister the most. She watched the game for a while, lamenting that the joys of childhood did not last longer.

Her growling stomach reminded her that the morning was passing and she still needed to have her breakfast and start her day's work. By the time she reached Mother Cloud Dancer's lodge, the hearth was long cold.

Libbie struck a flint and kindled the flames, then took out herbs for tea. As the fire grew, an eerie silence settled over Libbie, a quiet not even disturbed by the noise of wind or branches. She shivered, wishing Mother Cloud Dancer were with her, fearing something had happened to the old woman while she was wandering in the woods alone.

Libbie closed her eyes and concentrated the way the medicine woman had taught her. Instead of seeing images of Mother Cloud Dancer, she pictured her aunt, her mother and most clearly, her sister. The breath went out of Libbie. She collapsed forward, clutched her arms in front of her and tried to draw air into her lungs. She could feel herself shaking but could do nothing to stop it.

Winters had Annalee.

* * * * *

"Walks-in-Two-Worlds, I can see that you know." Chief Soaring Eagle stepped into the lodge.

Bird-in-Flight followed him. She knelt beside Libbie and hugged her.

"Dear God, what have I done? Why did I think I could stand up to Winters? This is my fault. What am I going to do?"

"Mother Cloud Dancer will know what to do," Bird-in-Flight assured her. "She is walking with Grayhorse—he brought the news to us. He will tell you what he knows."

Mother and Grayhorse entered the lodge. Libbie could smell the horseflesh, as though he had ridden for days without stopping. She looked into his eyes, now etched with worry, saw the exhaustion there and something else. Helplessness, disbelief, terror. The emotions rolled off him in waves. Libbie clutched her belly, nauseous and dizzy from the combination of her emotions and his.

With Bird-in-Flight's help, Libbie rose to face him. Mother stepped to Libbie's side and silently wrapped a thin, fragile arm around Libbie's shoulders.

"Annalee," Libbie whispered.

"I'm so sorry, Miss Libbie. Scott and I did everything we could to keep an eye on 'er. But some of Winters' men..." He shook his head and looked away from her. "Scott's stayin' at your aunt's house and the Bluecoats are keepin' a close eye on 'em. Fox is takin' care of our horses and then we'll be off to the trainin' camp to get Sebastian. Fox thinks we'll need his help if we..."

Another sentence he couldn't finish. Grayhorse was tired, disappointed in himself and Scott, worried sick about Annalee but there was something more, something that interrupted his thoughts and made him censor his words.

She closed her eyes to try to sort out his emotions and their causes but she could not go into his mind, in fact could feel him actively pushing her out of it. She opened her eyes to find him staring at her with an intensity that embarrassed her.

"Sebastian and Fox will know what to do," Mother Cloud Dancer whispered to her.

The gentle voice pulled Libbie away from the horror and fear gripping Grayhorse. She nodded, then hugged her mentor, drawing strength from Mother's embrace. Mother was right. If anyone could find Annalee, it was the man she loved. He would do everything in his power to save her family. He had promised her.

"When did it happen?" she asked.

"Days ago," Grayhorse answered. "They left a note. She's worth more to Winters alive than..." He stopped again and this time she knew it was because he did not want to say the word that terrified Libbie.

She wiped her tears and stuck out her chin. She would be strong. She would have faith. She would believe Grayhorse's words and Sebastian's promises. The alternative was more than she could bear.

"I'll get my cloak," she said. "If the weather holds and we ride nonstop, we can collect Sebastian and be in Charlottesville in less than a week."

The men exchanged glances. Chief Soaring Eagle shook his head. "You cannot go to Charlottesville, Walks-in-Two-Worlds."

"Why not?" She glared at Grayhorse. "What are you not telling me?"

Grayhorse met her gaze. "The note that was left when she was taken said he wants you back in Charlottesville for a reunion with Annalee and the rest of your family."

"So I'll go there."

Grayhorse shook his head. "He wants all of you together in one place."

"Perhaps. But he wants me most of all. If it will save Annalee, we'll give him what he wants."

Mother Cloud Dancer sighed. "You cannot give Winters what he wants. It will not save your family. He will not keep his word."

She considered Mother's words. Her quiet contemplation was interrupted by a commotion behind Grayhorse.

"*Excusez-moi.*"

Grayhorse stepped away from the door and revealed Pierre de la Beaulieu, soiled and crumpled, standing with as much dignity as his current state would allow. He plucked his bent hat with its sagging plume from his head and bowed to Libbie.

"Pierre, what on earth are you doing here?" she asked.

"I have spent a great deal of time with your lovely family. When I learned of this horrible thing, I had to offer my services, humble as they might be."

He stood erect again, his hat over his heart and gave her a small smile. "You are looking very well, *chérie*. Your friends have taken good care of you, although their protection is at times misplaced." He glanced at Grayhorse. "But contrary to their beliefs, I am here to help. I am here to offer—"

"I know that you mean well, Pierre, that you all mean well but I can't hide up here in the mountains while that evil man has my baby sister."

Mother Cloud Dancer squeezed Libbie's shoulders. "We need a moment."

The men filed out of the lodge.

Mother looked into Libbie's eyes. "Listen to me carefully, daughter. You are worth more to your sister here than you are in Winters' clutches. You are the one who joined forces with the Fated One, you are the one who brought him here, now you must trust him."

"But I…" Libbie could not deny the wisdom of the words. "I'll go to Sebastian. I'll entrust him with this."

Mother Cloud Dancer raised a pointy finger. "Ah but he won't do it alone. You will need to help him. Together the two of you will penetrate Winters' mind and learn what he has done with the child."

"But my connections come through love. I can't connect to Winters."

"That is the skill you use best. But there are other ties that bind souls, such as blood and death. Tell Cole what you need and he will know what to do. Trust me, daughter. Trust him."

* * * * *

They arrived at dawn on the third day of the training exercises. Sebastian looked up from his cup of tea and sucked in his breath at the sight of Libbie in all her glorious color, galloping across the field. Far behind her, Fox and two other riders emerged from the tree line.

Sebastian's pulse raced, instantly responding to the nearness of her. But at the same time, his heart sank. He could see it etched into her face—the news was terrible.

Then she was upon him, leaning down from her saddle to cling to him. She tried to speak but gasped for breath, the words catching in her throat.

"It's all right, love, take your time," he whispered as he held her in his arms and stroked her hair.

"Annalee," she managed to say. "Winters kidnapped her."

Sebastian nearly choked on her words. He tried to form a reply but couldn't speak. He needed to come up with some plan, some way to find Annalee, to save her from an unimaginably terrible fate. Nothing came to his clouded mind. As he struggled to concentrate, to find words, the other riders approached.

Sebastian nodded to Fox and Grayhorse but set his jaw when he realized the third rider was not Fox's other son. The pompous French ass whom he had met months earlier sat rigidly on his mount. Seeing Sebastians' gaze on him, he bowed in the saddle, his movement sending his pathetically sagging hat with a sad vestige of a plume to the ground.

"Where is Scott?" Sebastian asked Grayhorse.

Grayhorse moved his horse closer to Sebastian's. "Protecting Mrs. MacRae and Miss Holling and overseeing the search."

"And why in the hell did you bring him here?" Sebastian nodded his head in Beaulieu's direction.

"Pierre wants to help," Libbie answered. "He has spent some time with my family. He saw the ransom note. Winters wants me there, in Charlottesville, in exchange for Annalee."

Beaulieu nodded in confirmation.

Sebastian felt a blinding rage building inside him. It was the same feeling he'd had that night when he'd found the decimated village. He turned on the Frenchman.

"I don't believe him," he muttered. "I wouldn't be surprised to learn that he's been working for Winters all along. He probably snatched Annalee himself."

Fox leaned forward and grasped Sebastian's shoulder. "No need to start somethin'. We know for sure Beaulieu didn't do it."

Beaulieu grunted. "It seems your friends have been watching me since the moment you left town. But it is for the best. At least now I shall not be falsely accused."

"Accused of what?" Swift Bow had come across the field on foot, the frozen ground crunching under his weight.

Red Wolf followed closely behind him and stood near the riders, his arms crossed over his chest, his long headdress flowing in the wind. Beaulieu shifted on his mount, obviously awed by the sight of the regal chief.

Libbie explained the situation, including Mother's directive that they send Sebastian to search for Annalee.

Swift Bow ran his hand through his sleep-rumpled hair. "I will wake the other braves. We will begin the search today."

Sebastian's mind was focused now, his purpose clear. "No. You must get Libbie back to the village and keep her safe."

Swift Bow threw back his shoulders.

Red Wolf raised a hand, signaling to the young brave to say no more. "It is important to keep her safe, Swift Bow."

"Of course. We will break camp and prepare the horses."

"I'd feel a whole sight better if Grayhorse stayed with Miss Libbie too," Fox said to Red Wolf.

Red Wolf nodded. "He is welcome to stay in our village." He touched Libbie's hand. "We will do everything we can to help you and your other family, Walks-in-Two-Worlds."

Libbie whispered a thank-you, then looked at Sebastian. "We need to speak privately."

Sebastian climbed on to Black Thunder behind her. She turned the horse toward the trees on the distant horizon. Beaulieu moved as though to follow them but Fox grabbed his bridle.

"You and I'll help the braves break camp," Fox told the Frenchman.

"What haven't you told me?" Sebastian asked Libbie as they approached the trees.

"We need more information. We have to get something, some clue from Winters."

"How will we manage that?"

"I need to go into his mind."

"No." The word popped out of his mouth before he even had time to consider it. "Libbie, who knows what horrors that mind holds? I can't let you do that to yourself. Besides, to connect to another's mind you need to feel love for them."

"I have to do it," Libbie said. "There might be no other way to save Annalee. Mother said that blood and death connect souls as well. She said you would be able to help, that you would know what to do."

He pulled her back against him, smelled her hair, felt her skin against his cheek. He wanted to protect her but she was right—they had to save Annalee.

"I know what to do," he whispered in her ear. "Go deeper into the trees. We'll need privacy."

In minutes, they were well hidden in the woods. Libbie pulled Black Thunder to a halt and Sebastian swung down from the saddle. He reached up to help Libbie dismount and caught her in his arms.

He held her tightly against his body. Their mouths met. The kiss was hard and deep and desperate. He pulled away from her, from the passion that he could feel pulsing through her. She needed the comfort and the release, as did he but they needed answers more.

Libbie nodded, not needing to hear the words to understand. Without speaking, they sat on the ground facing each other, legs crossed in front of them.

Sebastian held both her hands in his. "I need to prepare you, love. It could come as a shock." He took a deep breath to brace himself. "I'm going to bring someone to you. A spirit. Johnny."

She gasped. "Johnny? But how…" She shook her head. "I trust you and I know it's what we must do. But to see him, my brother, as a ghost…" She closed her eyes.

Sebastian kissed her hands.

"I'm ready," she said. "You're here with me and I'm ready for anything."

With that, Sebastian closed his eyes and hummed the strange, tuneless song of the medicine woman. He thought of Johnny, of the times they'd met, in life and in death, of the things the young man had said and done. And then Libbie's brother was standing there, just a few feet away from his heartbroken sister.

"He's here, love," Sebastian told her. "Johnny, your sister needs to speak with you."

Sebastian's hands became cold, ice cold and no matter how tightly she gripped them, Libbie could not warm them. And he was still and gray, as though the very life had flowed out of him. She was about to scream, to jump to her feet, when she felt a cool mist on her shoulder.

"Isn't she lovely, my sister." Johnny smiled at her. "Cole is fine, Lib."

That smile. God, how she had missed it.

"Johnny, I can't believe you're here, that I can see and hear you."

He nodded. "I owe you an apology for all those years of taunting you about your overactive imagination."

"You couldn't have known the truth. I didn't even know it. But I wish I had. I wish I could have made you believe me when I begged you and Papa not to go—"

"No, Libbie, there's no time for that. Cole can't stay like this for long. We need every minute you can get with Winters."

Libbie shook her head. "But now that you're here, you can tell me where Annalee is."

"It doesn't work that way. I see much less than you do."

"But still, there are so many things I want to ask you."

Johnny looked solemn. "You and Cole still have work to do. But I can't tell you any more about it than the medicine woman did. I can tell you that I love you and I miss you."

"Me too," she whispered, barely able to speak over the lump in her throat.

"And there is one thing about Winters. He has some connection to Grandfather's brother, Barnabus. Ask Mama and Aunt Caroline what they remember."

He faded, almost disappearing into mist. "Hurry, Libbie. Get to Winters."

Libbie closed her eyes, hating to do it, knowing that when she opened them again he would be gone. But she focused on Johnny, on his feelings and thoughts, on the connection that bound them.

She was with Johnny on the battlefield. Winters was there, ordering his soldiers away from Johnny, intent on killing him with his own hands. Libbie felt the bullet in Johnny's chest, felt him fall forward, felt the bayonet tip slice into his back. She opened her mouth to scream in pain but she had no strength to do it.

And then she was in an office. Winters' office. Looking through papers, deeds. Dozens of them. Anger. Something missing. *Norton, damn him. He'll get his. And so will she. She's been helping that little tart, I'm sure of it. Liberty MacRae slipped away from me because my own mistress wouldn't help me capture her.*

A cold wave washed over Libbie and jarred her back to her senses. She sat on the frozen ground holding Sebastian's lifeless hands. In front of her, he convulsed, sucked in his breath, then opened his eyes.

"Johnny's gone," he said.

Libbie nodded, unable to speak. She had to make sense of so much—of Johnny's words, of Winters' thoughts. Sebastian sat in silence, his hands now warming in hers. She looked into the depths of his eyes, then slid forward and leaned against him.

"I learned something," she managed to say. "His mistress. One of Winters' spies, one that he expects will help him get to me, is his mistress."

"Do you know who she is?"

Libbie shook her head. "I couldn't get her name. Only a sense of her. She's older than he is, not very tall. She has long hair streaked with silver."

Sebastian's arms tensed around her. "Libbie, do you know who you just described?"

"Many women, I'm sure."

"But it had to be someone who knew we were in Charlottesville. Almost no one knew until that last night. To get word to Winters' men that very night, with the Continental troops guarding the town, seems impossible."

"So you believe it was someone who knew about our being in town early. But how could anyone know? You're ever the stealthy spy and I went nowhere. Except the day we had dresses made."

She sat up straight and looked at Sebastian. "You can't mean Mrs. Mitchell. But she loves my family—Mama and Annalee. But it has to be! Sebastian, she helped him take Annalee! What are we going to do?"

"Fox and I will find out everything the woman knows and we'll find Annalee. We'll bring her home, safe and sound."

He helped Libbie into the saddle and guided them back into the field. The braves were all awake now, scurrying about in the pale morning light to tear down their camp. Sebastian packed his saddlebag and prepared his horse. Liberty silently watched as he finished the tasks and climbed onto his mount.

Sebastian gathered her reins along with his and led both the horses to Fox. The man needed no prompting. He was already shifting his saddle and bags onto the fresh mount that one of the braves had brought to him. "You and Swift Bow look out for Miss Libbie," Fox told Grayhorse. He glanced across the camp at Beaulieu. "And don't let that French ass hurt himself with a sharp arrow or some such nonsense."

Grayhorse followed his father's gaze. "He thinks he's going with you, you know. It'll break his heart to hear you don't want his help."

Sebastian scowled. "He'll get over it." Spotting Swift Bow, he motioned for Grayhorse to follow him, then dropped Libbie's reins and maneuvered his horse in Swift Bow's direction. Fox hung back with Libbie.

On the way across the camp, Sebastian whispered to Grayhorse. "There's more you want to say, I can see that."

"I fear there's not much time."

Sebastian glanced over his shoulder, glad to see that Libbie was speaking with Fox and not watching him now. "You think he'll kill her?"

"His men. There were eight of 'em. They overcame us—Scott and me and two scouts and held us while someone took the child. They're barbarians. No child is safe with them."

Sebastian looked carefully at Grayhorse, noticed the bruises on his throat and the stiff way he rode his mount. Bruised or even broken ribs, Sebastian guessed.

When they reached Swift Bow, Sebastian spoke quietly to him. "There are two things you must do."

Swift Bow nodded.

"First, keep a guard on Beaulieu at all times. Don't trust him for a moment. Second, keep Libbie in the village. Winters wants her more than anything else. He cannot get her."

"How long you really think we can keep her there?" Grayhorse asked.

"I think she'll listen to Mother Cloud Dancer. When she says it's time for Libbie to join us, you come with her. Do not let her go anywhere by herself." He took a deep breath, hating to hear his own words but knowing he had to make his point crystal clear. "If Winters gets his hands on her, he will kill her."

"I understand," Swift Bow said. "And Cole, remember that Walks-in-Two-Worlds is counting on you."

Sebastian did not answer as he trotted his horse back to Libbie's side. He leaned toward her and gathered her in his arms. Her hair smelled like wildflowers and cold wind. He breathed in the fragrance of it, then kissed her hair, her cheeks, her lips.

"Tell me love, have you had a vision of Annalee? Do you know if she's well?"

Libbie nodded. "She's scared but well-treated. The man who kidnapped her threatened and terrified her but he's gone. He left her in the care of a woman."

"Not Winters' men?"

Libbie shook her head.

Sebastian breathed a sigh of relief that the men who'd held Grayhorse weren't holding Annalee. "I'll bring her back to you, Libbie, I swear."

She nodded. "I love you and I trust you. I've trusted you with my life, now I'm trusting you with Annalee's."

He nodded solemnly as he pulled away from her. "I love you too," he whispered.

As Sebastian followed Fox into the trees, he thought of the peace that he and Libbie had come to know in these mountains, with this tribe, in each other's arms. And he offered a silent prayer to Mother Cloud Dancer, the Occaneechi spirits, the makers of the Fated Ones, whoever would listen, that he and Libbie would return to this peaceful world someday.

Chapter Seventeen

ഇ

Winters stepped into his office and pulled the door closed behind him. He glared at Norton, who sat stretched out in a chair, his boots tossed haphazardly on Winters' clean rug and his feet, barely covered by gray, hole-filled socks, stretched toward the blazing fire in the hearth. But Winters' gaze rested on the brandy glass clutched in his underling's hand.

Norton lifted the glass as if in a toast. He grinned at Winters. "Afternoon, Colonel. Hope ye don't mind — the corporal told me ta have a sit an' warm m'self."

Winters scowled and grabbed the snifter out of Norton's hand, then slammed it down on his desk. He picked up the open brandy decanter and reached for a clean snifter, then poured a large portion for himself. He took a large gulp and closed his eyes, let the smooth, warming liquid slide down his throat and opened his eyes again.

"We'll deal with your insubordination later," he said quietly.

At least Norton had the sense to sit up straighter.

Winters continued. "Right now, I need an explanation. Why did you fail? Why has Miss MacRae not returned to Charlottesville?"

Norton blinked and swallowed hard. "Well, sir, the weather's been 'orrible. Me best guess is that no one's got the news to 'er yet."

"The weather? Your best guess? You're slipping Norton. Such a pity. You used to be so reliable."

"I did everything ye told me to do, sir."

"You left the ransom note when you took the child?"

223

"O' course, sir. Kept it right 'ere in my pocket so's I wouldn't lose it. The bird'll be along soon. We're bound to 'ear of it anytime now."

"I'll hear of it. You won't be here. Leave tomorrow with the two men we discussed. Take care of that business, then stay at the inn just outside Charlottesville and wait for further orders."

"But what about the new soldiers that arrived, sir? Gordon's men, no doubt. They're bound ta 'ave an 'undred questions about me leavin' again so soon."

Winters wrapped his fingers more tightly around his snifter. Gordon and his snooping had become a major obstacle. The general hadn't been discouraged nearly as easily as Winters had hoped. "Did they see you come into camp?"

Norton grinned. "Course not."

"At least you did that much right. Stay in the room upstairs tonight. They wouldn't dare set foot in my quarters without my permission. Sneak out before dawn. The two men you're to deal with will be on sentry duty. You meet up with them, tell them I've changed their orders and get them away from here. You know what to do after that."

Norton licked his thick lips like a mountain lion savoring its kill. "Yessir. I know just what ta do."

Winters dismissed Norton and watched with disdain while the man scooped up his boots and ambled out of the office. After Norton shut the door behind him, Winters checked his desk. More scratches around the lock on the drawer. A minute later, Winters confirmed that Norton had taken the bait. He'd stolen the two bank notes that Winters had left there to tempt him.

"Damn you." Norton was infuriatingly smug. He really thought he could get away with it. If Gordon hadn't assigned a new batch of spies to watch the fort, Norton would already be dead. Winters smiled. His time would come soon enough.

Winters closed his eyes, mentally reached out to touch the minds of his dead minions, silently spoke to them.

Come to me tonight, my dear boys. Our usual place, just outside the west wall of the fort. I have a special job for you.

Winters opened his eyes and sighed. "You too, Liberty," he whispered. "Come out of your rabbit hole and join me for a happy little family reunion. Well, I'll be happy, anyway. You, dear cousin, will be miserable, like the rest of my wretched relatives."

He took a long sip of brandy, then slammed down his snifter on the windowsill. The glass exploded, sending fragile shards and thick liquid across the sill and down the wall. Tiny drops of blood dripped from his hand. He ran his finger through the drops, connecting them.

"And when I have had my fill of you, dear Liberty, your lover will be my slave and you will be dead."

* * * * *

Sebastian stared at the dark sky. Not a star was in sight but at least the snow had subsided. He sat down by the fire and prayed that the weather would hold for a few more days. And he prayed that Libbie was still safe with Mother Cloud Dancer, perhaps staring into the hearth, looking for his face.

"I love you," he whispered into the flames that danced in front of him.

As he sat very still, the dull sounds of the night drew him into their hypnotic trance.

Dull shrieks rose on the night air, like distant echoes muted by the snow-covered forest. They grew sharper, seemed closer, sounded like breaths drawn by horses ridden too hard by soldiers, red-coated attackers who pushed into the center of the burning village. The acrid smoke billowed around him, thick, black, choking. He turned his head, caught a breath. Saw the riders' impassive faces, intent on their work, unmoved by the screams of women and children. He saw the woman he had loved lying quietly in the midst of the chaos. Her son was being pried from her blood-covered hands by one of the soldiers.

The sound of hoofbeats faded, the smothering smoke dissipated. Sebastian was alone by a campfire in the foothills, far from that horrible scene of devastation. That night, he had only seen the aftermath of Winters' attack on the vulnerable Indian village. These new details of the massacre left him sick and exhausted. They also convinced him that the boy, his best friend's son, did not die with the rest of the tribe. Daniel was alive.

"Well now, you're lookin' like hell."

Fox's voice made Sebastian jump to his feet, his hand on his knife hilt. Sebastian relaxed when he saw it was his friend. He pointed to the sack Fox carried. "Is that dinner?"

Fox nodded and the two men set to skinning and cleaning the rabbits, then put them on makeshift spits of thin, dry branches. Only after they had sat in silence for several minutes, sipping homemade whiskey from a canteen, did Fox finally speak.

"Do you want to talk about it?"

Sebastian breathed deeply, pulling in the fresh night air. No more choking smoke. No more bloody faces with unmoving eyes. Still, he shivered at the memory of them. Beside him, Fox sat waiting. He was a matter-of-fact man who believed only what he saw with his own eyes and often even questioned that. Sebastian hesitated to broach the subject on which they had never agreed. But it was late and the dark night was full of ghosts and the vision had left him too tired to listen to his own better judgment.

"I have to find Daniel. I'm convinced he's alive."

Fox scowled. "Not this again!"

"I'm sure of it. I can't explain it in a way that would make you believe it." He shook his head. There were many things that Sebastian couldn't explain and Fox wouldn't believe.

Fox sighed, turning over the roasting rabbit. "Truth is, I want to believe the boy's alive. But what if he's not? What then?"

Sebastian understood. The only other people left alive to grieve for Daniel and his tribe had been Fox and his sons. In the massacre, Fox had lost his second wife and his sons had lost the only mother they could remember having. If they believed that Daniel had survived but then never found the boy, or worse, learned that he was dead after all, the grief might be more than any of them could bear. But despite his fears, Sebastian could not deny the boy's existence. He would prove it. And then it would be time to tell Libbie the truth. About everything.

* * * * *

Libbie sat back, gasping for breath. She felt Mother Cloud Dancer's frail hand. She wrapped her fingers tightly around it.

"Mother, what was that? Who was the woman we saw? And the boy? I don't understand."

"You do not need to understand it. That vision was not meant for you. You were merely the vessel."

"For Sebastian. It must be. And the woman...Sunflower." Was the boy the woman's son, Wes' son?

"You have not accomplished what you had hoped," Mother said.

Libbie fought back tears of frustration. "No. I still haven't found the pathway back into Winters' sick mind. It's so frustrating. I was there but I glimpsed so little. And now nothing."

Mother sighed. "Daughter, you only feel rage and pain toward him. I have told you that those emotions will not connect you in the way you need."

"Yes, you've explained—love, blood, or death. And Johnny was able to help us before. But he left me with that cryptic message about my family..." She shook her head. "I

227

can't do it, Mother. I know I promised to stay here but I have to go to Charlottesville, even if it means confronting that murdering bastard."

Mother nodded. "It is time. Not for confrontations but for leaving. Swift Bow will lead the escort party."

"But they need to stay, to train."

Mother frowned at her. "This is no time for foolishness. You will leave in the morning but you will not go alone. And there is something you must do before you go." She stared into the flames.

Libbie sat quietly, waiting.

Mother sat back on her haunches. "It is the Frenchman. He has come to tell us something but no one will give him a chance to speak. You will find out what it is, then tell the chiefs."

Libbie nodded. As strange as the request seemed, she knew if Mother decreed it, then it was meant to be. Everything Mother said came to pass sooner or later.

The thought made Libbie shudder. Of course the woman was not infallible. She couldn't be. There was one prediction that would not come to pass because Libbie would not allow it. She would never sacrifice Sebastian and the life they were meant to share to his "ultimate destiny". She would give up her own life before she would lose one more person she loved.

* * * * *

Sebastian's legs ached from crouching. He stretched slowly, being careful not to make the back porch boards squeak with his shifting weight, although it was possible no one was home. Mrs. Mitchell's coach was not in the carriage house and he had yet to see any movement in her house.

As he considered breaking into the house to find proof of Mrs. Mitchell's involvement with Winters, a barely perceptible movement caught his eye. He peered through the window into the kitchen. A small pinpoint of light pricked the darkness, grew larger, then filled the room. The young woman with mud-colored hair and a tired face who had lit the lamp now snuffed out her candle and primed the water pump. Sebastian spotted the tray of dishes she had placed beside the sink. His heart pounded. There were too many plates and glasses on that tray for one person.

With a quick glance toward the street where Fox watched from the shadows, Sebastian rose to his full height and tried the door handle. The entrance was locked but the latch was not sturdy. It yielded easily to some gentle prying and as the woman began washing the dishes, he eased into the kitchen. From his new vantage point, he could see how young the maid truly was — probably a few years younger than Libbie.

The thought of the woman he loved made him wince with the pain of missing her. A year ago, before he had ever laid eyes on her, he had existed only for moments like these, moments that brought him closer to Winters' demise. Now his hatred for the man was even more intense, if that was possible. But his mission to destroy Winters paled in comparison to his need to protect Libbie, to save her sister, to get her family out of his enemy's reach.

Sebastian moved silently through the kitchen. The woman's creased brow suggested she was absorbed in her own thoughts and he was able to stand close behind her without attracting her attention. In one fast motion, he wrapped an arm around her shoulders and clamped his other hand over her mouth. Her body went rigid and she twisted wildly, trying to escape.

With a sadistic whisper, he did his best to imitate Norton's guttural accent. "Where ya goin', ducky? Didn't ya miss ol' Norton, then?"

She relaxed. He could feel her lips forming a smile against his palm. Without dropping his hand from her mouth, he spun her around to face him. Her eyes flew open wide and she emitted a scream that was squelched by his hand.

Sebastian clenched and unclenched his jaw, struggling to control his rage. "So, you know Norton. You're working for Winters. Where is the child?"

He dropped his hand from her mouth but the woman made no noise. Her face was chalk white and she swayed unsteadily. Seeing her fear, Sebastian stepped closer, leaving a scant inch between them. "I want the child."

She took a step backward. "He'd kill me."

"You won't live long enough to face Winters. I'll kill you first."

"Mister, I don't know nothin' about Winters, except that Norton works for 'im and 'e pays a pretty penny."

"Pays you, does he? You could hang for what you've done, you know. Assuming I let you out of here alive. Does he pay well enough to compensate you for that?"

She wrung her hands in front of her.

Sebastian narrowed his eyes. "Where is she? In the basement? The attic? Take me to her right now!"

He reached out to grab her again, planning to shake the information out of her if necessary. But a scraping noise from a door at the other side of the room distracted him.

The maid glanced anxiously in the direction of the sound, then reached into her dress pocket. Her jaw dropped and she withdrew her empty hand.

"Lost your key? And to a child, no less. Good job, Annalee!" Sebastian crossed the kitchen in seconds, barely able to control the emotion in his voice as joy and relief swept through him. No slice of light glowed under the door. The poor child must be standing in total darkness.

"Annalee, it's Sebastian. Mr. Cole. Your sister sent me to help you." He pressed his palms against the doorframe. "Look for the small point of light. That's the keyhole."

On the other side of the room, Annalee's captor had inched closer to the hallway. Sebastian, no longer needing her cooperation and feeling no twinge of mercy, stopped her with his angry stare and a deep, feral growl. She sank to the ground, as though to beg. A small figure bustling into the room nearly tripped over her kneeling form. Mrs. Mitchell, Winters' mistress and partner in crime, had returned home.

"Mr. Cole? You've come for the child? But how did you..." Mrs. Mitchell pushed past the maid. Her eyes were wide and terrified. "I wanted to tell someone, I swear it to you. But they lied to me and they threatened me."

Fox had escorted Mrs. Mitchell into the house. He now stood behind the maid. His face was pale, his mouth twisted. Sebastian lifted his hand to stop the woman's babbling.

"What is it, Fox?" he asked.

The hulking man drew a long, uneven breath. "She didn't know nothin' about Annalee."

"Annalee?" Mrs. Mitchell's eyes were wide with surprise. "Anna's daughter? Everyone in town has been searching for her. What does she have to do with this?"

There was such sincerity in her questions that Sebastian nearly believed in her innocence. As another scrape came from the closed door, he glanced at it, then trained his gaze on Fox's face. Mrs. Mitchell and the maid stared at Fox as well.

"Tell him, Mrs. Mitchell," Fox told her. "Tell him what you told me."

She pressed her gloved hands to her cheeks and glanced at Sebastian before dropping her gaze. "Well, they told me the boy was an orphan and he was in danger. I agreed to take him in," she pointed to the young woman, "him and his nanny and agreed to keep them hidden. Then that awful man showed up — she called him Norton — and he said he'd gladly kill me if I ever breathed a word to anyone about the boy..."

Her voice faded. Two words echoed in Sebastian's head, "the boy, the boy, the boy".

Chapter Eighteen

ᔓ

The moon rode low on the horizon. Night was coming too slowly. Norton squirmed impatiently in front of the campfire, waiting for the right moment, the right depth of darkness, the element of complete surprise. He licked his dry lips and sipped strong whiskey from a small silver flask — a gift from Mary, to thank him for getting her a job. He drank just enough to warm himself, not enough to dull his senses. He wanted all his faculties about him. Sport like this did not come along every day.

Winters had withdrawn his execution order for one of the men, the one that Norton had planned to help step off a cliff. Still, Winters had insisted that Norton take the soldier with him and now the bastard had disappeared. Norton would track him down later, after he'd had his fun. In just a few minutes, Matthew Nichols would pass close by the camp as he scouted the area and Norton would make his move.

As thoughts of what was to come — the yielding flesh, the resisting bone, the seeping blood — washed over him, his body surged with carnal desire. It was a shame Mary couldn't be with him. He would give her the ride of her life on the cockstand that rose out of his anticipation.

Without a round, ripe body to pluck, his shaft chafed against his clothes and ached more with every heartbeat. He plunged his hand into his breeches and grasped the firm flesh. With closed eyes, he could see every detail — the bulged eyes full of fear and surprise, the thick tongue lolling out from between blue lips. He pumped his erection and felt intense pleasure center on it. In the gusting wind he could hear the dying man's pathetic begging, his last gasping breaths. With the image of the death convulsions, his pleasure peaked and his release poured out of him.

Norton breathed deeply and stretched his arms over his head. His body relieved, he could now focus all his attention on the task at hand. He took one last swig of the whiskey and sat very still, listening. A few minutes later, twigs snapped close by. Norton cracked his knuckles and rose to his feet.

* * * * *

The night patrols filed past Winters' office window. He leaned back in his chair and turned away from his desk to watch the line of red-coated boys. One of them might even prove worthy of being Norton's replacement.

When the line of soldiers disappeared from view, Winters rose and poured himself a brandy, then sank back into his seat and closed his eyes. He took a sip of his drink and opened his mind to his newest followers.

The Indians desperately needed to please him. Their greatest fear was failing him. They were ready to prove their usefulness to their master. They held a young soldier trapped between them, hovering at the edge of a cliff. The man was begging for his life. The mute Indian grabbed both the man's arms behind his back. The other Indian leaned into the young man and together they propelled the soldier off the precipice, into the abyss far below them.

Winters opened his eyes and raised his glass in silent toast to his new assassins. Now that they had proven themselves, had proven that they would truly kill for him, he had no need to recruit another soldier to be his second-in-command. With two large gulps, he swallowed his mellow aperitif and set the snifter on the windowsill. He checked his pocket watch, assuring himself that Norton's final assignment would soon be completed. Then Norton would meet his own fate and with that unsavory business out of the way, Winters would be able to focus all his attention on the family reunion with Liberty.

"Where are you tonight, dear cousin?" he wondered aloud. "No doubt lying in that miserable squaw-man's bed. When you're in my bed, I'll make you forget you ever knew him. And when I've tired of you, I'll let you live just long enough to see me take your lover's soul from him."

* * * * *

Libbie patted Black Thunder's mane while the tired horse ate her oats. Nearby, Swift Bow directed the set-up of the overnight camp. If Libbie had her way, they would ride night and day until Annalee was safe in her arms again. Looking at the thin moon and the few stars in the cloudy sky, she knew there was wisdom in Swift Bow's insistence that they stop, for their safety as well as for rest. But she would not give up on reaching Annalee through some means. She leaned against Black Thunder and closed her eyes.

There was a darkly shadowed room. Annalee sat in the center of a soft bed. She was steeped in fear, sadness, cold. And something else—a deep caring, a comfort, a friendship. There were voices coming from far away, new, strange voices. Annalee felt terror and reached for her new friend's hand. Then a voice was louder. It was a man's voice and it was familiar.

Libbie opened her eyes, hope and joy welling inside her. Her sister was safe, somewhere with other children or at least another child. And Sebastian was there. He had found Annalee.

The happiness gave way to a red haze. Not Annalee— their connection was now broken. It was something much closer, something sinister. Libbie's vision clouded over with crimson streaks. The streaks ran down her body, dripped from her fingers, pooled on the ground. Her stomach twisted with fear. Without a word of explanation to the braves, she climbed onto Black Thunder and charged off into the darkness.

She could vaguely hear a man's voice calling to her, ordering her to return but she couldn't move, couldn't change her course as she rode blindly away from the camp and into the dark mountains. She did not know what she would find at the end of her journey, or more frighteningly, whom. But one thing became clear as she approached her destination — she would not be able to get a better image of the attacker or the attacked until her visions guided her to the scene of the crime. The victim could not send her anymore information than that. The victim was already dead.

* * * * *

Daniel would be six years old by now, a witness to his mother's brutal murder, the prisoner of a sadistic madman, a child condemned to know more than any child ever should. As the seamstress's mouth continued to move, making sounds Sebastian could no longer hear, he leaned his shoulder against the doorframe for support. His legs turned to rubber. Spots danced in front of his eyes. He slid to his knees and pressed his palms against the door.

The key scraped along the wood again but the children, no doubt terrified and shaking, could not unlock the door.

"Pass the key under the door," he told them. "I'll unlock it from out here."

He heard frantic whispering on the other side of the door.

"I know you're frightened but you have to trust me," he said. "Libbie sent me. She asked me to find you. I promised her I'd take you home."

More whispers, then the sound of the key being pushed along the floor. The end of the long metal key poked out from under the door. Sebastian pushed down on it with one finger and pulled it toward him until he could grasp the key in his hand.

"I'm unlocking the door," he said. "Step back, just for a moment, while I swing it open. Good. Now come out."

Annalee stepped through the opening. Her clothes were dirty and torn but her face was freshly scrubbed and her hair was tucked neatly behind her ears, as though she had prepared herself as meticulously as possible for this moment. So they had planned this carefully, probably over days. Had they known he would be there that night, that he would distract their captors so they could make their escape? Had Annalee felt her sister watching her? Had Libbie been able to communicate to her that help was on the way? He wanted to ask Annalee so many questions but they fell away from his mind as the girl stepped tentatively into the kitchen.

Mrs. Mitchell's jaw dropped at the sight of her friend's missing child. Annalee shook when she saw the maid, who tried to back away from the scene. Fox blocked the woman's way, all the while keeping his eyes trained on the darkness behind the door. Sebastian reached out to comfort the little girl, whose face revealed her fear of all of the adults around her.

"Libbie sent me, Annalee," he told her again as he hugged her safely to his breast.

"And we're going to take you to your mama," Mrs. Mitchell added.

Sebastian leaned forward and pushed the door open wide to reveal the boy, tall and strong beyond his years, whom he had cradled as a baby.

"Danny," Fox choked.

The boy's gaze darted to Fox but his face did not register recognition. Sebastian's heart sank when he saw the child's blank stare as he glanced from face to face. But his gaze lingered a moment longer on Sebastian.

"It's me, Daniel. Sebastian. It's been a year and a half but I've been searching for you."

The boy nodded slowly. "Uncle Sebastian. Mama and Papa's friend."

Sebastian's vision blurred with tears that spilled unchecked onto his cheeks. He clung to Annalee with one arm and reached out for Daniel with the other. The boy hesitated until Annalee held out her hand to him. He took it quickly, gratefully but remained just out of Sebastian's reach. Sebastian wanted to wrap the boy in his embrace but he knew the child was not ready for it.

"She's gone," the boy whispered. "My mother is dead."

Sebastian nodded. "I know."

"They're all dead."

"I'm sorry, Daniel. But you're safe now. You and Annalee are both safe."

There was a commotion from the front of the house. Sebastian pushed the children behind him and Fox reached for the pistol in the holster at his waist.

"Adele, where are you?" It was a woman's voice.

Mrs. Mitchell pressed her hands to her face. "It's Mrs. Jackson."

"Colonel Jackson's wife?" Sebastian asked.

The seamstress nodded. "She knew nothing about the child, though. I mean, the children. I swear it. The Jackson's have paid me to take care of wounded soldiers before but not the children."

"You work for the Jacksons?" Fox asked. "Not Winters?"

Mrs. Mitchell stared at him blankly. "Who on earth is Winters?"

Behind him, Mary cleared her throat. Sebastian glared at her.

"She's tellin' the truth, sir," the maid said. "Missus Mitchell ain't never met Norton's boss. Didn't even know as much about 'im as I know."

Sebastian scowled. "Then who the devil is his—"

"Mrs. Mitchell!" The thin, hawkish woman from Caroline's party stepped into the kitchen. "What... Who... Children?"

Sebastian sighed. "It's a long story, Mrs. Jackson and you shouldn't be here."

Mrs. Jackson looked closely at him. "Mr. Cole? Pierre's friend? He's sent you to collect the guns, then?"

Fox furrowed his brow. "What's this about guns?"

"Pierre's guns," she answered. "They've been hidden in our root cellar. He said Mr. Cole would come for them, to give them to the Indians along the frontier."

"Beaulieu," Sebastian muttered. "That pompous ass. Did he mention this to you, Fox?"

Fox shook his head, then rubbed a hand over the back of his neck. "I'm not sayin' he wouldn'ta, though, if I hadn'ta made the rule about him talkin' on our ride. The rule was, he didn't talk, I didn't leave him alone in the mountains to get eaten by bobcats."

Out of the corner of his eye, Sebastian saw Mary brace herself against the wall. "I didn't know nothin' about guns. They told me about th' kid, then another one, an' about keepin' me mouth shut but not about guns."

Sebastian shook his head, amazed that anyone who had cavorted with the likes of Norton could feel squeamish about guns. "You said they but you told me earlier you'd never met Winters."

She shook her head. "Never did. Jus' th' la-di-da-like old lady that got me th' job wit' Mrs. Mitchell, so's I could bring the boy 'ere."

"But you were recommended by—" Mrs. Mitchell reached for Mrs. Jackson's hand. "She wouldn't."

"No," Mrs. Jackson agreed. "She couldn't."

"Yes, she did," Sebastian told them as the pieces fell into place for him. "She is his mistress."

"This damn mistress again," Fox said, then reddened as he glanced at the children. "Beg pardon. But who th' hell is she?"

"Don't you see, Fox? It had to be someone Libbie trusted, someone her family trusted." Sebastian turned back to Mary. "Someone like Mrs. Louisa Barton, isn't that right, Mary?"

When the woman nodded, Fox let out his breath in a long whistle. "Mrs. Barton. Well, damn me if I didn't miss it completely. I shoulda known she was up to somethin'. I never do trust those la-di-da types."

"She fooled us all, Fox," Sebastian said. "And now she'll have to pay. But first, we have to get the MacRaes out of town tonight, under cover of darkness. We'll take Mrs. Barton as well."

"What are you sayin', Cole? The whole idea is to get them away from Winters' spies and outta harm's way."

"We'll take Mrs. Barton with us. We'll give her an ultimatum—she can help us get that bastard, or she can go to the gallows for her part in helping him. And then there's Norton."

Fox grunted. "He's bound ta be skulkin' around somewhere nearby."

Sebastian glared at Mary. "Where was Norton headed the last time you saw him?"

She swallowed hard and stared at the table. "Well, um, 'e was off into th' mountains, said 'e had a real important assignment ta do for Winters."

"An assignment?" Sebastian could see the blush rise in Mary's cheeks. Obviously, she had some suspicion about the kind of assignments Norton carried out for Winters. His heart pounded as he thought about Libbie in the mountains with the Occaneechi.

He pulled Fox aside dropped his voice. "Norton could be after Libbie. I've got to get to her. Take the MacRaes to Jane's estate and wait for us there."

"Nonsense." Fox crossed his arms over his chest. "You'd only put Miss Libbie in more danger. If Norton spotted you, he'd know he was on the right trail. You come with me and let

Scott go get Libbie. He knows those trails a hell of a lot better 'an you and he can ride night and day and get to the village long before you or Norton."

Sebastian grimaced. "I hate it when you're right. Send Scott tonight. We've got to keep Libbie out of Norton's clutches."

* * * * *

Libbie's ride through the black night offered no landmarks or direction, no sense of time or place as she rode in a trance. By the time she pulled on the reins to halt Black Thunder, they were mere feet from a precipice. She climbed off the horse and stepped to the edge of the steep drop. The thin slice of moon provided precious little light but the body was there, the neck twisted into an impossible position, the nose and mouth still leaking thick blood which collected in large stains on the soldier's red coat, the eyes open wide and unseeing.

Libbie did not know how long she was there alone. By the time Swift Bow, Grayhorse and the others caught up to her, lofting lanterns high into the air to illuminate the scene, she had lost the scant contents of her stomach, then had collected herself and had said a prayer for the young soldier. With the light the braves brought, she could see him clearly now. And the cliff above them from which he had been pushed.

"It will take some time to climb down and get him and we won't be able to build a funeral pyre until daylight," Swift Bow said.

Libbie shook her head. "That's not his way. Leave him here — other soldiers will find him."

She jumped at the sound of a strange, distant noise. The braves had heard it too. They sat very still on their mounts. Libbie nodded in the direction of the sound, indicating that they must follow it.

With a quick acknowledgement, Swift Bow motioned for her and Grayhorse to stay behind while he led the braves into the nearby trees. She held her ground but not because of Swift Bow's order. The soldier's killers were still nearby. She could feel them watching her, waiting for her, but not to harm her. A wave of pain and desperation washed over her. They wanted her to save them, yet they knew she couldn't. As they pulled their energy away from her and faded into the night, she knew what they were — Fated Ones. But they had lost their free will and most of the vestiges of their humanity. These Fated Ones had failed the spirits and as punishment they had lost their souls.

Chapter Nineteen

ॐ

Libbie mounted her horse and she and Grayhorse wordlessly rode into the forest, picking up the path Swift Bow and the braves had taken. By the time she reached them, Swift Bow, still astride his horse, had his bow loaded and poised for attack. When Libbie came near him, he glanced in her direction, not bothering to hide his disapproving scowl, then turned his attention back to the small clearing in front of him.

None of the other braves looked at her. As she watched their lined faces, flashing eyes, tensed shoulders, all of their images bled together into a red haze. More death was near. Too near. Libbie inched forward to glimpse the horror she knew awaited her.

Instantly, she saw why Swift Bow held his arrow in check. Two men stood tangled together and eerily still, a thin shaft of moonlight glancing off their faces and distending their expressions into ghoulish grins. One man held the other in a rigid embrace, like a lover in the throes of ecstasy. They were too closely entwined for Swift Bow to get a clear shot at the aggressor.

Then he moved, the larger man who held the other in that lethal grip. Even from several hundred yards away from them, Libbie could make out their features clearly now. Matthew Nichols, the soldier who had helped her escape with Sebastian from Winters' fort, now stood alone with his killer. Libbie could see his features being swallowed in a red fog. Slowly, ever so slowly, Swift Bow pulled his bow taut and lined up his arrow with the killer's head. Norton.

Before Swift Bow could release the arrow, the fog around Matthew thinned into small wisps, then disappeared, only to emerge like bony fingers around Norton's neck. Libbie licked her dry lips and held her breath, waiting. She watched Swift Bow inhale, saw his fingers shift. In the split second before he released the arrow, an image flashed through her mind — one of Johnny, Tom and Winters. And near them was Norton, watching.

Swift Bow's pulled his fingertips across the bowstring. His arrow landed squarely in Norton's shoulder. Norton dropped to the ground, shrieking.

The hooves of the braves' horses thundered past Libbie as they charged toward the men in the clearing. She followed them more slowly.

As they approached, Matthew dropped to his knees. Two of the braves leapt from their mounts and knelt beside him. He nodded in response to their questions, dark color flooding into his cheeks that, Libbie now realized, had been pale from lack of air. Grayhorse leaned over Norton and planted his knee on the injured man's back to hold him in check.

"We'll take him with us, get as much information as we can out of him," Libbie told Swift Bow. "And we cannot leave him unguarded for one moment."

He nodded. "You will have to tend to his wound."

Her blood ran cold at the thought of laying her hands on Norton but she prodded Black Thunder forward and dismounted beside the man's prone form. By the time she knelt beside him, his shrieks had subsided to groans and his breath whistled through his clenched teeth. As she prodded the wound, he tried to shrink away from her but was held in place by the weight on his back.

"Ye bitch," Norton hissed. "Ye did this ta me."

She scowled at him. "One word from me and Swift Bow will end your miserable life as painfully as possible."

His eyes glinted — was it with amusement? A grudging respect? Libbie could not be sure and did not really want to know. Instead, she called on more two braves to kneel with her and keep him motionless. She withdrew her sharp, short knife from her boot and made an incision in his arm to widen the wound. After several long minutes of gentle poking and hard pulling punctuated by Norton's nerve-shattering shrieks, the arrowhead twisted free of the flesh.

Without being asked, Swift Bow dropped Libbie's medicine pouch on the ground beside her. When she finished cleansing and wrapping the tear in Norton's shoulder, she rose unsteadily to her feet and stumbled away from the braves, who set to tying Norton into Swift Bow's saddle. Bile rose in her throat as she thought about the demon now in her care. She had made a deal with the devil and there was no turning back.

"Thank you, Miss MacRae," a raspy voice said behind her. "If you and your friends hadn't come along, he would have killed me."

Libbie turned to see Matthew extending his hand to her. She placed her own shaking hand in his. "I was simply returning the favor. I haven't forgotten what you did for me. And for Sebastian. But you should have left Winters' command a long time ago."

"I thought I could get into his inner circle and get information for General Gordon. No doubt Lieutenant Cole is furious with me for staying there so long."

"You can discuss it with him yourself. We're on our way to Charlottesville to meet him. Come with us."

Matthew rubbed his throat where Norton had tried to crush his windpipe. "Thank you, ma'am. I'll do anything I can to help you stop Winters."

Behind her, Swift Bow announced that their prisoner was secured and the party needed to return to camp. Libbie swung up onto Black Thunder, who stood patiently beside Swift Bow's horse, where Norton was tied. A brave stood beside the captured man, holding the reins of the horse. Upon seeing

Libbie, the murderer wriggled himself as close to a sitting position as he could manage.

"You're always quite a sight, ducky, in that damn squaw getup," he said with a leer. "It's a shame, ain't it, that we 'aven't met in better circumstances. We coulda been a pair, eh?"

"If you hope to live through this night, you'll refrain from speaking to me," she retorted.

"Aw, an' 'ere I was, about to spill my innards out to ye about yer dearly departed brother. An' the other one—a fiancé, was it? Not that ye can be missin' that one much, now that ye've taken up with that Indian-lovin' Cole."

Libbie sat up straighter and kept her face an expressionless mask. "If you have something to say, come out with it. I will not tolerate your games."

He laughed, then grimaced with the pain of it. "Why is it all the birds in yer family squawk so damn much? Quite unattractive." When Libbie reached toward the knife in her boot, he shrank back a bit. "But there's somethin' else I know about yer family, somethin' ye don't. I daresay it's the reason those two boys n' yer old daddy are dead as doornails."

She clenched her teeth. "Out with it or lose your tongue. It's your choice."

"I guess livin' wit' the savages taught ye a thing or two," he said boldly but paled as he spoke. "But ye'll know sooner or later. I mean, I suppose the crazy bastard means ta tell ye."

She pulled the knife out of her boot, letting it rest against her thigh where it could catch the moonlight. He swallowed hard as he eyed it.

"Now, don't go gettin' any ideas. Can't believe anyone would be so anxious ta 'ear they're related to the likes o' Winters."

"Related? What does that mean?" Libbie's heart pounded as she remembered Johnny's cryptic message and something in the deep recesses of her mind whispered that this was it, the tie that bound her to Winters.

"I almost 'ate ta be the one ta tell ye but 'e's yer kin. Refers ta ye as cousin when 'e thinks no one's around. It's what 'e called yer brother that day."

"It makes no sense. Killing his own kin."

"Winters don't worry much about makin' sense. An' he killed the other boy fer the same reason."

"Tom wasn't related to us."

"Said 'e was about to be. Right there on the battlefield, promised yer daddy and yer brother 'e'd marry ye and look after ye as soon as…"

Norton's voice trailed off when he saw Swift Bow walking toward them. Quick as a flash, Norton convulsed. His tied feet slammed into his guard's belly, slamming the man to the ground. Norton was off balance but he clung to the rope that secured his wrists to the saddle and kicked the horse, spurring her into a full gallop.

Libbie gathered her reins and turned Black Thunder toward the bolting horse. Before she could nudge Black Thunder into action, Swift Bow was beside her, his hand on her bridle.

"No," he said. "You will not leave my sight again. You will not find yourself alone with a man like that."

Other braves had swung onto their mounts and were giving chase but Norton had too good a head start.

Libbie scowled at Swift Bow. "Black Thunder and I were the only hope of catching him. Now what will we do?"

"I am even more displeased than you are, Walks-in-Two-Worlds. It was my judgment that spared his worthless life and lost my horse. But it is done and now we must keep you safe."

She did not argue with him. It would do no good. When the pursuers returned without Norton or the horse, the group wordlessly reassembled and moved toward their camp.

As she rode with Swift Bow seated behind her, Libbie turned her mind to other horrible thoughts. She could see Winters, his scarred face twisted in delight, his bloody bayonet poised over Johnny's crumpled body. She could feel his thoughts, his anger, his hatred. And she knew it was true. Somewhere in her veins flowed a drop of blood that was kindred to one in Winters' despicable flesh.

* * * * *

Jane motioned to her servant to pour more port into Sebastian's glass but he shook his head. With a wave of her hand, Jane dismissed the servant, then turned her attention to her friend. He looked away from her and stared at the fire in the hearth. He could think only of Libbie, out there in the wilderness, sleeping on the cold, hard ground if at all, in constant danger from Winters and his lackey Norton.

"I should have gone after her myself," he muttered.

"We've already discussed this a dozen times." Jane punctuated her statement with an annoyed sigh.

Before Sebastian could launch them into the discussion again, Jane's servant burst back into the room.

"'Scuse me, ma'am," she said as she curtsied to Jane, "but I thought ya should know right away. My Daddy just saw a horseman ride in." She glanced at Sebastian. "It's Mr. Fox's son, sir. And the others that's with him is just down the road a piece."

Sebastian's heart pounded as he jumped to his feet and pulled Jane into an embrace. "Have you ever heard sweeter words in your entire life?"

He ran from the room, out the side door and through the garden to the stable. Jane ran behind him, calling for him to wait for her but he could not control himself. By the time he reached Scott, he was so overcome with happiness that he nearly knocked the man off his feet with a friendly slap across his back.

It took him a moment to catch his breath and form words. "Where is she?" he finally managed to say.

Scott grinned. "I'm glad to see you too, Cole."

Sebastian tried to apologize but Scott raised his hand. "Don't bother. I'll wager you drove everyone plumb crazy waitin' for us to get here."

Jane panted as she reached them. She nodded to the stableman, who tipped his hat to her, then took the reins of Scott's mount and led the horse into the barn. "Be prepared Greves, you'll have a full stable to tend tonight!"

"Yes ma'am."

Still breathing hard, Jane stood between Sebastian and Scott and linked her arms into theirs. "Did all go well on the journey?"

Scott set his mouth in a hard line. "It went all right, Miss Jane but there was somethin' that came up."

"What was it?" Sebastian demanded.

"Well, Miss Libbie and the braves ran across something unexpected. Or, I should say, someone…"

His voice was drowned out by pounding horse hooves. The silhouettes of six mounted steeds came into view. They were too far away for the stable lanterns to illuminate the riders' forms but Libbie was in the lead. Sebastian could see her streaming copper hair and glimpses of her figure's gentle curves when the wind blew her cape away from her body.

His stomach fluttered. His breath quickened. His body tensed in anticipation of holding her again. She stopped scant feet from him and threw her leg over Black Thunder, dismounting in one swift motion. And then she was in his embrace. Her supple body was warm against his. He pressed his lips to hers, tasting her, caressing her, cajoling the heat to rise from the depths of her flesh and radiate into him.

"You saved Annalee," she whispered as he kissed her face. "Thank you, Sebastian. I didn't think it was possible to love you more than I already did but now you've—"

He claimed her lips once more. The feel of her pressing into him filled Sebastian's heart and his senses. Slowly, very slowly, he came back to the moment and remembered that they were not alone. He lifted his head to find that Scott had turned his back to them and was earnestly exchanging chitchat with Jane. A bit farther away, Grayhorse, Swift Bow and the other braves climbed off their horses and spoke with Greves, who led a few horses into the barn. It was then that Sebastian realized something was amiss.

Swift Bow was holding the reins of a horse but another brave climbed out of the saddle. Sebastian took a step forward. Libbie held tightly to his arm.

"We lost a horse," Swift Bow said quietly.

Sebastian didn't like the grave expression on the man's face. "Because?"

Libbie stepped forward. "It was Norton. We... Well, I came upon him near our camp one night. Swift Bow hit him with an arrow and we tied him to a saddle."

"He escaped," Swift Bow finished.

Sebastian glanced from Libbie to Swift Bow and back again. "What was Norton doing there? Did Winters send him after Libbie?"

"Actually, he was trying to break my neck."

"Matthew?" Sebastian turned to see the soldier dismounting.

Matthew grinned. "In the flesh, sir. But I wouldn't have been much longer if Norton would've had his way."

Jane stepped forward and brushed her hand over Matthew's lapel. "I'm so pleased that you're well, dear boy."

"Lady Jane, it's a pleasure to see you again." Matthew bent over her hand and kissed it.

Sebastian exchanged a glance with Libbie and saw the question in her eyes about Jane and Matthew. He gave her a slight nod and she widened her eyes as though to say Lady Jane never ceased to amaze her.

Matthew dropped Jane's hand and spoke again to Sebastian. "Much as he blames himself, Swift Bow did nothing wrong. I've never seen anything like it, kicking a brave to the ground, then riding off tied to a saddle without so much as a finger to wrap around the reins."

"He's devil's spawn," Sebastian muttered.

"I should have killed him with that arrow, instead of wounding him. I had hoped he would be useful to us."

Sebastian slapped Swift Bow on the shoulder. "He wouldn't have given us anything useful. This might actually serve our purposes better."

Libbie furrowed her brow. "He'll head back to Winters and tell him I was headed out of the mountains. How will that help us?"

"There's a lot to tell you," Sebastian said with a sigh, "but it can wait until morning."

She nodded. "But tell me how the boy is doing? I know Annalee is well. I've felt it through her and Mama and Caroline. But she worries about the boy. Sunflower's son."

"How did you know?"

She frowned. "I saw your vision of the village. That night. It was horrifying. Then I recognized her son in a vision I had of Annalee."

"Daniel has seen too much, I fear."

"He's safe now," Libbie whispered. "We'll take care of him."

Sebastian hugged her and kissed her hair. "I hoped you would feel that way." He took her hand and pulled her with him. "There's something you have to see. It's in one of Jane's unused outbuildings—"

"Oh, no you don't!" Jane grabbed Libbie's other hand. "It can wait. This poor girl has been on that horse for days. First, a warm meal, then a hot bath and a reunion with her very worried family."

"Of course." Sebastian caught Libbie's hand and kissed it. "I'll come to see you in an hour or so. First I'll help Swift Bow and Greves with the horses." He dropped his voice to a whisper. "Then we'll have a more suitable and much more private reunion."

* * * * *

Libbie did not care to hold court in the bathtub but Lady Jane had made her position clear. Libbie was to eat, bathe and dress in clean clothes that her mother and aunt had brought from Charlottesville. And she was not to ask for her buckskins to be returned to her. Jane had carried them away herself, pinching them between her forefinger and thumb, muttering something about a fire.

Now Libbie sat submerged in a sea of soft bubbles while Anna and Caroline fussed over her. She listened, enraptured as they described their reunion with Annalee and praised Sebastian's heroism and lamented the betrayal by Mrs. Barton.

As they began to repeat themselves, Libbie's mind drifted to thoughts of seeing Annalee and the boy and assuring herself that the children were truly safe, then slipping away to find Sebastian for their private reunion.

"Liberty MacRae, I cannot believe you will not answer me."

Libbie jumped and came out of her reverie to see her mother, arms crossed in front of her, staring down at her. She glanced at Aunt Caroline but the woman frowned and offered Libbie no help.

Libbie cleared her throat. "What was the question again, Mama?"

Aunt Caroline covered her mouth with her hand. Libbie sank deeper into the bubbles, withering under her mother's stare.

"I asked about your wedding. When and where it happened. Why we weren't invited."

"Oh, Mama. I'd never get married without you there." The words were out of her mouth before she realized what she had done.

"Not married?" Her mother's voice was a hoarse whisper.

Aunt Caroline stood beside her sister and held her shoulders. "Now, Anna, I'm sure there's a reason Libbie ran off with the man and then didn't marry him." Aunt Caroline widened her eyes at Libbie, beseeching her to have a good explanation.

"Oh, I know the reason," Anna said.

Libbie's heart jumped into her throat. What kind of a woman did her mother think she had become? She shook her head, realizing that indeed she had become that kind of woman. Even worse, she didn't regret it, did not regret one second she had spent in Sebastian Cole's arms or in his bed. Libbie opened her mouth, ready to defend her choices.

"They were in imminent danger," her mother accused.

Libbie snapped her mouth shut.

"Admit it, Liberty. You hinted as much when we had that heart-to-heart talk."

Libbie closed her eyes. She would rather have admitted to her passionate affair than to the battle with Winters. "I'm afraid it's true, Mama. I was in danger. I am in danger." She opened her eyes. "None of us is safe."

"Winters. He killed Sean and Johnny, then kidnapped Annalee and left that bizarre ransom note." Anna's eyes flashed with fury. Then she slumped her shoulders. "But why? Why is he hell-bent on destroying us? Does it have something to do with the militia?"

"No, Mama. It's personal. It's about the Hollings. About your father's brother Barnabus."

She briefly told them what she knew about Winters being a relative and having something to do with their uncle.

Aunt Caroline took Anna's hand. "Maybe it was true, after all." She looked at Libbie. "Daddy got some letters from Uncle Barnabus after he gambled away his small inheritance. Barnabus said he needed money for his child, who was born out of wedlock. Daddy sent some money but after a while he got worried. If there really was a child, he didn't trust Barnabus to take care of him, so he offered to pay for the boy and his mother's passage to America. When Barnabus didn't send them, Daddy assumed he'd made up the whole story to get money from us."

"But if there really was a son, you think it's this Winters person?" Anna asked Libbie.

"And I think he blames our family for not helping him." As she spoke, Libbie rose from the tub, dried herself and reached for her clean clothes. "Winters has some twisted idea about retribution against us. But we're safe here. Lord Whitmore is too rich and well-connected for Winters to cross." It was an enormous lie but Libbie couldn't bring herself to tell the truth that night, when they'd just been reunited after so many months apart. Anna and Caroline exchanged worried glances while Libbie pulled on her clothes.

"There," Libbie said as she closed the last button on her bodice. "Clean and dressed. Now it's time to see Annalee."

"She's asleep," Anna said. "And we're not through with this conversation. If we're in danger, if you're in danger -"

"Please, Mama, not tonight." Libbie took her mother's hand. "I just want to look at her, to see for myself that she's all right. And then I want to get a good night's sleep with no nightmares about Winters."

Her mother nodded, then hugged her tightly.

A few minutes later, the three women entered the bedroom where eight-year-old Annalee slept. A lantern burned on the nightstand because Annalee could not stand to sleep in the dark, her mother told Libbie. In the soft light, Annalee looked like an angel. Libbie kissed her soft cheek.

"Be careful where you step," Aunt Caroline whispered. "The boy is over there on the floor. He sneaks in here during the night. He can't bear to be away from Annalee for too long."

Libbie stood and peered into the shadows, trying to see the child. She could only make out a bundle of blankets a few feet from Annalee's bed.

"Careful not to wake him," her mother whispered. "He needs his sleep. He's been through heaven knows what and now he spends every waking hour hovering over Annalee like a self-appointed protector. Such a sweet boy."

Libbie nodded as she crept closer to him. The child sighed and turned in his sleep and Libbie's heart stopped, then began beating again, pounding hard and fast in her breast.

It was not his straight black hair or light brown skin, which he must have inherited from his mother. It was something far subtler, a small movement or a tilt of his head as he slept. But the realization hit her like a bolt of lightning.

Dozens of questions tumbled over themselves in her mind. When? How? Why? Should she tell him? Could she? If Sunflower herself had taken the secret to her grave, should Libbie expose it?

Chapter Twenty

ℰℐ

As Sebastian checked the wagon full of supplies in the back room of the abandoned carriage house, he heard Libbie's voice clearly. She was speaking with Effie, Jane's maid, whose words did not reach him as well. The women were in the front room of the building and he could make out their conversation as they moved closer to him.

"But I jus' wanted ya ta know, Miss Libbie," the maid said. "It meant everything ta us. Kep' us alive."

"Yes, my father was a good man. And he thought the world of your father, as well. Greves was one of his hardest workers."

"Even when some o' th' white fields hands didn't wanna work nowhere near a negro, still your daddy found work for 'im. And yer mama taught me all I know about workin' for Lady Whitmore."

"I'm glad it's worked out so well, Effie," Libbie said. "Lady Jane runs an interesting household and I'm sure things wouldn't go as smoothly without you."

"Well, yer mama is ta thank. She's th' one who recommended ta Lady Whitmore ta hire us. Jus' wanted ya to know that some folks in these parts still know how special the MacRae name is."

Through the narrow doorway, Sebastian saw Libbie lean forward and hug the maid. Effie motioned to the back room, then left the building as Libbie came toward Sebastian.

He stepped forward and wrapped his arms around her. She leaned into him. Her still damp, curling hair brushed his chin and fell over his hands as he flattened them against her back.

"When Scott met up with us on the trail, he told us about Mrs. Barton."

"I'm sorry, love. If it's any consolation, she's trying to redeem herself. She's gone on a special assignment with Fox."

"What assignment?"

He shook his head. "It can wait. Grayhorse said that after your run-in with Norton, you seemed upset. Did something else happen?"

She squeezed him tightly. "He just told me something I didn't want to hear."

He rubbed her back. "What is it?"

She shook her head. "It can wait. You have something to show me?"

He led her to a wagon along the back wall and peeled back layers of blankets. "This is it."

Libbie stood on her tiptoes and leaned over the edge of the old hay wagon. "Pierre's guns! How did you get them so quickly? We just arrived with the news."

"We've had them for days. They were stashed in Mrs. Jackson's house. How did you know? A vision?"

She crossed her arms in front of her and fixed him with a withering stare. "No, actually, I heard about them. And you could have too—you, or Fox, or his sons. But no one would listen to poor Pierre."

"Darling, I'm sure—"

"Do you know that Fox even made up some ridiculous riding rule to keep Pierre from speaking on their journey? That long ride and the poor man was barely permitted to say a word."

Sebastian fought back a grin. "Well, Fox is—"

"And then you rode off, after giving Swift Bow and Grayhorse instructions to treat him the same way."

"Now, just a minute! Is that what he told you? Because I never suggested they shouldn't listen to him."

Libbie scowled. "And then, lo and behold, Red Wolf and Swift Bow conveniently forget every word of English that they know when they get near the man."

Now Sebastian did smile. "Perhaps it's that dreadful accent of his."

Libbie gave a fake laugh. "Perhaps it's that all of you men are jealous of his fine manners and dandy clothes."

"Jealous? Of those silly hats?"

She shrugged. "Jealous of the way he danced with me. Jealous of the kind of proposition you knew he would offer me when he got the chance."

Possessiveness seized Sebastian. He pulled Libbie into his arms. "What proposition?"

She pressed her hands against his chest. "First, tell me, how much time can I spend with my family before we take the weapons to the Occaneechi?"

"We won't take them," he whispered between kisses to her cheekbone, throat and earlobe. "Swift Bow and the braves will leave with them first thing in the morning."

Libbie pulled back from his embrace. "So we're not going back? We won't be with the Occaneechi when Winters attacks them?"

Sebastian held her hands. "Winters will send his men but he won't be part of the attack. He will only come out of his den when he believes he can get to you, when you're the most vulnerable and unprotected."

"But how will he know? Mrs. Barton's mission with Fox — that's to tell him that I'm here?"

Sebastian nodded. "She'll tell him that the MacRaes are back on the farm and that we've anticipated his attack on the Occaneechi and I've gone to help them. It will draw him out, lure him here where we'll ambush him."

She went so pale, he thought she might faint. He grabbed her around the waist. "Darling, you're exhausted."

"No, it's not that. He can't come here. We can't confront him on the farm."

"Libbie, you need to sit down. You don't look well. Did Jane make sure you had some dinner?"

"No, it's not that. We just… We need a different plan. I don't want Winters to come to the farm."

"It's the best chance we have against him. We need to use Winters' own obsessions with your farm and family and most of all with you, against him. Your family won't be there. We won't let them set foot on your land until we've dealt with Winters."

She furrowed her brow, then nodded slowly. "Yes, they won't be there. My visions have already shown me that detail has changed." She looked at him with wide, intense eyes. "We must draw him out soon. Before May first. If it's not that day, not the anniversary of Papa and Johnny's deaths, it can all be different."

"Slow down, love. I don't understand. Are you saying you've had visions of our confrontation with Winters?"

When she nodded, he was overwhelmed with the need to know what she saw. Would he survive the day? Would they have more time together? Of course not. The shock of it hit him squarely in the chest and made his shoulders sag. She had gone pale and had been terrified to draw Winters to the farm. Of course she had seen a tragic ending.

"We can change it," she whispered to him.

He closed his eyes, wanting to believe her words.

"You're right, I can feel it," she continued. "Facing him anywhere else will put us at a disadvantage we can't afford. But if we bring him here, we can control the day." She squeezed his hands and he opened his eyes to see her smile. "We can beat him, Sebastian, we truly can!"

Her face was so beautiful, her smile so true, her enthusiasm contagious. And he felt it too.

"Tomorrow, you'll tell me about your visions," he said. "We'll sit down with Fox and plan the battle our way. We'll have our vengeance and the very next day, we'll begin the next chapter of our lives together."

"Yes, tomorrow," she whispered, still smiling. She leaned against him and kissed him. "But tonight..."

He pulled her roughly against him. "Tonight, you'll tell me about the proposition from that French dandy."

Libbie's eyes danced as she threw back her head and laughed. "First, admit it. You're jealous."

"Fine, I'm jealous. Green with envy. Unable to think clearly with the burden of it."

"Well, I'm a too much of a lady to repeat the things Pierre proposed." She gave him a wicked smile. "I'll have to show you, instead."

* * * * *

Half an hour later, Sebastian sat on the floor with Libbie curled onto his lap. "I've missed you," she murmured.

He smiled and wrapped his fingers in her hair. "I could tell." He turned her face up to his and kissed her softly, slowly, until he could feel the heat of passion rising in her again.

He stopped kissing her and looked into her eyes. "Wait, love. You had something to tell me. Something about Winters."

She frowned. "There's no easy way to say it."

"Then swift and sharp, like cutting open a wound to clean it."

She took a deep breath, closed her eyes, then opened them again and looked directly at him. "He's kin. Reginald Winters is my kin."

Sebastian did not know what he had expected to hear but nothing he could have imagined came close to this revelation.

"No. It's not true. You can't believe anything that a man like Norton says."

"I know what Norton is but when he said those words, I also knew they were the truth. And there was something that Johnny said too, that day I came to you at the training field. Something about my great-uncle Barnabus and asking my family what they remembered about him. Johnny was my connection to Winters that day but he knew there was another connection as well. And there is. Blood."

Sebastian shook his head, barely able to put into words all the questions forming in his mind. "Barnabus?"

"My grandfather's older brother was Barnabus. He died just over a year ago. Barnabus stayed in England, of course, because he'd inherited the title —"

"Title?"

Libbie shrugged. "A minor one, with almost no money attached to it. That's why my grandfather came here. He did well as a merchant and even ended up sending money back to Barnabus, who'd drunk and gambled away his own money and his wife's small inheritance."

Sebastian thought of how untouchable Winters seemed to be. "With his title, Barnabus would have had connections in Parliament and some other high places. The same kind of connections that Winters has now. Barnabus' son, then? But why didn't you know him?"

"A son born on the wrong side of the blanket," Libbie explained. "Aunt Caroline remembers overhearing something about it when my grandfather and grandmother discussed it. Apparently, Grandfather agreed to send extra money for the boy and his mother. But Grandfather wanted the boy and his mother to come to the Colonies. He didn't trust Barnabus and also worried about his brother's notorious temper that was fueled by drinking. I remember those stories, myself, from Grandfather talking about his boyhood and our kin back in England."

260

Sebastian ran a hand through his hair, trying to process all of it. "But Winters took his commission in England. Did he grow up here, then?"

Libbie shook her head. "Barnabus said the boy and his mother had disappeared. Easy enough to believe, given that he was married, destitute, drunk and abusive. But according to Aunt Caroline, Grandfather doubted that the boy ever existed."

"But if he did exist, if he is Winters, why hold a grudge against your branch of the family tree?"

"Oh, I don't know." Libbie sighed. "Who knows what lies Barnabus might have told about us? Or maybe he told the truth but the boy believed that his rich American relatives were remiss for not rescuing him from what was probably a miserable existence."

A tear slid down her cheek. Sebastian wiped it away with his thumb.

"Don't do that," he whispered. "Don't feel sorry for the past. You weren't even there!"

"I know that." She nodded. "Of course I know that. But he's kin and he was wronged and now it has come back to haunt all of us." Libbie pressed her fingers over Sebastian's lips before he could protest. "I'm not defending him. He's evil and he has to be stopped. I just wish I could have stopped him before he got to my father and brother."

She wrapped her arms tightly around him and leaned her head against his chest. He hugged her, held her to him and tried to give her all the comfort and strength that she would need to face the battle in front of them, a battle against her own flesh and blood.

* * * * *

"Damn it, where are you?" Winters muttered.

He pressed his palm against the filthy windowpane and stared down at the courtyard.

More minutes ticked by and still there was no sign of her. First that cryptic note, now this waiting game. He picked up his riding crop and gripped it tightly. When she finally did arrive, she would regret having summoned him here.

A carriage, a finer sort than those that typically frequented the inn, rolled into the courtyard. He watched the familiar form alight from the carriage with the help of the burly hired driver. Louisa Barton walked to the tavern door, the driver preceding her, her bowed head covered by a broad-brimmed hat with a long veil. Winters lost himself for a moment in the matronly sway of her hips under her skirts.

He breathed deeply and relaxed his hold on the riding crop. She did have her virtues and he did have his needs, which she was always so eager to fulfill. By the time she tapped on the door, he had decided to allow her the chance to explain her behavior before whipping her.

As she entered slowly and shut the door, she glanced about the room. She studied his face for a scant moment before dropping her gaze to the floor. With shaking fingers, she plucked at her hatpins until she could pull the monstrosity from her head to reveal a tightly wound hair bun and a pale, frowning face.

"So?"

His single word made her flinch as though he had struck her. She cleared her throat.

"I have some bad news, terrible news, really."

"Well, you'd better get on with it, hadn't you? The gall you had, sending a messenger I've never laid eyes on before."

His fingers tightened around the crop again and her eyes widened.

"Norton was unavailable and I had to get the news to you."

He stared at her.

"Reginald, I hate to be the one to tell you this."

"Out with it!" He tapped the crop against his thigh for emphasis.

"The child."

A cold anger ran through his veins. "What do you mean, the child?"

"The MacRae girl. Her family has her."

"The child is back with the MacRaes?" Winters whirled away from Louisa and threw the crop against the wall.

Behind him, he could hear her whimper. He could smell her fear. Fear—the emotion he most liked to effect in her. It brought all her passion to the surface, made her flush and shake in his arms. He turned to see her flared nostrils, her heaving bosom.

"Undress."

Her hands quivered as they fluttered to her neck. "Wh-what?"

"Undress as you tell me more. Where is the family? Has Liberty returned to the nest? Is that bastard Cole with them?"

Her trembling fingers obeyed his command. Her voice cracked as she spoke. "Well, the family, um, they were going back to the farm. Th-they're being cautious but they thought they'd be able to defend their own land."

By the time she stopped speaking, her blouse, skirts and stays lay in a pile at her feet and she stood in her shift and petticoats. She bent to unlace her traveling boots.

"Continue," he said as he loosened his shirt.

She cleared her throat again and now her voice gained some strength. "Libbie is with them. I saw her, the night before they left. She thanked me for being there for her mother and aunt while she was away."

"How sweet. Now, off with those petticoats and shift. That's right, every last stitch of clothing."

He watched her expose her soft skin and ample curves. His loins tightened at the sight of her rosy nipples raised to hard points.

"What about Norton?" He stepped closer to her as he asked and to his delight, she took a quick step back.

"Gone. I don't know where. I haven't heard from him. That's why I had to hire a boy to bring you the message. But he'll keep his mouth shut. He—"

Winters grabbed her backside and pulled her roughly against him. "And Cole? Where is he now?"

She panted as he tightened his grip on her. "He took the MacRaes to their farm."

He stepped forward, forcing her to stumble backward and cling to him to stay on her feet. "So he's there with them now?"

She shook her head. "He was going to see that they arrived safely at the farm, then go back to the Indians. Something about weapons. Helping them train to fight with a lack of weapons."

He kissed her ferociously, his teeth catching her lip. "He's with the Occaneechi now?"

Now she was shaking. "Y-yes, that was it. Does that mean something to you?"

"Oh, yes." He nipped at her neck between the words. "It means that I've got them where I want them."

He'd send the regiment to the Indian village. Then he and his Fated Ones would go to the farm and get acquainted with Barnabus' family, his own flesh and blood.

Winters picked up his mistress and set her on the wide windowsill with her bare back pressed against the pane. "And now it's time to make my move."

He thrust himself into her and she yelped.

She held herself rigid. "No, Reginald. Anyone could see us through the window."

He licked her salty skin made slick from perspiration and thrust again, forcing her soft flesh to yield to his demands. "Doubtful anyone could see a thing through this grimy glass. And who gives a toss? No one here knows you. No one cares whether you leave this room alive or dead."

There it was in her eyes—the sheer terror he had longed to see. He ground his teeth and drove harder into her. In that moment, the pleasure of her trembling body was second only to the anticipation of destroying Barnabus' relatives.

* * * * *

As he awoke from his scant hour of sleep, Sebastian's eyes adjusted slowly to the sea of gray around him. Libbie had retired to her own room, as she did every morning at dawn before the rest of Jane's household was awake, but today she had left earlier. Perhaps it had something to do with her dreams. They'd kept her tossing and turning most of the night while Sebastian had watched her, wishing he could take away her fear and pain.

He swung his legs over the edge of the bed and stood up to stretch. Pulling his clothes from a chair by the bed, he washed and dressed quickly, hoping to catch Libbie walking through the halls or taking a cup of tea in the kitchen. As he passed the window, a sharp point of light in Jane's garden caught his eye.

The light swung in rhythm as it moved along the dark garden path, then disappeared into the woods. Sebastian stepped into his boots and pulled on his overcoat, then headed downstairs to the kitchen. His hand was on the back door when someone touched his shoulder.

"It's awfully early for a constitutional, dear boy," Jane said. She wore a frilly, filmy nightdress and robe and her hair was unbound and rumpled.

"It's awfully early to see you about," he answered.

She laughed. "I've not been abed. Or, at least, not to sleep."

Sebastian shook his head. "I suppose there's no hope that your husband concluded his business early and arrived home to share your bed last night."

"No, he did not. But when he does come home, I'll be here for him. I'm here for my husband any time he needs me. He just needs me so rarely."

"But young Matthew's needs are no doubt endless."

She laughed again, then frowned when she observed him more closely.

"Sebastian, where are you going at this hour?"

He shrugged. "Wherever Libbie has gone. Probably to the MacRae farm."

Jane touched his arm. "Winters will come soon, won't he?"

He nodded. "Not to worry. We'll be prepared for him."

"You'd better be. They need you—Libbie and the boy you saved."

Jane could not know how deeply her words cut him. Being reunited with Daniel, seeing his quick wit, his kindness, his protectiveness toward Annalee, had brought him more joy than he had thought possible. It only increased the happiness that he and Libbie shared. They loved each other, they loved Daniel. They were becoming a family. And still he had no answers about how long he could spend with them, how long he could stay in this world.

"Jane," he said quietly, "I love her. I've never felt anything like it. I—"

"Hold that thought, Sebastian. And stay right there. Don't leave, don't move!"

She disappeared for what felt like hours but was probably just a few minutes. When she returned, she held out her closed hand to him, then opened it to reveal his mother's sapphire brooch.

"You remember why she entrusted it to me?"

He smiled. "To wish you luck on your trip to America and on your marriage."

"The rest of it."

"To hold for me, until I met a woman I love, a woman I want to marry."

Jane smiled. "And then I am to make sure you give it to her. An heirloom from her future family."

Sebastian touched the carved gold edge of the pin, then picked it up and held it in his hand. "How did you know that I plan to marry her?"

Jane shrugged. "I have a way of knowing these things. Explain the story of the brooch to Libbie before you give it to her."

"Yes, of course."

"No, I mean before you even take it out of your pocket. Make sure she knows that I only wore it for luck and you only wore it that night of the dinner party for the same reason."

He furrowed his brow, thoroughly confused by Jane's odd command. "Or perhaps it was to hold my shirt closed. Why would any of it matter to Libbie?"

Jane rolled her eyes. "Men can be so obtuse. Really, Sebastian, you've never noticed how jealous she is of me?"

"Jealous? Libbie?" He shook his head. "Why on earth would she be jealous of you? I mean no offense, of course."

She scowled at him. "None taken, I think. But you and I were sharing secrets and exchanging jewelry and believe me, she noticed. She wasn't shooting daggers at me with her eyes for no reason at Gordon's and Caroline's parties."

So Libbie was not immune to possessiveness herself. The knowledge made him smile.

"Don't you dare!" Jane admonished him. "I would love a reason to plan a grand party and a wedding would be perfect. Don't you dare ruin it with your smugness!"

With that, she pushed Sebastian out the back door and shut it firmly behind him. He could not contain his laughter as he dropped the brooch into his pocket and headed down the garden path in search of the woman he loved.

* * * * *

Sebastian had to go on instinct, on the connection between them to find her. The world was a paler gray now that the sun had broken the horizon but she was much too far ahead of him to be seen. He followed her invisible trail, crossed a wide meadow, walked through dormant fields once tended by Sean MacRae's capable hands. He shrugged deeper into his coat, immune from the chill in the air but shivering from the company of all the ghosts tied to this land.

By the time he passed through yet another grove of trees and stood at the edge of a wide-open space, the light he'd seen from his window was no longer a pinpoint in the distance. It now blazed from the windows of a small cabin on the horizon. Minutes later, he knocked on the door. She opened it quickly, as though she had been expecting him. They stared awkwardly at each other for a long moment, then she held out her hand to him. He grasped it like it was a lifeline thrown to a drowning man.

"I'm sorry I didn't tell you where I was going," she said. "I just felt drawn here."

"And I felt drawn to you. I need to speak to you."

"We should get back. They'll be looking for us."

"Not yet. We have more than an hour until breakfast. This is important."

She hesitated, then stepped aside so he could enter the kitchen. The cabin was actually one large room with a cooking hearth and a table on one side and a bed on the other. She gestured for him to sit in a straight-back chair by the table, then sat beside him, holding his hands in hers.

"What is this place?" he asked. "I wasn't even sure I was still on MacRae property."

"You're not. This belongs to the Donnellys. Just Mr. Donnelly now."

"Do they live here? Did they?"

She stared down at the wide-planked floor. "Tom did, for a short time. He built this cabin about a year and a half ago, after the last harvest. The main farmhouse is just over the next hill. His father lives there and the field foreman and his wife. She's run the place since Mrs. Donnelly died years ago."

"That doesn't sound like a very crowded place for a farmhouse."

"It's not. It gets busier, of course, during the planting and harvesting, when all the field hands come. Still not that crowded, but I suppose Tom thought a new bride would want more privacy than that."

"I see." And he did. It made sense. They were neighbors, about the same age, their families knew each other well. "Did he get a chance to propose before he and Johnny left?"

She nodded. "I didn't accept, though. I loved him like a brother but not like," she looked up at him, "not like I loved you, even though we'd only met once and then I hated you."

He'd known she'd distrusted him but hated? That was the kind of word that a woman spurned used. So Jane was not at all off the mark.

He squeezed Libbie's hand. "Was he heartbroken?"

She shook her head. "I didn't reject him either. I didn't know what to say. If I'd have been honest, if I'd have said no, then he might still be alive."

A tear slid down her cheek. Sebastian wiped it away. "How can you say that? What could that possibly have to do with his death?"

"You know Winters is my kin and that he's out to destroy all of us. That's why he went after Papa and Johnny." She closed her eyes and pressed out more tears. "I saw them, saw their deaths," she whispered. "That day we came across the battle. I could feel them there, could feel what had happened to them."

Sebastian leaned closer to her. "They were there, love. I saw them—at least, Johnny and Tom. They were helping all those dead boys, all those lost and confused souls. They were good men, they still are. They're still doing important work."

She sniffed and wiped at her nose with her kerchief. "I believe you. That's exactly what both of them would do. But if Tom hadn't promised Papa and Johnny that he'd come back and take care of the MacRaes and marry me, Winters wouldn't have targeted him."

Sebastian pressed her soft hand against his cheek. "Libbie, you have to stop blaming yourself for other people's pain. This is not your fault. Tom died doing what he chose, saying what he meant. His soul is at peace, I swear to you."

She cried quietly for a few minutes, then wiped her eyes. "They're all at peace? Papa, Johnny and Tom?"

He nodded.

She laid her hand against his cheek. "But you're not. You can't be until—"

"Shh. Don't speak of it just now."

"But we must." Her cheeks flushed with color and her eyes shone. "I had questions for Mother Cloud Dancer and for Johnny. Questions about you, about your ultimate destiny. They couldn't answer them, but I can. Sebastian, Norton wasn't the only murderer who was out there the night we found Matthew. There was another dead soldier. Swift Bow and the braves assumed Norton did it. I know he didn't."

Uneasiness crept up Sebastian's spine. "Who, then?"

"Fated Ones. They were just out of sight, reaching out for me. They were desperate to be at peace but I couldn't help them. Winters has them somehow, controls them."

"Winters doesn't control me and he never will."

"I know that. I can feel it. He's part of your destiny and we have to destroy him. But I'm part of your destiny as well. Once we've beaten him, we can live in peace. Together."

There, she had said it. The same thing he had thought hundreds of times, the thing he wished could be true. But hearing the words out loud frightened him for reasons he couldn't explain.

"Libbie, we can't know that."

She sat up straight and stared at him defiantly. "We love each other. They've put us together, they've put us in Winters' path, they've made us follow this destiny. They have to let us have each other. They owe that to us."

An icy chill ran down his back. "Libbie, don't speak like that, please."

She opened her mouth as though to protest, then closed it and threw herself against him. He wrapped his arms around her. Touching her made the cold chill pass.

"What I do know is that we have this time," he whispered against her hair. "I want to make the most of it. I want to know that you are truly mine and I want you to know that you have my heart forever."

He pulled away from her but held her hands, then dropped to one knee. "Liberty Holling MacRae, will you —"

"Yes!" she threw her arms around his neck. "Yes, I'll marry you."

"It's customary to wait for the man to finish the question." He laughed as he hugged her back.

"Customary. Conventional. Ordinary. I don't want any of those things. I want you!"

"And I want you to have this." He reached into his pocket, then stopped, remembering Jane's warning. "But first, I have to explain something."

She sat quietly, eyebrows raised in curiosity.

Sebastian cleared his throat. "Well, it seems that my mother entrusted something to Jane after her wedding, when she was leaving to come to America. It was for luck on the journey. Then Jane was to keep it for me, if and when the time came."

"The time for what?"

"I'm getting to that. You see, it was given to my mother by the Coles when she married into the family. Because I'd been here so long, my mother believed I'd marry here. And she wanted my wife to have this."

He pulled out the brooch and placed it in her hand.

"Sebastian, it's beautiful! And familiar…"

"I wore it at Jane's insistence that night I met with Johnny after the dinner party. But Jane and I were not sharing jewelry and we were not sharing confidences. Well, we were but they had to do with the information I gave Johnny, not personal matters."

Libbie widened her eyes. "Jane? She's a part of all of your…"

"The things I do to save the lives of soldiers and civilians alike, yes. When she came to the Colonies and found out what I was up to, she took up the cause as well. More interesting than quilting, she always says."

Libbie nodded. "And a damn sight more important!"

She sat back and asked him to attach the brooch to her frock. As he did so, she touched his hair. "I wasn't concerned, you know, about you and Jane and the brooch."

He smiled but stayed bent over the pin so she wouldn't see it. "That's good to know."

"Well, not overly concerned, anyway."

When he looked at her, she was no longer smiling. He touched her cheek. She took a deep breath, as though drawing courage. "Sebastian, there's something else. It's about Daniel."

He held her hand tightly. "I thought we agreed. We need to take care of him. He needs us."

"Oh, yes! We will take care of him, I swear it. You're his…" She stopped, then continued more quietly. "You're his only link to his tribe and his mother."

"Thank you for taking him into your heart."

She hugged him. "How could I not love…" Another odd pause. "How could I not love Annalee's protector and new best friend?"

His kissed her hands, her cheeks, her lips. "Now, we just have to find the right time and place to tell your family about our plans."

Libbie sighed. "Yes. During some quiet time. We'll be very dignified. Given all the time we've spent together, I don't expect much resistance."

When she bent her head and kissed him, he pulled her hard against him. Their kisses grew frenzied, his need for her desperate. But the ghosts were not all exorcised, not yet.

She seemed to feel it too. "There's someplace else we can go. Follow me."

As they left the cottage behind them and crossed the wide field, the sun began its leisurely ascent.

"Don't worry," Libbie told Sebastian. "We'll be well hidden, even in bright daylight. And this secluded spot isn't far from the Whitmore estate. We'll spend fifteen minutes there, then be back in time for breakfast."

"Only a quarter of an hour? I was hoping for at least a half."

"Well, then we'll have to run all the way back to Jane's."

He pulled her into his arms and kissed her. "Then run we shall. It's my second favorite way to work up an appetite."

* * * * *

Libbie and Sebastian stopped outside the dining room doors. She checked her hairpins one more time as Sebastian straightened his waistcoat.

"There you are!" Jane came from behind them. She dropped her voice. "I've been looking everywhere for the two of you." She held up her hand when Sebastian tried to speak. "Do not insult me with your fabrications. I'm just pleased to see you both looking so well and happy this morning. But we've been holding breakfast for you."

"Is everyone here?" Libbie asked.

Jane nodded. "Everyone but the children. They ate some time ago and have gone off to the stables for an adventure with Greves."

"That's perfect," Sebastian said. "We need to discuss the Winters situation, make sure everyone is clear on their duties."

Libbie fought back a smile. "Just remember that they're not soldiers," she said as they followed Jane into the breakfast room.

Fox had returned from his trip with Mrs. Barton and rose to his feet to greet Sebastian and Libbie. Libbie bent to kiss her mother and aunt and took the empty seat between them. Sebastian sat between Fox and Matthew, directly across from Libbie. Their hostess took her seat at the head of the table, looking like a queen holding court.

After they had passed around platters of eggs, sausages and biscuits, Sebastian cleared his throat.

"I know that by now you're all aware of who and what Reginald Winters is," he started.

"Our relative." Anna shook her head. "It's awful."

Jane patted her hand. "It must be dreadful. But you mustn't blame yourselves. We don't choose our relatives, now do we?"

"But we can choose to shoot them," Aunt Caroline said.

"Ladies, please," Sebastian interrupted. "Now, we've set a plan in motion and soon Winters will arrive."

"We know you're luring him to the farm," Aunt Caroline said. "I just want to make sure that you're clear on the fact that I'll be there."

Anna sighed. "Really, Caroline, I do wish you would let the men handle such things."

"But Anna," Jane said, "I hear she's a crack shot. And I'm sure Sebastian will keep her safe."

"Well, Libbie plans to be there too," Anna told Jane.

Libbie had hoped they would not have to have this conversation again. "Mama, we've been through this. Aunt Caroline and I know what we're doing."

"Fox, has Sebastian told you that my stable man, Greves, has insisted on helping?" Jane said. "He'd do anything for the MacRaes. I wouldn't be able to stop him if I tried."

Sebastian cleared his throat loudly. "Could we perhaps discuss this in a more orderly fashion?"

"Perhaps Sebastian is right," Libbie agreed.

Fox shoveled a forkful of eggs into his mouth and swallowed it quickly, then lifted the fork in Aunt Caroline's direction. "Greves'll need a good rifle then, Miss Holling. Any chance you've brought any of yer wares with ya?"

Aunt Caroline actually blushed as she answered him. "Of course, Mr. Fox. Perhaps after breakfast you can join me at the carriage house and we'll have a look."

Under the table, Libbie nudged her mother's foot with her own and they smiled at each other. As Fox and Aunt Caroline discussed various types of gunpowders, Jane asked Matthew if he'd like to join her for some horseback riding that afternoon.

Across from Libbie, Sebastian covered his face with his hands, then looked up at her, beseeching her to help him get their attention.

She nodded and took a deep breath, then delicately cleared her throat. If it was their attention he wanted, it was their attention he would have.

"We're getting married," she said, speaking barely above a whisper.

Everyone in the room fell silent. Sebastian raised his eyebrows at her, then smiled and spoke quietly through clenched teeth. "What happened to finding a quiet and dignified moment?"

She smiled back at him. "Consider our audience."

And that quickly, the room was abuzz once more but this time, an extravagant wedding and a large party were the topics. Libbie could barely make out the details of the separate conversations but she did hear Jane rattling off a list of potential guests to her mother.

"It will be quite an undertaking," Jane said. "I do hope you'll allow me to help you with it, Anna."

"Of course," her mother agreed. "Just as soon as this mess with Winters is resolved, we'll start working on the details. And perhaps Libbie will have some ideas as well."

At that, Libbie held up her hand, once again halting the noise. She glanced at Sebastian, hoping that her next words would not be overly shocking to him. But it seemed that she had been waiting for one thing or another, usually something terrible, for the past year. She didn't want Winters to force her to wait any longer for the most important moment of her life.

"Tomorrow night," she said quietly. She looked into Sebastian's eyes and held his gaze. "If my fiancé is agreeable, I want to marry him tomorrow night."

Sebastian nodded, then stood and walked around the table to take her hand. He led her out of the dining room and closed the door behind them.

"I don't believe it," he whispered.

"I know. I can hardly believe it myself. Tomorrow."

He laughed. "I didn't mean that, love. I'd marry you in the next hour. I meant that you actually rendered them speechless!"

He bent toward her and kissed her as the silence on the other side of the door was shattered by all of their voices at once. He pulled her down the hallway with him, toward the door to the verandah. "Perhaps we should take a long walk. After all, we have some planning to do and just a day to do it."

She nodded and smiled as they stepped outside, then frowned. She had meant to tell him earlier, had actually tried to get out the words but hadn't succeeded. Now time was running out.

"What is it, Libbie?"

She took a deep breath and plunged into it. "There's something I need to know. Something about Sunflower."

He dropped his gaze to the floor. "I see. Yes, you would want to know such things before we marry. It was so long ago, so long before I met you."

Libbie shook her head. "I'm not jealous. I just need to know the truth. Were you involved with her? Before she met Wes, were you and Sunflower lovers?"

He nodded. "We were attracted to each other and we cared about each other. But the moment she met Wes, it was over for both of us."

"And her child was born early?"

"Yes. How did you know that—a vision? He was born in the seventh month. She and Wes had only been married six months at that point but it was of no consequence to anyone."

Libbie closed her eyes. "It is of great consequence. Daniel was not born early." She opened her eyes and looked directly into Sebastian's eyes. "He was born at full term."

He shook his head, disbelieving. "But that would mean... That would make..."

She nodded. "Yes, Sebastian. Daniel is your son."

Chapter Twenty-One

ॐ

"Just another minute," Libbie told Annalee as she secured small white flowers into her sister's hair. "There, now your hair looks just like mine!"

Aunt Caroline dabbed her eyes. "Anna, you have two beautiful daughters."

Anna waved her hands in front of her own face. "Stop that, Caroline, or you'll get me started again."

Libbie picked up her sapphire brooch. Anna took it from her hands.

"Let me do that, sweetheart." Anna fumbled with the clasp but finally attached it to the supple leather of the white dress Libbie wore. "I still don't understand how this Cloud Dancer woman knew she should send along wedding clothes with those braves who brought you here."

Libbie took a steadying breath, then spoke in a whisper. "Because she has a gift, Mama. The same gift I have."

Anna nodded. "That explains it. I'm glad that you found each other and she has taught you how to use it. I'm grateful to her for teaching you that it's a gift. Your father and I didn't understand it. We just worried about you so."

Aunt Caroline cleared her throat. "It's almost sunset, dear. Time for Fox to walk you down the aisle."

"Wait one minute!" Jane appeared in the doorway of the small room in the back of the chapel where the women had gathered. "Is there time for a good wish?"

Libbie smiled at her. "Of course, Jane. Come in."

Jane stepped into the room. "Thank you, my dear. But I haven't come alone. I believe there is one loved one still missing. And now I've brought her to you." Maggie stepped into the room and Libbie launched herself into her friend's open arms.

"Maggie, you got my note! I'm so glad you came."

Maggie squeezed her tightly. "I wouldn't miss it for the world. I'm just glad you invited me, after the terrible way I behaved toward Sebastian in Charlottesville."

"None of that matters now. And as far as we are all concerned, you are a part of this family. You belong here." Libbie took her friend's hands. "You look wonderful. The color has come back into your cheeks."

"And you are absolutely glowing. I now know how wrong I was. I can see how much you love him, how happy he makes you." She dropped her voice to a whisper. "But your note was so cryptic. There's something else going on."

"We won't discuss it," Libbie said. "Not here, not today. Come stay with us at Lady Jane's house. We'll explain everything tomorrow. I need you, Maggie."

"Anything for you, you know that."

They hugged again, then Aunt Caroline shooed Jane, Maggie and Annalee out of the room and followed them.

Now alone with Libbie, Anna reached up and touched one of her hairpins. "These pink and green pins are pretty but I have blue ones that would have matched your brooch better."

Libbie shook her head. "These are special."

"Well, then, perhaps you would wear these." Anna pulled a pair of stunning blue sapphire earrings out of her pocket.

Tears flooded Libbie's eyes. "Mama, the earrings Papa gave you on your wedding day. They're even more beautiful than I remembered."

"And they're yours. But you'll have to let Annalee wear them at her wedding when the time comes." Anna smiled but looked wistful.

"I miss him too, Mama."

Anna nodded. A few tears spilled onto her cheeks. "I wish he could be here." She hugged Libbie. "He would have so loved to be with you on this day."

Libbie closed her eyes and hugged her mother tightly. "He is, Mama. And Johnny too. In their own way, Papa and Johnny are both with us today."

* * * * *

Sebastian could not have imagined any sight more beautiful. As his bride walked down the narrow aisle of the small chapel to join him at the altar, a hard lump of emotion caught in his throat. It was almost too much to believe that just over a year ago he had not yet even met this woman who now had changed his life, in fact had restored it. Back then he'd had nothing but gray days and a bleak future of hatred and vengeance. But today was for love. The love of a man for a woman. The love of a woman for a man. The love of two people for the child who they would officially claim as their own.

Fox, clean-shaven and dressed in a suit of Lord Whitmore's that Caroline had chosen for him, cut a dashing figure as he escorted Libbie to Sebastian, then bent nervously to kiss her cheek. He took his place beside Matthew and Jane, in the pew in front of Greves and Effie, on Sebastian's side of the aisle. The MacRaes and Maggie sat nearer to Libbie. All eyes were upon the couple as Sebastian took Libbie's hands in his.

They stared into each other's eyes as the reverend read the scriptures and had them recite the vows. The minister said a prayer from the Bible. Libbie recited a blessing in Occaneechi. Then the reverend asked Daniel to join them.

Libbie and Sebastian each took one of the child's hands. Daniel's fingers wrapped around Sebastian's hand, closing around his heart. He could barely fight back the tears as he promised the boy that he would love him, protect him and rear him. Libbie made the same promises, then bent to give Daniel a kiss on the cheek.

"We're a family now," the boy said solemnly to her.

Libbie could not hide her tears. "Yes, Daniel. Now and forever."

When the boy looked up at Sebastian, he knelt down and took the child in a tight embrace.

"I love you, Daniel," he whispered.

"I love you," Daniel whispered back to him.

Sebastian picked up the boy and encompassed Libbie in the embrace. The reverend pronounced them man and wife and son and the small gathering of loved ones cheered when Sebastian touched his lips to Libbie's. In that moment, he could smell the candle wax, see her green eyes and blue brooch, feel Daniel's warm arm wrapped around his neck. His heart held more love than he had ever imagined possible. It was heaven, pure heaven, or at least the closest thing to it that Sebastian would ever know.

* * * * *

"I thought we would never make our escape from Jane's little dinner party," Sebastian said.

All that had been "little" about the affair had been the guest list. They'd had a six-course meal, served by liveried servants in the most opulent of the Whitmores' dining rooms, a room that was dripping with luxurious linens and sparkling chandeliers.

Now, finally, Libbie clutched Sebastian's hand as he led her up a small staircase and through a darkened corridor, to an unused wing in the Whitmore house. When he pushed open one of the doors lining the passageway, golden light flooded over them. They stepped into a room flickering with a warm glow from dozens of candelabras placed on every dresser, bedside table and vanity. Libbie brushed her hand across the velvet curtains that shrouded the four-post bed. Behind her,

281

the door clicked shut, then Sebastian's arms wrapped around her.

She turned toward him, still caught in his embrace, and tilted her face up to receive his kisses. They came slowly and softly to her lips.

"It's so beautiful," she whispered. "How did you manage it?"

He stopped kissing her and laughed. "Well, I must admit I had some help."

She reached up to pull his head down and kiss him again but he grasped her wrists and pressed his lips to her hands. "There's more," he whispered. "Come with me."

There was an anteroom Libbie had not noticed. More candelabras were arranged in a circle around the focal point of the room—a large porcelain tub with golden clawed feet jutting from the bottom and thick wisps of steam rising from the top. The candlelight bounced off a looking glass positioned in the corner and made the room look surreal, dreamlike.

Libbie took off her earrings and brooch and carefully laid them aside. From behind her, Sebastian gathered the hem of her buckskin wedding dress and lifted it and her shift over her head, then brushed his hands over her exposed back. Her skin tingled in the wake of his touch.

"No petticoats," he whispered as he turned her around to face him, kneading her shoulders as he surveyed her naked form. "Come. Get into your bath."

She obeyed, sinking one foot then the other into the steaming depths. She slid into the tub and closed her eyes, feeling breathless as the hot water embraced her. When she lifted her eyelids just enough to make out Sebastian's shape, he was shirtless. She closed her eyes again and waited to feel him climb into the tub beside her.

Instead, she felt his strong, sure fingers removing her hairpins, caressing her scalp. Before she could ask him to join her, he poured water over her hair, then rubbed soap into it.

She sighed and leaned back. His hands were gentle but firm and under his ministrations, the rest of the world melted away. After he rinsed her hair slowly, thoroughly, lovingly, he moved on to her neck and back. He covered every inch of her skin with sudsy caresses, sending tremors of delight into the core of her being. She moaned softly and reached her hands over her head to run her fingers through his thick, loose hair.

He kissed the nape of her neck, then nibbled her ear. "I have something to confess," he whispered. The words lifted her slightly from her pleasurable trance and she nodded for him to continue. "I have loved every moment of this day but I love this moment the most. Do you think me a cad for it?"

She giggled. "Absolutely. But I'm more concerned that perhaps you're a tease. Tell me, Mr. Cole, do you ever intend to join me in this tub?"

"Why, Mrs. Cole, I thought you'd never ask!"

His hands fell away from her and she heard the remainder of his clothes drop on the floor. She kept her eyes tightly shut and anticipated the feel of his hard body on top of hers. The water swirled and rose around her first. Then she could feel him — muscle and skin pressing on her. With eyes still closed, she wrapped her arms around his back and pulled him down toward her while raising her hips to meet his. Her own cries of pleasure flooded her ears as he plunged deep inside her. Water flowed up over her shoulders and splashed onto the floor.

He held himself taut. "Be still, my love," he whispered. "Otherwise, we'll have gallons of water to sop up."

"I don't care," she groaned. "All I care about is the feeling of you."

She did as he instructed, though. He grasped her buttocks and rocked her slowly against him. The water caressed her breasts as it flowed over her and lapped against the sides of the tub. A pleasure so intense that it bordered on pain rose inside her. The urge to move quickly and recklessly was nearly undeniable but she forced herself to follow Sebastian's gentle lead.

He moved with delightfully excruciating restraint until she could barely breathe. When she was sure that she could not endure the exquisite torture a moment more, her ecstasy rose to a fevered pitch and consumed her. She was no longer aware of where she was or what was happening around her, she was connected to nothing in the world except Sebastian. She clung to him, screaming his name, feeling him engorge and pulse inside her.

Gradually, she became aware of her surroundings again. Candles sizzled and sputtered as they tried to burn away the water droplets that had landed on them. One of Libbie's arms was slung over Sebastian's neck, the other floated on top of the cooling water.

"I love you," he whispered.

"I love you too." She smiled with the joy of saying the words to the man who was now her husband, but knew neither one of them would have needed to speak them. Their love was all around them, as if it were its own entity. With every fiber of her being, she loved this man and felt him loving her back.

Chapter Twenty-Two

ॐ

Libbie jolted out of her trance. Her heart pounding, her mouth dry, she looked around the room, hoping to clear her head. There was a blazing fire in the hearth, a sturdy divan under her, a fluffy white pillow supporting her head. She was in Jane's drawing room and the instant she sat up, Sebastian was by her side.

She reached for his hand. "The battle will start soon. The scouts have spotted Winters' men. Mother Cloud Dancer is consulting with Red Wolf and Soaring Eagle now."

"They're prepared, love, prepared as they'll ever be. They have Beaulieu's guns and the element of surprise."

She frowned. "And we'll surprise Winters and his Fated Ones. But what if it isn't enough? The things that man's twisted mind reveals. Even his own mistress — ex-mistress — fears him. I don't understand why she ever helped him. Whatever he paid her couldn't have been worth it."

Sebastian kissed Libbie's hand. "Maybe it was worth it at first. That and the adventure of it all. By the time she realized just how dangerous he truly is, she was probably in over her head."

"And terrified. And the way he relished her terror..." Libbie shivered. "God help me, I know that monster's deepest, darkest thoughts. I wanted to deny it but..."

Sebastian knelt in front of the divan and held her hands. "You are not him. Kin or no, you are nothing like him."

She nodded toward the hearth. "Stoke the fire."

"Darling, no more tonight. You've already done so much."

She laid a hand on his cheek. "Please Sebastian. We have to know where he is, how much time we have."

Sebastian did as she asked. Libbie stared into the flames.

Mother Cloud Dancer and the chiefs stood in front of her. Scott and Grayhorse were there, as well as the braves, preparing their guns, listening to the chiefs' instructions. Even Pierre was in their midst, preparing a weapon, swearing his allegiance to the tribe. Their anxiety was high but so was their faith in their ability to defeat the British battalion that would be upon them in a matter of hours. Mother nodded gravely at Libbie, signaling that they were ready.

Libbie blinked hard and squinted into the depths of the flames. The picture of the warriors faded but nothing replaced it. Several minutes passed. She was about to quit the exhausting task when one flame sparked and grew. She held her breath and waited. And there in the center of the fire emerged the outline of Reginald Winters. She focused on it, her mind tumbling into his.

He stood beside his horse. A cool damp breeze swirled around him. He peered into the soft light that comes just before dawn. Hours of hard riding had left his back and legs stiff and his scar ached, pulled by his dry skin after long exposure to the wind. But he relished every ache and pain, intent on the knowledge that it brought him closer to his prey. He turned, stared directly at Libbie, blew her a kiss. Hot, hard anger slammed into her, forced her to her knees.

Libbie jolted out of the vision. She was on the floor with Sebastian kneeling beside her, looking very worried.

"You screamed like you were in pain."

"He felt me," she managed to whisper. "Winters felt me. I don't think he felt my thoughts like I felt his but he knew the connection was there."

"And he was able to cause you pain?"

She furrowed her brow. "Not exactly. I just felt his rage and hatred so completely and I knew all his thoughts in that one second." She closed her eyes and shook her head, trying to order the foreign thoughts. "Two days. He's two days from the farm." She smiled. "May first is two weeks away but he'll be here in two days. We've done it. We've changed everything."

Sebastian smiled too. "You've done it. You've drawn him to you, the fly to the spider."

"Yes, well, I wish I were a venomous one. It would be one more advantage over him."

"Did you learn anything else?"

She nodded. "He doesn't plan to go back to the army. When he's done here, he'll go west and live off his spoils. His Fated Ones will go with him, to serve him for the rest of his life."

Sebastian exhaled slowly but did not speak.

"And one last thing," she said. "He's furious that Norton's still alive—he'd ordered his Fated Ones to kill him but we saved Matthew and apparently Norton as well." She shook her head. "Norton crossed him but I don't know why or how. That's all I can find out tonight."

"You've done well, my love. Just Winters and his Fated Ones. Three of them and six of us. And the element of surprise. I like those odds," he pressed his finger to her lips, "venom or no venom."

He looked away from her and stared into the fire. "As your husband, I could order you to stay here, with your family."

She crossed her arms in front of her. "You could try."

He smiled and took her hand. "Yes. And I would fail. I know that you're not one to take orders. You never were. And I married you despite it."

Now she smiled too.

"But you cannot blame a husband for wanting to keep his wife, whom he loves more than life, safe."

She touched hiss face, kissed his cheek. "We both know I can't stay out of this fight. It's my destiny too."

* * * * *

The campfire sputtered in front of him but still Winters could not keep warm. The overcast day would no doubt give way to a rain-soaked night. Finding it impossible to sleep more than a few hours, he waited impatiently in the mist for the sun to set. The Fated Ones hovered nearby. They never seemed to sleep, barely ate and traveled poorly in daylight hours. Despite their fervent efforts to obey his every command, the pathetic beasts' near-death states imposed great limitations on them and ultimately on him.

His battalion, which was at that very moment overwhelming the Occaneechi, had no such limitations. The soldiers would do what he had told them to do, surprise the tribe, kill them all, burn their village and hold Sebastian Cole captive until Winters arrived with Liberty in tow.

Winters shifted to his haunches, then rose to his feet and found a suitable spot to use as a privy. As he made his way back to the encampment, a distant noise attracted his attention. It was the sound of movement, perhaps of animals, perhaps of men. But it was drawing closer. He gestured to the Fated Ones to be on alert, then mounted his horse and moved cautiously into the trees.

For several minutes, he quietly maneuvered his mount, tracking the intruder, closing in on it. When he finally came upon it, his breath quickened. He made out the image of the horse first, then moved closer to see the man.

"Norton."

The rider jumped, jerked his head around and stared, slack-jawed, at Winters.

"Colonel, what're ye thinkin'? It's me, all right, an' on my way ta find ye at the fort. It's a piece o' luck, ain't it, that I ran across ye out 'ere."

"Yes, indeed. Bad luck for you but good luck for me."

"What say ye, Colonel? I don't understand."

Winters smiled and spoke calmly. "Oh but I do. Did you really think I wouldn't notice the missing deeds and bank notes? No one steals from me, Norton."

Color drained from Norton's face. "Oh, no sir, it ain't what yer thinkin'. I didn't mean no harm."

Winters snarled, then prodded his horse toward Norton's beast, which reared up in surprise. Norton lost his hold and tumbled to the ground with a loud grunt. A quick snap of Winters' crop against the riderless horse's flank sent her crashing into the dense forest.

"You don't know the meaning of the word honest, Norton. It was the reason I counted on you so much." He hopped off his own mount and strode toward the prone man. "And the reason I trusted you so little."

Norton pushed himself up to a sitting position. "Bloody jackass, tryin' to break me neck, are ye? I've half a mind to keep me information about yer pretty little cousin to meself."

"What you have is half a mind and even that has become a liability to me." Winters reached under his cape and withdrew his pistol. He drew back the gun and slammed the barrel into Norton's face. The man shrieked and crumbled to the ground.

"Come join me, my pets," Winters said quietly. In an instant his Fated Ones were at his side. "Bind him with ropes from my saddlebag. Tie one around his neck and give the other end to me."

The mist was retreating after all and the moon was cresting the horizon, infusing the beings with strength and energy. They made quick work of obeying Winters' orders. He smiled as the mute one handed him the rope tied to Norton's neck. Winters swung up into the saddle and tied the rope tightly to it.

"You've had your fun," he told his minions. "Now go pack up our camp while I have mine."

The Indians faded into the trees. Winters looked over his shoulder at Norton, lying helplessly bound on the ground. Norton clawed desperately at the noose to free his crushed windpipe, to breathe again. But his face turned crimson and his eyes bugged out when his efforts proved futile.

"I see we need to have our fun before you lose consciousness." Winters laughed as he kicked his horse's sides and sent the beast crashing through the underbrush.

Norton gurgled more loudly as the horse bolted through the forest, dragging him in its wake. A minute later, the noise ended abruptly. Winters glanced back once but the gruesome sight of ripped flesh hanging from nearly exposed bone was too distasteful for him to abide. Instead, he focused on the rocky path in front of him and spurred the beast to a full gallop.

After several minutes, Winters pulled the horse to a stop. Without another look behind him, he cut the rope from his saddle.

"Such a pity," he said out loud. "You were useful to me on more than one occasion, old boy. But no one crosses Reginald Winters and lives to tell about it."

Chapter Twenty-Three

❧

Winters' underlings flanked him as he sat astride his horse on the outskirts of the MacRae property.

Soon, my dear, soon we shall be together, he said silently to himself and for a fleeting second believed that she had heard it. He held his breath, waited. The very wind in the trees seemed to stop, as if the earth too, held its breath in anticipation of their reunion.

And then she was there, just as she should be. She was so far away that the figure could have been anyone but he knew it was Liberty. She was alone, surveying the property, perhaps considering the spring planting. *Don't trouble yourself with it, my dear. You won't be here to see it.*

She changed direction and the trees obscured his view of her. He shifted on his mount, repositioned himself to see her better but to no avail. As quickly as she had appeared, she was gone.

* * * * *

Libbie squirmed through the black tunnel that led from the dried-up well to a trap door under the barn. It had been an escape route decades earlier, when Indian attacks on farmers had been rampant in the area. Ghosts seemed to haunt the tunnel, seemed to reach out with their clammy hands to claw at her. But she did not fear them. She understood them. They were awaiting justice. They had come with Winters, these spirits of all the innocents he and his men had murdered.

The essence of Winters' Fated Ones followed her as well. They could feel her, could follow her like bloodhounds following a scent. She clenched her fists and took deep breaths, forcibly severing the connection they had made with her.

Libbie popped up out of the hidden trap door and stepped into the barn. She pulled her pistol from her boot and crossed to the open barn doors, waiting for the next signal from Fox or Matthew. It had been Fox's birdcall that had alerted her that Winters was there and had spotted her so that she wouldn't have to connect with his mind and risk exposing their plan. Now they would use their coded signals to track him.

Libbie leaned against the wall just inside the barn, her pistol dangling in her slack hand as she tried to catch her breath. The effort of keeping Winters' Fated Ones at bay was already draining her and their strength would only increase as the night deepened. Dusk was gathering and the moon was a pale shadow on the horizon. Libbie reached out to Sebastian, begged him to help her. She felt a caress up her spine like he had run his fingers over her. Energy flooded her body and calmed her racing heart and strained breathing.

With her strength restored, Libbie hid herself at the edge of the open barn door and braced her pistol in front of her. She watched the farmhouse. The kitchen window shade was raised. It was Aunt Caroline's assurance that inside the house, she and Greves were armed and ready. Satisfied that everyone was in position, Libbie opened her mind to Winters. She strained her eyes and her mind so as not to miss the subtlest indications of Winters' thoughts and movements. He was close now, so close. And he had found the tunnel. She could feel him lift his body inside the well, knew he was feeling the stones to find the one that moved.

All went black. Realizing she had squeezed her eyes shut, she now opened them and desperately scanned the property. Where was he? What had happened? What had jarred Winters so completely that it had broken her connection to him? She narrowed her eyes, focused her mind but still nothing. Suddenly a small spark, a connection. But not to Winters. To one of his Fated Ones, climbing quickly through the tunnel. Winters had managed some trick of the mind. He had a power of his own and knew how to use it against her.

Libbie agonized over her next move. If she stayed put, Winters' minion would be upon her any minute and given the brightening moon, she wouldn't stand a chance against him. If she slipped out of the barn without knowing where Winters was, she was an easy target. As she weighed her unappealing options, a small movement on the periphery of her vision caught her attention.

She tentatively stepped forward, focused her mind on Winters again and felt the faintest connection. She knew he believed all of this was meant to be. He'd just wanted her but then the boy had been there, wandering alone, looking for her.

Libbie gasped when Winters came into full view, slipped out of a copse of trees, then ducked into the high, dead corn stalks on the edge of one of the fallow fields. He was headed in the direction of Donnelly land. And with him, tucked under his arm, spindly legs dragging uselessly behind him, was Daniel.

* * * * *

Sebastian crouched on the high branch of an oak tree on the hill by the meadow, every fiber of his being intent on his mission. For so long he had waited for this moment and those that were soon to follow—moments when he finally made Reginald Winters answer for what he had done to Sunflower, Wes, Daniel. And now Libbie and her family. If only he had stopped that monster sooner, they never would have suffered at his hands.

Sebastian saw one of Winters' underlings close to the well. Libbie called out to Sebastian, needed his strength. He answered her call, using the channel she had opened between them to send love and energy to her. Just as he saw the slightest shadow in the barn that indicated that Libbie was in position, he saw the Fated One climb into the well. Sebastian couldn't understand how he'd figured it out, how he'd know where she had gone but he knew that even with her pistol Libbie couldn't hold him off for long by herself.

Sebastian leapt down from the tree, landed hard and was on his feet in seconds. Horse hooves pounded in the distance. Fox whistled two separate signals—he had fired and had hit his mark. Sebastian was at the edge of the trees, ready to dash out into the open and get to the barn, when he felt an overwhelming angst. It was the same feeling that had gripped him nearly a year earlier in Jane's garden. It was another Fated One and the connection was so great that the being seemed to have taken over not only Sebastian's mind but his body as well. He struggled to propel himself forward but fell to his knees instead.

Another gunshot and a puff of smoke rose out of the woods. Sebastian caught sight of a movement in the brush several hundred yards away. It was the Fated One that he had felt. He looked like a man, of a sort but one who was impossibly gaunt with long straggly hair and dark, dead eyes, who made Sebastian think more of a beast than a man. The Fated One was headed straight for him. With shaking hands, Sebastian gripped his rifle and sat back on his haunches. He fired a round into Winters' Fated One and the being sank to the ground. It broke the hold the being had on Sebastian. Sebastian felt his strength return and he sprang to his feet.

Seconds later, the Fated One was struggling to his feet and pulling on Sebastian again, draining him. It was then that Sebastian saw the two other gunshots that had torn into the Fated One's back. While bullets couldn't kill Sebastian, he still had enough humanity to feel all their other effects. This Fated One was too far removed from his human form to be affected the same way. The bullets were slowing his progress but it would take more rounds than Sebastian had time to fire to repel the being.

Sebastian pictured Libbie, crouched in the barn fending off the other Fated One. Her pistols and Aunt Caroline's shotgun wouldn't protect them from these monsters. Rage gripped Sebastian. The force of the emotion sent Winters' minion stumbling backward and broke the connection between them. Fox and Matthew galloped into view, guns blazing. Sebastian had to trust them to hold off the wounded Fated One as he dashed out into the open, headed for the barn and Liberty.

A second shot had rung out and then a third. *So, dear cousin, it was all a ruse, a trap. Norton had something to tell me after all.* With his hand clamped tightly over the child's mouth, Winters dragged Daniel through the grass, into the trees and finally to the edge of a clearing. He stopped and listened, straining to hear the slightest footfall or rustling leaf that would reveal the presence of one of his enemies. The sounds of the battle Liberty's protectors were mounting were far away from him.

"Come to me, dear Liberty," he said out loud as he dragged Daniel across the clearing toward the cottage.

Inside the cabin, he tied Daniel to a chair and gagged him. "No need to draw anyone else's attention," he said to the boy. He stared out the window. "Just hers. I know you'll be here, dear cousin. I sense your thoughts as clearly as you sense mine."

He smiled. In a matter of minutes, she would be his.

Emboldened by necessity, Libbie stepped outside and pressed her back against the side of the barn, still gripping her pistol. She inched around it, using her eyes to search for enemies, employing her mind to seek out Winters. She sneaked around the front of the house, then dashed toward the high stalks that had swallowed Winters and Daniel.

A quick movement to her right drew her attention. She threw herself to the ground as a bullet whizzed over her head. She heard it hit flesh and bone and looked behind her to see a dirty, grisly-looking Indian in torn buckskins sink to the ground. She risked a quick connection to his mind and realized that Aunt Caroline's shotgun blast had merely slowed him down. Still, if she and Greves could manage a continuous onslaught, Libbie could outrun him.

Libbie jumped to her feet and ran around the back of the house, shouting through the open windows. "Aunt Caroline, keep shooting him! Don't stop, no matter what!"

Libbie heard another shotgun blast and then another as she streaked across the open field and slipped between the cornstalks. She tried to reload her pistol as she went. The task proved impossible, so she flung the gun to the ground and grabbed the knife she wore at her waist as she darted through the stalks.

As she ran, she wondered where Sebastian was, prayed he was safe. But she would have to trust him to protect himself. She had to save his son.

Chapter Twenty-Four

฿ා

Gunsmoke hovered over the farm. The second Fated One, riddled with gunshot wounds, lay still on the ground. Sebastian could feel him, could feel the slightest heartbeat in his chest. In the distance, Fox and Matthew were still shooting at Winters' other underling, whom Sebastian could feel was in nearly the same state.

Sebastian ran to the barn and came to a dead stop in the doorway. He leaned against the frame, his worst fear realized. She was gone.

She came to him, as he knew she would. Winters could feel the hard ground under her feet, the cold air slapping her cheeks. *Come to me*, he said over and over, silently, not needing to form the words with his lips, knowing she heard him just the same.

He trained his pistol on the boy's head the moment he heard her footsteps on the front porch. She stepped into the house blade first, anger and determination evident on her beautiful face.

"Drop the knife, my sweet," he told her. "And remove the other one from your boot. Good. Now have a seat in that chair with your hands behind you."

He yanked hard on the ropes that he wrapped around her wrists, leaving crisp red lines on the delicate white skin. He walked in front of his two tied prisoners, his pistol once more aimed at the boy and wondered if he should kill him.

Libbie's gasp assured him that she was still attuned to his thoughts. He smiled, pleased with the decision that came so clearly to him. Before, there had been the issue of letting the boy live until he was of age to sign over his tribe's lands. Winters could not swoop in and lay claim to it as he had done to so many other tribes' properties. Gordon had been watching too closely, would demand an investigation and might learn far too much. But now, that land meant nothing to him. All that mattered was that the centerpiece of his vengeance was in place, tied in front of him with no chance of escape and soon his newest minion would be in his grasp.

"Sebastian won't let you out of here alive." Her voice was steady.

Winters stroked her cheek. Her flesh was soft under his fingertips. She jerked her head away.

"Ah, yes. Cole. That was a nasty trick you played on me, making me believe the MacRae women were alone on the farm." He grinned and stroked the scar on his chin. "It's enough to make a cousin proud."

He turned up the lantern on the table. The light bounced off the angles of her face. She was breathtaking. It was so fortunate he had not killed her in his fort. Now she and her lover would both belong to him for as long as he saw fit.

"Hmph. Cousin." She scowled as she said the word. "You've gone to a lot of trouble to avenge some sort of imagined slight from my grandfather." She leveled another calm gaze at him.

Her coolness infuriated him. He grabbed the arms of her chair and leaned into her face. "Imagined slight? Your grandfather's selfish refusal to help us when we were in dire straits killed my mother!"

Her jaw dropped. "Refusal? Is that what Barnabus told you? He was a liar, don't you understand? Grandfather sent money—"

"Stop it! I will not listen to your excuses! My mother died in destitution and is buried in a pauper's common grave. Your grandfather could have changed all of that. He could have changed my life!"

"He would have, if Barnabus had given him the chance."

He shook his head. "He would have nothing to do with his brother's bastard son. I heard Barnabus explain it all to my mother. A few months later, she was dead and I was left to fend for myself."

She inched her chair backward. "How can you blame my family for—"

"My family!" Winters shouted. "My only hope. My mother's only chance. Lost to us."

"Barnabus did this to you. You should have confronted him while he still lived."

"Stop it!" He slammed his fist against the table. "If you want the boy to live, don't say that cursed name! With her dying breath she made me swear that I wouldn't go after him, that I wouldn't bring him shame. But now he's dead and it's time for the rest of the Hollings to pay."

"Please don't hurt the child," she whispered. "He's not a Holling."

He looked at the boy, who stared back defiantly. Winters could almost respect that. "I know exactly who he is." He looked at Liberty again. "And I have very special plans for all of you."

"Special plans? You've been planning to kill me since the moment you knew I existed."

He knelt in front of her. "That was very short-sighted of me. Please forgive me my lack of imagination." He smiled when she looked away from him, unable to hold his gaze. "I've come up with something much more interesting for you."

He was disappointed that her face did not register fear. But they would have many months together. She would learn to cower in his presence. And then he would want her even more than he did at this moment.

"You will go away with me," he continued. "You will be my woman, my servant, my whore and anything else I want you to be. And your lover, your squaw-man, will have a front row seat for all of it. He will be my slave, my obedient minion. I will own his soul and I will break his spirit again and again. How do you think he'll react the first time I order him to watch me make love to you?"

She swallowed hard and glanced around the room. Perhaps he had managed to stir fear in her after all. He laughed. She could look for a means of escape as much as she wanted. It would do her no good this time.

Out of the corner of her eye, Libbie saw Daniel's fingers furiously working the ropes that bound his wrists. She averted her thoughts and hoped Winters did not realize what the boy was doing.

"You won't get Sebastian," she declared. "I won't let him come here to confront you."

"You can't stop him, lovey. It's his destiny. And when he chooses to save you and the boy, when he sacrifices his mission for his earthly ties, he will forfeit his soul to me, just like those who went before him."

Libbie held Winters' gaze as the ropes that had bound Daniel dropped to the floor. With a quick bend at her hips, she drew her knees toward her chest and kicked at Winters. Her feet landed firmly in his abdomen, knocking him to the ground.

"Run, Daniel!" she cried.

But the boy's eyes were glazed and unfocused. He looked at her, finally seeming to register her presence.

"To the door, Daniel. Unlatch it and run!"

He nodded, turned swiftly, bumped the table. The lantern crashed to the ground, spewing oil and sparks over the rough floor planks. Winters, oblivious to the threat, rolled right into the mess and grabbed Daniel, then jumped to his feet.

Winters saw the flames through Libbie's eyes just as he felt intense heat on his legs. With great effort, he turned to see flames leaping out of the smashed lantern and engulfing his foot. The fire's tongue licked at him with sharp, unbearable strokes. He held the boy with one hand and slapped at the flames with the other but was rewarded only with a burning sleeve and a blistered palm.

Libbie screamed with the pain that bit into his flesh. Her own skin remained untouched by the flames but her foot and lower leg felt seared. Daniel reached for her, trying to break free of Winters' grasp. She fought Winters' mind, tried to replace his thoughts with her own, demanded he release the boy. But his hatred overwhelmed her.

She heard Winters' silent entreaty to his minions. And then they were there, one holding Daniel's arms, the other gripping Libbie's throat. In that moment she knew Winters' full plan. He would force Sebastian to choose his own second death at Winters' hands in order to save Libbie and Daniel.

* * * * *

"Lieutenant! Lieutenant!"

"Matthew, where is she?" Sebastian ran into the barnyard and nearly collided with the young man, who had been patrolling the farm's perimeter in case Winters had managed to hide any surprises from them.

Matthew was panting. Blood oozed from a wound on his leg. Sweat dripped down the sides of his face, despite the cool, damp air. "I spotted…" He stopped to suck in air.

"Libbie? Winters? Where are they?" He grabbed Matthew's shoulders. "Answer me, damn it!"

Matthew pointed toward the fields.

"You saw her there? Or Winters?"

Caroline and Greves stepped out of the house.

"He's got her," Sebastian said softly.

Caroline inhaled sharply, then looked in the direction that Matthew indicated. "Our girl. You have to find her, Sebastian."

Sebastian took off toward the fields with no clear idea of where he was going. As he ran, he silently called to Libbie, begged her to complete the connection between them so that he could sense her. He felt her for a moment—felt her fear. But it was not for herself, it was for Daniel. Winters had them both. The connection ended.

Sebastian ran between the dead cornstalks in one of the fields and dropped to his knees. He tried to slow his breathing, tried to summon Sunflower.

"Our son," he murmured. "Help me find our son!"

"Come with me."

Wes stood in front of him, his hand outstretched. Sebastian touched the spectral hand, felt the cold mist as it wrapped around his own hand and hauled him to his feet.

"But why?" Sebastian asked as they ran. "Why did you come?"

"To be sure," Wes answered.

"Sure of what?"

"Sure that you can forgive me. Sunflower told me the truth about Daniel just after his birth. But I loved them both and you were so happy for us. It was selfish of me."

"It doesn't matter." Tears ran down Sebastian's face. "All that matters now is that we find our son."

As he spoke the words, they crested a hill and saw it. Tom's cabin.

"Save him," Wes said. "Save our boy. And save yourself, old friend. You'll know what to do."

Sebastian was alone, running toward his family, going to rescue them. He was also running toward his ultimate destiny, toward the moment that had been inevitable since the day he had gone over the edge of that cliff and died.

Sebastian's chest heaved. His legs ached. Sharp pain sliced through his abdomen. But he pushed himself harder. Something was terribly wrong.

Bursting through the tree line, into the open field around the cottage, he immediately saw it. Bright orange flashes rose and fell and made the windowpanes glow with a horrible brightness. Thick black smoke seeped through the cracks around the front door. His nerve endings ached from the sudden and overwhelming sensations.

Sebastian jumped onto the porch to find the heat there unbearable. There was no chance of entering through the door.

"Help." The voice was weak and raspy but easily recognizable as Daniel's.

Sebastian ran around to the back of the cabin. The fire had yet to spread there. He smashed the window with his arm, then climbed up into the house, feeling the cuts of the glass but not caring.

Smoke filled his eyes and lungs. He dropped to the floor and crawled closer to the flames. Libbie was tied to a chair, gasping, choking. A Fated One with bullet holes that still oozed blood had her by the throat. The other one, looking just as impossibly wounded, held Daniel a few feet from the flames.

Winters leveled a gun at Sebastian's head. "Just say the word, Cole and they'll live. Let me kill you. Beg me to take your life to spare theirs."

No! Libbie's connection with his mind hit him like a shot. She had gathered her strength. She was struggling, focusing, pulling energy out of Winters' minions. Winters felt it too and commanded his underling to tighten his grip on her neck.

Sebastian couldn't bear to see her lips turning blue and to hear Daniel choking and gasping for breath.

No! Libbie told him again. *Don't give him your life. I can destroy him. I can turn his Fated Ones against him.* She sent a vision to Sebastian, a vision of her and Daniel with Sebastian, all of them in the Occaneechi village, surrounded by loved ones.

Winters broke into the connection, showed Sebastian an image so horrifying that he doubled over in pain. Libbie with a broken neck, Daniel's charred body lying beside her.

"You can save them but time is almost up!" Winters hissed just inches from his ear.

Sebastian had no idea what to do. He could see no way to save his family without forfeiting his soul. Wes' words came back to him. *You'll know what to do.* But Sebastian didn't.

Libbie's mind and heart touched his. *I love you, Sebastian. Trust me to do this.*

He opened his heart to her love and he knew. "I love you, Libbie." He looked at Daniel. "And I love you." He looked back at Libbie. "Save my son. Take care of him."

Tears streamed down his cheeks as he mourned the life he wanted to have with Libbie and Daniel, the life he had nearly convinced himself he deserved. Sebastian lunged at Winters and knocked him off his feet into the flames. Daniel struggled against the Fated One who pushed him closer to the fire. Every fiber of Sebastian's being told him to rescue his son, to pull him free of the horrible being's grasp. He fought the urge, trusted her to save his son, trusted that if he did what the spirits had entreated him to do, his loved ones would live a full life.

Winters struggled to get to his feet and fend off the flames. Sebastian lunged at him again, this time catching Winters in his grasp and rolling into the flames with him, holding him there while the fire engulfed them.

Liberty could suddenly breathe freely but she felt flames lick Winters' skin, singe it, then suck him into unbearable agony. Daniel was behind her, cutting the ropes away from her wrists and ankles. Winters' minions were rolling on the floor, howling in misery as they suffered their master's fate.

"Noooo!" Libbie's voice was faint, fading. She struggled to remain connected to Winters' mind so she could force him to release Sebastian.

"Libbie, don't!" Sebastian called to her. "If you don't break the connection, Winters will take you too!"

"I won't do it, Sebastian! I won't lose you!"

"Please Libbie," he wheezed. "My son needs you. My soul cannot have peace if anything happens to him or to you. Please Libbie, for my soul."

Daniel coughed and sank to the floor beside her. Libbie jumped up from the chair and shook off the vestiges of her bindings. With strength that she didn't know she had, she picked up the boy off the floor and dragged him to the back of the cabin. When they reached the window, the thick black smoke thinned and she drew in a breath of nearly fresh air.

It was only as she climbed up onto the sill that she even realized what she was doing. Her mind had been slow to comprehend but her heart had understood the truth of Sebastian's words. Regardless of how much pain Libbie had endured at their passing, Johnny and her father were now at peace. But if she did not allow Sebastian to complete his path, if she selfishly stood in his way, his pain and heartache would be eternal.

Libbie rolled off the windowsill and onto the hard ground, pulling Daniel with her and cushioning his fall. The fire followed them. One flaming tongue darted out of the window above their heads.

Libbie grabbed Daniel under his arms and staggered backward, dragging him with her. With her last bit of strength, she pulled him far from danger, then fell to the ground beside him. She reached for the medicine bag at her hip and pulled it off its string, laying it on Daniel's heart.

Libbie barely managed to lift her head to take another look at the cottage. She prayed that she would see Sebastian there, somehow free of Winters' grasp, striding toward her and his son. She only saw flames. One great wall of fire, devouring everything in its wake. The cabin no longer existed and the souls inside it were no longer of this world.

Chapter Twenty-Five

&

Libbie opened her eyes once as Fox carried her.

"Just relax, Miss Libbie. I got ya," he said.

But he wasn't alone. Maggie was there and Bird-in-Flight.

"How—" Libbie croaked but could make no more sound.

Bird-in-Flight took her hand. "Mother Cloud Dancer said you would need us. We left the village as soon as the battle ended. We arrived just hours ago."

"But Maggie—"

"I know I promised to stay at Lady Jane's," Maggie answered, "but when we saw the flames, we knew we had to come."

"Daniel," Libbie wheezed.

"He's gonna be fine, Miss Libbie," Fox told her. "Greves has gone on ahead to the house with 'im. Now you close your eyes and rest. We'll get you to the medicine woman in no time and she'll fix you right up."

Libbie closed her eyes, felt the comfort of unconsciousness pulling at her but she fought it. "Sebastian."

"He'll come, Libbie," Maggie said. "Matthew has gone to find him. He might even be at Jane's house by now."

Libbie was going numb but she could feel the tears on her face. "No, Matthew. Don't look. The fire. Sebastian was in the fire. He didn't come out."

She heard their gasps of surprise but she had no strength to acknowledge them. She let exhaustion overtake her, knowing it would restore her strength, knowing she would need that strength to help Mother Cloud Dancer bring Sebastian back to her.

* * * * *

Her lungs, her throat, her nose—with every breath Libbie took, they tingled and burned. The cool air she drew into her body scraped across the raw, torn flesh. Libbie wanted to cry out but could not make enough sound, wanted to call Sebastian's name but could not find her voice. She struggled to move. Her fingers tightened around a soft leather pouch. Her medicine pouch.

"We're here, sweetheart."

Libbie felt the familiar touch of her mother's hand on her brow. She opened her eyes. Her mother's face came into view. Behind Anna was the familiar shape of Libbie's childhood bedroom.

"Mama," she mumbled but it only came out as a raspy breath.

"Do not try to talk, daughter." Mother Cloud Dancer stood on the side of the bed opposite her mother.

Libbie struggled to sit up while her mind filled with questions but her mother pressed her shoulders back down into the feather mattress.

"You lie still, young lady. I'll go get the tea Mother Cloud Dancer has prepared for you."

When Libbie's mother left the room, Mother Cloud Dancer took Libbie's hand and chanted a healing blessing for her.

Mother Cloud Dancer spoke in Occaneechi. "The battle went well. There were wounds, as there always are but our braves prevailed. As for Winters' men, that General Gordon did what he promised—sent his Redcoats to get them."

"General Gordon. Thank God he got Sebastian's message in time." Libbie drew a labored breath and her eyes welled up with tears.

Mother Cloud Dancer squeezed her hand. "I know, my daughter. Your heart is broken. But you made the right choice. The spirits are pleased. His soul is at peace. When you have regained your strength, you will see it too."

"No, Mother. We can bring him back. There must be a way. You and I—"

"No, daughter," Mother Cloud Dancer whispered. "There is no way. If there were, I promise you I would tell you. But it is done. All is as it is meant to be."

"But it wasn't May first," she said. "It was two weeks away. It wasn't even May first."

Mother Cloud Dancer's face showed deep concern but no understanding of what Libbie said. "It is only April. Be calm, rest."

Libbie sat up and shook her head, making tears zigzag down her face. "He can't be gone." Suddenly, there was nothing more important in the world than making Mother Cloud Dancer understand. "My visions of his death were on May first. But we changed it. We changed everything. It's not May first."

"My daughter," Mother Cloud Dance whispered. "You did change the course of events and that helped save Cole's soul. Now you must let him go, let him be at peace."

Libbie closed her eyes, feeling her last hope slip away, finally letting the overwhelming sadness consume her. "He's gone. My husband is truly gone."

"But you are not alone," Mother told her. "You have two families—this one and the tribe. And Maggie and Bird-in-Flight. They both love you. You will have a best friend in each world to help you."

"And a child in each world to protect," Libbie said.

"Yes. It is part of your destiny."

309

The emotions were too much. Exhaustion overtook Libbie. As she drifted toward sleep, she felt Mother Cloud Dancer kiss her cheek.

"My spirit will watch over you as well," Mother whispered. "It is your time, Walks-in-Two-Worlds. You are now medicine woman of the Occaneechi."

* * * * *

Something was different. Libbie could not pinpoint it but the world did not feel the same as it had during the night. She stretched her arms over her head and inhaled deeply. Her throat and chest tightened, then convulsed into deep coughs.

"Libbie, it's all right. Get it out." Her mother sat beside her on the bed and held her until she could breathe easily again.

"Mama, you look tired. Have you stayed with me all night?"

"That's what mothers do, dear, as you'll learn. And speaking of that, Daniel is anxious to see you. Annalee as well."

"Daniel. What have you told him about Sebastian?"

Anna shook her head. "We didn't have to tell him anything. He told us. He's strong, Libbie. He's suffering and he'll need you desperately but he's strong."

"And Annalee? And Aunt Caroline?"

"Just sitting on pins and needles, waiting to get in here. Perhaps this afternoon, if you're up to it. Jane sends her love and Greves and Effie are staying here for a while, until we're able to manage. Jane insisted."

Libbie squeezed her mother's hand. "He was her dearest friend."

Her mother's voice trembled as she spoke. "She's heartbroken. And consumed with worry for you. Like the rest of us."

310

"And Mother Cloud Dancer — where has she gone?"

Anna smiled. "She's been such a comfort to us. I invited her to stay longer but she left at dawn, on foot no less. I thought she might be visiting the old Occaneechi homestead. I sent one of the field hands with her but he came back an hour later with his tail between his legs."

"Their old village is in the direction of the mountains."

Her mother nodded. "Yes, that's right. That was the path she took."

Now Libbie understood what had changed, what energy had shifted in the world. "That's where she went. Back into the mountains. A part of her will always be with us. But Mother Cloud Dancer, as we knew her, will never return."

Look after him, Mother, she silently entreated. *Look after Sebastian until I join him one day.*

* * * * *

The month that had passed since she'd lost him had brought the full bloom of spring to the valley. It was hard for Libbie to ponder why she'd met Sebastian one spring only to lose him the next. Someday she would fully consider it, have it out with the spirits, perhaps even learn to forgive them. But today, the best she could do was seek out some small measure of comfort.

She walked along the dirt road, clutching the season's first wildflowers in her hand. She could not yet bear to go through the fields, where she would see the charred remains of the cabin. Her chosen path made the walk to the churchyard longer, as did the slow pace she maintained in order not to tax her lungs. By the time she reached the cemetery, the sun had fully cleared the horizon and had burned away the morning mist.

She had felt them walking with her, the loved ones she had come to visit. But she wanted to speak to them here, in this peaceful place, where no one would disturb her. It was Mother

Cloud Dancer who had told her that to see and hear the ghosts required an unusual gift but to be seen and heard by them required only an open heart.

She stopped at Tom's memorial stone first and placed some flowers beside it. "We're looking after your father," she told him. "I promise you that the MacRaes will always treat him like family." She lingered there a moment longer, then said, "Thank you for loving me. I'll always miss your friendship."

Next she went to her father's and Johnny's memorial stones, which were beside each other. She laid more flowers. "We did it, Papa. Sebastian and I have taken care of Winters. And General Gordon's an honorable man. He told the army the truth and they've cleared the MacRae name. We're no longer branded traitors. But of course you know that. Now I have something to ask of you. You and Johnny both."

She drew an unsteady breath. "I love my husband, Papa. And I miss him. I'll miss him every moment for the rest of my life." She knelt on the ground. "But if I know that you're there with him, if you'll help him find the peace he seeks, I can survive this."

She pressed her forehead against the rough, cool headstone. "Please, Papa, promise me."

* * * * *

A small animal scurried through the underbrush, running for cover. Its paws scraped across the ground. He could hear it. The woods smelled of fertile earth and wildflowers, the wind felt cool on his skin and tasted sweet on his tongue.

Sebastian moved forward slowly, acclimating himself to all the sensations the world offered him and stepped out from under the trees. The sun was warm and golden. But to him, it paled in comparison to the sight of her.

Her skin was pinker, her hair more coppery, her lips more red than he could have imagined. She fixed her gaze on him and rose slowly to her feet. The minute it took him to reach her felt like hours. His arms ached for her as he held them open to her.

She threw herself against him and clung to him. He squeezed her as tightly as he dared, relishing the heat of her skin. He kissed her with all of his passion, unable to go slowly or softly.

"Is it really you?" she said against his mouth.

He kissed her cheek and ran his tongue along the side of her throat, settling on her throbbing pulse.

She sucked in her breath. "Are you a ghost? An apparition?" she whispered.

"No, not a ghost." He pulled away from her and gazed into her eyes. "I'm flesh and blood. But not like before. Not a man living in half-measures, not a Fated One waiting to reach a predetermined end."

She placed a hand on each side of his face. "You've come back to me. But how? No, don't tell me. I don't even care. Just promise you won't leave me again. I love you, Sebastian. I love you!"

She kissed him, first softly, then more urgently. She tasted sweet, so sweet.

When they stopped to catch their breath, he pulled her tightly against him. "I love you so much. I swear I won't leave you. We've been given a gift. The spirits have rewarded us for our sacrifices."

"They've sent you back to be with me? To be my husband? To be Daniel's father?"

"Yes. To be a family. The spirits have shown me that there is still much work to do—lives to save, innocents to protect. But the only thing predestined for us now is to love each other for the rest of our very long lives."

Also by Nancy Hunter

ဆ

eBooks:

Taste of Liberty

About Nancy Hunter

Nancy Hunter is the pen name for author/freelance writer Nancy J. Yeager. Nancy spent her early years wanting to be an English countryside vet (a la James Herriot) and an adventure-seeking archaeologist (a la Indiana Jones). After studying biochemistry and earning an anthropology degree, she realized that her true passion is for writing fictional stories about smart, adventurous women and the men who are strong enough to love them. She writes in multiple genres, including historical romance with paranormal elements, urban fantasy, and women's fiction.

Nancy lives in Maryland with her real-life hero/husband, talented musician daughter, and many, many rescued cats.

The author welcomes comments from readers. You can find her website and email address on her author bio page at www.ellorascave.com.

Tell Us What You Think

Why an electronic book?

We live in the Information Age — an exciting time in the history of human civilization, in which technology rules supreme and continues to progress in leaps and bounds every minute of every day. For a multitude of reasons, more and more avid literary fans are opting to purchase e-books instead of paper books. The question from those not yet initiated into the world of electronic reading is simply: *Why?*

1. ***Price.*** An electronic title at Ellora's Cave Publishing runs anywhere from 40% to 75% less than the cover price of the exact same title in paperback format. Why? Basic mathematics and cost. It is less expensive to publish an e-book (no paper and printing, no warehousing and shipping) than it is to publish a paperback, so the savings are passed along to the consumer.

2. ***Space.*** Running out of room in your house for your books? That is one worry you will never have with electronic books. For a low one-time cost, you can purchase a handheld device specifically designed for e-reading. Many e-readers have large, convenient screens for viewing. Better yet, hundreds of titles can be stored within your new library — on a single microchip. There a variety of e-readers from different manufacturers. You can also read e-books on your PC or laptop computer. (Please note that Ellora's Cave does not endorse any specific brands.

You can check our website at www.ellorascave.com for information we make available to new consumers.)

3. *Mobility.* Because your new e-library consists of only a microchip within a small, easily transportable e-reader, your entire cache of books can be taken with you wherever you go.

4. *Personal Viewing Preferences.* Are the words you are currently reading too small? Too large? Too... ANNOYING? Paperback books cannot be modified according to personal preferences, but e-books can.

5. *Instant Gratification.* Is it the middle of the night and all the bookstores near you are closed? Are you tired of waiting days, sometimes weeks, for bookstores to ship the novels you bought? Ellora's Cave Publishing sells instantaneous downloads twenty-four hours a day, seven days a week, every day of the year. Our webstore is never closed. Our e-book delivery system is 100% automated, meaning your order is filled as soon as you pay for it.

Those are a few of the top reasons why electronic books are replacing paperbacks for many avid readers.

As always, Ellora's Cave welcomes your questions and comments. We invite you to email us at Service@ellorascave.com or write to us directly at Ellora's Cave Publishing Inc., 1056 Home Avenue, Akron, OH 44310-3502.

MAKE EACH DAY MORE *EXCITING* WITH OUR

ELLORA'S
CAVEMEN
CALENDAR

WWW.ELLORASCAVE.COM

ELLORA'S CAVE
Romanticon

Annual convention
for women who
refuse to behave

www.ECRomanticon.com
For additional info contact: conventions@ellorascave.com

Discover for yourself why readers can't get enough of the multiple award-winning publisher Ellora's Cave. Be sure to visit EC on the web at www.ellorascave.com to find erotic reading experiences that will leave you breathless. You can also find our books at all the major e-tailers (Barnes & Noble, Amazon Kindle, Sony, Kobo, Google, Apple iBookstore, All Romance eBooks, and others).

www.ellorascave.com

Made in the USA
Lexington, KY
31 March 2014